THE LOVE HACK

SOPHIE RANALD

Storm
PUBLISHING

Ebook ISBN: 978-1-80508-603-1
Paperback ISBN: 978-1-80508-605-5

Cover design: Rose Cooper
Cover images: Shutterstock

Published by Storm Publishing.
For further information, visit:
www.stormpublishing.co

ALSO BY SOPHIE RANALD

The Fall-Out

The Girlfriends' Club series
P.S. I Hate You
Santa, Please Bring Me a Boyfriend
Not in a Million Years

The Ginger Cat series
Just Saying
Thank You, Next
He's Cancelled

The Daily Grind series
Out With the Ex, In With the New
Sorry Not Sorry
It's Not You, It's Him
No, We Can't Be Friends

Standalone romcoms
It Would be Wrong to Steal My Sister's Boyfriend (Wouldn't It?)
A Groom With a View
Who Wants to Marry a Millionaire?
You Can't Fall in Love With Your Ex (Can You?)

*For my wonderful agent, Alice Saunders – cheerleader,
hand-holder and occasional finger-wagger extraordinaire.
Thank you for everything.*

ONE

Has anyone ever thrown up all over your desk before, Marion? I asked my boss silently. *Thought not. Well, there's a first time for everything. Maybe right there next to the vase of tulips.*

It was 10.30 on a Monday morning, and it was fair to say my week wasn't getting off to the best start. My hands, clasped tightly in my lap so Marion couldn't see how much I was shaking, were cold and slippery with sweat. My mouth was so dry it felt like my tongue was made of cotton wool. My eyes were prickling with tears – and not from the sunlight slanting through the blinds half-covering the window.

I felt like I was fighting for my life – or at the end stage of a computer game, and any second the screen would go blank and 'GAME OVER' would flash in front of my eyes.

All I could think of was the worst-case scenario: I'd be out of work, unable to find another job, overdue on my rent, forced to sell all my stuff, and eventually I'd get thrown out on the street. And I'd have to find another home for Astro, because there was no way he'd put up with sleeping rough like in *A Street Cat Named Bob*. Astro had many admirable qualities, but toughness and resourcefulness were not among them.

Mine neither, come to that.

'Lucy?' Marion, my line manager – at least, my line manager for now – asked gently. 'You seem shocked by this. Did the letter we sent you last week not explain the situation clearly enough?'

Well, it had, of course. It had been placed on my desk, right in the centre of my keyboard where I couldn't possibly miss it, with my first and last name printed clearly on the envelope. I'd shoved it into my backpack, pushing it right down to the bottom underneath the plastic box containing my lunchtime sandwich, below the cardigan I kept in there for when the office heating played up and the trainers with the broken laces that I hadn't got around to replacing.

I'd read it later, at home. At least, I'd peeled back the flap of the envelope, slipped out the piece of crisp A4 paper and seen four words: 'At risk of redundancy.'

'This is a very hard decision for us to make,' Marion went on. 'Believe me, we've done everything we can to keep the print edition of *Fab!* going. It's my baby, as I'm sure you know, and I know that the tech column is yours. But circulation has been declining steadily over the past three years. The Covid lockdowns hit us hard, and levels of commuting still aren't even close to what they were before. If people aren't using the Tube, then they're not picking up the mag in stations. And if the mag isn't getting into people's hands, advertisers don't want to spend money on space. You understand that, don't you, Lucy?'

I nodded mutely.

'Strategically, we've had to make tough decisions,' Marion went on. 'We've had to look at the overall state of the business, and future-proof it. Other people's jobs would be on the line otherwise. The whole survival of the business is at stake.'

Do they always say this? I wondered. *And what do they expect people to say back? 'Of course, I completely get it. The survival of Radiant Media is far more important than me being able to pay my rent and feed my cat. Don't you worry, Marion, I'll take one for the team.' As if. Said no one in my situation, ever.*

'What will happen, though?' I managed to ask. 'To *Fab!*, I mean. To my column.'

Marion looked down at the leather folder in front of her, resting innocently on the glass surface of the boardroom table. She didn't need to consult her notes – she knew what they said. For a second, I almost felt sorry for her. Then I went back to feeling sorry for myself.

'*Fab!* will be transitioning to online only,' she said. '*Max!* too. The men's magazine has taken just as much of a hit as we have. We've got to find efficiencies. Cutting print and distribution costs is the big one, but there are others, too. The magazines' – at least, the publications', the e-zines' – readership is distinct, but there's a lot of content they have in common: the nightlife pages, the arts coverage and, of course, the technology content. Our readership will be as well served if those are shared across the two publications – portals, as they'll become.'

So that was that. *Fab!*, the magazine I'd worked on for three years – but still felt a little thrill of pride over when I saw someone reading on the train, when I smelled the freshly printed pages and saw 'Technology Editor, Lucy Masters' on the masthead – was no more.

My job was as good as toast.

'I know this is a lot to take in, Lucy.' Maybe Marion had guessed that I could hardly hear her over the rush of blood in my ears. 'Do you have any questions?'

'I... You said... I mean, there's still going to be a technology editor, right? For *Fab!* and *Max!* together? I could do that, surely?'

Marion shook her head, pursing her lips with what looked like genuine regret. 'Lucy, if I could give you that role, I would. Believe me. But Ross McEwan, who as you know is your opposite number at *Max!*, has been in the post four months longer than you have. We've had to adopt a strict last in, first out policy. It's the only way to ensure fairness for everyone.'

Ross McEwan. I knew the name, obviously. I'd probably even seen the guy at Christmas parties and away days and the whole-company strategy breakfasts that had taken place on a quarterly basis for a year or so and then fizzled out. But for the life of me I couldn't picture his face. He was probably one of the guys with bad teeth and a patchy beard, I thought unkindly.

But I was in no mood to #bekind, a slogan that had been all over the pages of *Fab!* for the past couple of years.

'There have been other roles thrown into the mix,' Marion was saying. 'Fashion and style, for instance, will be kept sepa-rate across the two publications, so those section heads will retain their roles under the new structure, and besides...'

She looked at me and smiled benignly. And I could see her point. There I was across the table from her in my jeans and hoodie and glasses, my hair scraped back in its usual ponytail, not a scrap of make-up on my face. A spot was threatening to break out on the side of my nose, and my nails were clipped short and unpainted as they always were. I looked about as much like a potential fashion and style editor as Astro, my cat. Probably less so.

'I wouldn't want to write about fashion and style,' I admitted.

'Look, Lucy.' Marion closed her folder and put down her pen, resting both hands on the glass surface of the table as if she was reaching out to me, or making a confession. 'We don't want to lose any of our people. Especially not good people who have been with the organisation a long time. If it were possible to keep everyone, we'd do that. I'd do that. Over the past few weeks, I've fought and fought for every single member of the team. We just couldn't see a way around this.'

'Are you sure?' A new tone had come into my voice, no

longer calm-ish but almost pleading. 'Are you sure you've thought of everything? Could there be another way? Couldn't Ross and I...?'

'We considered a job-share arrangement of some kind. But it would mean both of you losing half your income, which would obviously not be ideal. And when we put the idea to Ross, he was very clear that he didn't feel it would work for him or for *Max!*.'

'I understand that,' I said. 'But maybe... something else?'

'Do you have an idea of what that might be?' Marion asked.

I cast around desperately in my mind but came up with a total blank. 'Not right now, but I...'

'This is only our initial meeting,' Marion said. 'As I think our letter made clear, you're legally entitled to a follow-up in three days' time. You're welcome to have a colleague or union rep present to support you. If you wish to bring alternative proposals to that meeting, they will of course be carefully considered.'

Translation: We're doing this by the book because we don't want you suing our arses.

And I didn't want to sue their arses. I didn't have the nerve or the desire, and I knew that, more importantly, I didn't have a chance of winning. Still, Marion's words felt like a lifeline, albeit a slender one that would most likely break and send me tumbling back into the abyss I could feel opening up under my feet, beneath the heather-grey carpet.

'I'll think,' I said. 'Give me three days, and I'll think of something. I promise.'

TWO

It was raining when I emerged from the Tube after work – a steady downpour that felt more like December than April and made me offer up a silent prayer to the weather gods to get their shit together before my sister's wedding in six weeks' time. Then, without waiting to see if they'd answer – possibly in the form of a lightning bolt striking me down for being so presumptuous as to tell them how to do their jobs – I pulled the hood of my coat up and ran for it.

The truth was, I'd wanted to run since the moment I'd left the boardroom, where Marion had remained seated at the table, her folder in front of her, waiting for her next victim. All I could think was, *I need to see my sister. I need Amelie.* And so I'd texted her, my thumbs fumbling on the keyboard of my phone, and asked if she was home, and if I could come round.

The flat Amelie shared with Zack was in one of those elegant, white, stucco-fronted Georgian houses overlooking a garden square in which cherry trees were valiantly flowering in spite of the chilly weather and persistent wind. But I barely noticed the attractiveness of the surroundings as I hurried up the slippery stone steps and leaned on the buzzer of flat 29A.

My sister was expecting me, and normally I heard the click of the lock within seconds, because she generally had something she couldn't wait to tell me. But this time, I waited, shivering, for a full two minutes – which might not sound like long but does feel like it when you're loitering on a doorstep wondering if the neighbours think you're a burglar or a Jehovah's Witness.

Six months earlier, I'd received a text from my sister asking me to come round 'soon as poss'. I don't believe in telepathy or mysterious sibling bonds or any of that twaddle, but as soon as I saw that message, I thought, *Oh. Zack's asked her to marry him.* The realisation had come with a surge of happiness for my sister – but only after a fleeting yet horrible sinking sensation somewhere within my heart.

She's leaving me behind. There'll be no coming back from this.

But that unhappy – and frankly selfish – thought had vanished as soon as I'd seen my sister's face, positively shining with joy, as radiant as the solitaire diamond on her ring finger. She'd squealed and I'd squealed and we'd done a little hopping dance around her kitchen – or rather, Zack's kitchen, because where they lived was Zack's flat, and the Smeg fridge and the wine chiller and the £2,000 coffee machine were, of course, all Zack's.

'I can't believe how lucky I am!' Amelie had gushed.

Of course, I'd shut that line of thinking down sharpish. It was just a step away from, *I can't believe I'm good enough for him,* and if Amelie privately thought that, she needed to stop thinking it, stat. My sister was one hundred per cent amazing, and as far as I was concerned, it was Zack who'd got lucky. Not that there was anything wrong with him – on paper, he was the catch to end all catches, with his lean, six-foot-something frame, his way of holding the attention in a room that I guess some people would call charismatic, his high-powered something-in-finance career that was the perfect foil for Amelie's job in PR for companies that did things in finance. Still, I felt that I'd never quite got him – and he certainly didn't get me. He definitely didn't get my jokes, laughing a beat too late before looking at Amelie, who would abruptly stop laughing herself then turn to him like a flower to the sun. But in the intervening months, her happiness hadn't dimmed, and Zack, too, seemed unable to believe his luck – and my own doubts had more or less melted away.

As for her leaving me behind – well. She'd done that years ago. Done it, by almost imperceptible increments, since the day she was born, when I was eighteen months old. She'd smiled, crawled, walked, talked, slept through the night and grown teeth and hair earlier than I had. She'd been cast as Mary in the school nativity play when my highest achievement had been playing a camel. She'd been to a school prom a year before I had, with her then-boyfriend – with whom, obviously, she'd had sex for the first time, when I'd remained a virgin for another four years.

And now, with a kind of inevitability that I accepted without really questioning it, because after all I'd had twenty-seven and a half years to get used to the situation, Amelie was getting married, and I was just as single as I'd ever been.

I'd always known that my sister was quite the catch. If my granny's insistence on repeating every time she saw the two of us, undeterred by Mum's glares and shushes, that 'Lucy got the brains, but Amelie got the looks' hadn't been enough to bring the reality of our difference home to me, then one glance in the mirror would have been.

I scrub up okay. I've got great hair – long, thick, dark brown and shiny, and it puts up with the benign neglect I lavish on it without complaint – but the rest of me is only really average. Okay skin, an okay figure, a too-big nose, and eyes that would be quite nice if they weren't obscured by my glasses and too sensitive for contact lenses.

Amelie, though – Amelie looks like I was nature's first attempt, then it stood back, looked me up and down and thought, *Not too bad, but next time I'll really nail it*. It was like I was a basic stoneware coffee mug – one of those you get free from Sports Direct, maybe – and my sister was the fine bone china version. All her proportions were subtly different: her eyes bigger and wider set, her cheekbones higher, her jaw more delicately defined, her nose a perfect ski-jump. Her legs were longer, her waist smaller, her teeth whiter.

In the face of all that, I don't think anyone would blame me for not bothering too much with my appearance, especially as I could never bother as much as Amelie did. Fortnightly mani-cures and pedicures, subtle eyelash extensions, expensive cuts and blow-dries in a salon every six weeks – how she found time for all of it, I never knew.

And even now, when at last the door I'd been waiting outside clicked open and I hurried out of the rain and down the stairs to the basement flat, I found her swathed like a ghost in a white waffle dressing gown and a sheet mask, the backs of her hands slippery with some sort of oil, her lips sticking out over a pair of plastic mouth-guard things.

She flapped her hands at me then leaned in for a forearm hug, leaving a smear of fragrant goo on my cheek, and gestured to the fridge. Obediently, I found a bottle of white wine and two glasses and carried them through to the living room, where I settled down on the squashy cream sofa to wait. Amelie was hovering in the kitchen doorway, eyes fixed on her phone, thumbs busily tapping away at the screen.

'What're you doing?'

She made a 'hold on' gesture and said something inaudible around her mouthful of plastic. Then she disappeared into the bathroom. I waited, my eyes falling on the engagement photo of Amelie and Zack that had pride of place on the mantelpiece. It wasn't a selfie taken in the first giddy moments after he'd said,

'Will you...?' and she'd said, 'Yes!' but a professional shot taken a couple of weeks after. Zack was in a suit and Amelie was in a pink dress, her perfectly lit face angled to gaze up at him, her smile radiant but not quite natural, as if she were saying, 'Cheese!' or possibly, 'Success!' I heard splashing water and the hum of an electric toothbrush, then drawers slamming in the bedroom, and a few minutes later she re-emerged, looking more or less normal again.

'Sorry.' She flopped down next to me on the sofa, glancing at her phone again. 'Just logging my macros. I've got enough carbs left for a glass of wine – hurrah. Not that I'd let some stupid app tell me I couldn't, even if I didn't.'

'Amelie, you don't need to bloody diet.'

'It's not a diet. Diets are so over. It's body recomposition through optimum nutrition. Duh.'

I glanced sideways at her. 'Sounds like a diet to me.'

'It's n— Okay, it is. But I feel a bit better if I call it something else. I tell you what, though, this wedding can't come soon enough. If I ever see a tuna and egg-white omelette again after the tenth of June, I'll legit cry.'

'But you don't need—'

'It's not about needing. Come on, Luce. It's just one day, and I'm chucking everything I've got at it because... well, because if I didn't, I'd look at the photos after and think, maybe if I'd put a bit more effort in, I could've looked better. And when something's going to be up on your living room wall for the rest of your life, you want to make damn sure it's as right as it can be.'

'I still think—'

'I tell you what though, it's a bastarding faff,' she carried on as if I hadn't spoken. 'The skincare, the Callanetics – apparently that used to be a thing ages ago, did you know? And it's back. It's meant to make you all lean and toned like a dancer. The damn Invisalign retainers. I haven't told Zack about them – once my teeth were straight I thought that would be it, but no, I have to wear those vile plastic trays every night forever. Except I can't wear them at night – I mean, I'm getting married. Who goes on honeymoon with those? So I try and wear them for eight hours during the day, except I'm constantly spitting them out when I have meetings.'

'Or need to eat.'

'Or to eat. So I've been having protein shakes, mostly. They make me feel like I'm receiving palliative care and they taste like chocolate-flavoured chalk.'

She heaved a weary sigh, and I poured wine into our glasses and handed her one, watching as she took a deep gulp and then another.

'Did you sort out the thing with the flowers?' I asked, remembering some crisis a week or so back, but unable to recall the details.

'Mum did. We can't have the original ones I wanted – the giant orange daisy things – because they'd have to be imported from China or something. But the florist showed Mum some alternative ones that we think will do. Honestly, I'm so done with it all now. I just want to be married to Zack. No one tells you when you get engaged that planning a wedding takes over your entire life, and before it even happens you're sick to death of it all and can't wait for it to be over.'

'Don't be daft.' Since Amelie's engagement, I'd seen her giddy with joy when she finally found The One – dress, that is – in floods of tears when her dream venue got snapped up before she could book it, and on the verge of a toddler-worthy strop when the invitations got printed in a shade she declared was peach rather than apricot. But this weary resignation was a new one, and it worried me. 'Look, you'll have heard this before, but I'm saying it anyway. It's just one day. Of course you want everything to be perfect, but in the grand scheme of things—'

'But that's what I'm saying. It's just one day. God! All this stress for one stupid day.'

'So stop. Step away from the tuna omelettes. Ditch the skin-care. Chill out a bit and just' – I produced a pretty poor attempt at channelling Elsa from *Frozen* – 'let it go.'

'Yeah, right. If I did, you'd have to listen to me whinge for years and years about how it could all have been perfect but it wasn't. This way, at least you only have to put up with my drama for forty-four more days.'

'Forty-five days. Trust me, I know. I've got one of those countdown apps on my phone.' I swiped the screen to life. 'Actually, forty-five days, five hours and eleven minutes until I get my sister back.'

Except I'd never get my sister back. Not really. In forty-five days and whatever else it was, she'd become Zack's wife first and Lucy's sister second, and that would never change back. And immediately after the wedding, she and Zack were decamping to New York for six months for him to work on some lucrative secondment and for her to be his trailing spouse.

'Have I really been that bad? I'm so sorry, Luce.'

'Utterly vile,' I confirmed, smiling.

Amelie grinned back. 'Well, if I can't be utterly vile when I'm getting married, when can I? Honestly, I'm sorry. It's just all so... It's a lot. Sometimes I wish we'd just decided, "Fuck it," and eloped to John O'Groats.'

'You mean Gretna Green.'

'Whatever.' Amelie splashed picpoul into our glasses and scooted round on the sofa so she was facing me, cross-legged. 'Anyway. How are things with you?'

I took a breath, ready to tell her the whole story of the barely read warning letter, my meeting with Marion and the prospect of being able to keep my job – well, *a* job, at any rate – if I could only think of something valuable I could bring to the Radiant Media party. But before I could get a single word out, I heard myself give a massive gulp that turned into a sob, and suddenly I was crying as if I'd never stop.

'Oh my God. Luce, what's wrong? Has something bad happened? Is it Astro?' My sister hauled me across the sofa and enfolded me in her white-towelling arms, and held me tight while I sobbed, patting my back soothingly then passing me tissues when the flood of tears eventually slowed down.

Once I was able to speak again, I poured out the whole story.

'So I won't have a job after next week. I'll have some redundancy money but it won't last long and I don't know what to do.' I finished self-pityingly, 'I can't believe this is happening to me again.'

'It's nothing like last time,' Amelie said firmly. 'What bastards, though. And this Ross? Who is he, anyway? The fucker.'

'It's not really his fault,' I said. 'He's been there longer than me. Last in, first out, they said. If only I could think of another job for me to do, but I can't.'

'You can.' My sister looked at me with the same steely determination I'd seen in her face since she was a baby, dead set on reaching the vase of roses Mum had put out of her reach on the coffee table and bringing the whole lot crashing to the floor. 'We can. Together. We'll think of something.'

'I mean, I could offer to make coffee for everyone and reboot the server when it goes wrong. But it's not like they'll pay me a full-time wage for that.'

Amelie tutted. 'Not that. Come on. You need to come up with something *wow*. You need to make them an offer they can't refuse.'

'Clean the bogs when the Beast of Cubicle Two's done a massive shit in there and there's a client due in five minutes?'

'No! I mean, I can see how they might go for that, but it's not exactly sustainable, is it?'

'Not really. But what can I do? I know about technology, and I can write about it in a way people understand. That's it. That's my skill set.'

Amelie put down her wine glass and reached over to the table, picking up a notebook covered in champagne-coloured satin with beads and sequins embroidered on it. The words 'My Wedding' were stamped on it in gold, and a slim gold pen slotted into its spine. She flipped the pages until she found a blank one, about two-thirds of the way through.

'Okay.' She poised her pen over the page. 'You can write. We know that.'

'But so can everyone else who works in the editorial department,' I pointed out, 'otherwise they wouldn't have jobs there.'

'Fair enough. So then the question is, what don't they write about now that people would want to read?'

'Everything I can do is covered,' I said glumly. 'Movie reviews, computing, gaming. And then there's a whole load of stuff I don't have a clue about, like fashion and recipes and things like that.'

'Does the men's magazine have a recipe page?' Amelie brightened. 'I bet it doesn't. You could do that. How to impress your date with your jerk monkfish in blue corn tortillas. The first time Zack—'

'Yes, except unlike Zack, I can't cook. So that's a non-starter.'

'Shhh. I said something a second ago that gave me an idea, and now I've lost it.'

'Something about Zack?'

'No, before that.'

'About impressing your date?'

'Yes! That's the budgie. Dating advice for men. Like, *Fab!* has an agony aunt, am I right?'

'Sure. We – they – get loads of letters.'

'And do the men have one? Hmmm? Do they?'

'Umm, no. There isn't an equivalent at *Max!* – I don't know why. Maybe they tried it and it didn't work.'

Amelie shook her head. 'Poor men. Honestly, you've got to pity the buggers. No wonder so many of them end up being incels or following Andrew Tate on TikTok or whatever. All they need is some good, straight-talking advice from someone who understands what women want.'

'Like a woman?'

'Yes, but no. I know men, Luce, and I know they don't listen to a bloody word women say. It would need to be a man – or, at least, a woman pretending to be a man, all brotherly, explaining to them what they're doing wrong in their dating lives.'

'You're saying I should pretend to be a man and write a dating advice column for *Max!*?'

'Exactly.'

'Brilliant.' I loved my sister and I knew her intentions were good, but I couldn't help sarcasm oozing from my words. 'Only one: I don't understand dating. Two: I don't understand men. And three: I don't know what men do wrong when they're dating because I never date them.'

'Doesn't matter. I do. Go on – ask me anything.'

'Uh...' I racked my brains and came up with very little. 'Okay. I'm a guy and I can't get a girlfriend. Why not?'

Amelie frowned. 'I'd expect them to give me a bit more to go on than that. But okay. When guys can't get women to go out with them, it's generally because their expectations of the kind of woman who might want to date them are completely unrealistic, or because they aren't even trying to make the most of themselves, or because they're just dicks, and women can tell. One of the three. Try another.'

A memory rushed into my mind and I tried to block it, but it was too late. 'I've been hooking up with a girl and I think she wants more. What should I do?'

'Hmmm. If you don't want a relationship with her, that's fine. But be clear about it, be kind, and above all don't be a dick.'

'You make it sound so easy.'

'That's because it is. Men are simple.'

'Not to me, they aren't.'

'But you want to find out about them, don't you? What makes them tick? They're just another puzzle, like those lateral-thinking games you were obsessed with when you were little.'

I smiled. 'I remember those! Like, why did the man take the lift up to the eleventh floor when it was raining, but get off at the third and walk the rest of the way up when it was sunny?'

'Exactly! So come on, let's write a proposal. Seriously, this is genius. There's no way they won't go for it.'

Amelie had already put down her notebook and whipped open her laptop, and I could see words appearing at the top of a blank document on her screen.

PITCH: 'ASK ADAM' WEEKLY COLUMN FOR *MAX!* ONLINE.

THREE

'They're ready for you now, Lucy.' Marion's PA gave me a tight smile and whisked away from my desk.

Knees trembling, I tucked my laptop under my arm and made my way to the boardroom. Marion was seated on one side of the shiny wooden table, flanked by a balding, sandy-haired man who she introduced as Greg, editor-in-chief of *Max!*, and a woman in a suit who was apparently in charge of advertising sales.

The air smelled of furniture polish, coffee and the deodorant I'd frantically applied in the ladies' loo a few minutes earlier, hoping it would mask the smell of fear. My fingers fumbled as I plugged my laptop into the jack that worked the big screen at the head of the table. When I took a sip of water, my arm jerked and sent a load of it dribbling down my chin.

'Thank you for joining us, Lucy,' Greg said, in a tone I guessed was meant to be reassuring. 'Marion tells us you have a proposal. We're looking forward to walking through it with you.'

Personally, I felt more keen on the idea of running away, as fast and as far as I could.

But I said, 'I appreciate you all taking the time to be here.

I'm Lucy Masters, and I hope you'll find the presentation I've put together of interest.'

Be keen, Amelie had advised. *Poised, but keen. And remember, you've done nothing wrong. They're going to love it.* I wished I felt anything like as confident as she'd sounded – in that moment, I felt small, scared and vulnerable, and the idea we'd come up with seemed flimsy and stupid.

My finger slippery on the trackpad of my laptop, I fired up the slide deck my sister and I had worked on, which I'd completed late the previous evening, fuelled by coffee, culminating in a panic attack when Astro had walked over my keyboard and almost deleted the whole thing.

The thought of my cat made me smile, and almost magically my nerves receded a bit. I looked at the opening slide on the screen, took a breath and began, struggling at first to get any words out through my chattering teeth.

'There's very little out there in the way of relationship advice for men,' I explained earnestly, beginning to get into my stride as I reached the third slide. 'There are Reddit subs, of course, and TikTok, but that only appeals to a very niche demographic. *Max!*'s readers are all ages, and at all stages of life. "Ask Adam" will offer advice on everything from first dates through to sharing parenting responsibilities and caring for elderly parents – a burden which falls predominantly on women, but which affects their partners and sons nonetheless.'

Even to my own hypercritical ears, it sounded pretty good, and I could see my audience going from sceptical to interested to impressed.

Then Greg said, 'Hold on. You'll be answering all this yourself? You? Posing as this Adam guy? What about the legal ramifications if something goes wrong?'

Fortunately, Amelie had anticipated that question. 'We'll include a disclaimer, obviously. That "Ask Adam" is first and foremost entertainment. It's intended to provoke thought and discussion. And if I find myself stumped by a question' – or rather, if Amelie, my secret weapon, found herself stumped – 'I'll reach out to experts. Psychotherapists, sexologists, even financial planners. People like that are always delighted to help if it means getting their name in the media.'

Marion nodded. The advertising woman scribbled some notes on her pad. Greg flipped through the printout I'd given them all, then asked a few more questions that I was able to field easily.

'Of course, we'll have to discuss this some more among ourselves,' he said, when I'd reached the final slide.

'And run some numbers on potential sales,' said the advertising woman.

'Of course, if this all goes through, you know how unhappy we will be to lose you here at *Fab!*, Lucy,' Marion said.

'You were going to lose me anyway,' I pointed out, emboldened by the success of our discussion so far.

A few days later, I had a follow-up meeting with Greg, who seemed delighted by the idea. The day after that, I signed a contract for my new role as sex and relationships editor at *Max! Online*. And the day after that, I packed up my desk, got in the lift and ascended two floors to take my place in my new team, a photo of Astro under my arm, my Venus flytrap in its pot balanced carefully on one palm, and my special coffee mug hooked over my pinkie finger.

I don't know what I'd expected to see when the lift doors opened and I walked out on to the *Max!* magazine floor. I'd been there before, of course, for meetings and to drop off a phone someone had left in our breakout room – just occasional forays into the world of our brother publication. Except now it was my publication, and *Fab!* wasn't mine any longer.

The floor was identical to the one below it. There was a

reception desk by the lift and meeting rooms to the left. To my right, rows of desks were arranged across a bright, window-lined space, with private offices for management and team leaders along one side. If the layout was the same, the client services and sales teams would be nearest the entrance, then art in the middle and editorial at the far end. Which meant I'd have to cross the entire space before reaching my own desk.

And the space was full of men.

I should have anticipated that, of course, but I hadn't – not really. I'd been too busy focusing on clinging on and not being let go. If I had anticipated it, maybe I'd have reconsidered the wisdom of my sister's idea – that joining this team would mean not only being the recipient of men's romantic dilemmas, but being surrounded by them at work every single day.

I could feel sweat springing out under my armpits as I walked across the floor, and the finger holding my mug seemed to be working very hard to stop it from falling. With an effort, I kept my face impassive and made my way to the end of the room, looking around desperately for Greg, or any other familiar, friendly face. But I recognised no one – well, I kind of recognised lots of them, but only in an amorphous, collective sort of way. The man blob. At last, I reached the far end of the room, the last pod of eight desks.

Seven were occupied, four by men and three by men's possessions: jackets over chairs, Costa take-out packets next to keyboards and chunky, expensive headphones. There was a dark-haired man with designer stubble and the air of cockiness men have when they're more handsome than anyone deserves to be – and they know it. There was a thin, fair-haired guy with glasses wearing a button-down shirt. There was a bloke in cycling gear, clearly just arrived for the day, hitching his backpack off his shoulders and letting his helmet fall heavily to the floor. And the fourth was just ordinary, middling-tall and middling-built with middling-brown hair that flopped down over steady, middling-coloured eyes.

They all looked at me as I approached, with not unfriendly curiosity. The dark-haired one cracked a dazzling smile, which I was willing to bet was a reflex on seeing a woman, any woman, in the split second before he categorised her as fuckable or non-fuckable.

The thin guy pushed his glasses up his nose and returned to his keyboard, hammering furiously away as if the deadline from hell was at his heels. Cycling boy picked up his bag again and headed past me with a nod, presumably heading for the gents' to change into something less budgie-smuggly.

And the middling-everything man pushed back his chair, saying, 'Hi. You must be—'

He sort of half-stood but then seemed to change his mind. Maybe he thought standing up to greet a woman was unacceptable in a modern workplace. Maybe he decided he couldn't be bothered after all. Maybe he suddenly realised his fly was open. I had no idea.

But whatever the reason, it worked out badly for him. By the time he sat back down, his wheeled chair had scooted further back than he'd realised. His descending bum just clipped the edge of the seat. The chair went one way and he went the other and ended up on the floor with a jolt that must have felt like his spine was going to shoot through the top of his head.

There was a moment of silence, then the handsome bloke let out a guffaw that practically took the roof off. The skinny dude joined in, and Mr Middling stayed down on the floor. I felt a rush of sympathy for him – what if he was hurt? What if he felt awful because everyone was laughing at him? What if he was going to actually cry or something? Then I realised that he, too, was doubled over with mirth.

'Smooth move, bro,' said Handsome.

'Give us some warning next time,' complained Skinny. 'We could've videoed that and made a fortune.'

'What did I miss?' Budgie, hearing the commotion, hurried back to the group, a clean T-shirt sticking damply to his chest.

'Ross arse-planted in front of the new girl,' said Skinny.

'Most spectacular pratfall, like, ever,' said Handsome.

'Uh... are you okay?' I asked.

Middling – who I gathered was Ross, usurper of the job that should have been mine – picked himself up off the floor. 'Only my pride's hurt,' he said. 'But that won't recover any time soon. Show's over, guys, pretend it never happened. As I was saying before I so rudely interrupted myself, you must be Lucy. I'm Ross.'

'Easy to remember,' quipped Handsome. 'Ross took a toss – gettit? I'm Marco.'

I realised after a second that he had extended his hand for me to shake, and I took it. But I wasn't really looking at him – I was looking at Ross. There was an amiable grin on his face. He seemed totally unfazed by his embarrassing mishap, by being a figure of fun in front of his colleagues and in front of me.

Was it a man thing? Or had he just decided, after his first glance at me, that my opinion wasn't worth bothering about?

'Chiraag,' said Budgie.

'Neil,' muttered Skinny, glancing up from his screen then glancing straight back, as if the sight of me was too awful to endure.

'I look after news,' Marco went on, 'Chiraag's sport, Neil's money and Ross is tech. At least he is when he's not crashing his hard drive. Simon and Barney are fashion and lifestyle, but they're out on a shoot today. The subs and production guys are over on the next pod and art's beyond that. Greg said to show you round but I guess you've seen it all now, right?'

'Uh, yeah.' I put down my bag and sat at the vacant desk, which was the one opposite Ross, placing my mug and the photo of Astro next to my keyboard. Then I opened a drawer and slid in my Venus flytrap. I'd take it home this evening, I decided.

Five minutes in these guys' company had taught me one important lesson. They hadn't been unfriendly or hostile or even overtly sexist – nothing like that. But I'd realised that if I did anything foolish – anything at all – they'd laugh at me.

As the only woman in the team, I was going to stand out enough as it was. I wasn't going to show weakness, and I was categorically not going to be laughed at. I switched on my computer, got it set up the way I liked and logged into my email.

It didn't take me long to discover some key things about my new colleagues. I learned that when there was a collection for someone's birthday, Neil took round the card to sign and the envelope for everyone to chip in a couple of quid, or even a fiver if they were feeling flush, but added nothing himself. I learned that Chiraag spent a good five minutes each morning painstakingly shaking a protein drink at his desk – the rattle of ice cubes and scrape of the metal blendy thing against the plastic container got very old, very quickly. I learned that when Marco sat down each morning, he'd spend a few moments artfully rearranging his hair, using his blank computer screen as a mirror before switching it on.

And I learned that Ross was the social one in the group. He suggested heading out to have a few pints and play darts, or go to a CrossFit session at lunchtime, or nip to the corner shop for mint Magnums when the weather turned warm and the afternoon was dragging. And because he was the one sat opposite me, he was the one I noticed the most. He ran his fingers through his hair when he was thinking, messing it up and pulling locks down over his forehead. He seemed to go from clean-shaven to designer stubble to not-so-designer stubble on roughly a four-day cycle, so clearly he didn't take his appearance particularly seriously. He had nice eyes, a clear, bright hazel colour. Like all the rest of us, he wore jeans, hoodies and trainers. When I'd brushed past him in the kitchen, I'd caught a waft of a clean smell coming off him, a mixture of laundry detergent and soap.

Although maybe that was just the free toiletries provided in the showers down at the CrossFit box – I had no idea.

I supposed that if I'd been in the market for meeting a man, I'd probably have stuck Ross on the shortlist and started inviting myself along to the pub and the gym. Okay, maybe not the gym – even the mythical in-the-market-for-a-man Lucy would have thought that was a bridge too far. I could see the appeal of Ross, objectively speaking, but I wasn't interested in dating anyone – especially not a man I worked with – so Ross was just another guy, another member of the male sex in which I had zero interest. Even if I was interested, there was no way I was going to allow even a flicker of that interest to show – I'd learned the hard way that that was a surefire route to humiliation and heartbreak.

And sadly, it appeared at first that men had no interest in Adam, my alter ego, either. Adam's debut was announced with great fanfare in the final print edition of *Max!*. A stock photo of a friendly, innocuous-looking bloke in his mid-thirties, looking serious and chewing a pencil, together with the Ask Adam logo, went out on *Max!*'s social media channels shortly afterwards, but the following week, no problems arrived in the designated inbox.

By Friday, I was beginning to worry that my new job was dead in the water before it had even begun.

But that wasn't my only concern. The regular Friday afternoon exodus was about to begin, and I was determined to get out of joining my new colleagues in the pub. I didn't want to go – but at the same time I did. I didn't want to be exposed to their chat, their questions, their banter. I wanted to go home to my silent, solitary flat and cuddle my cat. But then – maybe I did. Maybe it would be fun. There'd been nothing so far to make me think it would be anything other than fun.

I could feel tension ratcheting up in my body with every sound: the click of Neil's mouse as he shut down his computer; the rustle of Barney's rainproof jacket as he eased it over his shoulders; the squeak of Ross's chair wheels on the polished concrete floor; the crack of Marco's knuckles as he stretched luxuriantly overhead.

Then Ross's voice broke into my reverie, making me jump. 'Earth to Lucy?'

'Sorry,' I said. 'Did you ask me something?'

'Just what you're up to this weekend.' His eyes met mine over the top of our monitors and he smiled. Nice teeth. Middling-straight. 'Wondered if I might bump into you. You live near Dalston Lane, right?'

How the hell does he know that? I must have mentioned it in passing, perhaps when Chiraag was talking about his forty-five-minute cycle commute to work.

'Holly Street,' I confirmed.

'Wow! We're practically neighbours. Maybe I'll see you in A Bar with Shapes tomorrow night.'

I thought of the weekend stretching ahead of me, calm and featureless, the way I'd learned to like it. Sleeping in on Saturday, tinkering with the mod I'd been working on for *Elden Ring*, cleaning my flat, chilling out with Astro. A pretty solid weekend, all told. I was looking forward to it.

But, for some reason I couldn't quite identify, I didn't want Ross to be able to picture me like that, alone, when he was hanging out in cool places I walked past every day but had never been to, no doubt surrounded by his cool friends.

I heard my voice say, 'Got a date tomorrow night.'

'Really?' He raised his eyebrows. 'First date?'

'Um... yeah.'

'On a Saturday night? Punchy. He must be keen.'

Shit. Of course no one would give up a Saturday night for a date with some random they didn't even know if they'd like. Except me, apparently. If the date had existed, which it didn't.

'I guess he is. We met...' *Where the hell did we meet?* 'Online.'

Damn. That just made it a million times worse. Giving up a Saturday night for a date with some random off Hinge? That had gone beyond punchy and straight into desperate territory. Just as well it wasn't true, or I'd have needed to take a long, hard look at myself. Although, given I was fabricating a date with someone who didn't exist just so my work colleague would think I was more interesting than I really was, I probably needed to do that anyway.

'Going anywhere nice?' Ross asked.

Stop asking me questions! You're stretching my creative powers to their not-very-long limit, I thought. I racked my brains frantically for a second. Where did people go on first dates? I hadn't been on one since forever. Not even with Kieren. Where had Amelie gone on her first date with Zack? Now, *that* I could remember clearly – after all, my sister had snuck off to the loo to send me WhatsApp updates so frequently that Zack had assumed she had an upset stomach or was having the period from hell, and he'd asked if she was okay or needed to go home. Cue total radio silence from her and panic from me because I'd thought he must have murdered her.

'Cocktails,' I said. 'At the Savoy.'

'Wow.' Ross did the eyebrow thing again. 'Really keen. I guess there's no point asking you if you fancy joining us at the Prince Regent tonight for a couple of pints, then. Wouldn't want you to slum it down the local.'

Shit. It was an invitation. A backhanded one, but an invitation nonetheless. And it coming from Ross made it much harder to refuse, for some reason I couldn't quite pinpoint.

But I thought ahead to what would happen if I said yes. Once we were installed with our drinks, Ross would say, 'Lucy's got a hot date tomorrow night. Cocktails at the Savoy,' and everyone would press me for details about the fictitious man I'd met online, who was taking me to a fancy hotel bar on our first date. I'd have to lie – lie to Ross – and risk getting caught out in my lie if he questioned me about it on Monday and remembered the made-up details better than I could.

That alone would have been enough to make my decision for me. But it didn't need making, because I couldn't go anyway.

With a pang of something that felt almost like disappointment – although, given the excruciatingly awkward consequences of saying yes that I'd rapidly formulated in my head, it couldn't possibly have been – I said, 'Sorry, I can't. I'm seeing my family tonight.'

'Fair do's,' Ross replied amicably. 'Blood's thicker than water, right?'

'My sister's getting married,' I volunteered, as if that somehow made a difference. 'In a few weeks. I'm her chief bridesmaid, and we're going round to Mum and Dad's place for dinner. I expect she wants me to try on my dress for the millionth time to make sure it still fits, or something like that.'

Ross grinned. 'Tell me your sister's a bridezilla without telling me your sister's a bridezilla.'

I felt a flare of defensive annoyance. 'She's not. At least, not more than anyone else who's getting married. It's stressful.'

'Tell me about it,' he agreed. 'I was best man for my mate Duncan a few months back and it was carnage. His missus got so worked up in the lead-up to the day, they almost called the whole thing off. It was fine in the end, though. You'll talk her down.'

'Hope so.' I allowed myself a tight smile and turned back to my screen, trying not to imagine what Ross would look like in a suit.

Then, right on schedule, I saw heads and shoulders rise up around me like a man-forest as they all stood, put on coats, carried empty coffee mugs to the kitchen, powered down computers. Little knots of people crossed the office towards the lift, first a trickle, then a flood, then a final few stragglers.

'Have a good one, Lucy,' Ross said. 'Good luck with the date.'

I paused a beat, as if engrossed in my work, then said, 'Thanks. Enjoy the pub,' without looking away from my screen.

I waited until I was sure everyone had gone, then switched off my PC, picked up my coat and bag and left, turning out the lights and activating the alarm on my way out. Then I got the Tube to meet my family – the single daughter, cheerfully joining in the planning for her little sister's wedding.

FOUR

The next week, two things happened. Good things – or, at least, things that had the promise of becoming good. I spent Monday with almost nothing to do: Adam's inbox remained stubbornly empty, no matter how many times I checked it. When, at the weekly team meeting, Greg asked how the agony uncle column was going, I had to stammer out an admission that, so far, it was all uncle and no agony. Greg raised an eyebrow and said something about a slow burn, but I knew full well that if the column didn't work, he would can it and therefore also can me.

The only work I'd done was reading through endless back issues of *Max!* – trying not to admire Ross's grasp of his subject matter and elegant turn of phrase – helping Simon with some research into the apparently unstoppable rise of grandpa-core, and proofreading an article about NBA basketball for Chiraag. Oh – and making endless rounds of tea and coffee for the team. I hated not being busy – it made me even more self-conscious than usual; I imagined Greg coming up behind my desk, seeing my screen blank and idle, and telling me that this clearly wasn't working and I might as well pack my things and go.

So, on Tuesday morning at around quarter to eleven, when I

heard a voice behind me say my name, I started and felt a cold trickle of dread on the back of my neck. This was it – the axe was going to fall.

But it wasn't Greg. It was a guy I didn't know – a tall man with a luxuriant beard, carrying a tablet.

'Lucy?' he asked.

'Uh... hi,' I said. 'That's me.' Not that it would have taken Sherlock Holmes to work that out, given I was the only woman on the entire floor and therefore the only potential Lucy.

'I'm Shane, from IT upstairs.' He smiled. 'I understand there's a problem with your ItemProcSearch folder.'

'I'm sorry?'

'With your incoming email,' he translated.

'No, it seems fine,' I said. Just five minutes earlier, I'd received an invitation to the *Max!* monthly five-a-side football match, which obviously I would not be attending. 'I've been getting mail just— Oh, wait. You mean the other account?'

'AskAdam@MaxMag.co.uk,' he confirmed. 'The new address we set up for you.'

'Yeah, that's right. Only I haven't had any mail to that address.'

He nodded. 'Thought not. Mind if I have a seat?'

I stood up and he swung into my chair and scooted over to the screen, clicking the mouse and tapping commands into the keyboard. I half-watched, the way you do when an IT guy is doing stuff on your machine, wanting to make helpful suggestions but conscious that although I knew about technology, I clearly didn't know about this particular aspect of it, otherwise I'd have been able to rectify the problem myself.

I managed not to say, *Have you tried switching it off and on again?* I suspected Shane might have heard that joke before, once or twice.

After a minute or two, he gave a grunt of satisfaction. 'Yup, that's it.'

'What?' I asked.

'There was an error setting up the inbox. My bad. Messages were getting stuck in a hidden folder. I've cleared the cache so it should be sorted now.'

He stood up, and I thanked him and returned to my chair as he hurried away to his next rescue mission. The Ask Adam inbox was on my screen, containing just one message, from support@radiantmedia.co.uk, with the subject line 'TEST'. So it was working – great. But there was still no one who wanted to ask Adam anything – not so great.

Then, as I watched, another unread message appeared on the screen, below Shane's test email and therefore sent earlier. Then another appeared below it, and another and another. Then there was a pause, then four more landed on the screen. Another pause – and then a rush. Email after email, their subject lines in bold because they were unread, came flooding into the inbox.

I couldn't help letting out a whoop of excitement.

'What's up?' Neil asked. 'Won the lottery?'

'It's not all about money, you know,' said Marco. 'Maybe Lucy's hot date from Saturday asked her out again.'

'Or she read my column saying that skinny jeans are over and never coming back?' put in Simon.

'Or she's been offered a job somewhere she won't be surrounded by idiots,' suggested Chiraag.

'What's going on, Lucy?' asked Ross. 'Do we need to hit the pub after work to celebrate whatever it is?'

'Adam's in business,' I told them triumphantly. 'I've got a whole mailbox full of problems.'

'First time I ever heard anyone sound so happy about having problems,' Ross noted dryly, but I just grinned at him like a loon and after a second he grinned back.

I adjusted my glasses, flexed my fingers and turned to the

brimming mailbox, picking an email at random and clicking on it.

Dear Adam,

My girlfriend and I have been dating for two years and living together for one. She's always been a casual kind of woman – only wearing make-up when we go out, comfortable clothes, all that stuff. Low-maintenance, you know? Not that I mind – I think she's gorgeous and sexy just as she is. But lately, I've noticed that she's getting up earlier in the mornings and blow-drying her hair and doing her face before she leaves for work. She even bought a pair of high-heeled shoes to wear to the office.

When I asked about this change, she told me she's hoping for a promotion at work, but I'm not sure I believe her.

Give it to me straight, Adam – is she cheating on me?

Rufus, Dundee

Okay. I was clearly going to need a strategy. Perhaps I'd be able to at least frame a response to some of the emails before I needed to lean on Amelie for help. Maybe I needed some sort of a system – colour-coding them, or automatically filtering them by keyword so that anything containing the word 'penis' got diverted into a folder where I'd never have to look at it again. Or alternatively—

'Lucy?' Neil's voice interrupted my concentration.

'Yes?' I glanced at him.

He was holding his empty mug, and as I watched, he tipped it upside down in a meaningful manner. A dribble of cold tea landed on his desk and he wiped it up with his sleeve.

'I'm awfully thirsty,' he said. 'Any chance of a brew?'

Shit. Half an hour earlier, I'd have leaped to my feet, taken a round of drinks orders and hurried to the kitchen, relieved to have something to do. But now I did have something to do – something important, something that was my actual job.

I'd made a rod for my own back, I realised. All those helpful trips to the kitchen – all that checking whether Chiraag's lemon and ginger tea was strong enough and putting just one ice cube in Simon's glass of water – had come back to bite me on the arse.

I was the only woman in the team, and now it seemed I'd volunteered to keep all these men hydrated and caffeinated for the foreseeable future.

I wanted to say no – but at the same time I didn't want to come across as unhelpful, lazy or bitchy.

'Come on, mate,' Ross said from the desk opposite mine. 'Why's that Lucy's job?'

'Do you think she switches on the kettle with her ovaries or something?' asked Barney.

'Are you okay, Neil?' Chiraag asked with faux concern. 'Couple of weeks ago, you took your turn to do a round of drinks, same as all the rest of us. Now you seem to have lost the use of your legs.'

'Maybe Lucy gives him such a massive boner he's scared to stand up,' suggested Marco.

'Fine,' Neil huffed. 'Fine. Gotcha. I'll—'

'Don't worry.' Now it was clear everyone was on my side, I felt guilty about causing ructions within the group. 'I'll do it. Just this once, mind.'

I stood up and started gathering the empty cups. Opposite me, Ross did the same, collecting mugs from his side of the bank of desks and following me to the kitchen.

'Thanks,' I said. 'You didn't have to do that.'

'You didn't either,' he pointed out.

'I didn't mean the coffee,' I explained. 'I meant backing me up.'

Ross smiled. 'Reckoned it wouldn't do any harm. Give Neil an inch and he'll take a mile.'

'Well – thanks anyway. Guess you saved me from a lifetime of servitude.'

'Somehow, I can't quite see you in that role.'

His words brought back a flash of a memory I'd have preferred to forget – when I'd also found myself in a role at work I could never have expected.

I pushed it aside. 'Yours is a double espresso with a drop of milk, right?'

Ross shook his head. 'It's after midday, so I'll just have a tea, thanks.'

I grinned at him and quoted, '"No thanks, I can't drink coffee late at night, it keeps me up."'

'"Coffee's not coffee, coffee is sex."'

To my surprise, he'd got the *Seinfeld* reference right away. Only now he was talking about sex, and that felt awkward – almost too personal, like he was suggesting something, or I'd be giving something away if I responded in kind. But that was ridiculous. We weren't exchanging details about our favourite positions – we were just quoting characters from a TV show.

After a second, I forgot my caution and went for it.

'"Sex, that's meaningless."' I pressed the button to send a stream of coffee into my mug.

'"Food and sex. Those are my two passions."'

Oh, really? I thought. Then I reminded myself, *He's just quoting a show.*

'"To men, sex is an emergency,"' I said.

Ross laughed, then poured boiling water over a teabag, his brow furrowed. 'Damn, you got me.'

'Next time, I'll do my Soup Nazi routine.'

'I'm totally here for that.'

I arranged the drinks on a tray and Ross picked it up.

As we left the kitchen, I couldn't resist saying, "'I gotta get on that internet, I'm late on everything!'"

When we got back to our desks, we were still giggling. I couldn't help noticing that every time I looked up from my screen and met Ross's eye, he'd smile like we now had a shared secret. I found myself storing up more *Seinfeld* quotes in my mind, ready to produce them at opportune moments so I could not only beat him at the game, but make him laugh.

I spent the rest of the day reading through Adam's mail, feeling more and more bewildered by the minute. I'd known I didn't understand men, but I hadn't realised just how much there was to not understand. There was a guy whose girlfriend had dumped him and he didn't know why. I didn't know either, and therefore neither did Adam. There was a guy who didn't know whether the woman he fancied fancied him back – both Adam and I drew a blank on that one too. And there was Rufus, who wasn't sure if his partner upping her sartorial game meant there was another guy on the scene.

I mean, I could see where he was coming from. I remembered myself a few years back, buying a dress and tights to wear to the office when before I'd always gone in wearing jeans. It was a decision I had come to regret, and I'd reverted to hoodies and zero make-up – it was safer that way.

There was no way I was going to try and make myself look fanciable at work again, not even for Ross. Especially not for Ross.

But perhaps Rufus's girlfriend was telling the truth, and she was just trying to dress for the job she wanted rather than the one she had. I was stumped – and so was Adam – over and over again.

With each new message came a fresh awareness that I had bitten off more than I could chew.

FIVE

Dear Adam,

You might not be the best person to answer this, but I don't know who else to talk to. And my problem isn't about a girl, but – actually, it is. Only she's my daughter. My wife passed away a year ago and I miss her more than I can say. Now it's just my little girl and me. She's twelve and she's my world. We do loads of stuff together: I take her to football matches – and watch her play; she's a cracking midfielder – we cook together, I help with her homework. All the stuff it feels right to do as a dad. But here's the thing – now she's getting older, I don't know how to help her with all the stuff girls go through at this age. You know – puberty, periods, all those things. Even though we talk about everything else, I feel so awkward about raising this with her.

What should a father do in this situation?

Jonno, London

My mind was taken off my problems by Wednesday – not by anything lovely, but by the gloom of an impending visit to the dentist. I spent much of the afternoon fretting about cavities and periodontitis, so I was barely able to focus on the messages that were still trickling into my inbox at a steady pace from Adam's correspondents.

Then my eyes lit on one that made a bit more sense to me. As soon as I read Jonno's email, my heart went out to him. Here was a bloke who really cared about the woman in his life – even if she was still only a child. She'd lost her mother and he'd lost the person who I could tell just from reading his message had been his other half.

I copied and pasted his message into a fresh Word document and read it through again, thinking of my own father. He hadn't had to raise Amelie and me on his own – our mum had been there the whole time. But if he had, I knew he'd have done his best. And something about Jonno's email told me he'd do his best, too.

Hesitantly – my fingers clumsy on the keyboard so I made loads of mistakes and had to delete and retype almost every word – I started to write.

Dear Jonno,

It's a privilege to answer your letter in the first-ever Ask Adam column. Your love for your late wife and your daughter shines through in your words, and it's clear to me how lucky you are to have each other in your lives.

You sound like a great dad, but I get how daunting it must feel to be accompanying your daughter on the journey she's going through. Do you have women in your life you can reach out to for support – your female friends and family, her teachers, even a trusted colleague? If your daughter asks questions you can't

*answer right there and then, don't be scared to admit that, and
tell her you'll help her find the answers.*

*Keep talking to her, keep loving her, and I bet everything will
work out okay. You've got this.*

I'm very sorry for your loss.

Yours,

Adam

By the time I'd finished, I felt as knackered as if I'd written a
dissertation instead of just 150 words. I could have carried on
for longer, but the length of the Ask Adam columns had already
been agreed, and I didn't want some ruthless sub-editor cutting
down my reply.

I pressed Print, hurrying over to the printer and hovering
over the sheet of paper, then taking it back to my desk and
reading it over and over. It felt like enough – but at the same
time, not nearly enough.

'Ross,' I asked, 'have you got a second to look at something?'

He glanced up from his screen. 'Sure. Hand it over.'

I slid the sheet of paper across the desks between us. Ross
took it and looked at it, and I saw his face change from interested and curious to kind of closed. He picked up a red pen and
made a couple of small marks on the page, then passed it back
to me.

His corrections were minor – a rogue typing error, a comma
in the wrong place.

'What do you reckon?' I asked. 'Is it okay?'

He shrugged. 'Looks all right to me. Why don't you show
Greg?'

'Yes, I will, but – what do you think?'

'I'm not the best person to ask. It's fine, Lucy. Good job.'

He turned back to his work, and I heard his fingers rattling the keys. Just the previous day, things between us had seemed fine – we'd been bantering over coffee, even. But now he seemed cold, as if I'd done something to offend him. I had no idea what that could be, but clearly I wasn't going to get the validation I sought from him. So I made the corrections, printed the page out again and left it on Greg's desk.

Then I spent ages flossing and brushing my teeth before reminding Greg of the reason for my early departure and leaving the office.

After a mercifully drama-free appointment spent having metal spikes dug into my gums and listening to a lecture about brushing for a minimum of two minutes twice a day and cutting down on coffee, there didn't seem to be much point in going back to the office. I'd head home, I decided, and do a couple hours' work on the sofa – or, more likely, doomscroll through websites about feline dentistry and wonder whether I should be brushing Astro's teeth as well as my own.

But when I opened the door to my flat bearing a pack of special tooth-friendly treats from the pet shop, my cat didn't meet me at the door as usual.

'Astro?' I called, dumping my bag on the kitchen counter and heading through to the living room and then the bedroom. 'Where are you?'

There was no response. It was about half an hour earlier than I usually arrived home – perhaps he was sleeping in some specially designated afternoon nap spot I didn't know about? I checked everywhere I could think of – under the bed, in the wardrobe in case he'd got stuck there, out on the balcony. But no grey, furry form emerged.

My puzzlement turning to worry, I left the flat again and walked down the road a bit, calling, rattling treats and looking under parked cars. There was no need to panic, I told myself; it was still going to be light for a couple of hours. It was not unheard of – although unusual – for Astro to hop the few feet down from the balcony and take himself off for a potter in the neighbouring gardens.

But he never went far or stayed out long. He'd always been an unadventurous, homebody sort of cat. His formative months spent sleeping rough had clearly convinced him that the outdoor life wasn't for the likes of him, and the idea that he was out somewhere, lost and afraid, made me afraid too.

By six thirty, there was still no sign of him. I rattled treats, checked in neighbouring gardens and walked the length of my quiet street again and again, calling for him.

There was no answering meow.

Reluctantly, I ventured further down towards the main road, where I could hear the evening traffic – buses, cars, lorries, speeding bicycles – building up. There was a park where people let dogs play off their leads. There was an MOT garage with all sorts of dangerous places where he could have got injured or trapped. There were shops with wheelie bins out the back where foxes and other, more streetwise cats foraged after dark.

It was no place for Astro. But I had to keep looking because I didn't know what else to do. If I hadn't found him by nightfall, I decided, I'd return home and post on social media, perhaps design some posters to print out at work in the morning, probably call my mum and have a cry.

For now, though, I kept walking, looking, calling and increasingly panicking.

At this point, I'd exhausted the front gardens of neighbouring houses, the open space surrounding the next-door block of flats, the kids' playground and the car park behind the supermarket. Only the main road was left.

My heart in my mouth, imagining Astro's fluffy form limp and crushed by a passing car, I turned the corner. My throat hurt from calling and from the lump of impending tears. I didn't want to lose him – I didn't think I could bear it. He was my best friend, my companion, my responsibility.

Then, walking down the road towards me, I saw a familiar figure.

The long, denim-clad legs, the mid-brown hair sticking up at the front, the T-shirt with a Nine Inch Nails album cover on it, which I'd seen only that afternoon – although it felt like a lifetime ago.

It was Ross, on his way home to a flat that was only a few minutes' walk from mine. But more familiar still – although bewilderingly strange out of context – was the grey, furry form he had cradled over his shoulder.

I broke into a run, sprinting the short distance until I reached him, arriving panting and tearful.

'Lucy! There you are. Are you okay?'

'Just about. Not really. What the hell are you doing with Astro?' Then I realised how bad that sounded, and hastily added, 'Is he hurt?'

Shaking his head, Ross turned around so I could see my cat's face, disgruntled but unharmed. When he recognised me, he tried to wriggle out of Ross's arms. His hold was precarious, I realised, because he was carrying not only his laptop bag and the cat, but also a brown paper bag from which a familiar smell emerged: savoury and vinegary, making my mouth water when before it had been dry.

'He's fine. Here, can you grab him without letting him go?'

Carefully, he passed Astro to me. The cat protested briefly but allowed himself to settle in my arms. Overwhelmed with relief, I tried to squeeze him hard enough so as not to let him go, but not so hard as to hurt him.

'Where was he? How did you find him? I need to get him home.'

'I tried calling you.' Ross fell into step next to me. 'But you weren't answering.'

'No – I must've left my phone in the flat. I came out in a rush when I realised he wasn't home.'

'I stopped off at the chip shop to get some dinner,' Ross explained. 'And he was there. Carol there said he visits a couple of afternoons a week, just at teatime, and they give him a bit of cod.'

'They what? My cat's been sneaking out for takeaways and I never knew?'

Ross laughed. 'I recognised him from the photo on your desk, and then I saw your name on his collar. I thought I'd better bring him back because it's not safe out there, you know.'

Hearing the roar of the road behind me, I felt my knees threaten to dissolve into jelly. 'I know.'

'He's such a great cat,' Ross enthused. 'He let me pick him up, no problem. I was going to take him back to mine and give him some of my scampi if I couldn't get hold of you – I don't know your address and I didn't want to just abandon him.'

'He would've never wanted to leave,' I said, pushing aside the thought that if Ross had invited me back to his for scampi and chips, I would never want to leave either.

'I know, right? I'm crazy about scampi – I've been obsessed with it ever since I moved here from the States; it's not a thing there. But how awkward would that have been? "Dear Adam, I rescued my colleague's cat and now she's accusing me of catnapping."'

I laughed, the release of tension making the joke funnier than it might have been. '"Dear Adam, my colleague, my cat and I have found ourselves in a throuple. How can we make this work for all of us?"'

Ross grinned. 'And what would Adam say to that?'

I looked sideways at him, over Astro's soft head. Now that

we were nearing home, he was starting to wriggle in my arms, eager to prove that he knew his own way back and didn't need to be carried. But I kept hold of him, as if he was providing a shield between me and Ross – or between myself and my feelings.

'"Negotiating space for a third individual within your primary partnership can be satisfying for all parties,"' I began, trying to channel the Adam persona that I'd discovered only the day before. '"Such relationships are challenging, but they can also be rewarding. Open and honest communication is..." Here's my flat now.'

'Damn,' Ross said. 'I wanted to know how that was going to end.'

'I guess you'll have to wait until someone writes to Adam with that exact question, then.' Feeling myself starting to blush, I buried my face in Astro's fur and kissed him, relief that he was okay flooding through me all over again.

Ross reached out to scratch my cat behind the ears, in just the spot he liked. 'What'll you do about his takeaways?'

'Shit.' It had only just occurred to me that since this was something Astro had done before, it was therefore something he was likely to do again. 'I don't know. I can't let him – it's not safe.'

Ross nodded. 'I wouldn't be too keen on the idea if he was my cat. He's pretty special.'

'He is.' Confident now that Astro wouldn't run off, I gently put him down, and he twined around our legs, rubbing his cheeks against us and purring. 'He's just the best.'

I gave him a quick run-down of Astro's history, keeping it brief because I knew that usually once I started talking about him, it took me ages to stop.

'Maybe you could ring them and tell them not to serve him again if he turns up,' Ross suggested.

'Like being banned from your local Wetherspoons?'

'I guess. I'd be gutted if Spoons banned me, though.'

I laughed, pleased and surprised – I'd taken Ross to be more of a hipster-speakeasy kind of guy.

'Maybe I should keep him indoors for a week or so, at least while I'm out,' I mused. 'Maybe he'll forget about it then.'

'Especially if you got takeaway from there and shared it with him,' Ross suggested. 'Then he'd get the gain without the potential pain.'

I felt an involuntary shiver of dread. 'Don't even say that.'

'Sorry.' Ross squatted down and fussed Astro some more. 'We don't want anything bad to happen to you, do we? You must be a sensible cat and do what your mum says.'

Astro made a beeline for the brown paper bag and began sniffing it eagerly.

'Come on now, you leave Ross's dinner alone,' I scolded. 'Sorry. It'll be getting cold – we've kept you ages.'

'Doesn't matter. It's been worth it.' He grinned up at me then stood easily, lifting the bag out of Astro's reach. I wasn't sure why he'd been so weird earlier, when I'd shown him my answer to Jonno's letter, but the weirdness seemed to have well and truly passed.

'Thanks so much,' I said. 'Honestly, I'm so grateful to you for rescuing him. Anything could have happened.'

He shook his head. 'Don't mention it.'

'Well... I guess I'll see you in the office tomorrow. Enjoy your scampi.'

'I will.' He turned to go, slowly, as if he wasn't quite ready. 'They're on Deliveroo, you know. You could order in for you and Astro.'

'They are? Technology for the win, right?'

'Technology for the win,' he agreed.

Then he looked at me for a second and reached up as if he

was going to – something. Shake my hand? Hug me? But at the last moment, it turned into a fist bump.

My knuckles only touched his for the briefest moment, but it felt as intimate as a kiss.

SIX

It was a week and a half later, the following Saturday, and my flat was no longer quiet, no longer empty, and no longer tidy. In fact I don't think there had ever been as many people in it as there were that night. As many girls.

Normally, I'd call myself out for using that word – these were all adult women, after all. But that night there was something about my sister and her friends that was pure, one hundred per cent girl. My kitchen counter was strewn with make-up compacts, stacks of brushes, bottles of nail varnish, magnifying mirrors and even a ring light. The air was thick with the smell of hairspray and perfume. Half-drunk bottles of fizz and cans of hard seltzer were leaving sticky rings on every surface. Music blared from my speakers, almost drowned out by gales of giggles.

It was Amelie's hen night, and my flat had been chosen for the rendezvous and getting-ready point, owing to it being closest to the bar in Shoreditch where we were heading. And maybe owing to me being chief bridesmaid, I guess, although I'd had very little to do with the arrangements for tonight's festivities.

Originally, Zack had offered to pay for us all to spend a

week partying in Ibiza. But, to my surprise, Amelie had put her foot down – it was too much time to ask all her friends to take off work, and, besides, what she really wanted was a good, old-fashioned Saturday night out. Zack, apparently, had told her that whatever she wanted was what he wanted too, and so it had been settled.

The moment my sister had set up the WhatsApp group and written, 'I'll leave you girls' – see: girls – 'to it then and see you all at my hen do! Woooo!!' followed by a slew of emojis – pink fingernails, clinking champagne flutes, cocktails, hearts and of course the dancing lady – Amelie's friends had begun building up to a fever pitch of excitement.

Most of them were just names I'd seen on the WhatsApp group. I had no idea whether the tall redhead or the curvaceous Asian woman was Miranda. There were dark-haired twins who'd introduced themselves as Caitlin and Bryony, but I couldn't for the life of me identify which was which. A group of four stunning blondes, almost as indistinguishable from each other as the twins, had arrived together and dashed, shrieking, into the flat to greet their friends, barely glancing at me when I opened the door.

I knew Amelie, of course. And I knew Nush, her best friend since primary school, and Rosa and Eve, her university friends, who I'd met at various parties and dinners over the years.

But that didn't make much of a difference – the whole vibe was so unlike anything I normally experienced, they all might as well have been fragrant, blow-dried aliens who'd flown in from another planet for the occasion.

Evidently, there was a theme. What exactly, I couldn't put my finger on – angels maybe, or unicorns, or sparkles, or perhaps just pink. Whichever it was, the girls were attired in thigh-high slinky dresses, cerise glitter trainers, fluttery white feather boas and tops so skimpy they looked like they'd nicked a hanky from somewhere and stuck it over their chests with a couple of bits of Sellotape going round the back.

I hadn't got the memo – literally. Once the WhatsApp chat had started to escalate, I'd muted the group, only checking in once a week or so to ask if there was anything I could do, other than hosting the pre-party, and I'd been assured it was all under control. So I was wearing black jeans, purple Docs and a baggy charcoal vest top with the Metallica logo on the front. Actually, thinking about it, I was the one who looked like an alien, foreign and abandoned on their shiny pink planet.

Even Astro had taken disgruntled refuge in his favourite shelf in my wardrobe, where his furry form was half-buried by jumpers. Amelie was doing her best to look out for me, but it was her night, and understandably she could only give me regular 'Are you okay?' glances, or comforting squeezes on the shoulder, before flitting back to her friends.

Determined to conceal – or ideally drown – my awkwardness, I poured yet another glass of fizz and set to work ferrying empties to the recycling, wiping up spills and crumpling empty crisp packets.

'Is it time to go?' the tall redhead asked, checking her reflection in her phone's camera and topping up her lip gloss.

'Our table's booked for seven thirty at the restaurant,' said a twin.

'And then ten at the club,' said one of the blondes.

'We're getting an Uber, right?' asked another. 'There's no way I'll make it further than down the stairs in these shoes.'

'But Lucy's not ready yet,' Rosa pointed out.

'Yes, babe, you'd better get changed,' urged Eve.

All at once, a dozen pairs of eyes turned on me like searchlights.

'I wasn't going to,' I muttered. 'I was going like this. I haven't got anything pink.'

'Don't be mad!' protested one of the twins. 'You need to be on theme!'

'Hasn't someone got something Lucy can wear?' demanded her sister.

'Come on,' Nush said, grabbing my elbow firmly, her other hand clutching a squashy silver leather backpack. 'I brought a spare outfit. I always spill food on myself and end up looking like I've been in a fight with it. But you can borrow this. I'll just have to tuck a napkin into my top, won't I?'

As she frog-marched me into my bedroom, I heard my sister say, 'Only if you want to, Luce. You must wear whatever you're comfortable in.'

But it was too late. The door had closed behind us, and Nush had produced a sparkly silver garment from her bag. It looked about big enough to fit Astro.

'It's stretchy,' she encouraged. 'And besides, you're way smaller than me. I'd kill for your figure. Come on.'

Reluctantly, I perched on the bed and unlaced my boots, then pulled off my jeans and top and stood there in my bra and pants, resisting the urge to cover my boobs with a forearm like some swooning Regency virgin.

'I'm afraid it's a bit of a braless wonder,' Nush said, shaking the dress at me like a matador goading a bull. 'I mean, you can wear one if you want, but it'll show. And you really don't need to, you're...'

'Flat as an ironing board?' I joked, trying unsuccessfully to conceal my awkwardness.

She tutted and shook her head. 'Lovely and perky, you lucky thing. Try it. I won't look.'

She turned away as if this was a game of hide and seek and she was counting to a hundred. I unclipped my bra and frantically tried to figure out the dress, putting my head through first one armhole and then the other before I finally got it right. I pulled it down as far as I could, but it still barely covered my bottom. It was Lurex, mercifully lined at the front but with the back made up of little more than a series of criss-cross straps. The mirror in my bedroom was too small for me to see the full effect, but Nush looked delighted when she turned around.

'Oh my God! It's like it was made for you. Fabulous.'

'What shoes will I wear though?'

'Your DMs are perfect. Pure rock chick. Come on, stick them back on and we'll get Miranda to do your eyes. She's a genius with make-up.'

Seconds later, I was perched on a stool in my kitchen, with Miranda – who turned out to be the Asian girl – fluttering over my face with brushes and sponges while someone else opened another bottle and everyone exclaimed over how amazing I looked in Nush's dress.

'You'll want to do your own mascara,' Miranda said after a bit. 'I'm so cack-handed I'd probably poke your eye out.'

She held up a compact mirror in one hand and proffered a mascara wand with the other, and, as if mesmerised, I slid the brush over my eyelashes, trying not to blink before it dried, my glasses clutched in my lap. Miranda wafted her hands in front of my face a few times, then said, 'You're all good. My work here is done.'

I slipped my glasses on again and the room came back into focus, but Miranda had already snapped her mirror closed, Amelie was putting the last half-drunk bottles of fizz back in my fridge, and everyone was shrugging into tiny cropped coats, oversized biker jackets and one long swishy trench coat, and heading for the bathroom or the front door.

I said a hasty goodbye to Astro, assuring him I'd be home as soon as I possibly could, and waited for everyone to file out before locking the flat behind us.

.   .   .

Dinner passed in a blur of small plates, smiling waiters and cocktail after cocktail. Nush settled the bill, saying she'd do a spreadsheet afterwards and share what everyone owed on WhatsApp, because obviously we were all picking up Amelie's share. Then Eve produced a carrier bag and dished out shocking-pink sashes – emblazoned with 'Amelie's Hens' for all of us and 'Bride to Be' for Amelie – and pink deely boppers with, of course, cocks and balls on the ends of the springs.

'No one – but no one – is to tell Zack about this until after the wedding,' my sister shrieked. 'I'd get dumped for sure – he still thinks I'm classy!'

Through a haze of alcohol, as I slipped the headpiece behind my ears, I wondered whether this, rather than its proximity to Shoreditch, was why Nush had volunteered my flat as the getting-ready location. I tried, and failed, to imagine Amelie's friends giggling and dropping glitter eyeshadow and crisp crumbs all over her and Zack's immaculate kitchen. I tried to imagine him watching benevolently from a corner, or making himself scarce in the bedroom, or making cocktails for everyone, and that didn't work either.

But there was no time to try and jump-start my mind back into working order – the bill was paid and we were moving on.

All thoughts of my future brother-in-law vanished from my mind as we all piled, giggling, out into the street. One of the blonde women, who was apparently pregnant and therefore designated the Sober One, got her phone out and checked the directions to our next destination, and after a false start – sober or not, clearly she was no Christopher Columbus – we set off on the short walk.

There was a queue outside the club, but we had VIP tickets so were able to swan smugly to the front and get let in straight away. Inside, I found myself battered by noise and blinking rapidly as my eyes fought to adjust to the sudden darkness.

I hadn't been clubbing for a long time. Literally years.

Maybe back when I was at uni it had been a regular thing – probably not, though, as I'd been too skint for anything much apart from beans on toast to be a regular thing. When I'd had my first job and been living in a house share, we'd had wild nights out in town sometimes. But I couldn't remember the last time I'd been to a place like this – if I ever had.

The clubs I could remember had been dingy, sticky-floored warehouses with massive banks of speakers against graffitied concrete walls, lights suspended from steel girders on the ceiling and fearsome bouncers on the door. This, in contrast, was positively civilised. There were waitresses flitting about, holding trays of cocktails aloft. Tall white leather stools were grouped around shiny-topped tables and, apart from the dance floor, which looked like it was made of glass or some sort of translucent Perspex, there was carpet on the floor.

I was willing to bet there'd be loo paper in the toilets, and probably even soap.

'Shall I get a round of drinks in?' I suggested, emboldened, turning towards the bar.

'Don't be daft.' Nush leaned in close so I could hear her over the music. 'We've got a reserved seating area and table service. Come on.'

A woman in a black dress led us through the crowd to the back of the room, where a roped-off area held two tables, each holding a bottle of champagne in an ice bucket. There was a great view of the dance floor and the bar, where two bearded guys and a woman with a full sleeve tattoo and scarlet undercut hair were doing complicated things with cocktail shakers. The bar was topped with beaten copper, and rows and rows of bottles lined the illuminated glass shelves behind it. A small crowd of people were waiting to place their drinks orders, studying the menus, discussing the options with their friends, pointing at potential choices, then leaning in to give their order when they reached the front of the queue.

As I watched, a man in a white shirt reached the bar, leaned in to speak to the woman with the red hair, tapped his phone on the card reader, then turned to face the room while he waited for his cocktail order to be made, a long-necked bottle of beer already in his hand. He hitched his elbows on to the copper bar, crossed one leg in front of the other and leaned back, relaxed and graceful, his eyes scanning the room.

I froze in shock and then turned around so quickly I almost fell off my tall stool. It was Ross.

Shit. Ross. Seeing him here shouldn't have come as a surprise, really – I knew he lived locally, and I knew he had a penchant for trendy bars as well as bargain-basement pubs. But seeing him out of context was weird – even weirder than seeing him carrying Astro down the road had been. This wasn't a place where people rescued cats or checked each other's work or swapped quotes from old sitcoms while they made coffee.

This was a place where people came to drink and dance and hook up.

A waiter was hovering by my elbow, and Eve nudged me and asked what I wanted to drink. Blindly, I ran my eyes down the cocktail menu and chose at random – something involving Grey Goose vodka and plum saké. Then I drank what was left in my champagne glass and filled it up along with everyone else's, finishing the bottle.

When my drink came it was a clear, pale pink and lethally strong, but I drank it as if it was pop and ordered another. Around me, my sister and her friends were caning the booze too – it was a hen night, after all, with no place for moderation. But as they got more and more giggly and raucous, groups of them leaving the tables to hit the dance floor, taking their handbags with them and putting them by their feet in time-honoured fashion, I found myself retreating back into my shell, longing for invisibility.

The barely there back of my dress made me feel horribly

exposed, as if at any moment Ross would clock me, perhaps by recognising my shoulder blades. I felt like there was a target painted on my skin in between the criss-crossed silver straps. It was very, very important that I didn't turn around.

So I didn't. I sat there and drank another cocktail and then another. When Amelie's friends came to talk to me and make sure I was okay, I made myself smile and nod and say how much fun I was having.

But all I could think of was Ross behind me. The way the line of his throat had looked when he lifted his beer to take a swallow. The breadth of his shoulders when he stretched his elbows out over the bar top. The easy way he'd crossed one ankle over the other as he leaned back, his legs long and lean in his faded jeans.

He was probably behind me on the dance floor right now, surrounded by his mates like they thought they were some kind of big deal. His hair was probably flopping down over his face and getting all sweaty. He was probably making comments about all the women in the room, and he and his blokey coven were rating them out of ten.

He was probably dancing like he thought he was good at it.

And there was no way I was going to be able to pluck up the courage to go over and talk to him – not wearing a fuck-me dress and bobbing male genitalia on my head.

I glanced at my watch. It was half past midnight; I'd been sitting there for almost two hours and I realised I was absolutely desperate for a wee. If I got up, Ross might see me. But the illuminated sign for the toilets – a male and a female figure, their legs crossed in discomfort – was directly in front of me. I could get up, walk straight there and then return to my seat – although admittedly I might have to do that backwards.

Either way, I couldn't sit here any longer – the discomfort was too much.

I slid off my stool and then clutched the rim of the table as the room swooped and tilted around me. I was very, very drunk. Drunker than I could remember being in years. Getting to the loo was going to take some doing.

I took a deep breath, forcing my eyes to focus on the sign and my feet to move steadily forward, one in front of the other. And I made it.

Washing my hands at the basin, I saw that my face was swimming in and out of focus, my lipstick smudged, my eyes still huge and luminous from the make-up, my skin glowing. I pointed a finger at myself in the mirror, and it connected with my reflection's finger.

'You okay, Lucy?' Nush appeared next to me, concern in her face. 'I was dancing and I saw you'd gone. I was going to ask if you wanted to join us – the DJ's awesome.'

'Thanks,' I said. 'I'm okay. I don't dance. But I think I need some fresh air – I'm feeling a bit...'

'Come on.' Nush assessed the situation in a heartbeat. 'Some of the others are out vaping. Let's get you outside.'

She took my elbow and guided me back out, past our table and through the labyrinth of others, towards a neon Exit sign. As we passed the bar and the dance floor, I looked for Ross but didn't see him.

The cool night air hit me like a cold flannel to the face, and I realised with relief that I wasn't going to be sick – not now, anyway. Nush guided me to the group, where Amelie was surrounded by one of the dark-haired twins and Eve and Rosa. My sister was wreathed in smiles, and when she saw me she flung her arms round me and whispered, 'Thank you so much for coming. I know it's not your thing but I hope you're having an okay time. I love you, you know.'

'Love you more,' I whispered, feeling tears prick my eyes.

'Bryony's living her best life,' remarked the twin. 'Pulled some hottie on the dance floor and now look.'

All our eyes followed the discreet point of her finger. Separate from the crowd around the entrance, a few yards away, I could see the back of Bryony's neon-pink satin dress. Or some of it, at least. The rest was concealed by a man's arms, wrapped tightly around her slender body. Her head was tilted upwards and his downwards, and they were kissing like they were exchanging life force.

I couldn't see his face, but I didn't need to. The glimpse I'd had of him at the bar had imprinted on my mind the exact shade of his jeans, the precise fall of his white shirt.

It was Ross.

Almost as if it didn't belong to me, I heard a keening sound come from my throat, and without further warning I started to cry.

'I think we need to get Lucy home,' I heard someone say, then everything vanished and there was only the cold, damp pavement under my hands and knees.

SEVEN

I can't remember how I got home. Someone – Amelie, most likely, or maybe Nush – must have put me in an Uber then, after a whispered conversation, decided I couldn't be left on my own, and so came back to the flat with me, fed Astro and put me to bed.

Which was just as well, really, because when my cat finally coaxed me awake on Sunday morning by purring thunderously and licking my earlobe with a scratchy tongue, I got up, opened a pouch of food to put into his bowl and immediately ran to the bathroom to be sick.

It was only then that the full force of my hangover hit me. Doubly unfair, if you think about it, because a good spew is meant to make you feel better, not worse. I crouched on the mercifully cool bathroom tiles, hugging the toilet bowl and wanting to die for a good twenty minutes before thirst forced me to my feet. Whoever had escorted me home had taken off my shoes and my glasses but not my make-up or the silver dress. Glancing in the mirror, I froze with horror.

I looked like I'd been to a Halloween party, not a hen night. My face was chalky-white with smears of dull, greyish foundation clinging to my skin. My eyes were bloodshot and ringed with black mascara. My hair was a greasy tangle. The silver dress was rucked up around my hips and there was dirt on my knees and hands.

Seeing that brought back the last few moments of the evening. I remembered standing up and navigating to the loo in the club, and Nush escorting me out. I remembered the smell of Eve's grape soda vape. And I remembered Ross – Ross and Bryony, snogging the life out of each other.

I wondered if they'd gone home together.

I could see no reason why they wouldn't have – it would have been a totally normal thing to do, a mutually desired and enjoyable hook-up after a night out. Ross was single – the brief moments of connection I'd felt might have meant something to me, but why would they have to him? He had no feelings for me. He could snog whoever he wanted – more than snog, if he wanted that too.

We were colleagues, that was all – and there was no way I could allow myself to develop feelings for him, even if there was a chance they'd be reciprocated.

It had been a long time – months, maybe even a year – since I'd opened the white envelope I still kept in my bedside drawer. It had been there for four years; when I'd moved into my current flat, I'd considered throwing it away but decided against it. I needed it there – needed to remember the mistake I'd made, and remind myself not to make it again.

I didn't open it now. I just looked at it, and looking was enough to bring the memories of four-years-ago me rushing back.

I was twenty-five, and I'd just got my first job that had 'editor' in the title and moved out of a flatshare and into a place of my own. Looking back, it was inevitable that, alongside those firsts, I'd fall for a man for the first time, too.

The job offer had felt like my big break – junior lifestyle

editor on a national newspaper although the way it felt, they might as well have put 'head of the known universe' on my business cards. I could see my career path ahead of me as clearly as if it was illuminated by spotlights – the indefatigable thoroughness, the awards, the promotion, and the rest would be history.

Oh, and at some point along the way I'd meet a man. An intelligent, thoughtful, serious man, possibly with deep emotional scars that only I could heal. He'd have been worth waiting for, because God only knew I'd waited long enough. Throughout my teenage and university years and beyond, I'd watched in disappointed bewilderment as the guys I'd liked took one look at me and put me firmly in the friend zone, before asking for one of my mates' numbers or – worse – whether my sister was single.

It was with hope and confidence in my heart that I arrived for my first day at the *Sentinel*. Even though the first thing that happened was I was shown where the coffee machine lived, and the second was a lesson in how to work the printer, nothing could dampen my enthusiasm.

And then I saw Kieren.

I didn't know his name at that stage – he worked on the news desk, way over on the other side of the office. But it so happened that he was in the kitchen making himself a cup of tea at the same time as I was making a round of coffees, and I literally stopped in my tracks and stared at him, mesmerised.

He was thin and not very tall – maybe five foot eight or nine – and a few years older than me. He had dark hair, almost black as far as I could see, but it was shorn too close to his head to tell. He had a spade-shaped dark beard and piercing blue eyes and cheekbones you could open a letter with. He was wearing jeans and an olive-green sweatshirt and he smelled like he'd just finished a cigarette.

He wasn't conventionally handsome, apart from those eyes, as blue as spilled ink. But I felt powerfully, magnetically drawn to him – here, I was sure, was the troubled soul my own soul had been seeking.

'Can I help you?' His voice jolted me out of my daydream, making me blush and realise I'd been staring vacantly in his general direction.

'I was just...' *I was just imagining our married life, ten years from now.* 'I was just wondering if you'd like me to wash that mug for you?'

He looked at me hard, his blue eyes narrow and a faint smile on his lips. 'No one, but no one, washes my mug. Ever.'

He had an Irish accent. I felt my stomach do a slow somersault.

'Sorry,' I muttered. 'I'm Lucy. I'm new, and I was told to make myself useful, so I thought...'

'Lucy.' He nodded, like I'd confirmed a long-held suspicion. 'I'm Kieren. Northern Ireland editor, over on the news desk.'

'I'm on lifestyle,' I said. 'I started yesterday.'

'Welcome to the *Sentinel*.' He said it ironically, as if it was some kind of poisoned chalice, but then he smiled and it was like the sun coming out. 'If you get a free moment, come on over – I'm sure we can find a way for you to make yourself useful in news.'

So, after that, whenever I had half an hour free, I'd check with my team leader and scurry across the bullpen to the news desk, where I'd be put to work correcting the spelling of obscure politicians' names, the dates when by-elections had taken place, or the boundaries between local parish councils.

Eventually, as I proved myself to be not totally incompetent, I was given more challenging tasks.

'Cut this to fit, will you?' Kieren said one day, and I spent an hour engaged in a sort of word jigsaw, making an article about corrupt police officers in Belfast go from a thousand words to eight column inches without losing any of the facts.

At last, when I told him I was done, I watched breathlessly

as he scanned the copy on his screen, changing a word here and there, before smiling and saying, 'You did a great job. Quick, too. Thanks, Lucy.'

He might as well have told me I was the reigning queen of his heart, that's how happy his words made me. When he allocated me another, longer piece to work on, I agreed instantly.

It was a Tuesday afternoon, the day before the paper was put to bed, so when five thirty came, no one left their desks. At six o'clock, a few of the early starters began to pack up their things and go, but half an hour later the bullpen was still more than half-full.

I still had a good two hours' work left, I reckoned. My eyes were tired, my shoulders hunched and aching, but I kept going, the words on my screen like thousands of ants, crawling their way slowly upwards in an endless progression.

'Tea?' asked Kieren's voice at my elbow. 'You look like you need one.'

'Thanks.' I didn't like tea much – he brewed it so strong it was the colour of burnt umber paint, bitter and sharp with tannin – but I drank it anyway, because he'd made it.

An hour later, I looked up from my screen. The contact lenses I used to force myself to wear then were drying out, threatening to ping out of my eyes, so I blinked furiously to try and lubricate them and clear the cloudiness that had settled on them. The office had emptied dramatically, I realised – there were only a couple of guys left at the sport desk, two women on the subs station, Kieren and me. As I watched, the two subs nodded to each other, shut down their computers and left.

'How're you getting on?' Kieren asked.

'Getting there, I think,' I said. 'Almost done.'

Five minutes later, I stood up, stretching my fingertips high over my head, interlacing my fingers and pulling my elbows back as far as they'd go.

'Taking a yoga break?' Kieren asked.

I never quite knew whether he was joking or not.

'I reckon I've finished,' I said humbly. 'Unless there's anything else...?'

I looked around. The office was empty now, pools of shadow over the other pods of desks, only the news section illuminated.

'Time to call it a night, then.'

He stood and shrugged his battered leather jacket – it smelled of smoke, I'd noticed, and the same juniper scent I'd noticed on his skin – over his shoulders.

Then he hitched a hip on the corner of my desk and perched there, looking half at me and half at the words on my screen. His closeness made it difficult to breathe, like the strap of my bra had suddenly been pulled to a tighter hook.

'Lucy?' he said.

I half-turned, shy of meeting his eyes but at the same time longing to gaze into his face. 'Kieren?'

'You know – people here might not tell you this. But I'm going to,' he said.

I felt my heart hammering in my chest. He was either about to tell me I was going to be sacked or I had a terrible body odour problem – or it was something good.

The look on his face – his lips turned up at the edges – told me it was something good.

'You've got talent,' he went on. 'Real potential. A woman like you – smart, hard-working, driven, beautiful – you'll go far in this industry. I don't think you know it yet, but you will.'

No one except my mum and my sister had ever told me I was beautiful before. And that he thought I had a future in journalism was like rich, velvety buttercream on top of a particularly decadent cake.

'Th-thank you,' I stammered. 'That means a lot. It really does.'

'Now, that doesn't mean you should pull an all-nighter here

on your own,' he chided gently. 'Come on – home time. Get some rest.'

I logged off hastily, got up and fetched my coat from my own desk on the other side of the room, then followed him to the lift and waited while he set the alarm.

Maybe he would ask me out for a drink. Or just thank me for my help and the late night I'd put in. Or something else.

As it turned out, it was something else. He pressed the button for the lift and then, while we waited for it to inch its way up from the ground floor to the ninth, he turned to me, put his hands on my shoulders and kissed me.

I couldn't have been more taken by surprise if he'd slapped me. For a second I stood still, frozen in the circle of his arms, and then I responded. I couldn't help it. It was like weeks – even years – of pent-up desire were exploding inside me. His mouth on mine was the best thing I'd ever felt; the smell of his skin was intoxicating. I wanted to press my body hard against his, feel every bone of him pressing against me, never let him go.

But I had to, when the low ping of the lift ordered me to.

He looked at me, that crooked half-smile on his face, and asked, 'You liked that?'

I nodded dumbly and stepped ahead of him into the lift. On the way down, he kissed me again and I responded just as eagerly. Then we stepped out on the ground floor and I followed him out into the street.

'So did I,' he said. 'Talented, beautiful and sexy as hell. Wow.'

He smiled at me again, his face transformed like a Christmas tree when the lights switch on, then he turned and walked away. I must have walked away too, but it felt more like I was floating, borne away towards the Tube station on a cloud of happiness and excitement.

'Stupid, Lucy,' I said aloud now, throwing the envelope

back into the drawer and slamming it shut. 'Stupid, stupid. No crushes on work colleagues again, ever. Remember that.'

It was almost eleven o'clock before I managed to shower, pull on tracksuit bottoms and a jumper, and make my way back to the kitchen with my phone. Amelie's Instagram story from the previous day was almost fifteen minutes long, and I watched it all – a mixture of group selfies, videos, close-ups of cocktails and, towards the end, blurry shots of the dance floor and the street outside the club.

I carried on scrolling, then moved on to WhatsApp. As yesterday segued into today, the messages became less coherent and the photos less carefully staged. But there were a couple of candid shots of that kiss – Bryony's back and Ross's front, a streetlamp illuminating them like something off CCTV, or a crime scene photo.

> Now you can't say pics or it didn't happen!

Eve had written, with a load of laughing emojis and the devil for good measure.

I scrolled rapidly past, knowing that if I allowed myself, I'd return to the photo again and again, torturing myself with it even though I knew I had no right to find it painful. My sister's friends didn't even know who Ross was. They had no idea I worked with him. I hadn't mentioned it; he and I hadn't spoken or even made eye contact.

Rapidly, I scrolled to the start of the chat. About a dozen posts up from the final one, I read:

NUSH:

> Has anyone heard from Lucy? She was absolutely sparko when I left her place last night.

AMELIE:

> Nope. I tried calling but there was no reply.

True. There were a couple of missed calls on my phone, but I was too deep in the Fear to check who from, or listen to the messages.

MIRANDA:

@Lucy? Are you there? Are you okay?

NUSH:

I fed the cat and I thought about crashing on the couch but I didn't want to be a pain, so I got an Uber home.

AMELIE:

If I don't hear from her, I'll go round there. I'm sure she's fine.

ELSPETH:

I bet she's feeling better than me. I'm legit dying. I've had two bacon rolls and they're not even touching the sides.

Elspeth? One of the interchangeable blondes, I guessed.

AMELIE:

How about Bryony? Any update on the hot man she hooked up with?

I couldn't read any more. I muted the chat – the hen do was over, after all, and any further business would be conducted on the separate bridesmaids' group.

Then I messaged my sister and told her I was fine, just feeling as rough as I was sure everyone else was, and I'd speak to her during the week.

And then I went back to bed, pulled the duvet over my head and stayed there for the rest of the day.

EIGHT

Dear Adam,

I'm eighteen and I've never had a girlfriend – there, I said it. And it gets worse: I've never had sex, either. I've kissed a couple of girls but it's never led to anything else, and now I'm at the point where I can't ever see it happening. Is there something wrong with me? What can I do?

Charlie, Portsmouth

By the next morning my hangover had receded, but the sense of fear, sadness and shame lingered. I wasn't worried about what my fellow hens would think about my behaviour – Amelie was my sister, after all, and the rest of them were close enough to her that they'd forgive me pretty much anything by association. And anyway, I hadn't behaved badly. I'd been pretty hammered, sure, but then it was a hen night and everyone had been hammered, apart from the pregnant one.

It was something more than that – something deeper and more secret. It was to do with Ross – to do with the contact we'd had with each other's lives outside of work. But why did I feel so weird about that, I asked myself, as I stepped out of the shower, roughly towel-dried my hair and pulled on jeans, a T-shirt and trainers without looking in the mirror.

Just as if it was a normal Monday morning, I got the bus to work, stopped off at my usual place for a flat white to go, and walked through the bright morning to the office. It had rained during the night and the pavements were sparkling with puddles, the sky a clear washed-out blue and the air mild and fresh. It was the sort of Monday morning that inspires optimism, the promise of eating my lunch outside in a garden square, of walking home through the balmy evening instead of getting the bus, of sitting out on my balcony later watching the moon rise.

But I didn't feel optimism, only the same looming, shadowy dread with which I'd woken up that morning. And the feeling only increased as I approached the imposing red-brick building where I worked. It had been some sort of a warehouse, back in the day, or perhaps a factory, maybe where dozens of women in headscarves had laboured over cutting tables and sewing machines. Now we laboured over keyboards, but the building had retained its high ceilings and vast, steel-framed windows through which sunlight poured in the afternoons until someone complained they couldn't see their screen for the glare, got up and shut a blind.

Work used to be my happy place. I'd never dreaded coming here – until I'd moved to *Max!*. Now, I had to share my work-space with a bunch of men, one of whom was Ross. And I'd be faced with even more men and their man-problems flooding into the inbox of someone called Adam, who I had no idea how I was going to learn to be.

The confidence I'd felt when I'd replied to Jonno's letter had evaporated almost entirely. Greg's response had been enthusiastic – the copy had gone to the subs desk and on to the design department, and I'd been left with a sense of pride and satisfaction. I could do this. I could be wise and empathetic, even to men.

But now I felt completely different, and I knew deep down that it was because of Ross. I'd thought we were beginning to be friends and even allowed myself to imagine that there could be something more there. I'd thought I could trust him – thought he might be different from other men. But however much I tried to rationalise it to myself, what had happened between him and Bryony had left me feeling disillusioned and betrayed.

He was just the same as all the rest of them, after all. He'd take a casual hook-up without hesitation if there was one on offer.

I tapped in the code for the door at street level and stepped into the lobby, greeting the concierge with a smile and heading for the lift. But its door was closing as I approached, and I couldn't see who was inside. *What if it's Ross?*

Shaking my head, I turned away and walked up the stairs instead.

Ross was there already. As soon as I pushed open the heavy fire door, out of breath from my climb, I saw his head over the banks of monitors. It was like he was emitting a signal – a high-pitched beep transmitted over Bluetooth or something – that grew louder and louder the closer I got to him. The distance from the door to my desk felt limitless, as if it would take hours rather than seconds to walk across the polished concrete floor, pull out my chair and sit, mostly hidden from his view by my computer screen.

I crossed the room, silent in my trainers. My breath hadn't returned to normal – if anything it felt like I was climbing higher and faster than I already had. My heart was pounding in my chest and my legs felt limp as cooked spaghetti when at last I sat down, resting my insulated coffee mug on the desk in front of me.

The tiny sound of the mug meeting the wood made Ross glance up from his screen, and for a second his eyes met mine. And then a surprising thing happened. He blushed. A wave of colour rushed up his neck and over his face. I felt an answering flush burning my own face and looked away, hiding behind my computer monitor as fast as I could. We didn't exchange a word for the rest of the day.

And what was more, it seemed like every time I lifted my eyes from my screen to think, answer the phone or get up to go for a wee, Ross would look up at the same moment and our eyes would meet. We'd blush furiously in unison and then look away, and I'd feel ashamed and unsettled for ages until I was able to focus on my work again, lose myself in it and forget the second-long eye-meet had ever happened. And then, as if this was just a normal day in a normal week, I'd glance up again and – *bam* – the eyes, the blush, the excruciating awkwardness.

It was like it was Ross and I who'd snogged – or maybe more than snogged – on a night out, not Ross and a friend of my sister's who I barely knew.

But I knew one thing. Ross knew I knew. Even if he hadn't seen me out on Saturday night, he knew I'd been there and he knew the girl he'd hooked up with was my sister's friend. Otherwise why would he be like this?

Actually, even given that knowledge, why was he being like this?

I couldn't understand it. I knew why I felt toe-curlingly embarrassed around him, but that was me. I was the one with the social skills of a washing-up sponge, the one who died inside at the idea of a colleague – okay, a man who I sort of liked – seeing me out in a short dress and a cock-and-balls deely bopper, having a few drinks. That was normal for me, because that's what I was like. But Ross?

As far as I could tell – and certainly as far as the evidence from Saturday night had shown – he was a normal guy, natural and at ease in social situations, and he had nothing at all to be embarrassed about.

I didn't get it. But there were more pressing matters still for me to not get: the slew of emails that had landed in the Ask Adam inbox. Whatever Ross's problem was, it was only one problem compared to the – my inbox confirmed – 128 requiring my attention. I was going to have to pick two, edit them and come up with answers that wouldn't result in the meltdown of relationships, the abandonment of long-held dreams or the loss of jobs – particularly my own.

The responsibility weighed heavily on me, to say the least. It had never crossed my mind that there would be quite so many men out there with quite so many problems.

I'd have to read through them all, giving them due care and attention, eventually. But for now, I figured I might as well pick one that looked like it would be widely relatable, and try to come up with a solution. I scrolled through the unread messages and clicked on one at random.

To my surprise, I felt tears pricking my eyes when I read Charlie's brief message. I remembered myself at that age, and how I'd felt about my contemporaries, the Charlies of their day. All those boys: tall and short, fat and thin, sporty and geeky – all equally unfathomable and intimidating to eighteen-year-old me. I still felt that way about men, and I realised I badly wanted to save Charlie from the same fate.

I copied and pasted his message into a Word document and read it through again. Then I pressed Enter twice, typed *Dear Charlie* and hit Enter again.

Then I stopped.

Think, Lucy. What do you wish someone had told you eleven years ago?

First off, there's nothing wrong with you.

I didn't actually know whether that was true – Charlie could have all kinds of things wrong in his life that I didn't know about. But it felt important to say it. Then I channelled my younger self again, and carried on.

I bet there are loads of girls you know in exactly the same position as you. I bet they share their worries with their closest friends, like you've shared yours with me. And I bet their friends tell them they're great, they're hot, they're funny, and the right person for them will come along when the time is right – probably loads of wrong people, too, but eventually the right one. In the meantime, try and hold that thought. Girls aren't an alien species. They've got worries and insecurities, same as you. I wonder if you could try letting your guard down, trying to get to know girls, not treating them like they're armed guards standing in the way of you having sex? Even girls you don't fancy could end up being – wait for it – friends. And friendship could be the first step to achieving the romantic relationships you really want.

I was suddenly besieged by doubt. Before even hitting Save, I copied the text and sent it to Amelie, without explanation but with a row of question mark emojis. She replied in a few seconds.

> Great! I knew you could do it. Maybe also tell him not to be a dick? It's always worth reminding them.

I spent the rest of that week reading through all the questions in the inbox – that and puzzling over the behaviour of another man, the one at the desk opposite mine. Ross's demeanour, other than when he looked at me, seemed perfectly normal. Apart from the fact that he'd stopped talking to me. Before, he hadn't exactly chatted for England, but he'd made the occasional effort at conversation. Usually, when I stood up from my desk at five past one, he'd ask if I was going for lunch, and what I was planning to get. At six o'clock when we logged off, he'd wish me a good evening. If he got up to make a coffee, he'd offer me one. When I asked what he was having for lunch, he'd tell me what was in his sandwich and then quote *Seinfeld*: 'Women don't respect salad eaters.'

But he'd stopped doing those things – which was probably just as well, because if we actually spoke to each other, we'd probably both spontaneously combust.

By Friday morning, I'd realised that spontaneous combustion was a risk I was simply going to have to take, because the alternative – the oppressive silence, the face-searing blushes, the crick I was getting in my neck from looking up sideways from my screen instead of directly ahead, so as not to meet his eyes – was simply intolerable. And besides, I knew that Ross would be off on holiday for two weeks, so at least if my attempt to clear the air failed, I wouldn't have to see him for a whole sixteen days, and by that stage we'd have moved on from this cringy awkwardness – wouldn't we?

I'd do it at ten thirty, I promised myself – a reasonable time to get up and offer him a coffee. But then, inevitably, ten thirty came and I found myself sitting in my chair like I'd been glued there. Okay, ten forty-five, I told myself.

But at ten fifty – I know, I know – I heard a voice from the end desk.

'Holy shit.' It was Marco.

'What's up?' asked Barney.

'Bomb scare on the Underground. It's just come over the wires now. They've closed three lines and they're evacuating Bond Street station.'

My first thought was of Amelie – Bond Street was her nearest Tube stop. But hopefully she was safely home, working on the seating plan for her wedding reception or something.

'Good news for you, mate,' Neil commented. 'I mean, bad

news for anyone who's going to get blown to smithereens in the blast, but it'll make good copy, right?'

'Steady on,' Chiraag said.

I looked up. Opposite me, Ross was doing the opposite of blushing – in fact, he'd gone so greenish-pale he looked like a pistachio gelato.

'It's been a while since we've had anything like this,' Marco went on. 'Hopefully it's nothing.'

'And you'll be back to reporting on the much-vaunted benefits of Brexit,' Simon said.

Ross didn't say anything. He got up from his desk and walked away towards the toilets in a not-quite-straight line, like he'd poured whisky instead of milk on his morning muesli.

'It's a developing story.' Marco's eyes were fixed on his screen. 'Maybe I should start a live blog?'

'And then if it turns out to be a false alarm, we'll all look like right fannies,' Neil said.

'Greg's in a meeting,' Marco dithered. 'Otherwise I'd ask him what he reckoned.'

'I'd hold fire,' said Chiraag. 'See if other outlets are reporting it. There's nothing on the Beeb yet.'

I checked my own screen. 'The *Daily Express* is running with it. They're saying there could be thousands of deaths.'

Barney laughed. 'Too bad, Marco, you've been scooped already.'

'Hang on,' Marco said, 'apparently there's going to be a statement from the Metropolitan Police in a couple of minutes.'

I glanced over my shoulder, wondering why Ross wasn't here with the group, joining in the horror-tinged excitement that had livened up this otherwise ordinary morning. But I couldn't see him.

Marco was leaning in towards his screen, as if by getting closer to it he'd have a better view. His hands were poised over his keyboard like a pianist about to embark on a particularly challenging concerto. Then all at once he relaxed, pulling off his headphones and leaning back in his chair.

'It's nothing,' he said. 'Some idiot left a pallet full of – get this – frozen vegan burgers on the station concourse, and a passer-by alerted the peelers. Stand down, team.'

'Pity,' Neil remarked. 'I was hoping we might all get sent home early.'

'I was hoping thousands of deaths would be averted,' Chiraag said. 'Guess what I'd rather have happen?'

Relief-fuelled, good-natured bickering broke out, but I didn't stick around to listen to it.

I got up and walked towards the kitchen, in the direction Ross had gone. But the kitchen was empty. The gents' toilet door was closed, of course – not that there was any way I'd have gone in there to look for him.

Then the lift doors swished open and he emerged. He wasn't greenish-pale any more, but I could see beads of sweat on his forehead, and his shoulders were hunched like it was freezing outside instead of a balmy twenty-two degrees.

'Hey, Ross.' I stepped up to him. 'Are you okay?'

'Fine,' he muttered. 'Just went out to get some air. I felt a bit weird there for a bit. What's... Has Marco heard anything more?'

'It's all fine,' I said gently. 'False alarm. Absolutely nothing to worry about.'

'Are you sure?'

'Positive.' I told him about the vegan burgers and he smiled, colour returning to his face.

'Guess I'd better get back to work, then.'

Together, we set off back towards our desks, but as we passed the kitchen I stopped.

'Ross?' Now I could feel colour in my own cheeks – too much of it. That all-too-familiar blush was doing its thing.

'Yo.' He looked at me, and I saw the same thing happening to him.

'Fancy a coffee?'

He glanced at his watch. It was still before midday.

'Don't worry, you're safe,' I teased, remembering his strict watershed policy. 'So long as you drink it fast.'

He smiled. 'Thanks, Lucy. That would be great. Reckon my sleep is safe if I have it now.'

'I'm on it,' I promised, and hurried to the kitchen, feeling my burning face gradually return to normal. I made a flat white for myself and a double espresso for him and returned to our desks, carefully gripping the two white china mugs by their handles. I put mine down on my desk, then walked all the way round and placed his carefully in front of him.

'Thanks, Lucy,' he said again.

I wanted to ask him again if he was okay, to try and reassure him that whatever he'd thought was going to happen, it hadn't, and that everything was normal. But I sensed he wouldn't want me to – that whatever impulse had made him get up and leave would also make him reluctant to talk any more about it, to expose himself to the risk of too-edgy banter from the rest of the team.

So I began, 'Do you—'

At exactly the same time, he said, 'So do you—'

We both stopped, our words colliding in mid-air. I felt the blush threatening to overwhelm me again and saw the tips of his ears turn bright pink.

I waved my hand in a 'carry on' gesture, and he said, 'Do you have anything nice planned for the weekend?'

'Not much. Feels like I need a quiet one after my sister's hen do.'

I noticed his ears turning pinker and I looked away, hoping he'd recover.

'Did you have a good time?' he asked, after what felt like so long I was worried my coffee would be cold.

'It was great!' I managed to sound enthusiastic. 'Er... how about you?'

'Yeah, it was a top night. I didn't feel too good on Sunday though.'

'Me neither.' *Although that was mostly because I saw you kissing Bryony.*

He smiled in what I guessed was intended to be a rueful fashion. 'Guess you get to do it all over again at your sister's wedding?'

'Nah,' I said. 'I'm chief bridesmaid. I'll have to be the responsible adult in case my sister ladders a stocking or there's some emergency like that.'

'Hopefully there won't be. I guess you'll be able to tell me all about it when I'm back from Croatia.'

'I'll show you the photos,' I said. Then I smiled too and returned to my coffee and my work.

There, I told myself proudly. *You did it. You had a normal conversation like normal people and no one died. Strong work, Lucy.*

But I didn't feel especially proud of myself. All I could think of was that he was off on holiday and I wouldn't see him, or laugh with him, or make him blush, for a whole two weeks.

NINE

Dear Adam,

*I wanted to write to you after hearing a podcast recently by
Parker Goldstein, the tech entrepreneur. He was talking about
longevity and all the health and wellness stuff he does. If I'm
honest, when I got to the bit about how he wakes up at four every
morning, I almost switched off. But then he got on to sex. He
reckons when he's with a woman, he can last at least half an hour
from first penetration to orgasm. I'm not gonna lie, I'm more a
five-minute man myself. How do some dudes manage this,
Adam? What should I do differently?*

Finn, Leicester

'So' – Amelie tucked her foot up on the kitchen chair, resting
her chin on her knee and pulling the sleeves of her jumper over
her hands – 'let's take a look at these men, then.'

   'Men's problems,' I corrected. 'There aren't any actual men
here. Thank God. Where's Zack, anyway?'

   'Off manning. Playing squash, that is. He's in some league

and they're near the top of it, and he hates losing. I mean, it is peak man, right? Plus he says he's trying to stay in shape for the wedding. Not that a week will make any difference, but at least it gets him out of the house and leaves us in peace.'

I breathed a silent sigh of relief. When I'd asked Amelie if she was free to help me with some of the emails that had landed in Adam's inbox, I'd expected her to say she couldn't, given that her wedding was only days away. But she'd agreed enthusiastically, suggesting a 'working brunch' at hers – which had struck me as an excellent plan until I'd considered that Zack might be home. It wasn't so much that I wouldn't have welcomed his perspective – he was a man, after all – but more that I suspected that whatever insight my sister might have given me would have been altered by his presence, diluted, her attention diverted whenever he wanted to talk about his own experiences, or have another coffee, or be kissed.

'Mind if I have another croissant?' I asked.

'Knock yourself out.' My sister hadn't touched the pastries I'd brought – but then, I hadn't exactly tackled the egg-white omelette and sliced-up kiwi fruit with much enthusiasm.

'Right,' I began through a mouthful of crumbs. 'Where shall we start? Finn from Leicester do you?'

'Go on then.'

I propped my tablet more securely on its stand and scrolled through my emails. As soon as I'd seen Finn's, I'd known that this was a problem I'd need my sister's help with.

'So, here's what he says.' I cleared my throat. 'It's a bit cringe, sorry.'

I read out Finn's letter.

'Oh. My. God.' Amelie rolled her eyes so hard I almost expected them to shoot out of her head. 'That is literally the most tech bro thing I have ever heard. Has this Parker Whatsit ever actually met a woman? Does he seriously believe that we want to lie there while he stabs away like a bloody sewing

machine, getting sorer and sorer and boreder and boreder? Just
so he can show off about it on his wanky podcast? Jeez, I
despair.'

Not for the first time, I felt acutely conscious of the huge
gulf of experience that separated me from my sister.

'Really?' I asked. 'You mean most women don't... It's not
just me?'

'Categorically, one hundred per cent not just you. I mean, I
haven't asked all women. Possibly there are some who like being
pounded at like chicken thighs in cling film. But every woman
I've ever asked about it says the same thing – men who are good
in bed make sure the woman's orgasm happens – or orgasms,
plural, ideally – and then crack on with theirs and don't take too
long about it, so you can both have a nice cuddle and a pizza.'

'So most men don't... you know. Last ages?'

'Only the ones who've spent so much time wanking over
porn they need half an hour of death grip to get anywhere.'

'So I can tell Finn he doesn't need to worry?'

'Exactly. So long as he's not going from first kiss to blowing
his load in two minutes, obviously. If he's making sure his
partner has a good time and not being a selfish dick, he's golden.'

'Um... gotcha.' I typed a brief note in the Word document I
had open, hoping Amelie hadn't noticed me blushing.

How on earth, I wondered, was I going to translate her
matter-of-fact advice into a reply that would appear online for
thousands of men to read? And, worse, for my colleagues at
work to read, knowing that I'd written it?

For a moment, my mind veered to Ross. What was he like in
bed? Did he last ages, or no time at all? Did he know how to
give a partner pleasure? Did he even care, or was he confident
that there'd always be girls happy to go to bed with him, and if
one didn't enjoy it, another would be along soon enough?

And then I realised that, whatever answer Adam provided
for Finn about what worked for women in bed, Ross would

know that I'd written it. He wouldn't know about Amelie's involvement – he'd presume that I was speaking from my own experience, about my own preferences. The idea made me die a bit inside.

This was going to be even harder than I'd realised. Even harder than Parker Goldstein's Duracell-Bunny erection.

'Right,' Amelie interrupted my thoughts. 'Who's next?'

I ran my fingers down my screen, the email subject lines flickering and blurring. There were so many, and I had so little time with my sister.

Randomly, I clicked on an email and started reading.

'"Dear Adam, I'm twenty-six and just out of a long relationship. I guess it's so long since I've needed to put myself out there, I've forgotten how it's done, and I just need to get back in the game. But I've got one main question for you. How do you actually know if a woman fancies you? My confidence is at rock-bottom and I don't want to get knocked back or friendzoned. Is there any subtle body language I should look out for?" It's from some dude called Seb in Littlehampton.'

Amelie smiled. 'Oh, the poor flower. He doesn't want to actually get his big boy pants on and ask – he wants women to do all the work. Still, he's all bruised from his long relationship – wonder what happened there? – so we'll cut him some slack, shall we?'

'We'd better. If we tell him to grow a pair and google "women's body language", Adam will soon be out of a job.'

'Fair enough. So if he were to google – not that I'm suggesting that, mind – he'd find a whole load of stuff about a woman touching her hair, looking at him sideways from under her eyelashes, leaning in to listen to him and stuff.'

'Wait, what? So you're saying if I want a guy to know I fancy him, I basically have to preen and gurn like I'm auditioning for Princess Diana in *The Crown*?'

'Don't be ridic—' Amelie stopped abruptly, her hazel eyes

fixed on me as intently as Astro's when he wants a game of pounce. 'Lucy, are you saying you fancy someone?'

'No! Of course not. It was just theoretical.'

'Who is he?'

'No one. I told you.'

'And does he fancy you back?'

'No. I mean, I don't know. But it doesn't matter – nothing's going to happen. I don't want to date anyone.'

Amelie took a quick breath like she was about to ask another question – or more likely begin a rapid-fire interrogation. But she appeared to change her mind.

'Okay. Let's not bother about him, then. Back to our boy with the tender ego. Tell him that when a woman likes a man, she seeks him out, tries to spend time with him, laughs at his jokes and makes jokes of her own. But mostly, tell him that the quickest way to find out if someone's interested is not to play guessing games, but to crack on and ask. Do you... I mean, do you think he'll get that?'

'Uh, yeah. I'm sure he will.' I was partly relieved to have been let off the hook and, perversely, almost disappointed that Amelie hadn't pressed me on my work crush, even though there was absolutely no way – even if she'd threatened to attack my cuticles with her special clippy tool – I'd have admitted that I felt anything for the man Bryony had spent the night with. I added hastily, 'Shall we try another?'

'Hit me with it.'

'It's another sex one, I'm afraid.'

'More the merrier.'

I cleared my throat. '"Dear Adam, I'm thirty-four and obviously I've been sexually active for almost two decades now. But there's one thing that's always bothered me and I think I might not be alone here. You guessed it, the age-old question: does size actually matter? I like to think I'm average or thereabouts, and my partners have never complained, but when I look at some of the dudes in the gym locker room, I'm like, woah. And then obviously there's the guys you see on Pornhub and they're in a different league entirely. But give it to me straight, Adam – what are the chances I'm under-equipped for the job? Nathan, Maidenhead."'

'Oh, Nathan. Nathan, Nathan, Nathan.' Amelie poured coffee from the cafetière into our cups, the stream of liquid flowing slowly, as if her thoughts were too. 'Bless his cotton socks. Age-old question indeed. If I had a tenner for every man who'd ever asked me about that, let me tell you, I wouldn't be – but anyway. Back to Nathan.'

'Yeah. I mean, porn aside' – I bit my lip, not wanting to admit that I couldn't remember the last time I'd actually seen a penis – 'I thought they were all about the same size, at least when they're, you know, erect.'

'Growers and showers, you mean?'

I giggled. 'That's what they told us in sex ed at school, anyway.'

Amelie snorted midway through a sip of coffee and choked.

When she'd finished spluttering and I'd poured her a glass of water, she said, 'Well, of course that's what they're going to tell a bunch of eleven-year-olds in a classroom. Of course they are! What's the alternative? "Sorry, lads, some of you are going to end up with three-inch tiddlers and some with ten-inch schlongs, and there's not a damn thing you can do about it. Now, moving on to sexually transmitted infections..."'

'You mean it's not true?'

'Certainly not in my limited – okay, not that limited – experience, it's not.'

'Then why not just admit it? Women don't expect to all have boobs the same size, do we?'

'It's the male ego again, Luce. Poor dears have been conditioned by centuries of patriarchy to believe that men with bigger penises will get more women, have more power and make more money. And we women haven't helped, let's be honest.'

'Come on – surely this can't be women's fault?'

'Not exactly. But think about it – when a woman's been hurt by a guy, when she's feeling powerless and broken, what do her mates say?'

'Have a gin and tonic?'

'Yeah, that. But only after they've said, "Tell him he's shit in bed and he's got a tiny cock." It's our first line of defence.'

'So then there must be some truth in it.'

'Of course there is. Some guys have big dicks, some have small ones. Some look like a dog's been chewing it, most thankfully don't. They're all different, same as women's bits.'

'So what on earth do I say to this Nathan, then?'

'Here's the thing. Here's what no one ever tells men. Size. Does. Not. Matter. It's like I was saying earlier. If a woman climaxes, she literally doesn't give two hoots how big the man's willy is. And if she hasn't, or isn't ready, it's more likely to hurt if the guy's hung like a walrus. Not that I've ever seen a walrus's one.'

'A walrus's what?'

I jumped. I hadn't heard Zack come into the flat, but now the kitchen seemed full of his presence – the bag holding his squash racket landing with a thump on the kitchen table, making the teaspoons jingle on our saucers; the smell of his body, a mixture of deodorant, rain and sweat; the way Amelie's foot instantly slid off the chair, her posture tensing before she jumped up to kiss him, Adam's correspondents forgotten.

'How was your match?' she asked.

'Shit. We lost in three games and we've got no chance in the league now.'

'I guess it doesn't matter that much, since you won't be here,' I said politely. 'Are you planning to join a league when you're in New York?'

Zack shrugged. 'Maybe. Could be a good way to network with other expats – other citizens of nowhere.'

Amelie gazed up at him like he'd said something ground-breaking and profound. What was it about him, I wondered, that made her set aside all her cynicism about men, as if he was the first one she'd ever met?

Perhaps he was so gifted in the sex department that my sister had realised she'd never meet anyone as good again. But I'd never had the chance to ask her about that, and now that he was going to be my brother-in-law, I knew I never could.

'I should go,' I said. 'Thanks for the breakfast, Am. And for all the – you know – help.'

'You're welcome.' She walked me to the door and gave me a brief hug, but I could tell her mind was already elsewhere – on Zack, on their wedding, on whatever plans they'd make for the rest of the day now that he was unexpectedly home. 'Don't worry about the letter. You'll work something out.'

'Okay. Have a lovely day. I guess I'll see you on Friday – wedding eve, hey?'

'Wedding eve.' She leaned into me and whispered, 'Don't tell anyone, but when I think about it, I want to puke. That's normal, right?'

Was it? I didn't know. But I did know that the giddy happi-ness I'd seen in my sister when she and Zack were first engaged seemed to have faded now that the reality of marriage was actu-ally upon her.

'Am,' I whispered back, conscious of Zack just a few feet away, 'you know, if you're not sure, it's not too late to... You could always...'

But before she could answer, Zack called her name from inside and she turned away from me, the door closing behind her with a click that sounded like the most final click in the entire history of clicks.

TEN

Dear Adam,

I really fancy this girl I work with. Let's call her Girl A. She's everything I'm looking for in a woman – cute, smart and thoughtful. Unfortunately, I just can't help blushing and getting all tongue-tied every time I look at her. And it seems she has the same problem – although I've got to admit she looks a whole lot better when she blushes than I do. She scrubs up seriously well too: just the other night I saw her for the first time with make-up on and wearing a party dress, and – phwoar!

But that's not the only problem. On said night, I messed up really badly and kissed another girl. Maybe we should call her Girl B? It wouldn't have been a problem, because I'm single after all and as far as I know so is Girl B. But what I didn't know was that Girl A and Girl B (still with me?) were out together in the same group.

Told you I messed up. Question is: what on earth do I do now?

Ross, Dalston

Dear Ross,

I gazed at the picture of Adam on my phone. There he was, same as always, with his high fade and his neatly trimmed beard, leaning his chin on the heel of his hand, thoughtfully chewing a pencil. Every week, some graphic designer added a different bit of cartoony art to the picture to make it look different – today Adam had a thought bubble coming out of his head with a few hearts and a mathematical equation in it.

Only problem was... Ross didn't have a problem. Gazing at Adam's *Max!* column on my phone, I'd simply invented the problem I wished Ross had – and I was totally unable to imagine what Adam's response to it might be.

Wearily, I chucked my phone down on the duvet next to me and stood up. It was Friday afternoon. I'd had the day off work and spent it having a manicure with Amelie and her other bridesmaids, then inspecting the wedding reception venue with Mum, who was having a last-minute panic about the tablecloths and napkins not being exactly the same shade of rose gold.

'It looks almost beige to me in this light, Lucy,' she'd fretted. 'Do you think we should ask Amelie what she thinks?'

'Definitely not. She'll only panic and it's too late to do anything about it. No one's going to be looking at table napkins anyway, come on, Mum.'

In a few minutes, Dad would be here to collect me and my bridesmaid's dress, which was hanging on the back of my wardrobe encased in plastic, and take me to the hotel. Everything was packed and ready. My spare keys were with a neighbour, who would feed Astro tomorrow and Sunday morning.

It all felt very final, somehow. It wasn't me getting married – I had no justification for this sense of seismic shifting, of the end of an era. But it felt that way anyway. As of tomorrow, Amelie would be a married woman. I'd no longer be the closest person to her in the world. Of course, the process of her moving away from me had started long ago, probably even before she'd met Zack and certainly by the time they'd moved in together and got engaged.

But now it would be more than a gradual process – it would be a done deal. My sister would have two rings on her finger instead of just one, and she'd be heading off on honeymoon and then to live with Zack in New York for six months.

It would be the longest I'd ever gone without seeing her. She'd have all the excitement of a new city, a new husband, a new apartment to turn into a temporary home.

I'd have my own life, carrying on just the same, only without the presence of my sister just a Tube journey away.

I should have felt happy for her. I did feel happy for her. But I felt a deep, selfish, hollow sense of loss for myself.

A buzz from the bed next to me and the sudden illumination of my phone's screen interrupted my glum introspection. It was Dad come to pick me up, fifteen minutes early. I leaped off the bed, threw the last of my things into my bag, kissed Astro and ran downstairs, too rushed and excited now to think that the next time I saw my flat and my cat, my sister would be married and everything would have changed.

Since she was a little girl, Amelie had been clear about what kind of wedding she wanted. Admittedly, that idea had changed numerous times over the years: from marrying a prince in a magic castle to a secret elopement to being barefoot in a field with lambs grazing nearby – she'd been dating a vet student at the time; I expect he could have told her that the reality of lambs was a lot less romantic than her idea of them.

But since getting engaged to Zack, her dreams had settled on a London hotel, the flashier the better. Our parents could never have stretched to that, but fortunately Zack could, and it was his vision of the perfect venue too. So later that evening, I found myself stepping out of a lava-hot shower into a room that – while nowhere near as large and luxurious as the bridal suite my sister and brother-in-law-to-be occupied – was way posher than anywhere I'd ever stayed before.

The bathroom was all done up in marble, with gold taps. The bed was huge and covered by a duvet so smooth and white it looked like snow had fallen on it. Through the heavy drapes on the windows, I could see glimpses of a rose garden three floors below. On the table by the telly, there was a bottle of champagne in an ice bucket, and I resolved to treat myself to a glass while I got ready to go down for dinner.

Only I didn't get the chance. While I was rooting around in my bag for my make-up, there was a soft tap on the door. Mum come to discuss some last-minute emergency, I thought. Or Nush offering me her hair straighteners. Or Amelie, saying she'd forgotten her eyelash curlers – as if I'd be able to help with that.

But when I opened the door, wrapped only in a towel, it was Bryony I saw smiling expectantly at me.

At least, I immediately assumed it was Bryony – her twin sister had even less of a reason to come calling on me than she did.

'Hi, Lucy!' She reached over to hug me like we were best friends, but when I raised my own arms my towel came adrift and I had to clutch at it, aborting the hug. 'Isn't this fabulous! I'm so excited! Are you excited?'

'Yes!' I tried to copy her giddy, friendly tone. 'Really excited! Come in!'

'I brought a bottle of fizz.' She brandished it. 'It was in our room. How cool is that? Like being a VIP.'

I giggled – her enthusiasm was endearing and quite contagious. 'I guess we are VIPs. I've got one too, and glasses.'

'We'll open mine,' she said firmly, and did so, carefully
pouring some into two glasses.

There was no seating area – like I said, my room was posh
but not exactly palatial – so we perched on the edge of the bed,
next to my open wheely suitcase. The bathroom door was open
and steam from my recent shower scented the room; Bryony
smoothed her hair as if she was worried it would frizz.

'I'm really sorry to interrupt you,' she said, once it was
clearly too late for me to tell her that she was interrupting me.
'Is this a bad time?'

Well, it obviously was, but there wasn't really going to be a
better time, so I said, 'No, it's fine. We're meeting for dinner at
eight so I've got ages to get ready.'

Bryony glanced at her watch. Clearly her idea of ages to get
ready was different from mine. But she was already dressed, her
make-up perfectly applied.

'It's just that tomorrow's going to be so busy,' she said. 'I
thought we might not get time to talk.'

'Now is fine,' I assured her, smiling. 'Cheers.'

She leaned in, suddenly serious. 'I just wanted to ask you
about Ross.'

Of course you did. 'Sure. What about him?'

'Um... well, you know. At the hen, he and I kind of got
together. I didn't realise until the next day that you work together.' She gave a tinkly little laugh.

The next day. So they had spent the night together.
Unless they'd just exchanged LinkedIn profiles, which I
doubted.

'Yes, that's right.'

She laughed again. 'Haha, I mean, random or what?'

'He lives nearby. I expect he goes out in Shoreditch all the
time, so it's not that random.'

'So I just wanted to ask,' she carried on, as if I hadn't spoken. 'I mean, what's he like?'

I shrugged. 'Nice guy. Good at his job. I haven't worked there very long so I don't know him all that well.'

'Oh, right. So you don't know if he, like, does that kind of thing often.'

I couldn't resist. 'What kind of thing?'

'I mean, he and I...' She flushed. Compared to Ross's and my epic blushes the previous week, it was a pretty poor effort, but credit to her for trying. 'You know, slept together. I just wondered if that's something... You know... if he's one of those guys who's got a different girl on the go every week or something like that.'

Suddenly, I felt a bit sorry for her. 'Honestly, Bryony, I've got no idea.'

'Did he say anything to you about me?'

'We work together. We're busy, and we're not close.'

Her face fell. 'So he didn't?'

'He's been on holiday this past week,' I explained. 'In Croatia. So I haven't seen him.'

'Oh!' She brightened. 'So that might be why he hasn't returned my calls.'

Calls? How many calls? But I said, 'Yes, that might be why.'

'That makes me feel better.' She tipped up her glass and necked what was left in there, which was about half. 'You see, I really liked him. I know it was just the one night, but you know how sometimes you think this one might just be special? And then I didn't speak to him and I thought maybe I was wrong. But you've given me hope! Thanks, Lucy.'

She reached over and gave me a fragrant hug.

'It's my pleasure,' I managed to say.

'Put in a word for me, won't you? Next time you see him?'

'I'll try.' Given I could barely offer the man a coffee without having a near-death experience, it wasn't looking good.

'Thank you.' She went all serious again. 'Bloody weddings. They just make you realise how shit it is being single, don't they?'

Before I could respond, she stood up and swished out, clutching her half-drunk bottle of champagne.

ELEVEN

'It's T minus seven,' Amelie said. 'We need to leave in, like, ninety seconds.'

She was standing in the centre of the bridal suite. Her dark hair was piled on top of her head, a few artful tendrils arranged around her face and shoulders. Her slender arms were encased in lace so perfectly fitting it looked like it had been painted on by a henna artist working in white. Her skin was glowing with make-up and, I suppose, happiness. The full satin skirt of her dress fell in sculpted folds from her small waist all the way to the tips of her pearl-embroidered shoes.

She looked like an angel and sounded like a sergeant-major. I was overwhelmed with love for her.

'Hold on,' Nush said. 'Let me blot your lipstick one more time.'

'Lucy, are you sure you remember which way to give your sister the bouquet?' Mum fretted. 'We don't want the back of it showing.'

'Do you need another squirt of deodorant?' Miranda asked Amelie. 'You were sweating like a horse earlier. Sorry, but you were.'

'I feel more like a dog being gussied up for Crufts,' grumbled Amelie. 'Come on, people. We need to make a move. Now.'

'Let me check your bag one more time,' urged Bryony. 'Tissues. Lipstick. Perfume miniature. Tampons.'

'Vape?' asked Amelie.

'You can't vape on your wedding day!' Mum protested.

'She can do whatever she likes,' I said. 'Including being late. Remember? That's what you've been saying for the past week. It's a bride's privilege to be late on her wedding day.'

'At the rate you lot are going, Zack will have got fed up, gone back on the apps and found someone else to marry before I get to the damn altar.' Amelie did a final pirouette in front of the cheval mirror, her veil drifting behind her. 'If you lot don't get cracking, I'm going to go down on my own.'

She strode to the door and flung it open, and we all followed: Nush, Miranda, Bryony and I in our rose-gold satin shifts and Mum behind us in olive silk with a massive hat that only just fitted into the lift. The smells of air freshener, our clashing perfumes and the roses in our bouquets made me want to sneeze. My shoes were pinching my feet and I felt sick with nerves.

Dad was waiting for us outside the function room. When he saw us, he took the hankie out of his breast pocket, blew his nose then tucked it back again, making sure the folds were in the same place.

'Good girls,' he said. 'You look very nice.'

Mum reached out and brushed Amelie's cheek with her finger, like she was a priceless china doll about to be displayed on *Antiques Roadshow*. 'Good luck, sweetie. You're the most beautiful bride I've ever seen.'

Amelie hugged her, leaving a lipstick smear on Mum's cheek that would be joined by many others and show later in all the photos. 'Love you, Mum. See you on the other side.'

She took Dad's arm, we all lined up behind her and the
Arctic Monkeys' 'I Wanna Be Yours' began to play. We entered
the function room, moving sedately through the banks of
flowers towards Zack, waiting patiently next to his best man at
the end.

Afterwards, I couldn't remember much about the wedding
ceremony. I suppose they're all much the same, aren't they,
while also being unique. Each time, two people say words that
have been chosen for them, whether by the church or the state
or a Google search. Each time, someone they love nervously
does the reading they've chosen. Each time, the couple make
promises to each other that they profoundly believe in the
moment, and some of them they'll keep and some of them they
won't.

It was a beautiful wedding, everyone said afterwards. But
all weddings are beautiful, aren't they?

After I'd got my reading over, I found my concentration
drifting. My eyes wandered to the rose garden outside the
window, the lilac feathers on Zack's mother's hat, the beads of
perspiration on the back of Nush's neck. I breathed in the
smells of flowers, the foundation the make-up artist had caked
on my face, and the promise of the wedding breakfast drifting
from somewhere else in the hotel. I listened to the celebrant's
cheerful but serious voice, the strains of Bach played by the
string quartet while Zack and Amelie signed the register, the
faint hum of traffic when the door to the street outside was
opened, which vanished as soon as it was closed again.

And then it was over. My sister and Zack were married.
They turned to face us, alight with smiles, and walked back the
way they'd come, almost running this time, Zack holding
Amelie's hand and her bouquet aloft. Everyone crowded out
into the rose garden. Petals and rice were thrown. The string
quartet set up and started playing again, waiters circulated with

trays of champagne flutes and canapés, and the photographer and videographer moved through the crowd, occasionally issuing instructions but mostly aiming for the informal reportage shots my sister had ordered.

Everyone chatted and laughed and ate and drank. Zack strode around glad-handing the guests, looking like he'd been made king of the world. Amelie's friends and their boyfriends stood in a huddle, making sure they were closest to the door that the booze and food were coming out of. Someone snuck behind an oak tree and lit a fag – I could smell the acrid smoke drifting above the scent of rose petals.

I wasn't sure what I was supposed to do. My duties were over, for the time being. At some point that evening, I'd need to slip a lace garter on to my sister's thigh for her to remove and throw to the assembled single men, but that was hours away. I checked my bag – the garter was safely there. I checked my phone – I had no new messages.

All at once, I felt lonely. I'd never wanted a wedding of my own – not since I'd graduated from playing with Barbies and moved on to Nintendo when I was about nine, anyway. I didn't want a boyfriend, still less a husband. But I couldn't help wondering how it would feel to have someone choose you, above all the other people in the world, to be with forever. I imagined the glimmer of desire I'd felt for Ross, magnified by thousands so it was like a steady, burning flame. And then I remembered what hurt and heartbreak felt like, and imagined that magnified by thousands too, should it all go wrong.

I went in search of my sister. She didn't seem to be mingling with the crowd or being congratulated by our uncle and aunt or in the gaggle of her laughing friends. I asked the photographer if he'd seen her, and he said no, but if I found her she was to come out straight away, because they wanted to get the formal shots done before it started to rain. I wondered if she'd gone to the loo, but I'd been under strict instructions to accompany her if she did, to make sure she didn't wee on her dress.

But I tried the toilets anyway, and I found her there. Actually, they weren't so much toilets – although of course they fulfilled that mundane function too – but more a kind of posh powder room, with little brocade armchairs, bowls of potpourri and flattering foxed glass on the mirrors. Amelie was perched in one of the armchairs, her phone in her hand.

'Hey,' I said. 'Are you okay?'

'I'm fine. It's just, no one seemed to want to talk to me.'

'What? What do you mean?'

She smiled forlornly. 'It's like, I'm the bride and they don't want to monopolise me. They think I must have more important people to talk to than them. So I was standing on my own for ages and it was really cringe, and I didn't want to drink any more because I'm already a bit shitfaced. And Mum's confiscated my vape. So I came in here to sit down for a bit.'

I sat next to her. 'Do you need a wee?'

She shook her head. 'I went already. You could check my dress isn't all pissy, though.'

She stood up and twirled, and I inspected her skirt. 'You're all good.'

She moved over to the mirror and did something to her lipstick, then adjusted one of the tendrils of hair, which was sticking to her neck.

'Do you think Zack's happy?' she asked.

'He looks over the moon to me. Like he's won the lottery. Absolutely made up.'

She nodded. 'That's good.'

'We should go and find him. He'll think you've done a runner.'

'I nearly did. Before we walked in, I was so scared I legit almost called it all off. But Dad was gripping my arm like I was under arrest, so I couldn't.'

'Just as well. Mum would've died of shame and Zack would have been heartbroken.'

'I know. But, you know, I could be in an Uber right now, on my way to Heathrow to go and live on a desert island somewhere.'

I realised she really was a bit drunk. 'You'd hate living on a desert island. Come on, we should go back. And you should have a glass of water.'

'I'll only need to wee again.'

'I'll help you next time. We'll have a code word.'

'The purple crane flies at daybreak?' she suggested.

I laughed. 'Got it.'

Then she reached over and gripped my hand. Her fingers were ice-cold and clammy. 'Lucy, I need to tell you something.'

'Of course. So long as it's not that you want me to come and live with you on your desert island, because—'

'No, it's not that. It's—'

But then the door opened and a gaggle of women – partners of Zack's friends, I guessed – entered, and Amelie was showered with kisses and compliments and congratulations, and as soon as she could extricate herself, we went back out and found Zack and the photographer, just as the first drops of rain began to fall.

It was late in the evening before I found myself alone with my sister again. The photographs had been taken, the wedding breakfast consumed, the speeches made – 'Zack got GenBot 2.0 to write his, you know,' Nush whispered to me as the guests laughed politely at his tired jokes – the cake cut, the first dance danced and the bouquet and garter thrown – there was a bit of a scrum for the bouquet, but Bryony won.

Now, it was almost ten thirty. Some of Zack's friends were settling in for a good old session, ordering bottles of champagne and spirits and testing the bartender's cocktail-making skills. Amelie's mates were on the dance floor, their shoes kicked off, throwing shapes and laughing. Mum was deep in conversation with Zack's parents. Dad, who for some reason I'd never understood hated weddings, was sipping coffee, his chin dropping lower and lower towards his bow tie. Amelie and Zack were standing together by the open door to the rose garden, holding hands.

The rain had stopped and a fresh breeze was blowing into the room, dispelling the smell of food, flowers and perfume. People were beginning to leave, saying their goodbyes to our parents, Zack's parents or the bride and groom, whoever was closest. I was wondering whether I could slip away too, or whether I should make a token effort to join the group of dancers for a few minutes first.

Then Amelie leaned up and kissed Zack on the cheek before dropping his hand and turning back to the room. She glanced around, a slightly glassy smile on her face, before her eyes lit on me and she hurried over.

'Come upstairs with me,' she said. 'I need to talk to you.'

'But what about Zack? I can't gate-crash your wedding night, you weirdo. And it's not like you need a chaperone or anything.'

'Don't be mad! Zack's coming up in a bit. I told him I was going to take my make-up off and get ready for bed. He's waiting for the big reveal of my wedding negligee.'

It was the first I'd heard of this and I wasn't sure I wanted to know, but I asked anyway. 'Wedding negligee?'

'Snoopy T-shirt,' she said. 'The boning on this basque is digging in something chronic and the lace is itching my armpits, and if I don't get into something comfortable soon I'm going to claw my own skin off. Let's go.'

She grabbed a bottle of champagne from the bar and led me

to the lift, and a few moments later she beeped us into the bridal suite with her key card.

Housekeeping had clearly been in and done their thing. The bed was turned down, the lights dimmed and the curtains drawn. There were chocolates on the pillows and fresh fluffy robes hung on hooks in the bathroom. On top of the snow-white duvet, red rose petals had been scattered in the shape of a heart.

'Quick, get rid of those,' Amelie ordered.

'What? Why? Aren't they romantic?'

'I think so, but Zack will think they're tacky. Just do it, Luce, please. We haven't got much time.'

I scooped up the rose petals and chucked them down the loo – a mistake, as it turned out, because several of them refused to flush and floated on the surface of the water like splats of blood. Then, while Amelie stood in front of the mirror yanking pins and grips out of her hair, I carefully undid all the tiny buttons down the back of her dress, one after another.

'Isn't this Zack's job?' I asked, kneeling on the floor with her bum by my face while I wrestled with the little loops of satin that encased each miniature pearl.

'He's even more cack-handed than you. He'd snap a button off for sure. Ah, that's better.'

Amelie pulled a brush through her hair and scraped it up with a scrunchie, then stepped out of the dress and sat on the edge of the bath, easing off her shoes, unhooking her suspenders and reaching behind her to release the clasps on her basque.

I hung the dress up, back in its protective sleeve, while she rummaged in her bag for her Snoopy T-shirt.

'Want to open the fizz?' she asked. 'I'll make a start at getting this slap off.'

Through the open bathroom door, I could see her peeling off her false eyelashes and wiping oil-soaked cotton pads over her face. They started off pristine white and ended up a muddy greyish-brown. By the time she'd finished, the bubbles were dying away in our glasses.

Amelie came back into the bedroom and sat on the bed, her legs crossed. I handed her a glass and joined her, watching as she took a huge gulp of champagne as if it was the first thing she'd drunk for hours.

'God, I needed that,' she said.

'So...' I took a cautious sip from my own glass. 'What's this all about?'

'I need to tell you something,' she said.

I felt a cold hollowness in my stomach: whatever it was, it couldn't be good news. Surely if there was something wrong between her and Zack, she wouldn't have gone ahead with marrying him?

But she went on: 'It's about Adam.'

'Adam? What about Adam?'

'Zack,' she explained patiently, as if reminding me of something I'd known for years, 'doesn't know about Adam.'

'Well, I mean, why would he know about Adam? We've only just started being Adam. And I guess Zack doesn't read *Max!* – I mean, why would he? I bet he reads *The Economist* or something.'

'He does, actually. I tried it once because I thought I'd be able to have an intelligent conversation with him about inflation and interest rates, but it lost me after the contents page.'

'Anyway' – to be perfectly honest, I wasn't that interested in Zack's reading habits – 'what's Zack got to do with Adam?'

'The thing is,' she said, crossing her legs and looking intently down at her French-manicured nails, 'Zack doesn't know about Adam, so he doesn't know you're Adam. And he doesn't know I've been helping you.'

'Okay. So tell him – or don't tell him. I don't understand why it's such a big deal.'

'I can't tell him. Adam's meant to be a secret. Especially Adam being a woman is meant to be a secret.'

'I know it is,' I admitted, 'although to be honest I've never understood why you thought it was such a big deal to keep it quiet. Why wouldn't the guys who read *Max!* want to take relationship advice from a woman? Horse's mouth, right? But Greg agreed it should only be shared among the core team, so I just went along with it.'

She looked at me pityingly. 'Luce, have you ever actually met a man? They don't listen to their mothers, they don't listen to their wives. Why the hell would they listen to you?'

This seemed like a fair point. 'Okay, fine. But still, there's no reason for Zack not to know you're helping me be Adam. He's your husband, after all.'

Amelie twisted the gold band on her finger. 'I suppose he is now. And the thing is, you're not meant to keep secrets in a marriage.'

'So tell him. I don't get it.'

'Lucy, come on. Okay, I'll explain like you're five. Zack wouldn't want me being involved in sorting out other men's problems. He'd get jealous. He'd think I was focusing on them when I should be focusing on him. And anyway, I'll need to spend time with Zack. I'm his wife. I'll need to meet his work colleagues and his friends and sightsee with him and host dinner parties and stuff.'

'Dinner parties? I thought you got married, not stepped into a time machine and travelled back to the 1950s. Anyway, you can't cook.'

'Exactly. I'm going to have to learn. I won't have time to do the Adam stuff on the side like we said.'

There was a definite awkwardness in her admission – like she was ashamed, almost, of what she'd said. I wasn't Zack's number-one fan, but my sister loved him and he seemed to worship her. It was the first inkling I'd had that there might be imperfections in their relationship. And that wasn't a subject I wanted to explore – not on her wedding night of all nights.

'So you're saying I have to do it on my own?'

She nodded. 'I'm afraid so. You've got this, Luce. You'll be fine. And if you get stuck, you can ask one of those neckbeards you work with to give you a hand.'

Thinking of Ross, I bristled. 'They're not neckbeards.'

'I bet they are. I bet they're—'

I could tell she was trying to change the subject, and I wasn't going to let her. 'Am, I can't do it without you. You know I can't. I don't understand men.'

Amelie sang the line from *The Sound of Music* about how I was totally unprepared to face a world of men.

'Exactly,' I said. 'So I can't do it on my own. You have to help me.'

'Luce, you've got to. You're smart, you'll manage it.'

'But Amelie, I can't. Seriously. Please don't abandon me.'

'Lucy, I forbid you to guilt-trip me on my wedding day. Don't you care about the happiness of my marriage?'

Guilt-tripping was evidently allowed for one of us, but it wasn't me. I was about to protest again when I heard the click of the door unlatching. Zack walked in, his hair standing on end and his tie askew. He smelled of cigar smoke.

When he saw us he stopped dead on the threshold. 'Am I interrupting something?'

'Luce was just helping me undo my hair and get out of my dress,' Amelie said.

'I'm on my way now,' I assured him, scrambling to my feet and putting my glass down on the coffee table. 'I'll leave you two to your wedding night. And congratulations.'

My brother-in-law and then my sister embraced me, gushing with thanks for the role I'd played in their big day. I said goodnight again and let myself out, and as I left I saw Zack pulling my sister close, kissing her passionately.

'You're irresistible in that top,' I heard him say as the door thunked closed behind me.

I stood by what I had said. I didn't understand men – not one tiny bit. And now, I was all on my own with thousands upon thousands of them and their respective problems, without the secret weapon of my sister to help me.

TWELVE

Dear Adam,

So, I've been dumped. Happens to the best of us, right? Back on the horse, etcetera. But I really thought that this woman was the one. We'd been together for two years. We were talking about moving in together. My parents loved her. I thought her friends and family liked me. And then – bam – she's off travelling in South-East Asia for a year. I suggested going with her but she wasn't having it. She said we'd grown apart and she wanted to follow her dreams. There's another man, isn't there? I think I've been played for a fool and I don't know what to do next. I'm thirty-one and I feel like a lost puppy.

Mitch, Carlisle

It was Sunday, a week since Amelie's wedding, and I felt just like a lost puppy myself. The previous week at work had gone okay – I'd been busy enough, typing up the responses to the queries that Amelie had helped me formulate, saving one of them for future reference so that Adam's readers didn't start to think he was some sort of penis specialist.

Each day, I'd stopped for coffee on the way to the office as usual and got the lift up to the *Max!* floor without having to worry about sharing it with Ross, because he was still on holiday. I'd filed my copy with Greg and waited for him to roll his eyes in disgust at what I'd written, but he'd only responded, 'Nice work.' But when I'd tentatively asked him how the Ask Adam column was landing with readers, he'd pushed his glasses up his nose and said, 'It's early days yet,' which did my self-confidence no good at all.

Now, alone in my flat with Astro sleeping behind me on the back of the sofa, I found myself less interested in the new release of *Resident Evil 4* and more compelled to get out my phone or laptop and see what new problems had landed in Adam's inbox.

I came face to face – well, face to screen – with Mitch, his globetrotting ex and his broken heart. And I had absolutely no idea what to say to him.

'What do you reckon, Astro?' I asked. 'What would Amelie tell him?'

But Astro only twitched a paw, deep in a dream about chasing squirrels.

'Well, I know how to get your attention, anyway,' I told him.

I was hungry, and there were fish fingers in the freezer and a loaf of fresh white bread on the kitchen counter. Maybe some carbs and essential fatty acids would kick my brain into gear – and if not, they'd at least stop my stomach from grumbling.

While I waited for the grill to heat up, spreading butter and mayonnaise on the bread, adding just a squiggle of ketchup and thinly slicing a pickled cucumber – I'm no chef, but I do know how to make the perfect fish finger sandwich – I thought of my sister. Not just what advice she would have given to Mitch, but about her. What was she doing right now? What time was it in the Bahamas? Was she lying on a beach somewhere with Zack rubbing sunblock into her back? Was she having fun?

Was she missing me as much as I missed her?

An unexpected tear splatted down on to the kitchen counter and I blinked, grabbing a square of kitchen roll and blowing my nose furiously. This was no good whatsoever. Amelie wanted me to be happy, not moping because she was off being happy.

Snatching the grill pan out of the oven just in time, I assembled my dinner and returned to the sofa. Astro, smelling fish, immediately roused and planted his front feet on my lap, begging shamelessly for scraps as I ate.

When I'd finished, I put the plate on the floor for him to lick clean and opened my laptop again.

Oh Mitch, you poor boy, I imagined Amelie saying. But what would she say next? I knew she'd been disappointed in relationships, but as far as I knew she'd never had her heart properly broken – she'd been more in the business of breaking other people's.

But my heart had. I hadn't forgotten the pain, but I'd buried it deep inside me, determined that it would never happen to me again. Now, if I was going to be able to help Mitch – or at the very least do the job I'd been hired to do – I was going to have to delve into that hidden place, remember how it had felt and tell Mitch what he needed to hear.

I started typing, my fingers hesitant on the keyboard at first, then picking up pace.

Dear Mitch,

Well, you've been through the wringer, haven't you? When you believe that someone is your person and it turns out they don't feel the same, it hurts. There's no getting away from that.

But here's the thing: if she decided you weren't the man for her, that means she wasn't the woman for you. No amount of compromising or begging or even writing to me is going to change that fact. You're going to have to move on, and deep down I suspect you know that.

There are many positives to draw from your situation. The people closest to her approved of you – that means you're a decent guy. You sustained a relationship for two years. You had sensible plans to take it to the next level. You're young. You've got everything going for you, Mitch.

As for what to do next – channel that lost puppy and lick your wounds for a bit. It's normal to feel self-pity in your position. But don't torture yourself – if there's another guy on the scene, you can't change that. And delete her from your social media if you can – watching her live her best life will only be painful for you and sustain the hope that she might change her mind about you. Because she's already made it clear: you're not the man for her.

So, when you're ready, dust yourself off. Check that broken heart – you'll likely feel the pieces coming together again. Have fun with your mates. Get out in the fresh air – I know I sound like your nan, but it helps.

I guarantee you, before long, someone else will come along. She might not be Ms Right; she might just be Ms Right for Now. But she'll show you that there are other women out there who appreciate your many excellent qualities. Eventually, you'll look back on this and you'll wish your ex well and maybe even admire her for having the courage to pursue her dreams.

Yours,

Adam

Feeling like I'd been through the wringer myself, I snapped my laptop closed. As soon as I put it down on the floor, Astro jumped up on to my lap, and I flicked on the telly. But I didn't return to *Resident Evil*; instead I scrolled through Netflix until I found *The Last Letter from Your Lover* and had a good old cry watching it until it was time for bed.

Over the next few days, I found myself looking at men a bit differently. On the bus in the morning, I sat next to a guy a few years younger than me who spent the entire journey scrolling through Tinder. Surreptitiously, I watched over his shoulder and wondered why it was that he swiped right on the blurry photo of a girl with glasses and a halo of blonde curls, but left on the slender, tanned brunette with the trout pout. Did he think picking the brunette would be punching? Did he just like women with curly hair? Had his previous girlfriend been a slim brunette who'd cheated on him with his best friend?

In the queue for my morning coffee, I overheard a guy asking his colleague how his wife's pregnancy was going, and I listened, fascinated, as the colleague embarked on a soul-baring description of how hard it was to see her being sick all the time and how much he longed for the baby's arrival but feared that their relationship would never be the same again.

Actually, that was my interpretation. The actual conversation had gone more like this.

'So, how's Lisa getting on, mate?'

'Still puking twenty-four seven. They say it's morning sickness but it lasts all bloody day, doesn't it?'

'Feel ya. With Marie it was the evenings, right until the ninth month. Couldn't keep anything down except ginger biscuits.'

'Jesus. Well, at least we've only got six months to go, right?'

'Yeah, then the sleepless nights and shitty nappies kick in.'

'Right. Remind me again why we thought this was a good idea?'

Then they'd ordered their coffees and started talking about a PowerPoint presentation they were working on instead.

At work, I overheard Chiraag on the phone to his mother. Evidently she was organising an anniversary party for his grandparents and wanted Chiraag's opinion on everything from the gift to the buffet. Chiraag, I knew, was an only child – no doubt if he'd had a sister this burden would have fallen on her. But as I listened to him spend fifteen minutes at a stretch saying, 'I really don't know, Mum. I'm sure Nan will be happy with whatever you decide. So don't spend six hours making samosas, buy them in. Yeah, I know yours are better – sorry I suggested it,' I felt as if I was getting a glimpse of a family life I'd had no idea about – pressures on his emotions and time I'd been unaware of, and probably wouldn't have cared if I had.

That same day, I – or rather Adam – received an email that left me more perplexed than usual. Working during our lunch breaks was frowned upon by Greg, but it was raining so I ate my sandwich at my desk instead of going out, and the call of the inbox was strong. I flicked it open on my phone and opened the first of the five unread emails that had arrived during the morning.

Since Ross had returned from holiday, the awkwardness between us seemed to have settled down somewhat. We still avoided making eye contact except when it was absolutely essential, but we were back to saying good morning and offering to make hot drinks for each other, and able to discuss work problems without breaking out in a storm of competitive blushing.

So, when I looked up and saw that Ross, too, was eating a sandwich and scrolling idly through his phone, I felt as if I could make conversation with him without either of us dying of shame.

'Hey, Ross?' I said.

He looked up, a triangle of ham and cheese sandwich halfway to his mouth. 'Mmmm?'

'If you fancied your mate's ex, and she fancied you, would you think it was okay to ask her out?'

He looked startled, then grinned, and I wondered whether anyone, ever, had managed to see that smile and not smile back. 'If I fancied... who?'

'Just theoretically. Say your friend had been going out with a girl – not seriously, but exclusively – for maybe six months, a year or so back, and you were all part of the same friendship group. Now you and this woman were getting close and you'd both told each other you liked each other. Okay to do something about it, or not?'

'How seriously are we talking here?' He hesitated, then went on, 'L-word territory, or not?'

I couldn't help wondering whether he'd ever told a woman he loved her. He must have done. Who was she, and when, and had she loved him back?

'I dunno, Lucy. It's a tricky one. I guess you should think about your mate's feelings before thinking about some girl you like.'

'So that's a no, then?'

'But on the other hand...' He took a bite of his sandwich and chewed thoughtfully. He managed not to look gross when he was eating, I noticed – no spraying crumbs everywhere, or anything like that. 'On the other hand, it's not like they were married or anything. Or were they?'

'Not married. No kids either.'

'And their break-up, was it, like, acrimonious or amicable?'

'Fairly amicable, as far as I know.' Louis from Manchester

certainly hadn't mentioned anything about it not being amicable.

'Then I'd say it's more of a grey area. I mean, in an ideal world, no one would date anyone their mate had been with, because of the potential fallout.' He shrugged ruefully, like the conversation had got more serious than he'd expected. 'But we don't live in an ideal world, do we?'

In an ideal world, you'd have not snogged Bryony. 'Not so far as I can tell.'

'Well, then.' I heard him breathe in, and he carried on, almost reluctantly. 'Maybe the thing to do is have a word with your mate – talk to her, see how she'd feel about it. And if she's okay with it, then you're free to make a move on this dude. Sisters before misters, right?'

Damn it! I was blushing now. 'Hold on! I said theoretically.'

He laughed. 'Okay, fine. Theoretically then, Lucy, have a chat with your mate, and if she's okay with it, then knock yourself out. And good luck.'

'Ross, honestly.' I hadn't expected the conversation to take this turn. 'I'm not talking about me.'

'I see. So you're "asking for a friend"?' Then I saw realisation dawn on his face. 'Oh wait, it's one of those Ask Adam questions, isn't it?'

'Yeah, as a matter of fact. And it's a guy wanting to date a girl whose ex he's friends with, if that makes any difference.'

He thought for a moment. 'Maybe it does. It shouldn't but it might. Guys are more territorial about shit like that.'

'Oh for God's sake. Don't pull that caveman, men are from Mars, women are from Venus stuff on me.'

'I wasn't! I was just saying, in my experience, a man might not take it as well as a woman. Women are more emotionally mature.'

'Oh right,' I scoffed. 'And you can't multitask and we can't read maps?'

'Hey, I never said anything about maps. You asked me my opinion, and I'm telling you.'

Which was true, of course. 'Sorry. Okay, thanks. I'll tell the guy to talk to his friend, and if he's cool with it, give it a go.'

Ross raised an eyebrow. 'Yeah. Sounds like a plan to me.'

I was saved from having to say anything more by Ross's phone trilling softly on the desk next to him. He put down the remaining corner of his sandwich and answered it.

'Hey, Bryony. How's it going?'

Then he stood up so quickly his chair went skidding into the sub-editors' pod behind him, and he hurried off to the area by the lifts where we all took calls when we didn't want to be overheard.

I bit my lip, remembering the conversation I'd had with Bryony the night before the wedding. I'd promised to put in a word for her, and I hadn't. I couldn't even tell myself I hadn't had a chance – I'd just spent five minutes discussing Louis from Manchester's love life – which I wasn't convinced Ross believed wasn't my own – with him. But that was different. That was – as I'd said – theoretical. His... thing, whatever it was, with Bryony was anything but.

Still, I'd promised to do something and not done it. And that wasn't cool. According to the code Ross had alluded to, I should have been bigging her up to him at every opportunity.

So why hadn't I?

I hadn't wanted to. It would have been all kinds of awkward. He'd have blushed; I'd have blushed. The tenuous normality that had been re-established between the two of us would get thrown all out of kilter again. But then, it just had been, by me going and asking him theoretical questions about one of Adam's correspondents.

I had a duty to say something. It was going to be difficult, but I was going to do it. Just as soon as an appropriate moment arose, whenever that might be. Maybe in a week or two.

My brain might have been all set to procrastinate, but apparently my mouth had other ideas. A couple of minutes later, Ross returned to his desk and sat down, glanced at me, then put his phone back where it had been, next to his keyboard. I could see the beginning of a blush stealing up his neck, but he picked up his sandwich and took what I guessed was meant to be a nonchalant bite.

'Ross?'

He raised both eyebrows this time, chewing.

'I'm sorry, I couldn't help overhearing. Was that Bryony you were talking to?'

He nodded and swallowed.

I felt myself starting to blush again, but I pressed on. 'I mean... that's the girl you met when I was on my sister's hen night. You know she's a friend of my sister's?'

He nodded again.

'Are you seeing her?' I asked. My voice sounded like it was coming from a long way away. 'Not that it's any of my business.'

'No, you're all good.' He glanced at his phone as if expecting it to ring again and rescue him from having to talk to me. 'We've been texting. We've been out. So, seeing each other...? Yeah, we kind of are.'

'You should go for it. Honestly. Bryony's lovely. She's really nice and...' What the hell could I say about her? I barely knew the woman. 'Lovely.'

Ross nodded, his face seeming to close off again. 'Good to know. Thanks, Lucy.'

And then our eyes slid away from each other's faces like ice cubes on a glass tabletop, and we both turned back to our screens and worked in silence for the remainder of the afternoon.

THIRTEEN

The following Sunday evening, I found myself – or rather, Adam found himself – with a clear inbox. I'd filed that week's answers to Greg on time and received the usual monosyllabic response. I'd read through all the incoming problems and decided which of them were on the shortlist for a reply the following week, although I hadn't drafted my answers yet, in case anything juicier arrived in the meantime.

So it felt like a usual Sunday evening at home, or what used to be a usual Sunday evening before Adam and his... followers – Clients? Patients? I wasn't sure what to call them – had become part of my life. I was on the sofa with Astro lying on my feet. A half-eaten carton of chicken and cashew udon was on the coffee table next to me, the lid propped on top of it to prevent Astro rummaging through the bits of bean sprout and carrot for fragments of chicken, like a cat fishing for koi carp in a pond.

My phone was on the sofa next to me, dark and silent, and the telly was on, tuned to a repeat of last year's *Eurovision Song Contest*, which I wasn't really watching. And then I felt a vibration coming through the cushion next to me, shortly followed by the buzz of my phone.

I snatched it up and saw an incoming call from Amelie.

I hadn't heard from her in over a week. She'd read my messages giving her updates on my progress as Adam, although I'd carefully avoided asking for her advice on a couple of the problems he'd been sent. But she hadn't responded in much detail at all. Just the briefest acknowledgments:

> All good here, miss you.

> Can't read now, will try tomorrow.

> You've got this Luce, don't worry.

But of course I was worried. Not so much about my ability to fly solo as Adam without driving his correspondents to drink or to involuntary celibacy – for now, at least, I was reasonably confident that wouldn't happen on my watch. But about my sister. Her silence was unusual; Amelie was normally a multiple-times-a-day texter. Sure, she was on honeymoon. But even given the five-hour time difference, I'd have expected her to be sending me gushing updates on what she and Zack were up to – how glorious the weather was, how delicious the food, how beautiful the tropical fish they saw on their scuba dives, how off-the-scale the sex.

But there'd been nothing. And now she was calling me. I was sure something was wrong.

I snatched up my phone and hit the green button, after missing it a couple of times in my haste. Amelie's familiar face filled the screen. She was half-sitting, half-lying on what looked like a deck chair or a sun lounger. She was wrapped in a fluffy white towel with the neon-yellow strap of a bikini top emerging from it and circling round her neck. Her hair hung in damp tendrils around her face. Bars of sunshine fell over her in alternating dark and light stripes.

'Jesus,' I said. 'I thought you'd been eaten by a shark.'

She giggled. 'Almost was, yesterday. At least, I thought it

was a shark but apparently it was only a dolphin. Still, I'll take it as a near miss and tell my grandchildren about it one day.'

I could only just hear her, so I turned up the sound on my phone. 'Why are you whispering?'

'Zack's in the shower and I'm just outside on our balcony. We've called a screen ban for the honeymoon so I have to sneak online whenever he's not around. Otherwise I'd be on social media all the time and he'd be on Teams. It's better this way.'

'Are you having a nice time?'

'Off the scale. You should see our suite – there's a free-standing bath that's so massive I can only lie down if I jam my feet in Zack's crotch, otherwise I'd drown. We've been having cocktails at lunchtime every day, and yesterday I ate so much lobster I thought I'd legit burst. And isn't it incredible how you don't get hangovers on holiday?'

'Amazing,' I said, although I hadn't been on that kind of holiday in the longest time.

'Anyway,' she said, leaning into the screen as if she was sitting next to me on my sofa, not thousands of miles away, 'how's it going? How's Adam?'

'Busy. I think I've been doing all right. Listen, while you're here, what advice would you give a bloke who—'

'Stop.' She held up a hand. 'Luce, we discussed this. I'd love to help, but it's a slippery slope. I tell you what advice you should give this guy, and the next thing you'll be asking me about the next one and the next, and we'll be back to square one and Zack will probably divorce me.'

I thought, not for the first time, that if Zack would even consider divorcing her over something so trivial, he needed to take a long, hard look at himself. But I'd agreed to stop asking her for help with Adam, and I wasn't going to break my promise.

'Fine,' I said. 'Your loss. And it was a really juicy email, too, you'd have loved it. But I'm not going to tell you now, even if you beg me.'

Amelie laughed, softly and breathily. 'No begging. Not a chance. But speaking of blokes, there's another one I wanted to ask you about.'

I suspected I already knew who she meant. But I asked anyway. 'There is? Who?'

'Your man at work. Ross. Is he—' She stopped, and I saw her glance away, towards the dark shadow on the edge of the picture, which I assumed was the interior of their hotel bedroom – or suite, rather.

'Is he what?'

'Zack's finished in the shower. I heard the water stop. Bollocks – he normally wallows in there for hours like a walrus, but we haven't had lunch yet so he must be rushing. I'll call again when I can, okay?'

'Okay.' I hesitated. Amelie was fine. She was having a wonderful time on honeymoon. She hadn't been eaten by a shark. But still, I was worried. Something about her – the whispers, the clandestine video call, the fact that it had taken, presumably, a three-line whip from Bryony for her to contact me at all – concerned me. It wasn't normal. It wasn't like my sister. 'Are you sure you're okay?'

'Course! I'm brilliant. Speak soon, love you, Luce.' She was still whispering, but so quickly that the words ran together. *SpeaksoonloveyouLuce.*

'Love you. Bye.'

The screen went dark again. I looked at it, puzzled. A ban on work and social media when on honeymoon made sense, in a way. It was a time when, I supposed, you wanted to be gazing into each other's eyes, not at your TikTok feed. A time when you were meant to be practising sex positions, not selfie angles.

But even so. Amelie used her phone a lot, but she wasn't obsessive about it. When we met up, she'd talk and listen, her phone on the table next to her, vibrating or lighting up intermit-tently, and she'd barely give it a glance. If I were Zack, I wouldn't feel excluded or threatened by that at all.

So who had imposed this so-called ban, and why?

For the first time in months, I flicked open the Instagram app. I never posted on there myself – what would I post? The world only needed so many cat photos. Actually, that number was pretty high, given the two dozen or so exclusively cat-related feeds I'd followed when I'd first opened my account a few years back. But that didn't mean I wanted to join them – Astro was a companion, not a celebrity, and everyone who loved him already knew what he looked like.

And there was nothing remotely Insta-worthy in the rest of my life. I went to work, I came home. I ate takeaways or things on toast. I rarely bought new clothes or wore make-up. There was no aspirational, hashtag-worthy content whatsoever being generated by my life.

I didn't want to be going out for cocktails that cost north of twenty quid each on Friday nights or spending three quarters of an hour doing my face or eating Buddha bowls or having every-thing showers on Monday evenings. I liked my life. But still, I didn't want to be reminded, in unfiltered real time, how different it was from those of other people my age.

But now, I felt the need to look.

There was Nush's carefully staged selfie of Amelie and her bridesmaids in the hotel before the wedding, glowing and smil-ing. There were Amelie and Zack next to each other in their business-class seats en route to their island paradise honeymoon – presumably before the screen ban had been imposed. There was Miranda at the hairdresser, having violet streaks added to her glossy almost-black hair.

And there was Bryony, in a post from Friday night. It wasn't just one image, but a whole slideshow of them. Her in her bedroom, wearing jeans and a white broderie crop top, her hair artfully tousled round her face, her even white teeth showing between taupe-painted lips. *Date ready!* she'd posted, with a selection of emojis ranging from the clinking champagne glasses to the boyfriend and girlfriend.

She must have posted at the end of the evening, I thought. No one – not even her – would feel confident enough to post the boyfriend and girlfriend emoji before even leaving the house for a date.

But, swiping through the slideshow of images, I saw that her confidence had been justified. Evidently the evening had involved a walk along the South Bank of the Thames, which had taken them past the London Eye and then through the forest of fairy-lit trees by the Tate Modern, and finished with Tower Bridge in the background. Then they'd moved on somewhere for cocktails. He'd had what looked like a dry martini with an olive in it, and she'd had something clear and pale pink, with a flower floating in it. After that they'd gone for burgers, and she'd persuaded her date to pose with her for a selfie, both of them clutching cheese-dripping, glossy-bunned towers that looked like they should by rights have been impossible to lift with one hand. The wall behind them was bright red and displaying vintage vinyl LPs. They were both grinning delightedly.

It was Ross, of course. Ross and Bryony, on the date they must have arranged in a few minutes when he'd been away from his desk, leaving his sandwich behind – their #datenight having #allthefun in #magicalLondon.

Bryony's face, alight with excitement and promise – *This date! This man! This moment!* – reminded me all too starkly of how I'd felt after that first kiss with Kieren.

The morning after it happened, I was late for work. I texted my line manager and told her my bus was stuck in traffic, but the truth was I'd overslept – and overslept because I hadn't been able to get to sleep the previous night. Instead, I'd lain there, the duvet pulled up to my chin, remembering and remembering that kiss.

And not only the kiss – the things that had gone before it. The things he'd said to me – talented, beautiful, sexy. The memory made me tingle all over. Part of me felt that if nothing like that ever happened to me again, it wouldn't matter. I'd have this to cherish and remember always.

But a much bigger part was avid to hear him say those things again, to kiss me again, to have him there next to me in my bed, to wake up with him in the morning.

When I arrived at my desk, I forgot all the guilt and stress of being late, because there, just visible underneath my keyboard, was a page torn from a spiral-bound reporter's notebook. At the bottom of the page was a letter K, bold and slanting, written in the familiar blue ink of Kieren's fountain pen, the same colour as his eyes.

I made myself wait to read it until after I'd switched on my computer, made coffee and checked my email. I didn't mind waiting – the anticipation was glorious, electric.

And it was worth waiting for.

The first thing I saw was my name – the L was tall and slanting too, same as his own initial at the bottom of the page. The letters our names started with were next to each other in the alphabet, I realised, as if it was some kind of sign.

Lucy, I've been thinking about you all night. Who taught you to kiss like that? Whoever he is, I want to shake his hand – or maybe kill him. Come over and see me when you can – I want to look at you.

K

That was all, but it might as well have been a love poem going on for verse after verse for all the delight it brought me.

I got up and walked slowly across the office. Kieren was

already at his desk – he'd have been there for hours; he was always one of the first in. I could see the back of his head, the dark hair, the faded collar of his green corduroy shirt, the leather jacket slung over the back of his chair.

As if sensing my approach, he stopped typing and turned around.

'Good morning.' He smiled.

'Good morning.' I felt an answering smile spread over my face.

'Sleep well?'

'Not really.' It was like we were speaking in code, our words concealing a wonderful shared secret.

'Me neither.'

His eyes travelled up and down my body, his smile intensifying as he looked at me. I felt something deep inside me soften, as if I was melting or evaporating.

'Need a hand with anything?' I asked.

It was a question I'd posed to him often, but today it felt loaded with innuendo, and I saw him register that, his eyes sparkling with humour.

'Not right now. Maybe later?'

'You know where to find me,' I said.

Then I turned and walked back to my desk, slowly, allowing my hips to move in a way they never normally did, knowing that he'd be watching me all the way.

I struggled to get any work done that day. Every time I tried to focus my eyes on my screen, I saw his face. When I got up to go to the bathroom, the kitchen or the printer, I felt him watching me. Whenever I heard someone approach my desk, I prayed that it would be him – even though I knew it wasn't, because the sound of his footsteps was already as familiar to me as the opening bars of a favourite piece of music.

He didn't speak to me again until the evening, when it was just about time to go home. I didn't want to go home, though – I wanted to stay and stay, until it was just us left, until it was time for what had happened the previous night to happen again.

And it did.

Just before six, I heard him behind me. Perversely, I didn't turn around but kept tapping busily away at my keyboard, savouring the anticipation of him talking to me.

'Lucy?' he said at last.

I typed a couple more words, then stopped and swung my chair around.

'Hey, Kieren.'

'Do you have half an hour?'

'Of course.'

'I don't want to keep you.'

I smiled. 'I don't mind being kept.'

Again, I felt that electric sizzle between us – the innocuous words meaning something completely different. I stood, and instead of following him back across the bullpen to his desk, I walked ahead, letting him look at me.

He pulled a chair over for me and we sat down, our heads close over a pile of proofs. I can't even remember what was on them – they might as well have been blank pages. Because after a couple of minutes, I felt his hand on my thigh, under the desk where no one could see. It rested there for a moment, then moved slightly upwards, pushing my skirt higher.

I stifled a gasp and saw him smile, then I bent my head determinedly down again, watching the ink from his pen marking the paper. Around me, I could hear computers shutting down, people beginning to leave, the swish of coats, voices calling out goodbyes.

At last, there was silence – apart from my breathing, faster than usual, almost ragged.

'Looks like we're the last ones standing,' Kieren said.

'We aren't standing,' I pointed out.

He laughed. 'Figure of speech. But we can stand if you like.'

'Or lie down,' I suggested boldly.

'Lucy.' He shook his head. 'Don't say that. One, you're torturing me. Two, I wouldn't disrespect you like that. Not here. And three—'

I never found out what three would have been, because I kissed him, turning my chair so my knees were outside of his, putting my hands on his shoulders and pulling him in close.

The kiss went on and on, and I didn't want it to ever stop. His stubble was harsh against my face, but his lips were so soft they felt almost liquid. His shoulders under my hands were lean, almost bony. The skin of his neck was smooth as velvet.

My entire body felt suffused with desire, like every cell had been charged with electricity. I didn't want the kiss to end, but at the same time I wanted more – I wanted to feel every part of our bodies touching, not just our lips. I wanted to taste more than just his tongue. I wanted to see his hands on my bare skin, not just feel them through my tights.

But you can't carry on kissing forever, however much you want to. It either leads on to more, or it ends.

This ended.

'Come on, princess,' Kieren said at last. 'We should get you home.'

'Why?' I asked, teasing him. 'I don't want to go home.'

He laughed. 'You minx. Do you think I want you to? But I can't bear this much longer, and like I said – I'm not doing anything here. You're worth more than that.'

His words were so sweet they overpowered the bitter disappointment of stopping. He helped me into my coat, walked with me to the lift and kissed me again on the way down, and again we parted in the street.

Again, I made my way home on a cloud of bliss, like it wasn't the Tube transporting me but some kind of magic carpet.

Now, I realised that must have been how Bryony had felt, heading home after her date with Ross. *If* she had gone home, that was – it was equally possible that she'd gone back to his, and her magic-carpet Tube journey had only happened the following morning.

This, I told myself, swiping away from the images and dropping my phone on the sofa, *this is why I never go on social media*. I stood up so quickly Astro leaped off my feet and squawked in protest as I took my leftover chicken to the kitchen.

I wasn't in the mood for a tear-jerking romcom that evening. Tears felt too close to the surface to need any help, and letting them fall would have brought me no comfort. Instead, I raided my bookshelf for my battered Terry Pratchett collection and read *Witches Abroad*, my all-time favourite, right the way through. I knew the story so well I could practically have recited it from memory, but it still transported me to a different world: a world where Ross and Bryony weren't an item, or perhaps one where, if someone was writing my story, it would end with, 'And they lived happily ever after.'

FOURTEEN

Dear Adam,

I'm writing to ask you about an issue I'm having with my wife. I got into cycling recently and now I'm hoping to do my first Ironman triathlon next year. I train every Saturday for up to six hours, and every Sunday for about four, and a couple of evenings during the week. Unfortunately, my wife hates it. And I see her point – we've got young kids, and she thinks I'm missing out on family time and leaving her to deal with all the weekend stuff on her own. But my training matters to me – I know I'm the cliche of a middle-aged man in Lycra, but without the Lycra I'd be just another middle-aged man. Why can't my wife understand how important it is? Or am I the arsehole here?

Mark, Sheffield

The following Friday felt like a bit of a red-letter day – or, more accurately, a lack-of-red-face day. I didn't blush once when I spoke to Ross at work. In fact, I managed to smile brightly every time we made eye contact. I made a point of offering him a coffee every time I went to make a cup. In a meeting, when he said he was having problems sourcing the new U-Turn turntable to review for his column, I said, 'I have a contact at the manufacturer from when I was at *Fab!*. I'm sure I can get hold of one for you,' and it landed on his desk that afternoon.

When it arrived, he sort of sidled up to me in the corridor outside the breakout room and said, 'Thanks, Lucy.'

'What for?' I asked, my eyes wide with faux innocence.

'For helping me out there.' He ducked his head. 'I'd have been stuck without a column this week if you hadn't stepped in.'

I smiled sweetly. 'You'd have got there in the end. You're a smart guy.'

Then I turned and strolled back to my desk as if our interaction had meant nothing to me.

And it did mean nothing. Ross had a girlfriend. Ross was now one hundred per cent off-limits – not that he had ever been on-limits, or would have been the slightest bit interested in me anyway.

But all the same, I felt a warm glow of pride and happiness.

Five fifteen came and Marco stretched his interlaced hands high over his head and cracked his knuckles. I did my best not to wince; they were his joints, after all.

'Pub?' he suggested, standing up.

'For sure,' said Barney. 'Not the Sun, though – the beer was warm there last week.'

'And they overcharged me for a round,' added Neil. 'How about the Mason's Arms?'

'No good.' Marco shook his head regretfully. 'Company my ex works for always go there on Fridays, and I can't risk bumping into her.'

'Why?' Chiraag asked. 'What did you do to her?'

'More like what did she do to me,' Marco said. 'Seriously, if I see her I won't be answerable for the consequences.'

I swallowed, opened my mouth and said, 'The Barley Mow's meant to be decent.'

My words seemed to hang in the air, silent now except for the distant hum of the servers. I waited for shock, incredulity, contempt even.

But Neil said, 'Oh yeah, it's under new management, isn't it? Good shout.'

'You joining us, Lucy?' asked Marco, as if it was a mere formality and I always came along to the pub on Friday nights.

'Sure,' I said. Out of the corner of my eye, I saw Ross's startled face.

Then, as if it was what I always did, I picked up my bag and headed to the bathroom. I had no make-up in my bag, so I made do with brushing my hair, putting on some lip balm and clearing the fingerprints off my glasses.

A few minutes later, we all stepped out of the lobby into the sunshine. Simon and Barney strode ahead, like men on a mission. Chiraag, Marco and Neil followed more slowly, and Ross fell into step next to me at the back, as if that was what he always did.

'So how's Adam?' he asked. 'Solve any notable bloke problems this week?'

'Yeah,' I said. 'There was a guy whose girlfriend dumped him because she said he was rubbish in bed.'

'Ooooof. What did you tell him?'

'That he probably was, and he should quit watching porn and download a diagram of female anatomy before he tries dating again.'

Glancing sideways, I saw Ross's eyes widen. 'Seriously? That's a bit harsh.'

'Okay, I didn't. I told him people often say hurtful things at the end of a relationship because they're hurting themselves, and only he can know how much truth there is in what she said. But I told him he should take this as a teachable moment and think about whether he was selfish or overly demanding, and try not to make the same mistakes again.'

'Okaaaay,' he said. 'You know what? It sounds like you're getting good at this.'

'I try my best,' I acknowledged modestly.

By then we'd reached the pub, and everyone filed in.

'G and T, Simon?' Marco asked. 'Pint of Guinness, Ross? Orange juice and lemonade, Chiraag?'

They all nodded, seeing no reason to deviate from their usual Friday routine.

'Let's grab a table,' Barney said. 'They'll be ages at the bar, look at that queue.'

'What can we get you, Lucy?' Ross asked. It might have been the dim light in the bar, but I could have sworn he was blushing again.

'White wine, please.'

'Sauvignon or chardonnay?'

'Uh... chardonnay. Thanks, Ross.'

Should I, as the newcomer, have offered first? For a second I felt myself shrivelling up inside. But no one seemed to think anything was wrong. So after a bit I relaxed, took a sip of my wine and even ate some of the cheese-and-onion crisps Marco had bought.

'So, anyone got any good plans for the weekend?' Neil asked.

I opened my mouth, wondering if I was going to have to invent another date somewhere fancy, but was rescued by Chiraag getting in first, with a long explanation of the triathlon training session he was doing. He went into a whole load of detail about intervals and VO2 max and slow-release carbohydrates, and under normal circumstances I'd have tuned him out.

Now, though, I remembered the letter I'd received earlier in the week, from Mark in Sheffield. My initial instinct had been to tell him to stop being so selfish, see things from his wife's point of view and put his Ironman ambitions aside until his children were older.

I shifted up closer to Chiraag and leaned in to hear what he was saying over the background hubbub of voices and clinking glasses, even though it meant turning my back on Ross and Marco, who were standing at the bar.

'My trainer's got me doing an hour solid on the erg at home, facing a blank wall,' he was saying. 'No telly, no tunes, nothing. She reckons it'll build mental strength.'

'God, that sounds awful,' I commented.

Chiraag looked at me like I was the last person he'd have expected to express an opinion. 'You know, it is and it isn't. It's pretty brutal at the time, I'm not gonna lie. But afterwards I feel amazing – until it's time for my ice bath, that is – and even during it...'

'During it, what?'

'This is going to sound all kinds of wanky, but bear with me. There are moments when it's almost... I dunno. Meditative? Like it's just me and my body and there's no space to even think.'

'Wow.'

He grinned, ducking his head and taking another sip of his OJ and lemonade. 'Told you it was wanky.'

'It's not. It's really interesting. How did you get into it?'

He did the thing with his head again, and I waited for him to speak. It was almost like he was trying to decide whether to give me the TL;DR version or the real deal.

I got the real deal.

'At school, I was the fat kid,' he said. 'You know I don't have any brothers and sisters, right? And my mum – cooking's her love language. By the time I started uni, I'd turned into a right chonk.'

'So what changed?'

'I wish I knew.' He spread his hands, palms upwards, almost

spilling his drink on me. 'Sorry. It was like I'd developed this persona – chubby Chiraag, always the clown of the group. When I went out with my mates, I'd play wingman because I didn't think girls would be interested in me. And then one morning – literally, just like that – I decided it didn't have to be that way. My dad's type two diabetic and I was heading that way myself. My grandpa's had problems with his heart for years. I decided I was going to change.'

'And you did – just like that?'

He laughed. 'I wish it was that easy. It took me two years to lose twenty-five kilos and get fit enough to run a half-marathon. And then I celebrated with an extra-large Papa Johns pizza and backslid a bit.'

'Papa Johns, though – can't say I blame you.'

'I know, right? But I got back on track. And I realised fitness was something that makes me happy. It makes me feel good about myself. I'm proud of my body for the first time ever. Not just how it looks—'

'You do look great, to be fair.'

His eyebrows shot up in surprise. 'Thanks, Lucy. That – and compliments like that – it's a bonus, you know? But it's really about how I feel. It's changed me for the better.'

'I can tell. You must be really proud.'

He smiled self-deprecatingly, and for a second I saw the old Chiraag, the awkward fat boy who watched his mates get all the girls. 'You're a good listener, Lucy. You should be a journalist or something.'

'I try my best.'

He finished his drink, looked at his watch and said, 'I guess I should make a move. Five o'clock start in the morning.'

'It was great chatting to you. Sleep well.'

To my amazement, he leaned in and dropped a kiss on both my cheeks, then turned and said his goodbyes to everyone else.

I headed to the bar to get a round in, picking the spot closest to where Ross and Marco were standing, Ross's back to me.

'So you're out with your hot hen again this weekend?' Marco was saying.

I edged closer, straining to hear their conversation.

I couldn't see Ross's face, but I imagined him smiling. 'Round to hers for cocktails tomorrow. Her sister's going to be there and some of their mates and their other halves.'

Nice, I thought bitterly. *Cosy. Next he'll be meeting her parents.*

'Nice,' Marco echoed. 'So it's going well then?'

'Yeah, kinda,' Ross said.

I was listening so intently I could hear the scrape of his trainers on the floor as he shuffled his feet. Then the barman leaned over and asked what he could get me, and for a second my mind went blank before I gabbled out the order.

'Not sure, really,' Ross was saying.

Damn, how much did I miss?

'I mean, I like her. She's a nice girl. But I feel like she's more into me than I'm into her, and I don't know whether I should say anything about that.'

'Say what?' Marco laughed. '"Babe, you're all right for a shag but this isn't going anywhere?" Go on, try it, and let me know how hard she kicks you in the nuts.'

I heard the shuffle of Ross's feet again and imagined him grinning ruefully. The barman passed our drinks across the bar, and I tapped my phone on the card reader he held out to me.

'Feel kind of bad,' Ross was saying. 'Like, I asked her out. We haven't had the exclusive talk exactly but she's not seeing anyone else and I'm not either. But it—'

A blast of laughter from a few places along the bar drowned out whatever he said next, and then Marco said, 'Pint?'

Ross said, 'Yeah, go on then. Thanks, mate.'

So I moved away from the bar, carefully clasping the three

glasses in my two hands, and delivered the drinks to Simon and Neil, who were discussing the garden shed Neil was planning on building that weekend.

By the time I finished my drink, I'd decided it was time to leave, so I put my glass down on the bar and returned to the table where we'd left our bags. Ross was there, slinging his black canvas messenger bag over his shoulder. I could see the worn place on his T-shirt where the fabric had rubbed away after years of the same treatment.

'You calling it a night?' he asked.

'Yeah, I think so. Two large wines is one thing, but three equals a sore head tomorrow.'

'Wise words. Want to walk with me?'

I wasn't sure that was a smart idea, but since we were going in exactly the same direction, there was no getting out of it.

'Sure,' I said.

We left the pub, stepping out into the balmy evening, and headed north, threading our way through the throng of Friday-afternoon drinkers and commuters. It was a while before the press of people thinned enough for us to fall into step side by side.

'Looked like that was quite the heart-to-heart you and Chiraag were having back there,' Ross said.

'Not really.' I had no way of knowing how much of Chiraag's life story Ross was party to, and I wasn't going to betray his confidence. 'He was just taking about cycling.'

Ross rolled his eyes, grinning affectionately. 'As he does, as often and for as long as anyone'll let him. Just as well he's such a good-looking guy, otherwise you'd have been headed for the hills, with or without a bike.'

I half-turned to him, startled. Was it possible he could be a bit... jealous?

'He was talking about his family as well,' I said, surprised at the urge I felt to defend him. 'He's an only child, you know.'

'Yeah. Me too.'

'I can't imagine what that must be like. My sister and I have always been so close.' *Were we, though? Are we still?* 'Do your mum and dad live in London?'

He shook his head. 'Mum does. Dad's... not on the scene.'

Which could mean anything – or nothing. Emboldened by the wine and Chiraag's praise of my new-found listening-to-men skills, I pressed on.

'And you said... I think you mentioned you spent time in America when you were growing up?'

'I was born in New York City,' he said, adding with a hint of self-mockery, 'The Big Apple.'

'That's so cool! I've never been, but I'd love to. Do you go back often?'

'Used to. Now, not so much. Once a year.'

Once a year sounded pretty often to me. 'Planning to go this year?'

'I guess. Around the fall.'

Talking about his birth city had brought the hint of a transatlantic accent into his voice, which I'd never noticed before. The fall – how could he make one word sound so exotic, almost romantic?

Then I remembered that I was forbidden to think of anything Ross said or did as romantic. Ross, who had a date for cocktails with my sister's closest friends just the next day. But what was it Ross had said about Bryony? *She's more into me than I'm into her.* What did that mean? It wasn't like he was saying he wasn't into her, just that she was more into him. And surely these things could never be exactly equal? I remembered Amelie telling me once that she'd read a French saying somewhere about there always being someone in a relationship who did the kissing, and someone who presented their cheek to receive the kiss.

Her implication had clearly been that she expected to be

the kissee rather than the kisser, always, but then that was Amelie for you.

'Lucy?' Ross's voice startled me – we'd been walking in silence for a few minutes, and now we'd reached the main road where Astro's favourite fish and chip shop was, next to the supermarket.

'Oh God, sorry. I was thinking.'

He frowned, almost disapprovingly, and I felt a flash of panic as if I'd been thinking out loud and he knew I'd overheard his conversation with Marco.

'I'm going to duck into Tesco and get something for dinner,' he said. 'So I'll say goodbye.'

'Right, okay.' But I wasn't ready for our conversation to end just yet. 'What're you going to have?'

'Probably pizza.' He still wasn't smiling.

'Good shout. What flavour?'

'Ham and pineapple, most likely.' Now there was the faintest shadow of his usual grin, like he'd forgiven me for whatever I'd said wrong, and we were almost friends again.

'You're kidding. That's my favourite too.'

'I never said it was my favourite. It's just usually the only sort they've got left on a Friday night.'

I laughed. 'I walked right into that.'

'And now I know your dirty secret.' He hesitated, as if he wanted to say something else. *Want to come and help me eat it?* – *maybe in my wildest dreams.* 'Bye then, Lucy. Have a fun weekend.'

'You too. And... good chat.'

'Good chat.'

For a brief second, I hoped he might do the fist-bump thing again, or even kiss my cheeks like Chiraag had.

But he didn't. He just stepped towards the glass doors of the supermarket and they glided open, letting him in and a blast of refrigerated air out.

FIFTEEN

Dear Adam,

I guess this is one of the world's great philosophical questions, along with 'What is the meaning of life?' and 'Should you put cream or jam first on scones?', but bear with me because I need your help.

How do you know when a relationship is worth pursuing, and when it's time to jump ship and look elsewhere?

I'm asking because I'm seeing this girl, and on the face of it everything's great. I like her. She's funny, smart and sexy. But I'm not totally sure whether or not she's my person, if you know what I mean? The thing is, when I'm with her, I don't feel any kind of deep connection. We have a laugh, we enjoy each other's company, but that's kind of it.

What does it feel like when you meet the right woman for you, and do you necessarily know? Or do relationships get better with time and the spark ignites even if it wasn't there right from the beginning?

And if you think you've got that spark with someone, will they feel it too or is it sometimes a one-sided thing?

I don't even know why I'm writing this, Adam. But I'm gonna send it anyway. Help me not be a dick.

Anonymous, London

I looked up from the email on my screen, feeling the now-familiar weight of responsibility, coupled with a prickle of annoyance, settle on me. My anonymous correspondent claimed he didn't want to be a dick, which was very altruistic of him, but at this point it wasn't looking good. Also, something about his email felt familiar. Had he messaged Adam before? Was there already a document in my to-be-answered folder from him? If so, he had a bit of a cheek emailing again. Didn't he realise Adam was a busy man? Or were there multiple men out there going out with women who they liked but weren't sure were quite good enough to achieve The One status? And was that a sign of man's fundamental arrogance or of some systemic inequity in the dating world?

I knew what I wanted Adam to say to him: Mate, if you're not into her, you're not into her. No point in leading her on and future-faking. The kind thing – the right thing, the only thing – to do is let her down gently and follow your heart to the relationship you really want. Let her go – she's not the one for you.

But then, what if I was inadvertently ending a perfectly good relationship – one that could strengthen and grow with time the way a diamond forms over years and years – and breaking two hearts, just because I could? Just because of my own cynicism and bitterness towards men, because Kieren had treated me badly and broken my heart?

I remembered the letter I'd received a couple of weeks back, from Mark, the triathlete from Sheffield. I remembered how my first instinct had been to give him the telling-off of his life and order him to stop being so self-obsessed and start being a better husband and father. And how my conversation with Chiraag had given me a totally new perspective, and I'd ended up writing a much gentler, more considered reply, asking him to think about what he was getting from all those hours of training, what it meant to him, whether he could have a conversation with his wife about that and help her understand, so they could reach some kind of compromise.

I'd been really proud of that answer. It had felt balanced, wise and kind.

Now I needed to tap into that version of Adam – of myself – to respond to whoever Mr Anonymous was.

I performed my usual ritual of copying and pasting the text of the email, clearing all its formatting and saving a new document. Then I poised my fingers over my keyboard, waiting to channel Amelie, or Adam, or whatever part of me was beginning to have faith that I could actually do this, and give this man some advice that wouldn't ruin his life.

Then my computer pinged with a Teams notification, snapping my train of thought.

It was from Greg.

> Afternoon, Lucy. Got a minute?

My stomach lurched, but I typed.

> Yeah, sure 😊

> Pop into my office, if you don't mind.

Be right there.

I stood up. Ross glanced at me, then looked hastily away. Adrenaline coursing through me, I made my way to my boss's office, a shorthand notebook and pen clutched in my sweating hand.

'Afternoon, Lucy.' Greg's chair was pushed back from his desk, his glasses perched on his head. There were smudges of red ink on his fingers from correcting proofs. He looked tired and dishevelled, as he usually did by the middle of the afternoon.

'Afternoon.' I forced a smile.

'Take a seat.'

I took one.

'So, Lucy. I see from my calendar you've been with *Max!* for almost three months now. We don't normally conduct a formal review at this point, but I thought we should have a chat about how things are going.'

I nodded mutely, my mouth dry.

'You've settled well into the team,' Greg went on. 'I'm impressed with the quality of your writing, your organisational skills and your attitude. You're a valuable addition to *Max!*.'

'Thank you,' I said. 'I'm really happy to be here.'

I could sense a 'but' coming, and I was right.

'But...' Greg said, and part of my brain went, *Told you so!* 'The Ask Adam column has got off to something of a slow start. The response from our readers has been extremely positive, but the numbers aren't quite where we'd like to see them. As you know, an ever-increasing share of our revenue is derived from online advertising, which is dependent on click rates. And we're not seeing these increase at the rate we'd hoped for.'

'Does that mean—' I began, but Greg held up a hand to stop me.

'I don't want to worry you, Lucy. I believe in you – I believe

Ask Adam can be a great success. It's early days. We're just not quite there yet.'

'What should I do?' I asked. 'I mean, I'm doing my very best but if there's something I need to change, just tell me and I'll try.'

Greg smiled. 'I know. Your enthusiasm is one of the things that make you a real asset. And that's why I think you'll be willing to get behind what I'm about to propose.'

'Okay,' I said, thinking, *I'll do anything – anything at all. Just so long as I get to keep my job.*

And not get sacked and never see Ross again, said a little voice in the back of my mind.

'Here's what we'd like to do,' Greg said. 'We want to run some numbers, analytics, so we can see what type of questions are working best in the Ask Adam slot. Then we can focus on putting those out there, and increase the reach of the column over time, backed up by posts on our socials to draw readers in.'

'Great!' I said. 'That sounds like a plan.'

Greg nodded approvingly, and then he said, 'But. In order for that exercise to be meaningful, we need more data. As I said a moment ago, Ask Adam got off to a rather slower start than we'd hoped, so we're limited in the amount of engagement we have to run our analytics on. In order to build traction, we need more volume.'

'Okay,' I said again.

'Am I right in thinking the number of queries you're getting is still high?'

'Sure, and it's increasing. In the beginning I was receiving maybe ten letters a day, now it's at least twenty. There's no way I can answer them all. Of course, some of them are obvious nutters, or asking totally random things like who's going to win the Premier League, but most of them are legit problems.'

'That's what I thought. And that's why I'd like to increase the frequency of the Ask Adam column from twice weekly to daily, if you're up for that? It'll mean a lot more work for you, of course.'

'That doesn't matter. I can manage.'

Can I? Can I really? I'd stared at Anonymous's query for over half an hour with no clue what I was going to tell him. The only reassuring thing about it was that I had the luxury of time to mull over my response – now, I'd glibly robbed myself of even that.

'I hoped you'd say that. Thanks, Lucy. And, you know, onwards and upwards, right?'

'Onwards and upwards.' It felt more like a dismissal than an encouragement. 'But, Greg...'

He'd already looked away from me, down at his screen, but now he looked back, his eyebrows raised enquiringly.

'What if it doesn't work?' I asked tremulously.

'Then we'll need a bit of a rethink.' As if to lessen the harshness of the reality, he produced an encouraging smile. 'But we'll make it work. Chin up, Lucy. We've got this.'

There was nothing more to say. What on earth had I let myself in for? Still clutching my notebook, which now bore a soggy handprint, I left Greg's office at a purposeful walk – even though what I felt like doing was running away screaming for help like the building was on fire.

SIXTEEN

At home that night, Astro and I had a working dinner. At least, he tried to eat the scrambled eggs off my plate and I tried to work.

My meeting with Greg had jolted me. I knew he hadn't meant it to – I knew he'd meant to soften the blow of Ask Adam's disappointing hit rate, come up with a solution and reassure me that if I produced just a little more content, it would all come good.

But I couldn't share his optimism – if it had even been genuine, which I doubted. The new-found confidence I'd been feeling at my ability to be Adam, to answer men's problems in a sensitive yet forthright fashion, had been dashed. The numbers weren't stacking up. I wasn't doing a good enough job.

I wasn't good enough.

My heart sank as I flicked through Adam's inbox. As I'd said to Greg, there was no shortage of material there to work with. Young men, older men, single men, married men. Sad men, angry men, lonely men. Men who seemed to hate women and men who seemed to think women hated them.

There were so many of them. They all needed my help, and

right now it felt like I couldn't even help myself. Back when I'd embarked on this crazy scheme, I'd had Amelie as back-up, but now I couldn't even turn to her.

'Come on, Lucy,' I said aloud, repeating Greg's words to myself, 'you've got this.'

I opened the document where I'd saved the anonymous letter Adam had received earlier. At the time, it had seemed straightforward to answer. But now, my self-belief at rock-bottom, I had no idea how to respond to whoever he was.

End things with the girlfriend; don't end things. Hold out for someone you feel really passionate about; settle for someone you think is good enough. What was the right answer? Two people's happiness could depend on what I decided to write – and never mind that, there were scores of other men whose problems hung in the same balance.

'I don't know if I can do this, Astro,' I said.

Astro blinked slowly at me, his eyes like amber traffic lights.

And then I remembered Nush's hissed aside during Zack's wedding speech, telling me that he'd got GenBot 2.0 to write it for him, and how that had made me feel – not shocked, exactly, but kind of let down and disappointed that he couldn't have been bothered to do it himself, that he'd used a generative chat algorithm to do it for him. It was his wedding reception, after all. He literally had one job.

I literally had one job, too. Right now, though, I didn't feel like I could do it.

You can't get artificial intelligence to write Adam's column! Part of my brain recoiled from the idea in disgust. *It's cheating.*

It's not cheating. It's just getting help, same as Amelie helped me in the beginning.

It's probably copyright infringement. You'll get sacked.

I'll get sacked anyway if I don't come up with a way to answer these damn problems.

You'll get sacked in disgrace.

I won't use it to write the actual answers. I'll just ask it to give me a steer. It's no different from getting a steer from Chiraag before I answered Mark's letter.

It's lots different.

But I opened GenBot 2.0 anyway. I knew what it was, of course – I even understood the technology behind it because I'd researched it back in the happier days when I'd been technology editor of *Fab!*. I'd written an article about five ways it could help *Fab!*'s readers in their daily lives – from composing tricky letters to their line managers to highlighting the top summer fashion trends.

I knew it was a generative, language-based chatbot that had been trained on a vast input of text which it drew upon to produce language of its own. I had a vague idea that it could be trained still further by its users asking it follow-on questions that would refine the output it gave not only to them but to other users asking it similar questions. I'd delved into the theory behind how it worked – I could recall a load of stuff about machine learning, reward models and something called Proximal Policy Optimization, which I'd attempted to get my head around at the time but certainly couldn't understand now.

Although I'd tinkered about with it a bit, just to make sure it could do what I was saying it could, I'd never actually used the technology in my own work. I hadn't needed to – until today.

I wasn't going to feed any of Adam's readers' queries to the bot, I decided. There were probably terrible confidentiality implications of doing so, I thought, imagining Adam's readers discovering that their anguished words had been used to train a bot, suing *Max!* for some sort of data protection violation, and me losing my job and ending up exactly where I'd been back in April, facing homelessness and penury.

I wouldn't use their actual words, I decided. I'd do a kind of summary. Just to see how it worked.

At the bottom of my screen was a small, horizontal window. In it, I began typing.

I'm not sure if I'm really into my girlfriend.

Adam's anonymous correspondent hadn't actually referred to the woman he was seeing as his girlfriend, but I figured that it was acceptable shorthand for someone you'd been on a few dates with and were, to be old-fashioned about it, sleeping with. *I mean, come on.* She was a girl, and you didn't actually sleep with mere acquaintances, did you? Well, I supposed some people did, if I thought about it.

I like her, but I think she likes me more, and I don't know if it's fair to carry on seeing her. What should I do?

At the top of the screen, a black cursor blinked a few times. Clearly, the AI was giving my question some hard thought. Then, rapidly, words began to appear below it.

Choosing whether to continue a relationship is always a difficult decision. Your happiness as well as that of the other person are at stake here, and decisions shouldn't be made rashly. Here are some points for you to consider before you reach a conclusion.

So far, so diplomatic. I was impressed – especially when I read on. The bot had come up with no fewer than eight separate steps its correspondent might take in the course of his reflection, from considering what he really wanted in a relationship – 'a deeper connection, or something else', which I took to be PG-speak for no-strings sex – to turning to friends and family for deeper insight into his situation, to, obviously, having a conversation with the girl herself to try and discover whether their needs and priorities were aligned.

Remember, each relationship is unique. Take time to think through your options and you will come to a decision that feels right for you and your girlfriend.

'Damn,' I muttered. I was impressed. In less than three seconds, the technology had come up with an answer that – while a bit vanilla, if I was being hypercritical – was right up there with the best I could have written after agonising over my keyboard for the best part of an hour.

This thing had the potential to put us all out of jobs.

I read through the bot's response again. It was good stuff, though it could do with a polish, a bit of shortening and some of Adam's signature wit adding to it – it had, not surprisingly, neglected to warn its user not to be a dick – which would be easily remedied with a few taps on my keyboard.

I copied and pasted the text into a fresh document, did the same with the original question and read it all through again.

Tomorrow, I'd give it a final edit and send it on its way to the subs desk, just in case there were any finer points of style that had been missed between me and the bot. But the question was as good as answered.

This thing had potential. I could work with it. My life – or rather, Adam's life – was about to become a whole lot easier.

SEVENTEEN

Dear Adam,

I've read a load of stuff online recently – okay, mostly seen it on social media, if I'm honest – about vaginal gummies. Ever come across them? Apparently Gwyneth Paltrow is a fan. But when I suggested to my girlfriend that we might give them a go – because, let's face it, girls don't always taste that great down there – she went absolutely mental at me. She says if I don't like the way she tastes, I can damn well forget about going down on her ever again.

What's your verdict on this? Surely Ms Paltrow and a million TikTok influencers can't be wrong? How can I persuade my girl-friend that this would be a great way to spice – or rather sweeten – up our sex life?

Billy, Cumbria

Dear Billy,

Well, where to begin? Your credulous assumption that paid influencers know more about your sex life than your own partner does? The misogyny that absolutely oozes from your letter? Your basic ignorance of the fact that there's no need for women to go shoving anything up their vaginas unless they actively choose to? The simple truth that fannies should smell and taste of fanny, and if they don't, there's probably a medical reason why and your girlfriend might want to get checked out by her GP?

I suggest that you a. pause a moment and make a note in your gratitude journal for the fact that she allows you anywhere near her bits, and b. maybe try shoving a jelly tot down your penis and see how you like it.

No. On balance, Billy, I have just one simple, succinct piece of advice for you: don't be a dick – of any flavour.

Yours truly,

Adam

I stopped typing, my fingers aching from the speed at which I'd bashed out the reply and my heart actually racing, like it did on the frequent occasions when I walked up the stairs to the office rather than risk sharing the lift with Ross. *How dare he?* I fumed silently. *How dare this Billy try and shame his poor girlfriend into experimenting with something she doesn't want to do? How dare he have the utter cheek to suggest that some sugar-laden thrush-bomb is the only way to make her perfectly normal vagina acceptable to his hypersensitive man mouth?*

'Jeez,' I muttered, shaking my head.

'You all right there, Lucy?' Marco asked. 'You've gone all red in the face. And Ross isn't even he—'

Then he looked at me a bit more closely and shut up. There must have been something in my eyes that warned him now was not the time to share his observations on either the state of my complexion or the way I sometimes – rarely, hardly ever, these days, since I'd got Amelie's mate Miranda to give me a crash course in concealer application – reacted to our mutual colleague.

'You know what, Marco?' I said. 'I've been doing this job for three months now and men still amaze me.'

'We're pretty cool, aren't we?' Marco said, breathing on his nails and buffing them on the collar of his shirt.

'Cool?' I squeaked. 'You've got the brass neck to think that after reading hundreds of letters about erectile dysfunction and cheating and refusing to talk about their feelings, the conclusion I've reached is that men are cool?'

Marco grinned. To his credit, he looked a bit abashed. 'Well, you'd be a bit stuck without us, wouldn't you? I mean, the survival of the human race depends—'

'What's going on here?' Ross, returning late after his lunchtime CrossFit session, swung into his chair. 'Are you okay, Lucy?'

I closed my eyes for a second and breathed deeply. *In for five, hold for five, out for five, lungs empty for five.* Then opened them again and said, 'It's just as well I want to keep this job. Otherwise I might be tempted to tell some of the men who write in to Adam what I really, actually think of them.'

Marco and Ross exchanged looks that I hoped meant, *Don't mess with her when she's in this kind of mood.* I gave them a look back that I knew said, *Yeah, don't even go there.*

And then I did the breathing thing again and turned back to my screen.

The thing was, over the past months of being Adam, I'd noticed a bit of a shift in my attitude towards his correspondents. At first, I'd viewed them a bit like I imagine scientists must have viewed the Covid virus once they'd got its genome sequenced, or whatever they did. *So this is what the enemy looks like, up close and personal. Now let's figure out how to beat it.*

But, so gradually I'd barely even been conscious of it happening, my attitude had changed. It had started with the letter from the widower worried about his relationship with his teenage daughter. It had continued with the insights Chiraag had given me into Mark from Sheffield's possible reasons for spending so much time on his sport, at the expense of his family life. Even the first problem I'd given GenBot 2.0 to answer, from the man who was uncertain whether the woman he was seeing was right for him, had given me pause for thought.

They weren't specimens from the man blob, I found myself realising. They were people. People with problems, and complex inner lives, and feelings of insecurity and self-doubt just like my own.

And then someone like Billy came along and proved that, actually, some of them were just dicks, plain and simple.

Of course, I didn't publish the trenchant reply I'd composed to Billy. I read his letter again and considered toning my response down a bit, but the second reading made me every bit as cross as the first had, so I couldn't bring myself to come up with any soothing, understanding words for him.

Instead, I posted a precis of his letter into the screen of the AI program and let the bot compose a reply. Within about five seconds, it had come up with five paragraphs about the importance of not disrupting the vaginal microbiome, the wisdom of consulting a healthcare professional if either Billy or his partner suspected she might be suffering from some kind of infection, and the non-negotiable nature of holding a calm discussion, ideally outside the bedroom, when either partner wished to introduce any new sexual shenanigans.

Not that it used the word shenanigans, obviously; it hadn't been trained to. I added that in myself afterwards, together with a gentle prod to Billy away from the course of dickishness. GenBot, I reflected, wasn't too bad at relationship advice – but it had a lot to learn. If it was going to be any kind of valuable assistant to Adam, it would need to become a bit less moderate in its responses.

Still mildly seething, I saved the document to the *Max!* server for the subs to look at, took a sip from my water bottle and checked my phone.

In spite of all the excitement at work, Amelie hadn't been far from my thoughts. According to my diary and her Instagram, her honeymoon was well and truly over and she and Zack had flown – first class, natch – to New York, where they were installed in a fancy apartment in Chelsea, provided by Zack's work.

It was all there on my sister's stories: the champagne on the flight, the yellow taxi, the view over Manhattan, the squashy cream sofa, cousin no doubt to the one in Zack's London flat. As usual, exclamation marks and emojis were studded throughout her posts.

But still, I felt that something was... not necessarily wrong, but not completely right either. I'd messaged her several times suggesting a chat, and I'd been left on read. She hadn't responded as she usually did to the numerous comments on her social media posts. And in all the videos of the skyline and the front-row seats at *Hamilton* and the speakeasy cocktail bar and the rest of it, Amelie's own face was conspicuously absent.

So when I saw that I had two new messages on WhatsApp, my heart gave a little skip of hope – then lurched again when I saw that they were both from Nush.

Hey Lucy! How are you?! Hope work is good!

Nush was one of those people who couldn't resist an exclamation mark.

> Have you heard from Amelie?! We haven't!
> We're starting to get worried!

Her words brought my own concern back to the forefront of my mind. Although I'd never stopped thinking of my sister, my preoccupation with what had been going on in my own life – my feelings for Ross, unrequited and mostly unspoken, even to myself; Greg's bombshell about Adam's future; the unceasing flow of men's problems landing in my inbox – had all but drowned out thoughts of my sister.

I replied:

> You know what, I haven't. I'm going to
> FaceTime her! Tonight!

Nush's exclamation mark habit was contagious, I realised.

So, that evening, I made sure to leave the office on time. And, at home, instead of firing up my laptop to see what Adam's readers had in store for me or switching on my PS4 for a bit of soothing monster-murdering, I made sure my phone was fully charged and settled Astro on my lap.

On my first attempt, Amelie didn't pick up. So I tried again five minutes later, and then again straight after that.

And the third time, she answered – only without her video switched on.

'Lucy?' Her voice was as clear as if she was right there in the room with me instead of thousands of miles and multiple time zones away, but she didn't sound like herself. 'What's up? Are you okay?'

Now was one hundred per cent not the time to burden my sister with my problems – and not Adam's either.

'I'm fine,' I said. 'But what about you? I can't see you.'

'That's because I look like shit. I'm in bed.'

'In bed?' I glanced at my watch and rapidly counted backwards in my head. It was two o'clock in the afternoon in New York – Amelie should have been shopping or at a hot yoga class or having an omakase lunch with a new friend. 'Are you sick?'

There was a pause, then my sister's face appeared on my screen. The lighting was dim; I could see shadowy pillows behind her head and drawn blinds behind that. The soft furnishings looked like they were white or cream, and her skin was pale too, her hair a dark smudge.

'I'm not great,' she replied forlornly. 'I've got a stomach bug. Ever since we got back from honeymoon I've been puking. I think it's some sort of rare tropical disease and I'm going to die horribly, miles from home.'

I felt surprisingly encouraged by her words. Amelie had always been the most overdramatic of hypochondriacs – when she'd caught chicken pox at uni, she'd called our mum in tears and said she was going to scratch her own skin off and be scarred for life.

'Am, don't be daft. You won't die. But you should see a doctor, right?'

'I guess. I'll be all right. I need to get up in a bit anyway and sort out something for Zack's and my dinner.'

Now I worried. Amelie never cooked. Ever. Not even when she was feeling one hundred per cent great. I recalled the time, not long after she'd moved into her first flat share, when my sister had invited me and our mum and dad over for a celebration dinner to mark the occasion. She'd decked the whole place out with flowers and balloons, insisted that Mum take the place of honour on the only comfortable chair, made champagne cocktails with Angostura-soaked sugar cubes in the bottom – and then, when seven thirty came, proudly produced a platter of wraps and sandwiches from Pret left over from a work meeting.

'Come on – you're in Manhattan. You should be living on

smoked salmon bagels and ramen and cupcakes like in *Sex and the City*. Besides, you'd probably poison him.'

Amelie laughed – a faint, breathy sound, but a laugh nonetheless.

'Yeah, right. But Zack's working long hours and I'm not working at all, so it kind of feels like the least I can do.'

'Who are you and what have you done with my sister?' I demanded. 'Are you living in Stepford or New York City?'

She giggled again. 'You do make me feel better, Luce.'

'Then why haven't you been answering calls?' I asked. 'I've messaged, Nush has rung. Last time I spoke to Mum she said she was about to call the police, until I talked her down.'

'I texted Mum,' Amelie said. 'I told her I'm fine. I am fine. I've just not been well, and I'm missing home.'

'You could come home,' I suggested. 'Fly back for a weekend. We could all go out for cocktails. You could see Astro.'

I angled my phone so she could see him now, even though he was fast asleep.

'Awww, look at him,' she cooed, with a smile that looked more like herself. 'But I can't. Not now, anyway. I can't leave Zack.'

I felt a flare of annoyance. Where was Zack? At work, obviously. But hadn't he realised that Amelie was ill, lonely and homesick? And if he had, why wasn't he doing something about it?

'Zack's a big boy,' I said. 'He can look after himself. You need to look after yourself, okay?'

'I am. Honestly. Don't worry about me. I should get up now – I've been in bed for hours and I absolutely stink. I need to get these sheets off and wash them, and wash my hair.'

'Am? Are you sure you're okay?'

'Yes. At least, I will be. Stop worrying, Luce. That's an order.'

'But I... Okay. Love you.'

'Love you more.'

Reluctantly, I ended the call. But despite Amelie's command, I didn't stop worrying. I remembered the cloud of her hair against her pillow and wondered if she was still using the same violet-scented shampoo. I wished she wasn't miles and miles too far away to hug. I missed her so much it hurt.

EIGHTEEN

I got up off the sofa, immediately followed by Astro, loudly complaining that it was way past his dinner time. Not really focusing on what I was doing, I tipped food into one bowl, replaced the water in another and sorted out his litter box, then made myself a slice of cheese on toast and returned to my phone.

There was no point messaging Amelie again tonight. What with Nush, Bryony and Eve and no doubt loads of her other friends all trying to get in touch and Mum on red alert, she must have felt positively besieged. If she wanted to confide in me properly, she'd confide. And if she didn't, more drastic action might have to be taken.

I tucked my feet up on the sofa and stared at my phone until the screen went blank. Drastic action. I wasn't sure what that would mean if Amelie needed me, but I knew exactly what it had meant when I'd needed her.

When things with Kieren ended, I didn't tell my sister. I didn't tell anyone – not that there was really anyone to tell. My colleagues at work hadn't known anything was going on – not officially, anyway. Mum and Dad certainly hadn't known – I'd fondly imagined introducing him to them some day, and Mum looking all relieved and proud and saying, 'We knew you'd find someone lovely in the end,' and Dad shaking Kieren's hand and saying, 'You've caught yourself a catch there, young man.'

But it had never happened and, in hindsight, I suppose I'd known it never would.

At the time, though, I hadn't had the luxury of hindsight. All I'd had was the sound of blood roaring in my ears, the burning of unshed tears in my eyes and, most of all, a horrible sick feeling in my stomach that wouldn't go away however many times I puked.

And I puked a lot. As soon as I got home, closing and double-locking the door behind me like an animal going to earth in its burrow, I ran to the bathroom and was sick. When eventually I felt able to drink some water, that came straight up too. And so it went on for the next day and a half, until I gave up and stopped trying to eat altogether.

I told myself I'd probably come down with norovirus, even though I knew that wasn't true. I couldn't sleep. The days were an endless cycle of staring at my hands – which wouldn't seem to stop shaking – being sick and crying. Oh my God, the crying. I never knew it was possible to cry so much.

I was determined not to call Kieren, or allow myself to hope that he'd call me, so I buried my phone in my sock drawer and left it there on silent, and eventually the battery must have run down. I didn't shower for three days. I tried going outside for a walk, but I couldn't stop crying, and when I almost got run over by a bus, I decided it would be better if I stayed indoors. I felt like there was no point in living, but I didn't want to die enough for my demise to be the responsibility of some poor bus driver.

Eventually, on the third day, Amelie turned up. I didn't know it was her; in fact, I would have guessed it was almost anyone else but her, because the hammering on my door was more like a visit from the vice squad than a social call from my sister. So I didn't answer.

But the knocking went on, harder and louder, and after a bit it was replaced by the rattle of the letterbox and Amelie saying, 'For God's sake, Luce, open the bloody door. I know you're there.'

I knew she wouldn't go away, and deep down I didn't want her to think anything serious had happened to me, so I dragged myself off the bed, tightened the cord of my old towelling dressing gown and shuffled to the door, my whole body stiff and sore because I hadn't properly moved for so long.

The smell of her perfume met me as soon as I opened the door. It reminded me that, in contrast, I must have smelled absolutely horrible – I couldn't remember the last time I'd had a shower, never mind put my manky bathrobe in the washing machine.

But Amelie didn't even flinch at the sight – or smell – of me. She folded her arms round me and pulled me close, and the feeling of her cashmere jumper and her fragrant hair tickling my face predictably set me off again, and I burst into a storm of weeping.

'Come on.' Her arm squeezed round my shoulders, Amelie guided me into the flat and over to the sofa. I heard the tap of her heels on the floor as she bustled off to the bathroom, returning with a loo roll, which she thrust at me to blow my nose with, and then the click of the kettle switch and the roar of the heating water.

By the time I'd finished crying, there was a steaming cup of tea in front of me, so strong it was practically terracotta-coloured.

'I made one with milk first,' she said. 'But your milk's off, so you'll have to have it black. There's a ton of sugar in it.'

I took a sip, feeling my mouth pucker from the tannin. The smell of it reminded me of Kieren, whose tea was always steeped like that. Even now, I drew some comfort from it, as if it was bringing me closer to him again – as close as I was ever going to get.

'Now,' Amelie said, when I'd worked my way cautiously through about half the mug, 'are you going to tell me what happened?'

I looked down at my hands again, but I could feel my sister's penetrating, patient gaze on my face, and before long, without really wanting to, I found myself looking up at her.

'I'm so stupid,' I whispered.

'No, you're not. You're the one with the brains, remember? You're a lot of things, but stupid isn't one of them. Now come on, spill.'

Reluctantly, helped by another cup of tea and most of the rest of the loo roll, I told her.

'And you've been holed up here ever since on your own?'

I nodded.

'And you haven't eaten?'

'I had some biscuits, but I puked them up.'

'Right. There's no way you're going to start feeling better if you're half-starved. Let's get some calories in you.'

Amelie bounded up off the sofa and whisked through to the kitchen. Normally, I'd have followed her, making sure she knew where the plates were kept and telling her not to open the Tupperware with the cheese in, because it had been festering in there for ages and God only knew what state it was in. But that day I simply didn't have the energy. I just sat there and listened to her clattering around, and waited.

'Eggs,' she said a few minutes later, appearing with a heaped plate. 'One thing I can cook, right? So long as I use enough butter, not even I can fuck up scrambled eggs. There's no toast though – your bread's Alexander Fleming's wet dream. It's in the bin now.'

I took the plate, fork and square of paper towel from her, and cautiously scooped up some eggs. They were rich and peppery and delicious, and my appetite came flooding back as I inhaled the lot in record time.

'I'll have to find another job,' I said. 'I won't be able to pay the rent otherwise.'

'Yeah, you will, but there won't be any rush, right? Give it a couple of weeks. You're in no fit state to go to interviews right now. Speaking of which...'

She fixed me again with that steady, luminous gaze. Her eyelashes were curled and mascaraed, and she had some sort of highlighter thing on her skin that made it glow like a pearl. The last time I'd looked in the mirror, I'd seen flaky bits all round my nose and mouth, a massive spot erupting on my chin, and bits of days-old make-up crusted in the hollows under my eyes.

'Shower,' Amelie ordered. 'Now. And use that L'Occitane stuff I gave you for your birthday. You were saving it for best, weren't you?'

'Of course I was,' I muttered.

'Well, don't. It's there to be used when you need it, and you need it right now. Up you get.'

I realised that she was channelling our mum, who'd always been a big believer in tough love.

I got to my feet, swayed a bit with light-headedness and walked carefully to the bathroom, pulling my dressing gown off and letting it fall to the floor behind me. Then I closed the door and switched the shower on to boiling hot.

When I emerged twenty minutes later, wrapped in a cleanish towel with another round my hair, I found that Amelie had stripped the sheets off my bed and replaced them with fresh ones, opened the window to fill the flat with chilly early spring air, and switched on the washing machine. I didn't feel much better, to be perfectly honest, but the fragrance coming off my skin, the crisp, clean duvet cover and the cold breeze made me realise that feeling better was an option. Eventually, when I was ready.

My sister stayed late that evening, and we drank wine and ordered a curry and she listened to me talk and I cried some more. She left around midnight, literally tucking me into bed and ordering me to make sure my phone was charged and to call her if I needed her, however late it was.

Just before she turned off the light and let herself out, she said, 'Remember, Luce, the thing about men is they're dicks. Hold that thought and nothing they ever do will surprise you. It might hurt you, but it won't surprise you.'

I woke up the next morning feeling quite a bit better and sorted out a load of the necessary practical stuff I needed to do, like getting a sick note and starting to polish up my CV. The following day, I felt even better and managed to go out for a walk without any bus-related mishaps. I went to Amelie's birthday drinks alone, and although I didn't stay late, I managed to laugh and even dance a bit.

And the following Friday, Amelie turned up at my flat again. This time, she had something with her: a nylon shoulder bag, only its sides were made of mesh instead of solid fabric. I could hear rustling sounds coming from inside it.

'Close your eyes, Luce, and sit down,' she commanded, and I did.

I heard my sister whispering and the click of a plastic catch, and a moment later I felt sharp pinpricks on my thighs and a warm softness against my hands. My eyes snapped open.

In my lap was a kitten. He was smoky-grey with amber eyes, spiky whiskers and a tiny, upright tail. He was precious and purring and perfect and I fell instantly in love.

'Oh my God,' I breathed. 'Look at his little face. Where did you...?'

'Battersea Dogs and Cats Home,' Amelie said proudly. 'They're awash with kittens at the moment but he was easily the cutest. They called him Astro, but you can change it if you like.'

'I think he looks like an Astro. He's the best thing ever. I adore him. Thank you.'

'There's food and toys and stuff for him outside,' she said. 'I had to get a taxi here and the driver was none too pleased, until I tipped the hell out of him.'

All I could say, again, was, 'Oh my God. Thank you so much.'

'Now remember,' Amelie lectured once she'd stashed Astro's food in my kitchen, put his litter tray in my bathroom and filled a cereal bowl with water for him, 'this cat needs you. And you won't be able to look after him if you don't look after yourself. No more of this going into a decline nonsense, you hear?'

'I won't,' I said. 'I promise.'

And, of course, I didn't. My broken heart recovered in due course – although I wasn't sure my self-esteem ever would – and every time I needed to cry over Kieren and torture myself with the memory of what had happened, Astro would come and perch on my lap and purr and make me feel better. Whenever I needed to rake over it all, Amelie would listen and reassure me that none of it had been my fault.

Nothing about her kindness surprised me. She was my sister, doing what sisters did. But I knew that if she ever needed me like I'd needed her then, I'd do whatever it took to fix what was wrong – because that was what sisters did.

And now, she did need me – but I had no idea what to do to help her. I couldn't bring her a kitten, not to an apartment in Manhattan where she was only going to live for six months. There must be something else I could do.

Unconsciously reaching out my hand and caressing Astro's hard, furry head, I felt my heart reaching out to Amelie, all those miles away. I tried to reach out to her with my mind, too, although of course I didn't believe in telepathy, not even between sisters.

As soon as I've worked out what you need me to do, I silently promised her, *I'll do it. I've got you.*

NINETEEN

'What'll I do if no one wants to talk to me?' I asked Astro. He was lying on my bed, half-watching in case I stepped on his tail as I wobbled precariously, craning over my shoulder to see the reflection of my back in the mirror.

It was the beginning of September and I was wearing short denim dungarees, panic-bought the previous day in a smash-and-grab Primark trip, with a purple crop top underneath them and my trusty Doc Martens boots. I had no idea whether the look was even remotely appropriate for the work summer social, but at least it was different from what I wore to the office and my hair looked decent. Also, thanks to a TikTok tutorial Miranda had sent me a link to, I'd more or less nailed the summer's signature 'super-glowy, no-make-up make-up look'.

But none of that helped much. I was going to have to spend the day socialising with my colleagues. There'd be Pimm's to spill down my front and sausages in buns that would dribble ketchup down my chin if I so much as looked at them. There'd probably be rounders or volleyball or some such horror – the exact nature of the entertainment on offer was 'a surprise', according to Neil, who was on the organising committee.

But whatever it was, there'd be men. Loads of them, everywhere, all busy out-manning one another over who wielded the barbecue tongs in the most manly way and whose team came first in the touch rugby.

And one of the men would be Ross.

The thing was, the more time I spent sitting at my desk opposite him, the more I was coming to see him as a human being, rather than just another man. I liked the way he was always first to offer to help if someone was stuck with a work problem. I liked the way he always put a fiver in birthday collections, rather than Neil's paltry handful of small change. I even liked the way he still – sometimes although not always – blushed when he looked at me. I'd come to realise it mostly happened when I smiled, so I'd been trying to ration my smiles in case I exhausted his capacity to blush.

But Ross was still going out with Bryony, and I'd made a promise to myself years ago that I was never going to allow myself to be hurt by a man again.

The pain I'd experienced over Kieren had been more than enough to put me off for life: no matter how much I thought about it, I couldn't see what men – any man – could offer me that would be worth risking that again. I could change fuses myself and evict spiders myself and take my own bins out. I didn't need romantic candle-lit dinners or someone's lap to put my feet on when I watched television in the evenings. I didn't care if I went to weddings without a plus-one.

And sex? Whatever. With Kieren, as I'd had to admit at the time, it hadn't been all that. But even if it was, no orgasm I'd ever experienced was worth the hassle and pain and risk of heartbreak of actually getting a man to provide it for me.

I'd managed perfectly well for all these years and I intended to go on managing.

So why did Ross make me feel the way I felt?

I let my knees go bendy and flopped down on the bed next

to Astro, who bounced slightly as my weight hit the mattress, and looked offended.

How did I actually feel about Ross? It was surprisingly hard to pinpoint, because it was such a complex jumble of emotions. Sometimes he was an annoying bloke's bloke, like the time he took the piss out of Barney when Queens Park Rangers beat Charlton four-nil over the weekend. Sometimes he made me feel almost protective, like I had when he'd inexplicably freaked out over the terrorist attack on the Tube that had turned out to be nothing of the kind. And when I read his sharp, knowledgeable tech column in *Max!* every week, I felt a surge of something like pride.

And – yes, damn it – there was the way I felt when I saw him walk across the office in his gym kit, all loose-limbed and sweaty, or brush his hair back from his face, or grin when I made a joke. My assessment of his looks as middling might have been correct, but they were ordinary like perfect things are ordinary – a simple white shirt, or a fried egg with the edges crispy and the yolk still runny, or a daisy on a green lawn. Like when I opened the door to my flat and Astro came to meet me and everything was ordinary, because I was home.

'God, I need to get a grip,' I told Astro, who opened one eye and gave me a hard stare like he one hundred per cent agreed. 'Going around comparing a bloke to a daisy like I'm William fricking Wordsworth or someone. And I need to get going or I'll be late for this stupid party, not that that would be the end of the world.'

Astro blinked slowly at me and I blinked back, and we carried on doing that for a minute or so until he lost interest and went to sleep. Reluctantly, I stood up, checked my reflection in the mirror one last time, gathered up my things and left the flat.

By the time I stepped off the Tube at an obscure West London station I'd never heard of, let alone visited, before, the sky had clouded over and it was beginning to rain – only a thin drizzle for now, but it looked like the kind of thin drizzle that had big ambitions to turn into a proper downpour. It wasn't looking good for the barbecue and volleyball.

But, to my surprise, the pin on my phone led me to an industrial estate. Hulking warehouses surrounded a large car park, and there wasn't an open field suitable for a sporting event anywhere in sight. I wandered around for a few minutes, trying to locate the exact location of the pin, and eventually saw a small group of men clustered around a metal roll-up door, looking confused. One of them was Greg, my boss. Another was Ross.

'Lucy!' Greg reached out as if he was going to give me a hug, then changed his mind and patted me on the shoulder. 'Glad you made it. We're still waiting for about ten others and then we'll go on in and get you guys divided into teams. There'll be coffee and bacon rolls laid on before we get started.'

Teams. Apprehension flooded me again, coupled with awkwardness as Greg moved away, leaving me standing next to Ross and a couple of the guys from the art department.

'Do you know what they're going to make us do?' I asked.

Ross shrugged. 'No idea. Last year was clay pigeon shooting and it was a disaster. Well, it was for me, anyway. I just shut my eyes and blasted away and missed everything.'

This made me feel a bit better.

'At least it looks like we'll be indoors,' I said, shivering as a fresh breeze brought a gust of rain on to my shoulders, and wishing I'd brought a jacket.

'Here.' Ross rummaged in his canvas messenger bag and got out an umbrella. 'We might be about to get splattered with paintballs or something but we may as well be dry when we start.'

I moved under its shelter, which meant moving nearer to Ross. I'd never been this close to him before – although there were at least four inches between his bicep and my shoulder, I was close enough to smell whatever soap or shampoo he'd used that morning and feel a faint but welcome warmth coming off his body and meeting my bare skin.

'What would Adam advise in this situation?' he asked.

'What would... What?'

'"Dear Adam,"' he improvised. '"I'm heading on a corporate away day with a g— with my colleagues. How do I avoid making a total tit of myself?"'

I laughed. 'I mean, obviously I'd say, "Dear Ross, developing a non-fatal but highly infectious disease will allow you to get out of going to the horrible thing."'

'Bit late for that.'

'I'm afraid so. But Adam would probably say, "Dear Ross, team-building activities are meant to be just that. Be yourself, have fun, remember not to take any of it too seriously. And—"'

'"Don't be a dick?"'

'Exactly. So I'll be watching you closely for any signs of dickish behaviour.'

He grinned. 'Looks like we're going in.'

A metal door had swung open, and we all filed inside. A corner of the vast industrial unit had been cordoned off with hessian screens, and a table was set up with food and drink. The staff of *Max!* descended on it as if they hadn't been fed for weeks, and I joined in. Ross had been separated from me by the hungry throng, and I found myself eating my breakfast and drinking my coffee alone, which was fine with me.

After a few minutes, someone tapped a teaspoon against a coffee mug and Neil called for attention.

'Good morning, all, and welcome to the *Max!* summer social. In case you haven't worked it out yet, this year's activity is an escape room challenge. I've divided everyone into teams of three, so please listen up and I'll announce them in just a second.'

'Aw, why can't we choose our own teams?' someone grumbled.

'Because everyone would be fighting to have Lucy on theirs – duh,' said Chiraag from behind me, and I almost choked on my bacon roll.

But there was no time to ask him why on earth he thought that, because names were being called and people were moving to the end of the room in awkward little clusters of three, discussing strategy and analysing the various skills their team members boasted, before being hustled out through a gap in the sacking screen to begin their adventure. Eventually, only Ross and I were left, standing awkwardly by the food table.

'And finally, Ross, Lucy and... where is Declan, anyway?' Neil asked.

'Someone said he emailed,' Ross said. 'His boiler's fucked and he's got to wait at home for a gas engineer.'

'Bad luck,' Neil said. 'Looks like you'll be a team of two, then.'

I looked at Ross and Ross looked at me, and part of me went, *Nooooo*, but a bigger part went, *Yesssss!*

Then he grinned at me, a delighted smile full of excitement and promise, with not a trace of a blush on his face. 'Come on then, Lucy. Let's do this thing.'

We stepped forward, Neil parted the hessian barrier for the final time and we passed cautiously through. We were in a space designed to look like an old-fashioned library, with leather-bound books lining the walls, a desk with a green-shaded lamp on it and a heavy Oriental rug on the floor. Everything smelled old and musty, the way second-hand bookshops do, and there was a hint of potpourri in the air. At the far end of the room was an oak-panelled door with a brass lock, but no key.

'Right,' Ross said. 'So we find the key, and that gets us to the next stage. Easy, huh?'

'Piece of cake.' But I realised my hands were trembling. The more I looked around, the more possible hiding places I could see: the drawers in the desk, obviously, but also all the books, the carpet, vases and ormolu boxes and several huge bunches of actual keys on the shelves.

'Do we try the keys first?' Ross asked.

'No way. Clear misdirection. There must be at least forty of them and by the time we tried them all we'd have wasted loads of time.'

'So where do we start?'

'Where do people usually hide keys?'

'My dad used to put his car keys in the dog's bed overnight.' A smile flashed across his face and vanished almost straight away.

'Really? Was he vicious? The dog, not your dad, obviously.'

'Soft as butter,' he said. 'Both of them. Until... Anyway, he reckoned it was the last place anyone would look if they broke in.'

I was intrigued to pursue this line of questioning further. What if a burglar gave the dog a treat to keep it quiet and spotted the keys? Did his dad still do this random, slightly mad thing? What happened after 'until'?

But I knew if I started distracting him with questions, we'd never solve the challenge in time.

'There'll be clues,' I said. 'Let's look at the papers on the desk.'

There were almost as many of those as there were keys. Old letters, piles of invoices and several sheets that were blank.

'The blank ones, right?'

'Got to be. And the lamp.'

Feeling a surge of excitement, I held one of the blank pages up to the light, but nothing happened. I tried a second, then a third, then hit pay dirt. When the light hit the paper, faint lines appeared on it.

'Look here!'

Ross leaned in close, so close I could feel his breath tickling my hair.

'Looks like a floorplan of the room,' he said.

'And there's an X – look. Right there.'

I pointed to the spot on the map, and Ross did the same at the exact same second. Our fingers brushed each other's, and then we jumped away like an electric current had passed between us. The paper fluttered to the floor.

But there was no time for awkwardness. Together, we hunkered down on the dusty floorboards and pulled back a corner of the rug. There, taped to its underside, was a key.

'Yes!' Ross's grin flashed out again in the gloom. 'Nailed it! You're good at this, aren't you?'

'I think I played a game ages ago that had the same thing,' I said modestly. 'When you know, you know.'

I unpicked the tape and fumbled the key into my hand. We scrambled to our feet and almost ran the couple of steps to the door.

'You want to do it?' I offered.

'Nah, you worked it out.'

'Fine. I'm not going to waste time being polite.'

He laughed, and I slipped the key into the lock. It turned easily. We exchanged a half-high-five, our palms not quite meeting, and hustled through to the next room.

This had been arranged to look like the kitchen of some ancient manor house. There was a scrubbed pine table, a white ceramic sink beneath a window offering a fake view of a vegetable garden, and a trapdoor in the floor, an iron ring sunk into it.

I paused. 'God, this reminds me of a place we went to on holiday when I was little. Somewhere in Cornwall. The kitchen was full of clutter like this – my sister and I thought it was magical but Mum moaned about what a pain it was to clean.'

'I'm Team Your Mum,' Ross said. 'My flatmates call me Marie Kondo – I'm always tidying.'

I thought of his desk at work – the keyboard always arranged just so, the few papers he had on there stacked neatly in trays, his jacket on the coat rack instead of draped over the back of his chair like everyone else's.

'Fully house-trained,' I said approvingly. 'I like it. So what's our mission here?'

'Guess we need to get through the trapdoor,' Ross said.

'Right.' I gave the ring a half-hearted tug, but predictably it didn't budge.

I moved over to the sink, as if the backlit, painted view of the garden beyond would give me some sort of inspiration.

'Hey,' I said. 'That cabinet and the windowpanes – they're the same layout and dimensions.'

'So they are,' Ross agreed. 'You're a genius.'

I felt a glow of pride. 'I just like figuring stuff out. So I guess we open some of the drawers. But which?'

'We could try random ones and see what works?'

I gave him a withering stare. 'There's sixty-four of them. The number of possible combinations will run into millions.'

'Fine, whatever, Archimedes. So the clue must be in the window.'

I stepped forward and studied the painted view. 'What do the labels on the drawers say? Start from top-left.'

'Pepper,' Ross began. 'Salt.'

'Stop.' In the second windowpane, there was a distant view of the sea. 'Open that one, then carry on.'

We carried on, Ross opening drawers that matched the view of a wheat field, a honeycomb, a couple of roosting chickens, a dairy cow, a grapevine and a tree that I guessed was meant to be bay.

As soon as he tugged open that final drawer, we heard a grinding sound and the trapdoor in the floor slowly opened. I joined Ross at its edge, and we could see a ladder leading down into darkness.

'Awesome!' he said. 'Come on, Lucy, we're killing this.'

'You go first,' I said. 'I'm not sure I love this bit.'

'What? What's wrong?'

'I mean, isn't there something in the Health and Safety manual about climbing down ladders in the dark?'

He laughed. 'Guess not, or they wouldn't make us do it. Come on, it won't be far down.'

'No. You first.'

Honestly, I didn't know what had come over me. I mean, I wasn't crazy about heights, but I knew, rationally, that Ross was right – it would only be a few steps down. There'd be a light at the bottom. But somehow, looking at it, I couldn't quite work out how I'd arrange my hands and feet on the rungs, which looked like they were made of shiny brass, how I'd manipulate my body through the trapdoor, how I'd arrive at the bottom in one piece. Suddenly, all sorts of scenarios were rushing through my mind: the ladder breaking, my hands losing their grip and letting me slip into a bottomless abyss, the trapdoor coming crashing down on my head and knocking me unconscious.

'Shit. You really don't love it, do you?' he said. 'Right. Gotcha. I'll go first and I'll help you from the bottom.'

Nimbly as an acrobat, Ross grasped the top rung of the ladder and stepped through the gap. I heard an almost musical *clong* as his feet found a rung. Then his head disappeared from view, followed by his hands.

'You okay?' I asked.

'Sure.' His voice sounded surprisingly close. 'I'm almost – ah, I'm there. It's maybe twelve feet? Piece of piss. I'll be able to reach you right from the start.'

'Right. I'm going in.'

I took a big breath and swallowed, hoping the feeling that my stomach was going to shoot up into my mouth would go away. It didn't – but I had no option but to go down. Same as I'd seen Ross do, I knelt on the floor, gripped the top rung of the ladder and eased my feet back through the trapdoor.

'Keep feeling for the rungs,' he instructed. 'There. You've got the first one. Now, right foot down, left foot down – easy.'

My teeth were gritted, my knuckles white on the brass rail. Tentatively, I groped in the darkness with my feet, feeling first one rung and then the next beneath the heavy soles of my boots. My body followed until I was almost all the way through.

Then I let out a squeal of shock. A hand had grasped my ankle from the darkness below.

'Sorry!' I could hear concern in Ross's voice, but also amusement. 'I should've warned you. I'll hold your legs and guide you down.'

Shit. Did I shave my legs? I thought. But there was no time to worry about that. I felt Ross's hand moving from my left calf and then to my right, surely and competently, from one step to the next. I didn't dare look down, but I could see a rough brick wall in front of my eyes, steadily moving upwards as I moved down.

'You're three rungs from the end,' he said after a bit. 'You can literally let go your feet now and jump to the bottom if you want.'

I didn't want. Ross's hands had moved upwards now – politely bypassing my thighs and bottom – and he was holding me firmly round my waist. Gingerly, I stepped my feet down the final rungs – one, two, three – then felt the welcome crunch of solid ground under my left boot. My right joined it and then, stiffly, I released my hands from the ladder, feeling Ross release my waist at the same time.

'Phew,' I said. 'That was proper scary. Sorry to be such a wimp.'

I turned around, an embarrassed smile on my face. Ross was

smiling back – and then, to my amazement, he pulled me into his arms and hugged me.

'Well done,' he said. I could feel his lips moving against my hair. 'You're hardcore.'

'You helped me.' My own voice was muffled by his shirt. 'Thank you.'

'You're welcome. Now let's get on and smash this thing.'

He let me go and we stood in the gloom for a second, beaming at each other. My legs were still a bit shaky, but I didn't think it was from the climb any more.

Together, we turned around, ready to assess the next challenge.

It – and the following five rooms – passed in a bit of a blur. Afterwards, I could remember putting together jigsaw puzzle pieces to make one of a whole gallery wall of pictures, behind which was the key to the next room. There was a code we had to crack, where hieroglyphic symbols corresponded to letters of the alphabet and spelled out a line from a poem hidden in a book. There was an algebra problem whose solution was the code on a combination lock. There was a chemistry lab where the final key was hidden in a test tube of liquid, made invisible by its refractive index and revealed when the solution was changed by the addition of a specific chemical.

Ross got that one – I'd never even heard of refractive index, but he'd studied chemistry at A-level and explained it to me. Although, by that point, I had to admit being conscious of a different sort of chemistry – a kind of fizzing connection between him and me, the way our brains seemed to fit together like they were puzzle pieces themselves, so that when I got stuck Ross stepped in, and when he was at a loss the answer popped straight into my own head. Never mind the fact that I could still feel the places where his hands had touched my legs, my waist and my shoulders, like they'd also been coated with invisible ink that would leave a mark on my skin only I knew was there.

By the end, we were laughing as we entered each room, confident that none of the others had beaten us and this one wouldn't either.

It was no surprise, really, when we emerged from the final room to find all our colleagues, who erupted into cheers when they saw us. They were gathered round Neil, who was holding a stopwatch.

'Forty minutes and fifteen seconds,' Neil said. 'You beat the next-quickest team by a clear six minutes.'

'How the hell did you do that?' Chiraag asked. 'I thought our team had won it for sure.'

'Just natural talent,' Ross joked.

'Ross did the hard bits,' I said, remembering the climb down the ladder.

'Hey, don't throw shade on yourself,' reprimanded Greg. 'You can tell us your secrets over a drink. Grab your bags from the first room where you left them, gang, and let's go to the pub.'

Ross walked next to me, both of us still glowing with our shared triumph.

'That thing with the windows,' he said, 'that was genius. And you got it in like five seconds.'

'It took us at least fifteen minutes,' Chiraag complained. 'We'd have beaten you if it wasn't for that.'

'If it wasn't for Ross, I'd still be standing around at the top of that ladder, too chicken to go down,' I said. 'You took one for the team there.'

'No, I didn't.' Ross moved a fraction closer to me, so his shoulder brushed mine. 'It was totally worth it.'

'Why?' Marco asked. 'Did you get to see her knickers?'

'Shut it, you sleaze,' said Ross.

'I big brave man.' Chiraag stooped over so his knuckles

almost brushed the ground. 'I help frightened ladies down ladders. Then I—'

'Oh, piss off, the pair of you.' But I could see Ross was grinning.

What had he actually meant, though? Was he saying that he'd enjoyed touching me, or that it had been a necessary, unfortunate price he'd had to pay for coming in first? But I didn't need to analyse that now: we'd have the whole afternoon together, chatting, drinking beer in the sun, getting to know each other even better.

I couldn't believe I'd been dreading this day. It was turning out far, far better than I could have dreamed of.

But when I picked up my bag and checked my phone, I saw six missed calls from Amelie.

TWENTY

Dear Adam,

I'm twenty-seven and I recently moved in with my girlfriend.
We'd been dating for six months and it felt like time to take
things to the next level. I thought I was the luckiest man alive
when she agreed to go out with me. She's a fitness influencer and
she's absolutely gorgeous – my mates couldn't believe I managed
to find a girl like her and neither could I. But there's a problem.
When we were just dating, she always made the most of herself,
and every time I saw her she looked stunning. When I went
round to hers, her flat was spotless and she cooked incredible
food. But now we're living together, things have changed. She
spends the weekends in her workout gear with no make-up on.
She plucks her eyebrows over the bathroom sink. When she's on
her period she cries all the time. She leaves empty protein shake
containers all over the flat. Basically, my hot girlfriend has
turned out to be a hot mess. What can I do?

Karl, Belfast

I emerged from the stairwell into the office the next morning, out of breath as usual from the six-storey climb, at exactly the same time as the lift doors opened. Marco stepped out, laden with carrier bags from McDonald's, a cardboard tray holding five cups of coffee balanced on one hand and a clanking blue carrier bag looped over one arm.

'Morning, Lucy.' He looked briefly surprised to see me, then his normal megawatt smile broke out. 'You missed the hangover cure order. I've got sausage and egg McMuffins, extra hash browns and a double cheeseburger for your man Ross. This is a dark day. We'd have been better off with bloody marys all round if I'm honest, but Greg takes a dim view of drinking at work, especially at breakfast time.'

By the time this little speech had concluded, we'd walked the full length of the office. I put my bag down on my desk and surveyed the scene. Simon and Barney were unshaven, and I was pretty sure Barney's shirt was the same one he'd been wearing the previous day. Neil's usual pallor had taken on an almost green tinge. Ross was hammering away at his keyboard, then he paused, moved his finger to the Delete key, and held it there.

'We're not in a good way,' Marco continued. 'Not at all.'

'I can't remember getting home last night,' Simon said.

'I didn't get home last night,' said Barney.

'Our struggle is real,' Neil said. 'We're suffering.'

'Except me,' Chiraag chipped in. 'I did a twenty-k cycle this morning, and I feel great.'

'No one likes a show-off,' said Marco.

'What happened to you, anyway, Lucy?' Neil asked. 'One minute you were revelling in your moment of glory, the next – poof.'

'The mysterious case of the vanishing agony aunt,' said Chiraag.

Ross looked up from his keyboard. He didn't look at me

directly – in fact, he seemed to be avoiding looking at me at all. And he wasn't blushing; his face was pale and set.

'Something came up,' I said. 'I'm sorry I bailed on the drinks bit. I messaged Greg and said I'd catch up with you guys later, but – well, I guess I didn't. My bad. Looks like I had a lucky escape from the team hangover, though.'

'Speaking of which' – Marco dumped his burden of bags and cups on his desk – 'the cavalry has arrived. First aid all round. Coffee for you, Barney, tea for Simon, Diet Coke for you, Chiraag – smug git – full-fat Coke for you, Ross.'

Everyone collected their orders, thanking Marco before sitting down, the cloying smell of warm grease seeping into the air. But Ross didn't move from his chair.

I hesitated for a second, then passed the can of Coke, slippery with condensation, across the desk to him.

'Thanks, Lucy,' he said, but he didn't smile.

'You're welcome.' I sat down and switched on my computer, puzzled and hurt. Yesterday, I'd thought everything was okay between us – good, even. Today, it was apparently anything but good.

But as soon as I opened my email, I found myself distracted from my thoughts of Ross – and even from the other thoughts that had been plaguing me since the previous day. I needed – with or without the help of his chatbot assistant – to get my Adam head on, and the letter from Karl seemed as good a place as any to start.

My first reaction to his letter was annoyance – anger, even. *Yeah, Karl, you found a girl you thought was some sort of perfect Insta persona, and she turned out to be human – boo hoo, poor you,* I thought. *I wonder how different you are when you're slobbing round the house in your boxer shorts leaving dirty coffee mugs all over the place and farting in bed to the guy she fell in love with?*

I read the question again and rolled my eyes. Honestly, men – what was even the point of them?

And then I remembered Ross yesterday – his kindness, the way we'd vibed together completing the escape room challenges. *You saw the point of him all right, didn't you, Lucy?*

But now it seemed he couldn't see the point of me any more. Perhaps what had happened between us the previous day had just been a one-off – a never-to-be-repeated forty minutes of friendship. Perhaps all I was to him was an escape room teammate – useful in the moment, then relegated to the status of the geeky girl who sat opposite him in the office. And anyway, I reminded myself for the zillionth time, Ross had a girlfriend. Ross was off-limits. Any man I worked with was, but especially him.

So I'd just have to carry on as usual – being smiley and polite, and not allowing any sort of closeness to develop between us, ever.

Grimly, I turned to Karl's letter on my screen and started typing.

Dear Karl,

Well, you've had quite the rude awakening, haven't you? The perfect woman you thought you'd found turned out to be – newsflash – a human being. How disappointing for you. Maybe it's time you moved out and left her to be human in peace? Or buy yourself a blow-up doll for company, who'll be just the same every single day and who'll let you use her as a wank sock with a permanent smile on her plastic face. Perhaps you

Then I stopped. It was no good – I couldn't allow myself to take my own moods out on Adam's correspondents. It was unprofessional; it was unfair. I wouldn't let the shadow of gloom and worry that was hanging over me cloud Adam's judgment. If necessary, I'd have to turn to GenBot 2.0 and get it to compose a less trenchant reply, although that always felt like a bit of an admission of defeat, as if I wasn't capable of doing Adam's job – my job – myself. I sighed and eased a knot of tension from my shoulders, staring down at my keyboard as if it would somehow spring to life and type the words I couldn't find.

It didn't, of course. Instead, I found myself picturing the note I'd found from Kieren, after that second night when we kissed: the pale blue lines on the white paper, the darker blue slashes of the descenders of the capital K. I could almost feel how my heart had skipped seeing it, and the stomach-lurching excitement I'd felt when I'd read it.

Lucy, you're so beautiful it hurts my heart. And I want you so much it hurts my – well, never mind. Again tonight? K

And so it happened again – that night, and the night after, and almost every night for the next three weeks. The kisses in the silent office; the tumult of desire that swept over me like a tsunami; Kieren eventually, gently, insisting that we stop and go home; the notes on my desk the next day.

I didn't tell anyone what was going on – partly because I didn't fully understand what was happening between us. We weren't dating; we hadn't slept together. We'd only kissed. If Kieren had bundled me on to the floor and had sex with me, there's no way I'd have objected – I wanted it more than I'd wanted anything in my life.

But he didn't – not until almost a month after our first kiss by the lift.

It was a Tuesday afternoon and we were all on deadline, stressed and snappy. As a junior, my role was to step in and help whenever help was needed – and try to look busy when it wasn't. So when an email arrived in my inbox, I sprang into high alert – first with alarm and then with a kind of dizzy excitement.

It was from Kieren. The subject line was:

Can you stay tonight once everyone's done?

He'd never emailed me before. He'd communicated either by those handwritten notes or by walking across the office to find me.

My hand trembling so much I could barely control the mouse, I clicked on the email.

I don't think I can wait any longer, Lucy. I want you so much. Do you want me? K

I fumbled for the Reply button and typed one word:

Yes.

The rest of the day passed in an agony of anticipation. Every time it seemed we were about to be able to sign off and go to press, someone would find an error and it would have to be corrected, checked and re-checked, the pages processed again and sent off. Every time I turned to look for Kieren, his head was bent over his work, a dark line of sweat staining the back of his shirt.

At last, at almost nine o'clock, we were done. No one cheered – there was nothing to celebrate, just another deadline met, another edition put to bed. But I felt no release of tension – it had been building in me all day, a mix of anticipation and nervousness, and now I felt like it was reaching its crescendo. I waited, barely daring to breathe, as the office gradually emptied.

At last, some sixth sense told me that Kieren had got up

from his desk, and when I turned to look, I saw I was right. I stood up too. Our eyes met across the empty office and he smiled – a smile full of promise.

My weariness melted away. I stood up, my knees stiff from sitting for so long, and walked over to him.

'My God,' he said, 'you're the sweetest thing I've seen all day. A sight for sore eyes – literally.'

I laughed; my own eyes were dry and burning.

'Lucy,' he said, his face serious, the harsh light casting shadows on his skin, making him look older, and tired. 'Will you promise me something?'

'I... Yes, of course.'

'Don't tell anyone in the office about this. About us.'

It hadn't occurred to me to – up until that night, there'd been nothing to tell.

'I won't, if you don't want me to,' I said. 'But why?'

'You know what it's like. A hotbed of gossip. I'm older than you. I don't want to damage your reputation. I don't want people talking about you – seeing you like that. You're precious to me, and I want to keep this special, just between us. All right?'

'Pinkie promise,' I said, and he laughed.

'You're so cute. Come here.'

Pushing aside my apprehension, I stepped into his arms, waiting for his kiss. Except tonight there would be more than a kiss – I was about to have sex. Not for the first time ever, but for the first time in absolutely ages, with a man I fancied who must, surely, fancy me back – otherwise why was I here?

His lips met mine, and immediately I felt reassured – that familiar, magical kiss, the kiss I'd dreamed about for weeks. Just the same as it had been, although now there'd be no disappointment, no reluctant moving apart and going home.

This was the start of something new – something special, like he'd said.

I closed my eyes, letting myself get lost in his kiss, feeling the surge of desire it always awoke in me, tinged this time with additional excitement. My fingers found the buttons of his shirt and fumblingly undid them until I could slip my hands on to his chest – that smooth skin I'd yearned to touch, the hard arc of his ribs, the slight softness around his waist. He eased my dress up over my head and unhooked my bra, gasping as he touched my breasts.

'God, you're beautiful,' he said. 'Like a flower.'

He eased my tights over my bottom and down my legs, kneeling to remove my shoes. I heard the clink of his belt buckle and the swish of fabric against skin as he took off his jeans.

And then we were on the floor, the scratchy carpet harsh on my bare back, and he was on top of me, his hands on me, his penis thrusting hard against my thigh and then pushing inside me. I gasped, but the pain was brief and soon replaced by plea-sure – here it was. This was what I'd longed for, happening right now.

Afterwards, he held me close.

'Was that all right for you, Lucy?'

I nodded, unable to find words for what I was feeling. It had been all right. It hadn't been the magical experience I'd hoped for – but it would get better, surely? We'd learn each other's bodies, learn what worked.

'How about for you?' I asked shyly.

'The best,' he said. 'The very best shag with the very best girl.'

And then he said the words he'd said each time before.

'We should get you home.'

'Lucy?' Ross's voice jolted me out of the memory, making me jump and blush, as if he could somehow guess what I'd been thinking about. 'You got a second?'

'Sure.'

Feeling half-dazed still, not certain whether I was here in

the *Max!* office with Ross or there, back then, with Kieren, I stood and followed Ross away from our desks. He gestured to the door of one of the meeting rooms – not the one with the glass walls that anyone could see into, but the smaller one, where people went for confidential events like performance appraisals.

In that second, I suddenly felt as nervous as if I was going in for a performance appraisal myself.

Ross held the door open and I followed him in and sat down. He sat opposite me, and we looked at each other for a second, both apparently tongue-tied.

Then I said, 'So how was the rest of the party? The pub and the meal and everything?'

He shrugged. 'It was good. It was – you know – a pub and a meal.'

'I'm sorry I couldn't join you.'

Ross looked down at the surface of the table, as if he was wishing he'd written what he was about to say in a notebook and brought it in with him for reference. Then he said, 'Lucy, I have to apologise.'

'You what? Apologise for what?'

'For making you feel uncomfortable. What I did yesterday – I didn't think at the time. It was inappropriate.'

'What you... I'm sorry, I don't understand.'

He looked up again, his eyes meeting mine. 'In the escape room, touching your... uh... your legs. Without asking. And then talking about it in front of the others. It wasn't cool. I'm sorry.'

I couldn't help it – I laughed. 'Ross, me leaving after the escape room was nothing to do with what happened in there. And you did nothing wrong. You were helping me. I didn't mind. If I had done, I'd have said something.'

He blinked. He looked like a flat-earther who'd just seen images of the planet from space or something. Or maybe not, because I didn't think flat-earthers were that easy to persuade, even when confronted with reality.

'You mean you... Then why...'

I cupped my hands around my water glass. I didn't owe Ross an explanation – I'd already explained myself to Greg, who was my line manager and whose business it was. But suddenly I felt the need to explain – more than that, actually. To confide.

I said, 'My sister called me. I don't know if you remember – she got married back in June?'

He nodded. 'Is she okay?'

'Here's the thing,' I went on. 'We – her friends and I – we hadn't heard from her in a while, and we were worried. She and her husband are living in New York for a bit, because he's working out there. And we've been trying to get hold of her for ages, but she wasn't really answering our calls. And then yesterday, when I came out of the escape room, I saw she'd been trying to ring me, so of course I had to call her back.'

Ross nodded, that look of dawning comprehension still on his face. 'Is she okay?'

I shook my head. 'Not really. She's having a shit time out there, as far as I can tell. She's really bored, and I think really lonely. Zack – that's her husband – is working long hours and she's stuck in the apartment on her own and she hates it, and she's homesick and missing me and her friends, and...'

And I want to be there with her, but I can't.

Just forming the words in my head made me feel like I was about to cry. There was a box of tissues on the meeting-room table, I supposed for when appraisals were going badly. Ross got up and fetched it, his free hand hovering over my shoulder for a second before he moved it away, put the tissues within my reach and sat down again.

'New York's an amazing city,' he said gently. 'I used to spend the summer there quite often. There's so much to do.

Why doesn't she do the tourist thing, explore a bit, the Met, Central Park, shopping – all that stuff? She'd feel at home really soon.'

'That's what I said to her. But she said she feels nervous leaving the apartment, which is really weird. It's not like her. I'm worried.'

'So you had to speak to her yesterday and try and find out what was going on?'

'That's right. And afterwards – well, I was on FaceTime with her for about an hour. And after that I didn't really feel like a party. So I just went home and let Greg know why. It wasn't anything to do with you, I promise.'

Ross smiled, a slightly sheepish, dialled-down version of the smile I'd seen the day before – but it was a smile, at least. 'I'm sorry about your sister. But I'm glad I didn't offend you.'

'Thanks. I don't know what to do, really. I offered to go out there and visit her, and I suggested if she hates it she could come back home for a bit, but she said no. She said she's just going to have to get used to it. And besides, you know... work.'

'Yeah,' he said. 'Work.'

We both looked towards the door, and then we both stood up, left the room and headed back to our desks. My concern about Amelie was still at the forefront of my mind, but I felt better for having shared it with someone. Ross knew something about me now, and I got the feeling he understood, and I'd be able to talk to him about it again if I wanted to. And I knew a bit more about him, too – just tiny nuggets of information: his childhood in America, the family dog that had guarded the car keys each night. But it felt like something – like we'd been drawn ever so slightly closer to each other.

When I returned to Karl's email, I felt quite different about it. Sure, he was being a dick and I needed to tell him that. But the tone of my response changed.

Dear Karl,

Moving in with a partner is always challenging. When we're dating, we show off our best selves, and now your girlfriend is showing you another side of herself. It's good that she trusts you enough to let you see that, don't you think? And don't you find that when you two go out together, you get to see the glamorous, groomed side of her that first attracted you? Remember, Karl, women are people too. She's not a blow-up doll. She doesn't have to be perfect – or maybe she is perfect just as she is, eyebrow tweezers and period pains and all. If you love her, you'll embrace all those aspects of her.

And if you don't – well, you'd be being a bit of a dick, wouldn't you, Karl?

Yours,

Adam

Full of a smug glow born out of having poured the milk of human kindness all over the possibly undeserving Karl, I saved the document and literally dusted off my hands against each other. *A job well done*, I thought. I should have been filled with gratitude for Ross's timely intervention proving that men could be – and often were – decent.

Then I thought, *Hold on. He felt bad about touching my legs yesterday. Presumably he felt bad about hugging me as well. What does that actually mean?*

My mind whirled into overdrive. He regretted it, therefore he hadn't enjoyed it. I'd checked the previous evening and my fears had been well founded: I hadn't shaved my legs. That would have grossed out finnicky Karl for sure, and it had probably grossed Ross out, too. And besides, it wasn't as if he was single and free to go around touching all the legs he wanted. He was still going out with someone, with Bryony. I needed to keep my guard well and truly up and save my interest in men for whichever dick-adjacent loser was next rash enough to confide his poxy man-problems in Adam.

But nothing could have prepared me for the email that landed in Adam's inbox just a few days later.

TWENTY-ONE

Dear Adam,

I'm a pretty together guy, if I say so myself: good job, great flat, nice car – it's a Porsche Macan, far superior to the Cayenne in my humble opinion – and a wife who worships me. I never thought I'd find myself writing to an agony uncle – but here we are.

Where to begin? I guess with my wife, who I just mentioned. She's a great girl and, like I said, she worships me. I really don't want to do anything to hurt her. But marriage isn't turning out quite like I expected. We're living in a city she doesn't know well and she's struggling to settle in. I've recently been promoted at work and I'm leading a team out here, so I need to prove myself, and that means putting in the hours, both in and out of the office. I'm putting the effort in to show my value to my managers and my direct reports, as well as the wider firm, and I'm doing pretty well at it if I say so myself.

When I got together with my now wife, I thought she was pretty sorted. She's gorgeous and smart and sassy, and I thought she'd be a real asset to me in my life and career. But since we got married, she's changed. She's become really clingy and needy, and nothing I do seems to make her happy. I don't know what her problem is – she's got a great life here and doesn't have to work beyond doing the basics to keep things ticking over at home and occasionally turning up on a night out and being a credit to me with my colleagues. But she doesn't seem that interested in doing either of those things.

Normally, I'd let a lot of this slide – even the fact that our sex life hasn't exactly been up to standard since we got back from honeymoon. But the problem is, at work I've run into an old girlfriend of mine. We split up when she got transferred to a different location, and I met my wife shortly after. But now my ex is back in my life, and if I'm honest I feel like I've made a mistake.

My ex is everything I thought my wife was – sassy, driven, sociable and of course hot. I never thought of myself as a cheater, but what if I just ended up with the wrong girl, and now I've got the opportunity to put that right? That wouldn't really count as cheating, would it?

Help me out here, Adam. I want to do the right thing for myself.

Anonymous, Citizen of Nowhere

I read the email, then read it again. I could literally feel cold sweat breaking out on my palms, and my teeth were chattering even though the office was just as warm as usual. I stood up, my legs unsteady, and walked to the loo, locking myself in a cubicle, sitting on the closed toilet lid and shaking.

It's Zack, one part of my mind screamed. *It's totally, one hundred per cent Zack.*

It can't be, said another part. *It's too much of a coincidence. He doesn't even know Adam exists.*

Come on, coincidences happen. And all the facts match – the wedding, the move to a different city, the car, the unhappy new wife. It's Zack, and the wife is Amelie.

Nonono. It's not possible. Mostly because if it were true, I'd have to do something about it, and I had absolutely no idea what that could be.

Feeling like my brain had just been put through a smoothie-maker, I stood up again, unlocked the cubicle and washed my hands. My eyes stared back at me in the mirror, maybe a bit wider than usual but otherwise normal. My hair hadn't abruptly turned white or anything. But it didn't feel that way – it felt like the whole landscape of my life had shifted, like when you arrive on a new level in a computer game and you've got to adjust to the fact that you're not on the deck of a ship any more, but in the middle of a desert.

Still dazed, I returned to my desk, for once not noticing whether Ross was looking at me or not. I sat down and read the letter again, anger beginning to replace my shock. 'Citizen of nowhere' indeed. Who did he think he was?

And then, beyond a shadow of a doubt, I knew. That phrase: 'citizen of nowhere'. I remembered Zack using it months before, in his and Amelie's London apartment. I'd suppressed an eye-roll at the time, because it was such an up-himself thing to say – not that anyone would have noticed. Zack never noticed anything I said or did, and when he was around Amelie, she seemed incapable of noticing anyone else.

I was as sure as I could possibly be that he'd written this letter to Adam. That the clingy, needy wife in danger of being betrayed by her new husband was my sister.

I remembered my conversation with her the previous day. She'd sounded so down, so unlike herself. *Nothing I do seems to make her happy.* Yes, that sounded pretty much like the unfamiliar version of Amelie I'd encountered on our hour-long Face-Time chat.

The Amelie I knew would be relishing life in a city known to be even more buzzy and exciting than London. She'd be booking shows and going to the kind of restaurants you had to spend hours glued to social media and then pounce in seconds to get a table at, and shopping till she dropped. She'd be making new friends at hot yoga classes and going for runs in Central Park.

She wouldn't be moping alone in her apartment – unless something was very wrong.

Unlike me, Amelie understood men. If her husband's head had been turned, if he was having – or even considering – an affair, she'd know about it.

But would she know what to do about it? It was so huge – such an unexpected betrayal on such a grand scale, after such a short time – that I suspected not. I imagined that anyone, even my savvy, take-no-prisoners sister, would be blindsided, paralysed by what she knew or suspected.

She needed help. She needed me.

But I didn't know what to do.

But you've got a secret weapon, Lucy. Remember?

I felt a trickle of relief. I had the oracle of GenBot 2.0, Adam's virtual assistant, which I turned to for problems I couldn't deal with on my own, and this one was the very definition of that.

I tapped on the tab, kept permanently open on my browser. There was the blank window at the bottom of the screen and basically the whole of human knowledge waiting in the background to help me.

I typed, making a few mistakes because my hands were still unsteady, and I had to delete and try again:

I think my sister's husband is having an affair. What should
I do?

As always, the answer took just seconds to appear and, as
always, the response was comprehensive but concise.

This is a complex and worrying situation. If your suspicions are
correct, it could have serious implications for both your sister
and her husband.

1. Gather evidence. Don't confront your sister or her husband
until you're sure.

2. Communicate with your sister and listen to what she has to
say before voicing your own suspicions and presenting her with
the proof.

3. Respect her boundaries and privacy.

4. Consider counselling for yourself, and recommend it for your
sister and her husband.

5. Don't take sides, but be there to support her.

Don't take sides? Ha – as if. If Zack was cheating on Amelie,
there was only one possible side for me to be on, and it wasn't Zack's.

But gathering evidence was going to be more of a problem.
When Amelie had first started dating Zack, she'd shown me his
LinkedIn page, just so I could admire the chiselled jaw and
designer suits of her new boyfriend. I remembered thinking at
the time that I'd never seen a more innocuous, buttoned-up
profile in my life. Presumably Zack thought he was being
professional; personally, I'd thought he just came across as dull.

But the point was, his online presence wasn't going to give me the clues I needed. Gathering evidence was going to be hard. And so was being there to support her.

I was in London. Amelie and Zack were in New York.

It was a problem – but hardly an insurmountable one.

Gather evidence. Be there to support her.

The bot's advice was clear, even though it hadn't said so in so many words. I was going to have to do what army generals do when national security is threatened and put boots on the ground. Okay, it had also said to respect her boundaries and privacy, but what did boundaries matter at a time like this? She needed me, just like I'd needed her when she'd turned up to my flat and taken charge of me when my heart had been broken by Kieren.

I was going to have to visit New York, and soon.

I could work remotely, I knew – people sometimes did if they were on holiday and an emergency cropped up, or even if they just wanted extra time away without eating into their annual leave. Ross had, for the second week of his two-week jaunt to Croatia earlier in the year. There was even a clause in my contract about it – I'd just need Greg to sign off on it, and given I'd been consistently delivering my daily Ask Adam column since its frequency had been increased, I saw no reason why he'd refuse. I could afford a flight – just. I'd need somewhere to stay and someone to look after Astro.

The latter felt like more of a challenge. My neighbour, who I'd asked to drop in and feed the cat when I was away for Amelie's wedding, had moved, and I didn't know the new person who'd moved in. I could ask Nush, but that would mean telling her why I was planning an urgent trip to New York, and she'd fly into a panic and probably want to come too, which would only complicate things.

I needed someone who lived nearby. Someone who knew

Astro. There was so much I needed to plan, and I needed to plan it fast.

I looked up from my screen. Opposite me, Ross was typing busily.

'Ross?'

'Hold on.' His keyboard rattled for a few more moments, then stopped. 'Lucy.'

'Where's good to stay in New York?'

'Depends what you want. The Four Seasons, obviously, but that's top dollar.'

'Okay, where's good and cheap?'

'Brooklyn, maybe? I can help you find somewhere that's not in a sketchy area, if you like.'

'Thanks, that would be great.'

'Why? Are you planning a holiday?' Understanding dawned on his face. 'To see your sister?'

'That's right. I think I need to go out there, like, now.'

'Okay. Want to sit down after work and do some research? We could go for a coffee.'

'Thanks.' Relief flooded me. 'Oh, and, Ross? There's one other thing.'

'What's that?'

'You remember Astro...'

TWENTY-TWO

Dear Adam,

*I'm writing to you about an issue I'm having with my girlfriend.
She*

Dear Adam,

*Please could you settle a disagreement between me and my wife?
She says I'm the arsehole here but I dis*

Dear Adam,

*I've done a bad thing and I don't know whether I should say
something to the women involved. You see, I was*

'Ladies and gentlemen, we will shortly be beginning our
descent into John F. Kennedy Airport. Please make sure your
seatback is in the upright position, your tray table is stowed and
your seatbelt is securely fastened.'

The Tannoy announcement jerked me away from my laptop screen. I'd promised myself that I wouldn't work during the flight, to make the most of my first solo long-haul travel experience, but it hadn't turned out that way. Wired from the stress of navigating the airport on my own; being asked to take my Docs off to go through security, which meant spending ages undoing all the laces with an impatient, tutting queue building up behind me; then panicking on at least five separate occasions that I'd somehow lost my passport – I'd been a bundle of stress by the time I boarded the plane.

That stress had only been compounded when I thought of all the work I had to get through. Of course, I was in New York to see my sister, attempt to discover the truth about what was going on with Zack – if it was Zack – and hopefully resolve things between them, one way or the other. But I still had my job to think about: the backlog of emails that had gone unanswered because the only one I'd been able to think about was from Anonymous, Citizen of Nowhere. The need to prove to Greg that I could do this. The challenge of turning the answers GenBot 2.0 produced into something that sounded like advice Adam would give.

I'd necked two gin and tonics, devoured a soggy hummus and carrot wrap, then stared at my screen until I'd fallen asleep, only to wake in a panic an hour before landing and stare at it some more.

To be fair, I hadn't slept much the previous night. After work, Ross and I had gone for coffee, which had turned into a pint, which had turned into a shared olive and 'nduja pizza and a bottle of wine.

While we'd eaten and drunk, he'd downloaded some of his extensive knowledge of New York City, and I'd tried to commit as much of it as possible to memory, notes on my phone and five pages of scribbles in a spiral-bound notebook.

'I mean,' he'd said, leaning across the table, his elbows on either side of his pizza plate, 'I know you're going out there for a reason, and an important one at that. But you'll have five days there, right? You may as well make the most of it.'

'I don't know if I'll have five days,' I'd objected. 'My first priority is to find out if there's anything actually going on with Zack and this ex-girlfriend of his. Then I'll need to see Amelie, and either tell her or not tell her – I'm not sure yet. But if it turns out he is cheating on her, and I decide I do need to tell her, she might want to come straight home with me.'

Which was why I'd freaked out about having to spend a fortune on a flexible return ticket. Fortunately, Ross turned out to be a seasoned traveller and knew all the tricks for getting the cheapest deal possible, otherwise my plan might have been scuppered before it had even begun.

'But you'll still have to eat and drink, right?' he'd argued. 'There's just so much. Salt beef bagels at Katz's, the Chelsea food market, the street food, the cocktails. Go on, Lucy – you've got to go to the Campbell Apartment and have a dry martini, just for me.'

'The what?' Pushing my pizza aside, I'd scribbled in my notebook. I'd wanted to show willing – let Ross see that I was paying attention to his proposed itinerary – but the truth was, I couldn't imagine myself going to a food market, never mind a swanky cocktail bar, on my own.

'Campbell Apartment. It's in Grand Central Station. It's... I won't spoil it, you'll see it for yourself. And you can see the Empire State Building and Central Park and go shopping at Macy's and Bloomingdale's.' He hesitated, then added, 'And visit Ground Zero, obviously.'

I'd nodded, scribbling again in my notepad, then Ross had shyly produced his phone and showed me a link to an app where he'd marked all his suggestions on a map for me, with little notes about why they were so cool. Fascinated as always by new technology, I'd downloaded it and exclaimed over it a bit, thanking him over and over.

But I still wasn't sure I'd want to pay a visit to the scene of that long-ago tragedy, however historically significant it was. And given the stress that the flight and the relatively affordable studio apartment I'd found on Airbnb – not really allowed in New York, Ross had explained, but people still did it anyway – would place on my finances, I couldn't imagine myself doing any kind of massive department store haul. But I could browse, I supposed, if I had time, and get a present to bring back to thank Ross for his help.

I'd taken a gulp of wine and, to my surprise, heard myself say, 'I wish you were coming with me.'

He laughed, but there was something forced about it.

Too far, Lucy! my mind warned me.

'Yeah, I'd be a great tour guide,' he said. 'But, like you say, you're there for a reason. So you'll need to get from Brooklyn to Wall Street if you're going to go full gumshoe on this Zack. Let me show you how the subway trip works.'

He took out his phone again, and I shuffled my stool around so I could see the screen. Patiently, he explained the journey step by step, telling me how to pay on the subway and reassuring me that it was perfectly safe, even if I was travelling alone late at night.

'And remember, you can FaceTime me any time you like,' he said. 'It's a big city, but it's just as easy to get around as London. You'll have a ball.'

I wondered whether talking about New York somehow brought his own background to the surface. But there was no time to ask him to say it again, or teach me more phrases that would make me sound less like a limey – if Americans even called British people that any more – because our waitress was hovering to see if we wanted more drinks or the bill.

'Let me get this,' I said. 'Please. It's the least I can do. And now I guess it's my turn to show you stuff.'

'Right,' he agreed. 'Astro 101? Let's go.'

Letting him into my flat had been the weirdest thing. Apart from my dad and the plumber I'd had to get round one time when my kitchen tap sprang a leak, and the estate agent when I'd first moved in, I'd never been alone with a man in there before. It felt weird – but also not weird, because the man was Ross.

When he heard my key in the door, Astro came running, eager for his dinner. I reintroduced them, and Ross squatted down and scratched Astro behind the ears the way he liked, and I let Ross give Astro his food to cement their relationship. Then I showed him where everything was, apologised for the fact that he'd have to scoop the litter tray out twice a day, and demonstrated my cat's favourite pouncing game involving his yellow mouse with the feathery tail.

And then I'd handed him my spare keys and said, 'I guess that's everything. Sorry, I don't think there's an app for cat-sitting.'

'I guess I'll manage without one. Uh... good luck, then, Lucy. And bon voyage.'

'Thank you. For looking after Astro and – you know – everything.'

'Keep in touch, all right?'

'Of course.'

I opened the door and we stood there for a second, me on the inside and Ross on the outside and Astro kind of snaking between our legs. I thought, *Is he going to hug me? Is he?* Then I remembered his awkwardness over the unsolicited physical contact at the escape room and realised I was going to have to take the initiative – either that, or go unhugged.

So I raised my arms and spread them out, and Ross stepped

in and wrapped his arms round me, and we stood there for a moment, our bodies almost but not quite touching.

Then he'd moved away and so had I, we'd said goodnight and I'd gone inside and started packing.

And now I was here. Looking out of the window of the plane, I could see Manhattan and what must have been Central Park spreading out below me – a vast rectangle with a sparkling lake at one end, surrounded by a grid of streets and building upon building, like a square of graph paper that had been partly coloured in with a green marker pen.

Then the aircraft circled away, and wispy clouds obscured my view. But I could feel the descent, slow and steady, one wing then the other dipping. I was three thousand miles away from Ross – but, weirdly, it didn't feel that way. I was arriving in a city he loved – a city that was far more his, I sensed, than it was Amelie's, even though she was there and he wasn't.

And then, with a gentle bump and a sudden deceleration that made my seatbelt cut into my tummy, I was there, too. I waited patiently for permission to undo my belt, stand up and retrieve my bag from the locker overhead, and then I followed the slow-moving line of people to the front of the aircraft, through the door and into a long tunnel.

Half an hour later, I'd retrieved my bag, bought a bottle of rum at duty-free for no particular reason except that I was travelling and that was what travellers did, and was making my way to the train station. *Don't get a yellow cab*, Ross had advised. *They're cool, but the drivers are grumpy gits, the traffic is terrible and they'll charge you a fortune.*

His instructions had given me the knowledge and confidence I needed to get where I needed to be without gazing fixedly at Google Maps and looking like a tourist, which I felt proud of in a silly and random way. And the email my host had sent me gave clear instructions on how to locate the apartment.

The building was a red-brick apartment block on a tree-lined street, just a few minutes' walk from the subway station. Across the road was a deli, and at the end of the block a corner shop – a bodega, as Ross had said they were called. It was mid-afternoon and the streets were quiet – or what I imagined quiet would be for the city that never sleeps. A couple of women with babies in buggies were power-walking along the pavement – sidewalk? – a guy was arranging cloths and glasses on tables in a restaurant, and a man was strolling along, patiently waiting while his dog sniffed and peed against a lamppost.

But I didn't want to linger – I wanted to investigate the place that was going to be my home for the next few days. Furtively, I entered the passcode into the keypad outside the main door, and it swung open. After retrieving the key from a lockbox, I hefted my backpack higher on my shoulder, climbed to the second floor – third in American, as Ross had explained – and slotted the key into the door of apartment 3B.

It turned obligingly and I stepped in. The flat was tiny – its ceilings were almost as high as the floor area was wide. But it was spotlessly clean, and sunlight streamed through steel-framed windows on one wall and reflected dazzlingly off the parquet floor. There was a cream IKEA sofa-bed next to the window and a tiny kitchen next to the door, just beyond a smaller, sliding door that I imagined led to the bathroom.

There was a wardrobe and a glass coffee table with a money plant in a brass pot on it, a few framed theatre posters on the walls, a wall-mounted TV – and that was it. It was tiny and perfect and, straight away, I imagined myself living here, waking up in the morning with someone next to me in the unfolded sofa-bed, making coffee in the drip machine I saw on the kitchen counter, going out for pastries and exploring the city.

Except, of course, there'd be no room for Astro here, that was for sure. So it would never work.

Swiftly, I unpacked my clothes and arranged the contents of

my washbag in the bathroom, which was small and windowless with a shower over the stainless-steel bathtub. I investigated the kitchen cupboards and found plates, glasses, coffee mugs and cutlery – two of everything. There was everything I needed and nothing I didn't – except maybe someone to share my adventure with.

But Ross was sharing it – albeit remotely. So I sent him a picture of the apartment and a brief message saying I'd arrived safely and everything was great. I was itching to head out, explore the neighbourhood, find some food and plan my next move.

First, though, I had work to do. I might have been in a foreign city, but I was still working and Adam was still on duty. So I perched my laptop on my knees and turned to my over-flowing inbox.

There was an email from a guy who, at five foot five, was demoralised by the number of women on the apps who only wanted to date tall men, and was considering lying about his height on the basis that, once they met him, they'd be so blinded by his personal magnetism they wouldn't notice his small stature.

You think a lie is a good basis for starting a relationship? I thought. *Don't be a dick.*

There was an email from a sixteen-year-old who knew he was gay but hadn't come out yet and had fallen in love with his best friend. My heart twisted in sympathy for him – he might be a dick or he might not, but he needed considered advice. I wasn't in the right frame of mind to deliver that right now, so I saved the text of his message to my folder of problems I was definitely going to address in the next few weeks.

There was an email from a father who'd recently started dating a woman and wanted to know when and how to intro-duce their kids to each other, which would definitely need input from the child psychologist I contacted when I had a problem I felt neither I nor Adam nor GenBot 2.0 was qualified to respond to.

But I kept coming back to the message I was sure Zack had written. I was going to answer it – I felt compelled to. But I didn't know what to say.

I pasted the message in its entirety into GenBot and waited for it to respond. After a few seconds, it produced its usual brief, mild-toned reply.

Your situation sounds complicated... It's normal to experience temptation in a relationship... Talk to your wife and find out what's troubling her... Don't embark on an affair without ending your marriage first...

'For God's sake,' I snapped. 'Come on, AI Adam. Get with the programme.' I typed in response:

But can't you see what a dick this man is being?

The algorithm returned:

He comes across as somewhat materialistic.

And he's thinking of cheating on his wife!

Betrayal in a relationship is never an advisable course of action.

So why are you being so sympathetic to him?

I am a generative, language-learning model. If you have relation-ship concerns, I recommend seeking counselling.

'Oh, fuck off.' I snapped my laptop closed, picked up my

bag and the keys and headed out. But before I descended the stairs, I made sure I had Ross's app open on my phone, and I was surprised to see I had a message from him.

Glad you got there safe. Thinking of you. xxx

I could see straight away how many kisses there were, but I counted them all the same.

TWENTY-THREE

I had a plan, and I believed it was a good one. I'd grab something to eat, then get the subway over into Manhattan. Although I longed to go straight to Zack and Amelie's apartment and see my sister, I had an even higher priority. I needed to find the building near Wall Street where Zack's office was, lurk outside until he emerged, then follow him and see where he went, with whom and what happened next. I had my phone for directions. I had my sunglasses and a hat to make myself less recognisable – although I was confident that, out of context, the chances of Zack recognising me were slim.

But it didn't quite work out that way.

The first part of my plan went flawlessly. I walked out into the sunny afternoon, carefully locking the apartment behind me and making sure the street door was securely closed, too. Then I walked round the block and found a tiny restaurant – not much more than a hole in the wall, with bench seating at the window and a couple of handkerchief-sized tables in the shadowy interior – with a long line of people snaking outside the door and round the corner.

Given it was mid-afternoon, I reckoned that boded well for

the food, so I joined the queue, earwigging intently to see what other people were ordering. But I needn't have bothered, because the place only sold one thing: artisan hot dogs, which was fine with me. Actually, it would have been fine even if they weren't artisan. Eventually, I reached the front of the queue and ordered a large one, plus a double-thick chocolate milkshake.

That was my first mistake. I ought to have realised that this was New York, where portion size reached a whole new level. The hot dog was the size of my forearm and the milkshake came in a vast paper cup, the straw sticking proudly upright because it was mostly ice cream.

Daunted, I perched at the counter and started eating. It was one of those times when you know you're hungry but you don't realise exactly how hungry until the first bite of food passes your lips, and then you go into a kind of feeding frenzy and eat and eat like a python until your ribs are groaning and your spine is sticking out at the back.

I devoured the whole thing, slurped the very last dregs of the milkshake and only then realised how extremely full I was. Of course, the sensible thing would have been to take a gentle stroll to digest it all, but I was overcome by a wave of tiredness that, combined with my extreme fullness, made lying down feel like the only option.

I staggered back to the apartment, kicked off my shoes and lay down on the bed, thinking I'd be good to go after a forty-five-minute nap.

And then I woke up to find the apartment in darkness. For a moment, I thought I was back home, and I even sat up and called Astro because I thought it must have been him that had woken me. And then I remembered where I was, and my phone told me it was four in the morning.

So much for catching Zack in between his working day and whatever he had planned for the evening. I'd wasted most of the afternoon and all night, and now I was wide awake with no idea what to do. Going back to sleep was out of the question – I'd been out like a light for twelve hours, and according to my body clock it was time to start my working day.

I showered, dressed and went outside. The morning was still cool, and the world was dark and silent. I could hear the faint hum of traffic, and around me the occasional window flickered into brightness as someone got up for their early yoga class or because their baby was crying, or whatever. But I felt as if I had the world to myself.

Since I was up, I might as well get some sightseeing in, I reckoned. So, using my phone as a guide, I walked in the direction of the Brooklyn Bridge. It was further than I'd expected, and quite eerie walking the streets alone, but I wasn't afraid. The sleeping city felt welcoming and benign, as if this morning had been created just for me.

At last I reached the bridge and stepped out on to the wooden walkway beneath the cobweb of metal struts. The sky behind me was just beginning to brighten, turning from deepest black to midnight blue, with a widening vein of violet visible between tall buildings.

But I didn't look behind me; I looked ahead, and I walked.

And after a bit, the most extraordinary thing happened. One by one, the glass towers of Manhattan in front of me turned to flaming torches as the sun emerged. I thought of Dick Whittington in the fairy story, imagining the streets of London paved with gold, only this wasn't London, and it was skyscrapers I was looking at, not cobbled streets. Still, I found myself holding my breath as I walked, amazed that something so beautiful could happen every day, every time the sun rose.

I found myself involuntarily smiling, so that the occasional passer-by looked at me and smiled back, sharing my delight in the glory of the morning. And I realised that – despite my worry about Amelie, my uncertainty about how this rashly planned trip would pan out, and my knowledge that my feelings for Ross were likely to go unrequited – I was happy.

I'd embarked on a new job, and despite its challenges I was doing my utmost to make it a success. I'd travelled alone to a strange city and I was enjoying myself.

I could look back now, at what had happened with Kieren, and feel almost like it had happened to another person.

The envelope in the drawer next to my bed containing his notes hadn't got any new additions after the night we first slept together. When I arrived at work the morning after the first time we'd had sex, I was sure there would be one there – I remembered I'd spent the whole time getting ready for work and the journey to the office looking forward to seeing it, imagining what it would say now that our relationship had moved on to the next level.

But there was nothing there. I moved my keyboard aside to check, then lifted it up in case the note had somehow got stuck to its base. Nothing. I pushed back my chair to look on the floor under my desk, but there was no white piece of paper on the floor. Then I noticed my colleague Misha looking at me curiously, and I called off my search, swallowing my disappointment and going off to make coffee as if nothing was wrong.

He was at his desk – I could see him there, working, his dark head bent just the same as usual. I realised that with my disappointment had come a wave of anxiety – what if he was ill, or some accident had befallen him and he hadn't made it to work?

But he was here. Just the note wasn't.

As the day wore on, I felt my bewilderment crystallising into an agony of self-doubt. I must have done something wrong. Something about the sex must have disappointed him. Evidently, what I'd thought of as a consummation had been a disaster – a failure. My failure.

But I was wrong.

This time, it happened earlier – towards the middle of the after-noon. With it being a Wednesday, the day after the paper had gone to press, the office was quieter than usual. The editor-in-chief was off, along with a few of the other senior people. Those of us who were working had less to do than usual, so I felt justified, once I'd plucked up the courage, to walk over to the news desk and throw out a general offer of help, carefully not aiming it specifically at Kieren.

But it was he who responded. He turned those deep-blue, slightly narrowed eyes on me and said, 'Actually, I could use a hand. Thanks, Lucy.'

I waited, my heart hammering. He stood up and said, 'Let's grab a tea first.'

I noticed the glances of his colleagues following us, without any real interest, as I walked with him down the office. But he didn't turn into the kitchen. He led me into the cluttered little room opposite it, where the seldom-used binding machine and stocks of stationery were kept.

And then he closed the door.

'What...?' I began. 'Kieren, what are you...?'

He placed a finger over my lips, smiling, then moved it away and kissed me, one hand in the small of my back and the other behind my head, his fingers buried deep in my hair.

I thought, *This is crazy. This is insane.*

But my doubts were overwhelmed by relief that he still wanted me. *It's just a kiss,* I promised myself. *It's stupid and risky, but it's just a kiss.*

I was wrong about that, too.

Seconds later, I felt his hands pushing my dress up and pulling my tights down, a finger caressing me, gently but urgently.

'We'll have to be quick,' he murmured. 'You up for this?'

Afterwards, I thought I should have said no. Of course I should have. But I was too bewildered. I didn't want to cause a scene. And, in a way, I was up for it. I wanted him. I wanted him to want me. Just not like this.

He put his hands under my thighs and lifted me up, so suddenly I gave a gasp of surprise. Before I could I figure out what was happening, he'd pressed my back against the door and I felt his cock inside me. Instinctively, I wrapped my legs around his waist and my arms around his neck, amazed at his strength.

It didn't last long. After a few seconds, I heard his breathing turn ragged and felt him shudder inside me, and a few seconds later his penis slipped out of me and he let me down to the floor.

'Sorry,' he said. 'Proper knee-trembler, that one. God, you're so sexy, I couldn't have carried on longer even if I wasn't worried about getting caught.'

I straightened my clothes hastily. 'I'm still worried about getting caught.'

'We won't,' he promised. 'I won't let that happen to you. Trust me.'

'I do trust you,' I said, wondering even as I spoke whether that was true.

And then he said, 'We should get back to work.'

The memory made me shiver, although here in New York the day was already warm. I could feel the Lucy I'd been then somewhere inside me still, shy and awkward and unsure how to interpret men and their actions, but at the same time longing to be worthy of a man, the way other women were.

I didn't feel that way any more, I realised. Although I was single, I didn't care if I stayed that way – I didn't need a man in my life to be happy and fulfilled. But, thanks to Adam and all the men who'd poured their problems and their secrets out to him, I was starting to understand men a bit more. I even liked some of them. Especially Ross. Our friendship might be recent, but it meant a lot to me. I couldn't remember ever having had a close male friend before, and now it looked as if I did. But why did it feel as if friendship wasn't really what I'd hoped for from him?

But I didn't like Zack. Obviously.

In the heart of the Financial District, I found the building where he worked – a glass tower among a sea of other glass towers, all so tall they gave me a crick in the neck when I looked at them. I loitered on a corner and watched men and women in suits, laptop bags slung over their shoulders, coffees and mobile phones in their hands, hurrying in through the glass doors into the vestibule, then on towards the rank of lifts – elevators? – that would take them up to the desks where they'd spend the day doing mysterious things with spreadsheets.

Even if I was lucky enough to spot Zack going into the building, it wouldn't help – I couldn't exactly follow him, and even if I could, all I would find would be him sitting blamelessly at his desk, going into meetings and chatting to colleagues round the water cooler. Even if there was something going on with him and this other woman, they were hardly likely to sneak off for a shag in between answering emails.

So I turned away and headed off on the itinerary Ross had planned out for me. I looked at the Stock Exchange Building and the Oculus Center and the 9/11 Memorial, remembering the seriousness on his face when he'd said I should see it. Then I made my way by subway to the Metropolitan Museum of Art, but I didn't go in – I just joined the crowds of tourists perched on the stairs and had a bit of a rest, wishing that my sister was sitting there next to me, imaging her remarking that art gallery shops were always far better than the art galleries themselves.

I bought a giant, salty pretzel and ate it in Central Park, then wandered round there for a bit before heading down Fifth Avenue, stopping to gaze into shop windows but again not going into any. I did go into the Empire State Building, though, all the way to the top, where I admired the dizzying views all around me and took a selfie to send to Ross.

What with that, and the notes he'd put on the app that made me giggle, it felt almost as if he was there, exploring his home city with me, telling me stories about growing up there, where he'd been to school, where he'd learned to play baseball, where he'd thrown a ball for the family dog to chase.

I wished I knew more about his childhood so I could imagine it better. Better still, I wished he was actually there, being a real tour guide instead of a virtual one.

But he wasn't. And anyway, the only man I needed to be thinking about right now was not Ross but Zack.

I got the subway back to Wall Street, and by five forty-five, I was back on the corner outside Zack's office, where I waited. And waited, and waited. A few people trickled out through the glass doors, but many more were still going in, presumably returning from high-powered off-site meetings to go back to their desks and carry on working.

I'd made a serious miscalculation, I realised. Zack didn't get paid the big bucks to knock off work after eight hours like a normal person. I didn't know what to do. I walked round the block – another error of judgment, because obviously if he was going to leave work at a sensible hour, he was bound to do it in the few minutes when I wasn't watching the door – then waited another half-hour, then eventually gave up and got the subway back to Brooklyn, tired and hungry and frustrated.

My initial plan was no good. I was going to have to come up with a better one.

TWENTY-FOUR

Dear Adam,

My girlfriend and I have been dating for two months. I know it's not long in the scheme of things, and neither of us wants to rush into anything until we've got to know each other better – she's twenty-nine and I'm thirty. I really like her; she's beautiful and clever and kind and basically everything I'm looking for in a partner.

There's just one thing: I'm not sure whether she's as into me as I'm into her, especially when it comes to sex. We've kissed and stuff, but when I suggest taking it further she backs off and says it's too soon.

Like I said, I'm fine with taking things slow. But does that mean never having a proper sexual relationship with her? Because if so, I'm not sure I can do this, even though I like her so much and can see myself falling for her and even being with her long-term.

I know you're going to suggest I try talking to her, and of course

I've done that. But she just kind of shuts down – the only time we come close to having a row is when I attempt these discussions. She accuses me of only wanting her for sex and not being interested in her as a person, and that's just not true.

Could there be something she's not telling me, or are we just not compatible? Be honest with me, Adam, I can take it.

Kit, Essex

I read Kit's letter and then read it again. I knew pretty much what the AI version of Adam would say to him: a carefully considered list of numbered steps recommending communication, other forms of intimacy and the possibility of accepting that the relationship wasn't meant to be. I suspected I knew what Amelie would say: *Maybe he's just a really crap kisser and she doesn't want to find out he's a really crap shag as well?* But I felt so overwhelmed by the sheer number of messages I still needed to respond to that I couldn't begin to frame a response to any of them. When I poised my fingers over my keyboard to begin typing, they kind of seized up, the way I'd felt one December when I was still working at *Fab!* and the heating had gone on the blink and we'd all been so cold our fingers just wouldn't move.

It was late, anyway, I told myself – almost nine in the evening. I was back in my Brooklyn Airbnb and, given I'd been up since the early hours of the morning, I was just about ready to go to bed.

The only thing was, after a full day and a half in New York, I was no closer to achieving my goal than I'd been when I arrived. I felt like I should be doing something, planning something, making some sort of progress with my plot to locate Zack and see whether my suspicions about him were correct. If I couldn't make any progress, I had no idea what I'd do. Give up and go home? Go and see my sister anyway and give her the hug I was longing for? Just get in touch with him and flat-out ask him?

None of those felt like the right thing to do. Perhaps if I slept on it, the solution would come to me during the night, the way solutions are meant to but rarely in my experience do.

Oh, and the only other thing was, I really wanted to check in with Ross and tell him how my day had been. But he hadn't responded to the picture I'd sent him earlier, and it was even later in London now, gone midnight, and he had work the next day so I couldn't possibly call him now.

Frustrated and indecisive, I snapped my laptop closed and found myself pacing around the tiny apartment. Then I remembered how tired my legs were, and the blisters on my heels reminded me of their presence, so I sat down again just as my phone buzzed with an incoming FaceTime call.

To my surprise and relief, it was Ross.

The image on my screen was gloomy, so I couldn't quite make out the background. 'Hi, Lucy! I wasn't sure you'd pick up. Hold on.'

I saw the picture move, blurrily, revealing a view of Ross's denim-clad legs and a patch of wall, and then a light snapped on and I suddenly knew exactly where he was. He angled the phone away from him, and I saw Astro, in his favourite spot on my sofa, his head heavy and his eyes half-closed in sleep.

'Awww! There he is!' I cooed delightedly. 'How's he doing?'

'He's great. I got here about eight and gave him his dinner, and we've just been hanging out. I hope you don't mind me staying so long. I was worried he might be lonely.'

'No, it's cool. I appreciate you looking after him so much. Is he okay?'

Ross told me how Astro had eaten his food, then sat on his lap for a bit, then played one of his favourite games. He detailed how much water he'd drunk and assured me that his litter tray had been used, and explained that, judging by the amount of fur on my bed, the cat had spent most of the day asleep. Reassured, I asked him about his day and got an update about the office, and how everyone was managing perfectly okay without me.

Then Ross asked me how New York was, and I launched into a long account of my exploration of the city.

'Only I'm getting precisely nowhere with stalking Zack,' I said. 'I hung out outside his office for ages and I didn't see him. By the end, it was like all the men coming out of there looked the same; they could've all been clones of him. But none of them was actually him. So I'm kind of stuck.'

'Hmmm.' Ross leaned back on my sofa, and I saw Astro's tail move through the picture as he walked over his lap. 'You know what I've noticed about your cat?'

We were meant to be talking about my brother-in-law. But it was never hard to distract me into talking about Astro instead of... well, practically anything.

'He's the cutest and the best cat in the entire world?'

'I haven't met all of them. But on the evidence, yeah, I'd say so. But what else?'

'He's got exceptionally long whiskers?'

'He has? Yeah, now you mention it, they are pretty impressive. And?'

'He's an incredibly noisy eater. He sounds like someone in the seat behind you on the bus chewing gum.'

Ross laughed. 'Well, I didn't like to mention it. But there's another thing – something relevant.'

'Okay, you're going to have to tell me, otherwise I could carry on all night.'

'He's a creature of habit. Like, I've only been looking after him a couple of days, but I've noticed. As soon as I walk in the door, he goes and jumps on the kitchen counter, because he did that the first time and I gave him treats. And he sleeps in the

exact same places – back of the sofa in the mornings, your bed
during the day, and so on. And he always washes his face with
his left paw.'

'He does?' I was intrigued. 'I never noticed that. Adorable –
a left-pawed cat.'

'Cute as fuck,' Ross agreed. 'But anyway, my point is,
people have habits too. They might only last a couple of months
before they change and move on, but for a while, you can
depend on someone doing the same thing this Wednesday as
they did last Wednesday.'

'Like you going to CrossFit every Thursday lunchtime and
buying a salt beef sandwich on your way back to the office.'

Ross looked startled, then a bit as if he might be going to
blush, but the light wasn't good enough for me to see.

'Yeah,' he said. 'A bit like that. See, you're good at this detec-
tive thing. Anyway, my point is, if you can find out where Zack
was after work six days ago, chances are he'll be there again
tomorrow.'

'Good thinking. Only problem is, I don't know where he
was last Thursday night. Unless you have access to a time
machine you never told me about.'

'Don't need one. You just need his social media.'

I tried not to roll my eyes. Did he think I was some kind of
amateur? 'Tried that. He's got LinkedIn and that's it.'

'Bollocks. Everyone has social media. What's the point of
having an attractive wife and a swanky apartment and a six-
month secondment to New York if you can't show off about it to
the guy who got picked for the football team instead of you
when you were fourteen?'

'Honestly, he doesn't.'

'You haven't found it, that's all. He's probably got it set to
private, with a name that makes it hard to find.'

I thought about this for a second and had to admit it made
sense. When I'd initially looked for him on Instagram to see if

there was more to this man my sister was so smitten with than a well-cut suit and an extensive network of connections I hadn't looked particularly hard. I'd been mildly curious, that was all – and then when I'd drawn a blank I'd concluded he wasn't on there. And then, when he and Amelie got serious and moved in together and later got engaged, it would've seemed weird and stalkerish to ask.

If only I'd known then that just a few months later, I'd be stalking the man for real.

'Okay, maybe you're right. But I can't exactly ask now, can I? "Hey, Zack, it's your sister-in-law and I'd like to follow you on the Gram." "You would? Why?" "Just, I'm here in New York and I want to know where you might be tomorrow evening so I can catch you out with another woman." "Oh sure, knock yourself out. It's @PhilanderingBastard."'

Ross laughed. 'Okay, fair enough. So you have to find someone who already follows him and figure it out that way.'

'Yeah, that makes sense. Only, Amelie follows about three thousand people. When she was planning her wedding she went mental on it. It would take me ages to go through them all.'

'That makes it more challenging,' he admitted. 'But there'll be a way. Leave it with me.'

'Are you sure?'

'Give me until lunchtime tomorrow, your time. I'll call you then, and if I haven't found anything, we'll come up with another plan.'

My eyes strayed from his face to the clock at the top of my screen, and I realised how late it was. We'd been chatting for almost half an hour, so it would be nearly three in the morning, London time.

As if on cue, Ross gave a jaw-splitting yawn and said, 'Sorry.'

'No, I'm sorry. You must be knackered.'

'I'm all right. I should probably get home to bed, though.'

For a second, I considered saying, *You can stay if you want. Sleep in my bed, with Astro.* Somehow, imagining him waking up in my flat made me feel less far from home, almost like I was there with him. Like we were going to get up together and get in each other's way while we dressed for work, and have Astro tell bare-faced lies to one of us about not having had his breakfast when the other had already fed him.

But I couldn't let myself think that way.

So I said, 'Thanks again for looking after the cat. And thanks for the chat.'

'It's my pleasure. It really is. Night, Lucy.'

'Night,' I said, and his face vanished from my screen as if it had never been there.

TWENTY-FIVE

It was just after two o'clock when I found myself in a crowded deli, balancing a tray containing a sandwich that looked like it could single-handedly end world famine and a Diet Coke, wondering where on earth I was going to sit to eat it. Someone was just getting up from the only spare table, so I hovered for a second then sat down as soon as I could. To my surprise, a couple of women in the queue turned and glared at me like I'd done something terribly wrong. I glanced around, embarrassed, but it seemed like that was the system – you looked round, you hovered, you sat. Maybe they were just having a bad day. Or, if they'd taken against me for some other reason, there was nothing I could do about it.

So I took a slurp of my drink and a bite of my sandwich, got my phone out and settled in for what was clearly going to be a marathon eating session.

Just as I was chewing my first delicious mouthful, stingy with mustard and sharp with pickle, my phone rang and Ross's name popped up on FaceTime.

My first thought was, *Great! He'll be so pleased to catch me here, at the place he recommended.* Then I thought, *Shit, have I got mustard on my chin? Should I message and say I'll call him back?* Then I remembered that he might have news on Zack, so I answered the call immediately, propping my phone up against a sugar canister, relieved that my headphones were already in so at least I wouldn't give the women in the queue another reason to hate me.

'Hey, Lucy.' Ross wasn't in my flat this time; he was outside somewhere, sitting on a bench in the early-evening sunshine. 'How's it going?'

'Good,' I muttered through a mouthful of sandwich, then swallowed. 'Sorry. Yeah, great, thanks. I saw the Statue of Liberty this morning, and now I'm having lunch.'

'You sure are,' he said. 'And you're in Katz's, aren't you? How's the pastrami?'

'Off the scale.' I held the unbitten half of my sandwich up so he could see.

'Oh my God. I'm so jealous. Which table are you at?'

'I don't know. Do they have numbers? It's kind of in the middle.'

'Show me.'

So I angled my phone around a bit to take in the room, puzzled but humouring him, because he seemed so vicariously excited by it all.

'Lucy! Mate, do you realise you've got the table?'

'What table?'

'Look above your head.'

I obeyed and saw what I hadn't noticed before: a sign suspended from the ceiling, which read, 'Where Harry met Sally... hope you have what she had! Enjoy!'

Right. That explained the daggers looks from the two women in the queue. Presumably they'd planned to film themselves faking orgasms over their lunch and put it on their TikTok or something, and I'd come along and ruined it. Well, I was sorry about that, but realistically what could I do? I was here, they were already sitting somewhere else, and the queue was building so quickly that I knew if I stood up, someone else would grab my place before the two women even noticed my random act of kindness.

'So I have,' I said to Ross. 'How cool is that?'

'Awesome,' he agreed, grinning.

Suddenly, I knew what I was going to do. I was here in Manhattan, in this iconic eatery, with the right sandwich, sitting at the right table, with a captive audience of not only the two disgruntled women but also Ross.

Ross loved old movies. Ross would think I was confident and hilarious. The women whose table I'd unwittingly stolen would be mollified. It would be rude not to.

I took a bite of my sandwich, chewed and swallowed, and then let out a theatrical moan, throwing my head back in bliss.

'Yes!' I said, running my hands through my hair. 'Oh God! Yes! Right there!'

I moaned, gasped and moaned again, sliding lower in my chair. 'Oh yes! Yes, yes, yes!'

My eyes were half-closed in theatrical bliss, but I could sense heads turning to look at me. I was in the zone now, so I carried on.

'Oh my God! That's so good! Oh yes. More, more, more!'

Another loud moan, a few more gasps and sighs, and I reckoned I was done. I sat back upright, pushed my hair back, dabbed my lips with my napkin and turned back to my screen.

Ross was looking at me, perplexed but half-smiling. 'Lucy? Are you okay?'

I glanced around. People at the neighbouring tables were staring, some discreetly and some less so. One of the annoyed women hastily put down her phone, but I was pretty sure she'd been filming me.

My giddy excitement evaporated as quickly as it had

arrived, replaced by a prickle of doubt – maybe I'd gone just a bit too far. But it was okay; it was only Ross watching me.

Ross and a roomful of strangers.

My face burning, I took a gulp of Diet Coke. 'I'm fine. I was just... you know.'

Ross cleared his throat. 'Anyway. I've got news for you.'

I felt a surge of excitement that almost – but not quite – wiped away my embarrassment. 'You found Zack's secret Instagram account?'

'I did. And I can reliably inform you that every Thursday at about eight, when he's finished work, he goes to the Campbell Apartment and has a dry martini, straight up with a twist.'

'Seriously?' Typical Zack, ordering the most James Bond cocktail in the world.

'Seriously. At least, he has done for the past three weeks. "Hashtag thirsty Thursday" might move on somewhere new after a while, but it would make sense for that to happen on a monthly basis. So tonight, if you go there, odds are you'll spot him.'

'Amazing! Thanks so much. I can't believe you— How did you find out, anyway?'

'Easy.' He smiled smugly. 'Bryony told me. She's followed him on Insta for ages. I didn't tell her why, just mentioned that a friend was in New York and looking for somewhere cool to drink and I'm kind of out of touch because I haven't been there in a year, and she said Zack had raved about this place and showed me his grid, and here we are.'

'Right.' My mouth felt all strange and numb, like after I've been to the dentist, and I was struggling to get the words out. 'Looks like you nailed it. Thanks, Ross. I'd better go now... You know...'

I gestured vaguely at the people standing around waiting for a table.

'Gotcha. Let me know how it goes, okay?' He sounded just

the same as usual – well, just the same as he'd sounded recently, since things had stopped being weird between us.

It looked like they'd just got weird again.

'Will do,' I said, although I had no intention of speaking to him ever again, unless it was strictly necessary, like at work.

I ended the call and unpropped my phone. Then I looked down at my sandwich. Almost all of it was left, but I didn't feel in the least bit hungry any more. It felt like a massive waste of food, but there was no way I could eat it, and no way I could take it out and give it to some homeless person, half-chewed as it was.

So I just abandoned it, along with my half-drunk Diet Coke. I tucked a ten-dollar bill underneath the sugar canister, slipped my phone into my bag and left.

And then, although my feet were still hurting from the previous day's marathon sightsee, I walked and walked, barely noticing or caring where I was going.

I'd made a fool of myself. I'd let myself believe that I could be the kind of woman Ross might fancy – an extroverted, self-confident woman who travelled abroad on her own, who was capable, sassy and sexy.

And to try and prove it, I'd faked a bloody orgasm for him, on camera, in the middle of one of New York City's top sight-seeing spots.

I'd forgotten – or let myself forget – that he had a girlfriend. My sister's friend.

She'd shown him Zack's grid – that meant in person, not over WhatsApp or whatever. He was still seeing Bryony. It was early evening in London, so he was probably on a date with her right now. I imagined the two of them sitting together in some trendy bar somewhere, drinking cocktails, and Ross saying, 'Hey, don't suppose you know of any good places like this in New York? My mate's over there at the moment.'

Mate. He'd even called me mate. I bet he didn't call Bryony mate.

And then I'd seen fit to stage a spot of amateur porn while she went for a wee or out for a vape.

Or worse still, sitting right there opposite him while he looked at my fake O-face on his screen.

I couldn't do this. I was no better at relationships with men now than I had been four years ago, when I'd let Kieren use me and humiliate me.

I deserved to be alone – and it was just as well I was used to it, because clearly that was how I was going to stay.

My furious speed-walking had carried me quite a way from Katz's Deli by now, and I realised I was lost. I didn't want to sightsee any more; I wanted to go home. Except, of course, home was thousands of miles and many time zones away. I wanted my sister, except I was hiding a secret from her that I couldn't reveal until I'd confirmed if it was true.

Blindly, I walked down into the nearest subway station, figured out the best way back to Brooklyn and boarded a train.

Half an hour later, I was back in the apartment, my laptop on my knees. I'd been neglecting work, but I was going to make up for it now. I was going to compose a reply to Kit, and I didn't need any AI to help me do it.

Dear Kit,

I'm sorry to hear your girlfriend won't put out – that must come as quite the blow to your male ego. I suppose you think that now you're dating someone, you get the whole package – someone to listen to your problems, someone to show off to your mates, someone to meet your physical needs.

And now she's not playing ball. Isn't that a shame?

You know, Kit, this is something I've said before in this column. Women are people, too. I know it's hard to understand, but they've also got needs, desires and – wait for it – boundaries. And there you are, chip chip chipping away at hers, and she's pushing back.

And you don't like it one bit, do you?

There's something I'd like you to think about for just a moment, Kit. When a man wants sex and a woman says no, and the man pushes for it anyway and insists – because after all he's a nice guy, or he bought her dinner, or they're married, or whatever – there's a word for that. It's not a word you want to use in the context of your relationship, is it?

So give that some good thinking, Kit, back off from this poor woman and stop being a sex pest.

Oh, and don't be a dick.

Yours,

Adam

I'd been typing at warp speed, and the tips of my fingers felt almost bruised from bashing the keyboard so hard – but it had barely relieved my feelings. I saved the document, deciding to wait before filing the copy to the subs desk just in case there were any more pearls of wisdom I needed Kit to hear.

I was done with him, for now. Maybe later, I'd have another look in Adam's inbox and see if there were any other men who deserved a piece of my mind. Fuming, I thought of all the measured, kind responses I'd sent, both with and without the bot's help. All those men I'd tried to understand and sympathise with – and for what?

They were all just the same. All of them – including Zack, who my sister had fallen in love with. And Ross, who I'd allowed myself to think might like me despite the fact that he was not only miles out of my league but also dating someone else.

I couldn't deal with Ross now; I felt too bruised and humiliated. But Zack?

Brother-in-law, I'm coming for you, I promised.

I closed my laptop, stripped off my clothes and showered, then carefully made up my face, blow-dried my hair and put on the black dress I'd packed just in case I ended up going anywhere smart. My trusty Docs would have to do – I had no other shoes with me except my battered Converse.

With my hair done and my legs out and dark glasses hiding most of my face, I was confident Zack wouldn't recognise me. To him, I was just Amelie's plain, frumpy older sister. He had no reason to expect to see me – no reason to expect that I was coming to get him and give him his just deserts.

My bag slung over my shoulder again, I left the apartment and headed back into Manhattan, towards Grand Central Station and the Campbell Apartment, feeling like Uma Thurman in *Kill Bill* only without the hair, the yellow jumpsuit or the legs to go with it.

TWENTY-SIX

My feeling of righteous fury lasted all the way to Grand Central Station, but as soon as I stepped through the doors of the Campbell Apartment, it vanished abruptly. It wasn't easy to feel righteously furious and like a total fish out of water at the same time, and I definitely didn't nail it.

The place was as intimidating as anywhere I'd ever been. It was full of Manhattan's most beautiful people, up there with the most beautiful in the world. Back at the Airbnb, I'd been reasonably happy with my make-up and New Look dress, but here I felt drab and dowdy. It was just like all the times when Amelie had persuaded me to meet her for somewhere fabulous for cocktails, and I was inevitably early and she was inevitably late, and I had to sit there waiting, panicking that my cocktail order would have involved some massive faux pas and it would turn out to be bright blue with a paper umbrella in it. Except then, I'd known that eventually my sister would turn up and make everything all right, and now I didn't.

I waited by the door – resisting the urge to abandon my plan and flee back to Brooklyn – and gazed around me at the room, no doubt looking like a rabbit caught in headlights. The place was gorgeous. Tall, steel-framed windows filled one wall, still bluey-bright with the last of the daylight, casting long shadows on the floor. Away from the windows, the room was dimly lit, with ranks of leather barstools lining a long counter and tables for four and eight in the rest of the space.

I panicked. I'd be sat at the counter with my back to the room, which would mean having to turn around constantly to see if Zack had arrived.

So, when the beautiful girl on the door came over to seat me, I found myself blurting out, 'Table for four, please.'

She wasn't to know I wasn't being joined by three glamorous friends. Once my bum was on the seat, they weren't exactly going to throw me out – or were they?

At least the fact that the sun hadn't yet set gave me an excuse to leave my sunglasses on. Kind of. More likely, people would think I had some kind of disfiguring eye infection.

By the time I was seated at the table, perusing the encyclopaedic cocktail menu with its eye-watering prices, I was in a right state. And the perusing turned out to be hard work, because I could barely read the menu through my dark glasses.

So, when a waiter came to take my order, I said, 'A dry martini, please.'

Great – now I wasn't just stalking Zack but channelling him by ordering his favourite drink too. Oh well, I thought, hopefully my martini order would summon him from the ether – or rather, from that glass-walled edifice in the financial district – as if I was some kind of psychic medium or something.

My drink arrived, and I apologised guiltily for the lateness of my fictitious friends, then took a large gulp. The alcohol simultaneously stripped what felt like an entire layer of cells off my throat and emboldened me. Now I wasn't just an awkward tourist sitting alone in a flash bar wearing a cheap dress, but a cocktail-sipping femme fatale.

I took another gulp, then another, then finished the complimentary bowl of olives the waiter had brought, and ordered another of each. If I kept the orders coming, I figured, they'd mind less about me hogging an entire table to myself.

And then, realising it was almost seven thirty, I focused my attention on the door. There were fewer touristy-looking people in the bar now. The ones that had been there – distinguishable from locals, I'd realised, by being either more smartly or much more casually dressed – had departed, presumably to go off to dinner or the theatre.

And now, a trickle of office workers was beginning to gather, along with a smattering of couples who looked like they were on dates. Of course, there was some crossover, like a Venn diagram: couples in business suits, both clearly having recently left their desks, but who were nonetheless sitting with their knees touching, making eye contact and giggling.

But none of them was Zack. Maybe Ross had got it wrong, and #thirstythursday changed location on a more frequent basis than monthly.

I didn't want to think about Ross just now. Just forming his name in my head filled me with a turmoil of conflicting emotions – shame, anger, guilt and something else that might have been regret.

I'd messed up. I'd misread the situation badly, and I probably owed both him and Bryony the apology of the century.

I forced my mind away from Ross and my eyes back to the door.

And then I saw Zack.

He stepped in through the glass doors, tall, handsome and confident. He still had a trace of his honeymoon tan – or maybe he'd been topping it up taking strolls in sunny Central Park while Amelie languished in their apartment alone. He was wearing a suit, dark charcoal grey with a chalky pinstripe, but no tie, and his shirt was undone to reveal a couple of inches of chest, dark hair springing through the gap. His hair looked like it had been recently cut and was swept back from his brow. Even at this distance, I could see the ice-blue of his eyes.

I thought how proud Amelie would be, walking into this fabulous place with her handsome husband; how excited she'd feel to be spending the night with him, talking, laughing, drinking, and then leaving at the end of the evening with him on her arm – *Look! I married him! He's mine!* And how proud Zack should have been, arriving with his beautiful wife who'd chosen him out of all the men in the world she could have taken her pick from. Who'd followed him across the world, leaving her friends and family behind to be by his side.

But the woman with Zack wasn't my sister. She was a tall blonde, her hair hanging poker-straight down the back of her navy-blue shift dress, held away from her face by chunky black sunglasses. She was carrying a cream-coloured leather bag and wearing nude stilettos that made her slim, tanned legs look even longer. Her face might only have been averagely pretty, but her make-up was so perfect, her Botox and fillers and whatever else so subtly done, she looked model-flawless.

My heart ached for Amelie, who was far more beautiful but not here.

I watched from behind my own sunglasses as the two of them made their way to a table on the opposite side of the room. Zack sat with his back to me, which was a relief. I waited until they'd got their drinks order in, just in case they decided to sack it off and head somewhere different, and then I turned to my phone, scrolling rapidly through Zack's LinkedIn connections to see if I could find her picture.

It didn't take long. Brooke MacIntyre, a senior analyst at Spelman Global, the same firm where Zack worked. I scrolled rapidly though her CV – an undergraduate degree from Harvard then a master's from Yale, then a string of appointments at various financial institutions before she'd arrived at

Spelman Global two years earlier, splitting her time between its offices in New York, London and Hong Kong.

The timing just about worked – that would have been shortly before Zack had met Amelie. I could just imagine it – the flirtation, the meeting of minds, the few passionate nights together before she moved on to her next location; the regretful goodbye, the promise to stay in touch. And then, for Zack, out of sight and out of mind, and my sister, equally beautiful and smart, had come along.

This was no work meeting – I was sure of that. The two of them had cocktails – dry martini for him, the twin of my own drink, and what I guessed was a dirty martini for her, cloudy with several olives skewered in its depths – and although their phones were out on the table, they were barely glancing at them. They were looking at each other – exclusively and obsessively.

Hopefully, I thought, sinking lower in my seat and adjusting my dark glasses over my eyes, that would mean they were unlikely to clock me.

I watched Brooke tilt her head back, her pale sheet of hair falling away from the razor-sharp line of her jaw, and laugh at something Zack had said. I imagined him responding, gratified his joke had landed, with a wolfish grin of pleasure. I saw her take an olive out of her drink, nibble the edge of it and pass it over to him, as if it was too delectable a morsel not to share – or possibly as if she was a woman so self-disciplined in her eating habits that consuming a whole olive would count as shameful gluttony.

Zack took the olive, nibbled a bit from the other side, then passed it back to her, fingertip to fingertip. The two of them burst out laughing, like this was a ritual they'd begun some time ago and had now honed to hilarious perfection. They carried on until there was no meat left on the stone, then Brooke fished out another and the process began again.

Honestly, that told me all I needed to know. *Who the hell sucks an olive pit that's been in someone else's mouth? That's seriously gross – unless you're cool with a level of physical intimacy that goes way beyond sharing snacks. Would I take a bite of Chiraag's half-eaten sandwich or finish Neil's leftover cereal? God, no. If Ross offered me a sip of his cappuccino, would I—* But that was neither here nor there.

This wasn't about Ross, and I wasn't here to think about him anyway.

I kept watching Zack and Brooke. They'd finished their first round of drinks and moved on to a second, and evidently the olive game was over for the evening. They were leaning in towards each other, talking, their faces so close I could see where his dark hair and her blonde tresses touched each other. And that wasn't the only thing that was touching. Their elbows were in contact on the tabletop, the backs of their hands occasionally brushing as they gestured.

But it was Brooke's eye contact that said the most – the steady, intent stare of a woman who simply didn't want to look at anyone or anything except the man opposite her. I wondered how it felt to be looked at like that; I wasn't sure I'd ever know, or wanted to find out.

I stayed there, watching them, for another half-hour, then I figured there was probably nothing more to see. I'd already found out what I'd wanted to know and seen what I'd come to see. So I asked for my bill and paid it, adding a hefty tip to the already astronomical total. Then I picked up my bag and left, going via the restroom to avoid walking past their table.

And by the time I came out, it had happened. They were kissing. Of course they were – there was nothing surprising about it at all. *Two people look at each other like Astro looks at a catnip mouse and share saliva through the medium of a bar snack, it's only a matter of time, right?*

Even so, the sight stopped me in my tracks. They were still

seated at their table, their chairs at right angles to each other, their elbows still on the tabletop, their knees still touching. Only now Zack's hand was buried deep in Brooke's hair, her fingers were hooked into the belt loop of his trousers, and their lips were interlocked in a kiss that looked like it would never end.

Like I said, I'd known it would happen. I'd been so certain I hadn't even thought I needed to stick around to witness it.

But now I had, it was as shocking as a kick to the kneecap. The man who'd promised, just months before, to love and cherish my sister – to forsake all others – was snogging the face off his beautiful blonde colleague in a bar.

I felt sick. Empty and furious and helpless. And I didn't know what to do. I couldn't go over there and confront him – what good would it do? I'd just be causing a scene in a public place. It wasn't like I could make it unhappen and everything would be okay again.

So I walked slowly to the exit and out into the dark street. It was nine o'clock. I'd got what I'd come for: to gather evidence, like the advice from the bot had said. I had done that, and now I needed to break the news to Amelie.

TWENTY-SEVEN

When I arrived at Amelie and Zack's apartment building in Chelsea, still almost hyperventilating with shock and anger, a woman was just leaving, a small white dog that looked like a series of cotton-wool balls joined together under her arm. She gave me a half-recognising smile and held the door open for me, so I smiled back and slipped into the lobby.

From a surprise point of view, good: I was going to see my sister for the first time at her door, rather than over the security video. From a time point of view, bad: I'd missed out on valuable seconds that I could have spent not having broken the news yet.

But I was here now and there was no point in delaying further. I stepped up to the lift and pressed the up button, and the doors opened immediately – bad – so I stepped in and pressed the button for the fifth floor. Seconds later, I was in front of the apartment, a blank, glossy, teal-coloured door with a brushed-steel number screwed on to its surface.

I took a deep breath, knocked and waited.

There was total silence for a few moments. The corridor was quiet and somehow sterile – there were no cooking smells; I couldn't hear any TVs playing or voices laughing. It was like being on a stage set waiting for the curtain to rise.

Then the door opened and Amelie stood there, a look of blank enquiry on her face that was immediately replaced by surprise and then delight.

She squealed and hopped and flung her arms round me and hugged me so tight the breath whooshed out of my lungs. She smelled different – presumably some fancy new American shampoo she'd starting using. She felt thinner than usual, her shoulders almost frail under the free hand I used to return her hug.

'Oh my God. Lucy. It's actually you. Is this real?'

I said, 'I thought I'd surprise you.'

'You have. Oh my God, it's the best surprise ever. How did you find out the address? Did you ask Zack?'

Shit. I wasn't ready to tell her I'd just seen her husband – not yet. 'I asked Mum. I didn't want him to know I was here either.'

That at least was true. But her excitement made me feel like the biggest fraud ever.

'Come in. Let me show you our flat.'

She let me go, then changed her mind and hugged me again before letting go properly, turning round and leading me into the hallway. She was wearing stone-coloured yoga pants and a cropped cream jumper with overlong sleeves that almost covered her hands. In the gap between the trousers and the top I could see the knobbly ridge of her spine. Her hair was damp, piled on her head with a scrunchie, and she wasn't wearing any make-up. Her skin was pale and there were dark circles under her eyes.

Still, she shone with pleasure at seeing me. I wondered how long that would last.

'So, here's the kitchen,' she said. 'It's just one end of the lounge, really, like you saw in the photos. Come on and I'll show you the rest.'

The blinds were closed so the apartment was shadowy, but Amelie did something with a remote control and they whooshed up, revealing a view of another glass building opposite and the black, skeletal shapes of trees against the navy sky.

'They're all the same, I imagine,' she said. 'I mean, not down to the cushions and things like that, but essentially, it's like a filing cabinet for expats. Or like being in *Married at First Sight*. Here's the bathroom – all the towels and everything were here when we moved in, it was so weird. And that's the bedroom but I can't show you because it's a total pigsty. But look at the amazing storage in the hallway – all the cleaning stuff and the ironing board and everything just vanishes behind these sliding doors, and that's where you keep your coats and things in winter, isn't it genius?'

'Amazing,' I enthused, my stomach feeling heavier and heavier by the minute.

'Have you eaten? I had a salad earlier and I've got nothing in. But there's wine? Or water?'

'Water would be great.'

She poured two glasses from a filtered jug and handed me one. Then we sat down next to each other on the sofa, and I realised that now I had no choice but to tell her why I was there.

'So, how are things?' I began. 'You look...' She looked tired, drawn and too thin, and I was worried. But I wasn't going to jump right in and say that. 'You look like you've really settled in here. Tell me all about everything.'

Amelie shrugged, taking a sip from her water glass.

'There was nothing to do really,' she said. 'I mean, I was all excited about going to Crate, Bath and Barrel or whatever it's called and picking stuff for the flat and making it all homey, and even having some of our things taken out of storage and shipped over, but it was all here. Literally every last pillowcase. So it's been a bit of a letdown on that front.'

'But what about the other fronts?' I pressed. 'How's Zack? What's being married like?'

'Honestly, it's pretty much the same as not being married.' She returned her glass to the coffee table and gnawed at a ragged cuticle for a second. 'Only we see even less of each other. Zack only ever gets home at stupid o'clock, and after the first week I gave up waiting for him and started going to bed. I've been so fucking tired. But he says that's what it's like here – everyone works long hours and if you don't, you look like a slacker, so...'

Yeah, Zack, I thought, *a slacker's exactly what you looked like earlier, snogging your colleague in a bar. A sleazy, cheating, rat-faced slacker.*

'Why've you been so knackered?' I asked. 'Are you over that stomach bug thing you had?'

She looked down at her hands and half-shrugged. 'Kind of. Mostly. But tell me about you, come on, Lucy. What made you decide to come out here on your own? I can't believe you did. Who's looking after Astro?'

'Ro— A colleague. He lives really close by so it's no bother for him.'

'Are you sure he works in online journalism and isn't actually a fully qualified vet?' Amelie teased. 'You must really rate the guy to trust him with your cat. But anyway, how's work going? How's being Adam? Do you know absolutely everything about the male psyche now?'

Here it was – the opening I'd been searching for. I needed to take it, right now, otherwise my sister and I would still be making chitchat about bed linen and cat-sitters in half an hour, and I wouldn't have told her what was going on or found out what was wrong with her.

'So here's the thing, Am.' I took a big gulp of water. 'The

Adam column's been going really well. I've discovered this amazing hack, which I'll tell you all about some other time. But Adam got – I got – an email last week that was kind of different from all the others.'

'Different how? Did it say, "I've realised I've been a dick to women all my life and that's why I can't sustain a satisfying and meaningful relationship. Tell me how to be better"?'

I laughed. 'Nope, haven't had that one yet. But it was weird, and I think you'll get why I thought so. Hold on, I'm going to read it to you.'

Amelie watched, her face curious but unconcerned, as I rummaged in my bag for my phone and then rummaged through my phone until I found the letter from Adam's anonymous correspondent.

I started reading it aloud. When I got to the bit about the Porsche, a little smile flickered on her face – *That's the same car as Zack's got*. Then the smile disappeared at the mention of moving to a city his wife didn't know well, and was replaced by a frown when I read the words 'putting in the hours'. When I reached the bit about the wife being clingy and needy, Amelie had started gnawing her cuticle again, so I stopped reading.

She tilted her head like she was waiting for me to go on, then when I didn't, she said slowly, 'So let me get this straight. You had a letter from a guy who sounded a bit like Zack, and he thinks his marriage might be going tits up, so you came out here to tell me I need to get my shit together or Zack's going to get fed up with me?'

'No!' I was appalled at how badly she'd misunderstood – how badly I'd handled things so far. 'It's not that. It's... The thing is, Am – and I don't want to read you the next bit so please don't make me – he goes on to say he's back in touch with an ex-girlfriend at work and he thinks he might still have feelings for her, and I really didn't want that to happen to you.'

Her face had gone all still now. 'So you came out here to tell me to get my shit together or Zack'll fuck another woman?'

'Amelie, no. Honestly. I... By the time I'd finished reading that, I was about ninety-nine per cent sure that the guy writing the letter was Zack. And I was really, really worried. Not that you were doing anything wrong, because you're not, but that he was – or was about to. So I... I mean, the advice Adam gave was to support you, so here I am. And also to find out whether my suspicions about what he was getting up to were correct or not, and I thought that the best way to do that would be to come over and see you. So – you know – here I am.'

'I see.'

I saw, too. I saw that this wasn't landing a bit well. I wished I knew how to backtrack and explain properly, but I didn't.

'So you thought you'd come and ask me if I think my husband's having an affair?'

'No, I—' *Don't mention the bloody sleuthing, Lucy. Not now.* 'Well, do you, Am? I mean, if you think about what that guy wrote to Adam, does that sound to you like something Zack might write?'

Her face was still all stony and her voice was cold. She didn't even look – or sound – like my sister at that point. 'Zack has many colleagues he works closely with. Some of them he's worked closely with in the past. He's probably dated at least one of them. So circumstantially, if you wanted to make the fact fit your pet theory, you probably could.'

I really, really wished I could turn this around – or, even better, turn around myself, walk out of the door, go downstairs, press the buzzer and try again from the beginning.

As gently as I could, I said, 'Am, I'm so sorry. I'm messing this up. I love you. I came here because I love you and I was worried about you. And now I know I was right to worry. It's not just about Zack – what he is or isn't doing. It's about you. You seem sad. You said you were homesick. You've lost weight.

If there's something wrong, please talk to me. Forget about Adam. I'm your sister and I'll do absolutely anything to make you feel better.'

At last, the rigid mask that Amelie's face had become seemed to crack, then dissolve. She made a sound that started out as a croak and turned into a wail, and then she buried her head in her hands and burst into tears. I scooted across the sofa and hugged her tight, stroking her back and shushing her until the first flood of sobs started to ease off. Then I dashed into the bathroom and brought back a fancy, gold-foiled cube of tissues and put them on the sofa between us, and held one of her hands while she mopped her eyes with the other.

'What's wrong?' I asked. 'Please tell me. Whatever it is, it can't be that bad.'

Amelie looked at me, her eyes all red and damp and her mouth turned down like the sad-face emoji. 'I'm having a baby.'

My heart soared and then immediately plummeted again. This was the best news – but it had come at the worst possible time.

'Am! You're pregnant! No way! I mean, that's... You do want to be, right? You've always wanted babies.'

'I do,' she said. 'Like, yeah, I've always wanted kids. But maybe not right now. Not here. God, Luce, I've been so fucking sick you wouldn't believe. I've been puking twenty-four seven. That's why I've hardly left the apartment. And I've been so lonely. And I haven't told Zack yet because I wanted telling him to be a happy thing, and right now I feel so awful I don't know if I even want to keep it. I mean, if I feel as sick as this, does it mean there's something wrong?'

'Of course it doesn't mean there's something wrong! I'm not a fricking midwife, but come on. Look at the Princess of Wales – sick as a dog all through her pregnancies and her kids are fine. Have you seen anyone?'

She shook her head. 'Our health insurance is through Zack's

work and I haven't got the details and I didn't want to ask him because... you know.'

'But you were being sick the whole time! Surely he'd want you to see a doctor? In case you'd picked up some rare tropical disease on honeymoon, like you told me.'

'I'm not so bad when he's here. It's in the mornings mostly and he's already left for work. And the afternoons, if I'm honest. And by the time he gets in at night, like I said, I'm in bed already. That's the only time it stops. So he knows I haven't been well but he doesn't know it's been this bad.'

'Do you know how far along you are?'

'I think it must've happened on honeymoon, so, what – two and a bit months? I wanted to tell him properly, with like balloons or something, and make it all special. But how could I do that when I'm feeling so vile and wishing it wasn't happening?'

Shit. Shit shit shit. How on earth, knowing this, could I tell her the full extent of what I knew about Zack?

I said, 'I really think you need to get checked out. Tell Zack about the spewing – you don't have to tell him about the baby, although if he's got any sense, he'll work it out. Ask for your health insurance card or whatever you need. Find out who you need to see. I'll come with you, if you want. It'll be okay.'

And then we can work out what to do about Brooke bloody MacIntyre.

'You're right,' she said. 'I do need to talk to him. I've honestly just been feeling so awful and sad, I haven't been able to think straight. I'll ask him tonight and I'll google how you get to see a doctor here, and we can go tomorrow.'

'That sounds like a great plan. And maybe you and I can go out tomorrow, if you're feeling up for it, just for a bit of a walk or whatever.'

Amelie was feeling stronger, more herself. We had a plan.

That was what mattered – the rest could all wait. Relief washed through me: I'd done the right thing, coming here. I was here for my sister. And then it all went pear-shaped.

Amelie said, 'Hang on. You said, back then, about finding out if your suspicions were correct. What suspicions, exactly?'

'Just... You know. The letter. The colleague. It doesn't matter really.'

'It does matter. When did you get to New York? What've you been doing?'

'Um... couple of days ago. Just sightseeing, really.'

'Luce. You've been here a couple of days and you only came to see me today? Why?'

My tongue felt like it was tying itself in knots. Lying to Mum to get Amelie's address – I'd told her I wanted to send her flowers – had been bad enough; lying to Amelie was impossible. I was right when I'd observed that she was more herself – the take-no-prisoners Amelie was, if not back, a whole lot nearer to the surface than she'd been when I'd arrived at the apartment.

'You know... what the advice said, about seeing if it was true, what the letter said. If it was Zack who wrote it. But it wasn't, obviously.'

'Why obviously?'

'Because you trust him. He's your husband. And you're having a—'

'Lucy. Me being pregnant changes the future, but it doesn't change the past. If Zack was cheating on me, me being up the duff wouldn't make him uncheat. And besides, that's not what you said when you walked in here. You came out to New York to find out if what you were worried about was true, didn't you? Not just to see me.'

'Well, I—'

'And it took you two days to get in touch. Therefore, you were busy doing other stuff. Like stalking Zack. Weren't you?'

I felt like a specimen in biology class, pinned between two sheets of glass, a microscope trained on me. Amelie's pregnancy was a surprise – a surprise I wanted to welcome, but wasn't sure I could. It changed things, but it also made me realise how totally ill-prepared I'd been for this encounter with her. I'd imagined coming to the flat, all guns blazing with righteous indignation, breaking the news of Zack's infidelity to Amelie and then... what?

Now that I was actually here, I could barely recall what I'd expected to happen. That she'd react with gratitude towards me and fury towards Zack, and I'd whisk her away, rescuing her from a future with a liar and a cheat who she couldn't possibly still love now that she knew the truth.

But now, I realised that what I wanted – perhaps even my duty, as her sister – was to protect her from the truth. Except she wasn't going to let me do that.

'What did you do?' Amelie pressed remorselessly on. 'Did you hack his phone or something?'

'No, of course I didn't.' It was a denial, and an honest one – but as soon as I said it, I realised it was an admission of something else.

'So you followed him. You figured it out, like one of your lateral-thinking puzzles. My sister, the clever one. Let me guess – you went to his work and you couldn't get in, because the security's so tight. So you looked on his social media to see where he'd be going after work, and you went there. The Campbell, right? That's where he's been the past couple of Thursday nights.'

Amelie's voice wasn't raised, but I could see she was blazing angry. I felt helpless, ashamed and afraid – what had I started? Why the hell hadn't I thought this through? Why hadn't I stayed in London with my cat and left Amelie to work out for herself what was going on, and been there to pick up the pieces afterwards? Then, at least, her anger would have been directed at Zack instead of misdirected at me.

She was going to get the full story out of me, whether I liked it or not. So, I figured, at least I could try and tell it my way – try and minimise the fallout.

'Okay,' I said. 'You're right. That's exactly what I did. Maybe it was the wrong thing to do, but it was what Adam said to do and I didn't have a better plan. I went there and I waited for him and eventually he turned up.'

'He turned up with a woman?'

I nodded miserably.

'Who? Don't tell me you don't know, because you do.'

'Brooke MacIntyre,' I muttered.

'Right. And what happened?'

'Nothing,' I lied desperately. 'Well, hardly anything. They had a couple of drinks. They looked like they were friends. Having a good time, you know? I watched them for a bit then I left.'

Amelie shook her head and folded her arms, her hands buried deep in the sleeves of her jumper. 'Does not compute. They kissed, didn't they? Or she was all over him like a rash. Or they left together, or something. If you hadn't seen anything, you wouldn't be giving me chapter and verse of this letter that whoever it was wrote to Adam.'

'Okay. They kissed. I saw them. Amelie, it was probably nothing. It was probably just—'

'And what's this about following Adam's advice, anyway? You are Adam. You decide what advice he gives. It was you telling yourself that the right thing to do was come out here and stalk my husband.'

'It wasn't!' I blurted out. 'It was the bot. The AI Adam.'

'The what?'

'I've been using one of those generative chat things, GenBot

2.0, to help with problems when I'm stuck,' I said. 'Just to give me ideas. Because I kind of understand men a bit now, but sometimes I think I still don't understand them at all. So I don't always know how to answer their questions. You know that. That's why I needed your help. But then when you couldn't help any more, I had to find another way, and that was it.'

'So let's get this straight.' Amelie fixed me with her clear, hazel stare. Her eyes were still red from crying and it made the irises look brighter, almost green by contrast. I could feel my own eyes beginning to sting with tears, and I wondered if they looked a different colour from usual, too. 'You've just blown my marriage apart on the basis of some AI-generated nonsense. You're telling me I need to leave the father of my child because of fucking GenBot. Nice work, Lucy.'

'I'm not telling you that you need to leave him,' I protested. But it was hopeless. There was no point trying to justify what I'd done, or convince Amelie that she needed to focus her anger on Zack, or Brooke, or anyone but me.

'Damn right, you don't understand men,' she went on. 'Or you'd know that this stuff happens. It doesn't mean anything. Once I tell him about the baby, he'll kick this Brooke to the kerb so fast she won't know what's hit her. I'll see to that. I might never forget it, but I'll probably forgive him, if he begs hard enough.'

'But what about...?'

'You?' She shrugged, a weary movement of her thin shoulders under the cream cashmere. 'I don't know, Lucy. You've done enough damage for the time being, don't you think? You should probably go.'

'Amelie, please. I'm sorry. I didn't want to damage anything. Forget I ever came. Forget I ever saw anything.'

She looked at me coldly and got to her feet. 'Don't be stupid. How can I ever forget this?'

I stood, too, desperately reaching out to hug her, but she

shifted away like she was made of smoke, and my arms closed around nothing.

'Goodbye, Lucy,' she said.

Blinded by tears, I turned and left the apartment. By the time I made it out into the street, I was sobbing so hard it felt like I'd never stop.

TWENTY-EIGHT

All the way back to Brooklyn, my mind refused to allow me to think clearly about what had just happened – how badly everything had gone wrong. What an utter, clumsy fool I'd been. I should have talked to Amelie first, before embarking on my stupid espionage campaign. Or I could have talked to Zack, long ago, when I was first worried about her, and perhaps he would have listened, spent more time with her, given her the opportunity to tell him she was pregnant.

And then not snogged his ex. For fuck's sake.

In spite of the horrible weight of guilt I was feeling, I was aware that, however idiotic I'd been, however badly I'd mishandled the situation, ultimately Zack was to blame for this, not me. I'd been rash and foolish; he'd cheated on his wife. I'd come rushing out to help my sister without thinking through the possible consequences; he'd abandoned her in an unfamiliar city while she was homesick and vulnerable.

But that didn't change the outcome. My sister wasn't talking to me, and it felt as if she might never forgive me.

We'd had rows before, of course, like all sisters do. But never one as awful as this. The epic fallout of 2018 when I'd borrowed her Fenty Beauty lipstick to wear to a festival and it had melted in my handbag was nothing in comparison. The night before my A-level maths exam when she'd come home late from a party and stayed up until four in the morning playing music and chatting to her friends and I'd called her a selfish bitch seemed like a minor tiff next to this.

This felt terminal, and I didn't know what to do. I couldn't ask the AI version of Adam, because I no longer felt like I trusted it after the mess it had landed me in. I couldn't confide in Ross, because after what had happened in Katz's Deli, he must have suspected that I had feelings for him that he could never reciprocate.

I should have known better. I should have known that I wasn't cut out to be the cool girl, the sexy, daring girl. If Kieren had taught me one thing, it was that.

The relationship – thing, situationship, whatever it was – between us had lasted six months. A whole half a year. After the second time in the office, he acted totally normal. Again, there was no note under my keyboard the next day. But this time, I wasn't tortured by doubt about having done something wrong – and I was no longer worried that it wouldn't happen again.

And it did. The following week, when we'd been working late on a deadline, he did message me – a brief note over email asking me to stay late with him.

I'd replied with just one word – yes. A small word, but it had meant more than that; it had signalled a willingness to continue doing what we'd been doing. And we did continue. A handful of times, I went back with him to his flat after work – but not often. Mostly, we had sex in the office. It made me cringe, now, to remember it, but at the time it had felt illicit, thrilling, powerful. *He must really want me*, I'd rationalised to myself, *to take such risks*.

Because it was risky. Mostly, it happened in the office after everyone had gone home – on the sofa in reception, in a meeting room, on his desk chair. But sometimes it would be the middle of the day when he summoned me with an email, or his eyes, or just a few words. And then it was in the stationery cupboard.

I knew it was wrong; I knew it was stupid and dangerous. But I didn't know how to stop it, and part of me didn't want to stop it. For the first time in my life, I was the sexy girl, the girl a man couldn't keep his hands off, the girl with the power to ignite desire.

But, increasingly, it didn't feel right. I believed no one at work knew – certainly, I hadn't told anyone. But as the days began to grow longer and winter felt like it was finally drawing to a close, I did tell my sister. We were round at our parents' place for Sunday lunch, and while we were stacking the dishwasher I leaned in and whispered, 'So, I've kind of been seeing someone.'

'Seeing someone? Like, a man?'

I nodded.

'Seeing like as in having sex?'

'Yes.'

'Ooooh! Who is he?'

I told her. His name was Kieren, we worked together, he was a journalist. I bigged up his attractiveness, although the qualities I admired – his lean jawline, his incisive writing style, his air of being a slightly tortured soul – were attributes I knew my sister would totally not see the point of.

'So when do I get to meet him?' she asked.

'I don't know. We've kind of...' *We've never actually been out. Not together, as a couple.*

But I couldn't bring myself to admit that to my sister – I knew what her reaction would be. *You what? Like, never? Luce, that's not seeing someone, that's being someone's booty call.*

As soon as I imagined her words in my head, I shut them off. More than that – I rewound the tape and erased them.

'Luce? You've kind of what?'

'It's tricky,' I said, 'because of work, and me being still in my probation period, and him being older and a section editor. I don't think he wants people in the office to know.'

Amelie raised one of her carefully shaped eyebrows. 'Okaaay. Fair enough. Although, to be honest, Luce, I'd question whether, if he doesn't want people to know he's doing something, he should be doing it in the first place.'

'It's not like that! I don't report to him or anything. And I'm not doing anything I don't want to do.'

'Cool,' Amelie said. 'So if he doesn't want people at work to know, how about people not at work? You're coming to my birthday drinks next month, right? Why not ask him along?'

The idea of Kieren surrounded by Amelie's friends was almost impossible to imagine, but there was no way I could tell my sister that.

'Okay,' I said, although I felt far from certain. 'I'll ask him.'

More than a week passed before I could find the courage – a week in which I was barely alone with him, anyway. Finally, the next Monday evening, I got my chance. I was in the kitchen, rinsing coffee mugs and scooping up used teabags, when Kieren walked past, his bag slung over his shoulder.

'Knocking-off time,' he said casually. 'You coming?'

'I... Yes. Just a second, I need to finish in here and get my things.'

He nodded. 'See you downstairs.'

So this would be one of the nights when I went to his flat – almost a luxury, compared to our hurried, furtive encounters in the office. By now, I knew the ritual. The Tube journey, the walk to his house, the climb up the stairs, the glass of wine, the sex. I resisted the urge to mention anything about my sister or her birthday until afterwards – then, I'd learned, Kieren was at his most mellow. So I waited. I'd never been eager for sex with him to finish before, but that day I was. Rather than wanting the intimacy we had to last as long as possible, I was eager for a different kind of closeness.

'Kieren?' I said, as soon as I dared, just as I was feeling him easing his body away from mine.

'Mmmm?'

'What are you doing next weekend?'

'Doing?' he laughed. 'Same as I always do. Pub on Friday, football with the lads on Saturday. Getting over my hangover on Sunday. Why?'

'It's my sister's birthday and she's having a party on Saturday night. Do you want to come?' The words came out in a rush, before I could reconsider them.

Now he did push me away, but not roughly. He sort of turned me around and held me at arm's length, looking at me.

'Do I want to come to your sister's birthday party?' he echoed.

I nodded, feeling a dark foreshadowing of what was to come, wishing I could unsay what I'd said and go back to how things had been a few seconds before.

'Is that what you think this is?' he asked. 'The kind of thing where I meet your family and buy you flowers and in a year or so we shack up and have a couple of kids?'

'No! I never thought that. I just thought…'

'Lucy.' I remembered how it had made me feel the first time he said my name, how it had felt when he called me princess. I didn't feel that way now. 'I thought you understood. This was never going to be a boyfriend-girlfriend thing. I thought you were on the same page as me. I don't want a woman. I've my career to think about. I don't have time for that. But I enjoy the occasional fuck. I thought that was what you wanted, too.'

'I do.' My tone was almost wheedling. 'But I thought we could see each other sometimes, too.'

'Well, we can't. Jesus. A girl like you, I thought you'd be grateful for what you could get. Seems I was wrong.'

'I am grateful' – *Well, you shouldn't be!* screamed the voice I'd been ignoring, outraged – 'I just wanted...'

'More. Well, you're not getting it. It's this or nothing – take your pick.'

To my shame, I heard myself say, 'It's okay. Forget I said anything. We can carry on as we are.'

His hands released their grip on my shoulders and he sat up. 'I don't think so. This isn't what you're after – you've made that clear. It's enough, now, before you get yourself pregnant or something and try to trap me that way.'

I was so appalled and stung by his words I was unable to come out with any of my own. My face flaming, I struggled into my clothes and left, without saying goodbye. Somehow, I made my way home, and it was only once the door was closed behind me that I allowed myself to start crying.

And now here I was, back in my Brooklyn Airbnb, once again returning home in tears. I flung myself down on the bed, my whole body limp with shock and fatigue. I didn't think I'd be able to fall asleep, but somehow I did – only to jerk awake again a few hours later, my heart hammering in panic.

I had a deadline. I was meant to have filed an Ask Adam column the previous day, and I'd completely forgotten about it. It would be the start of a working day in London now. If the subs hadn't already gone to Greg and asked when they could expect to receive my copy, they'd be doing so any moment.

And I still hadn't picked out a question to respond to, never mind written Adam's carefully considered response.

I sat bolt-upright in bed and switched on the light, all prospect of sleep now vanished. Greg had been generous enough to allow me to work remotely from New York on the basis of the personal crisis involving my sister, which I'd explained to him as thoroughly as I could while omitting as much detail as I could get away with.

By missing my deadline, I'd not only be putting my career in jeopardy but also taking advantage of his kindness, and there was no way I wanted either of those things to happen.

If you get the sack, you'll never see Ross again. The thought turned up unbidden.

It would probably be no bad thing, the other part of my mind argued back. *And anyway, you might crack an invite to his and Bryony's wedding, so you'd get to see him then.*

Shut up! You're no help.

But actually, my internal conflict reminded me that I had a lifeline. I'd posted the problem Adam had received from the anonymous correspondent I felt sure was Zack into GenBot 2.0, just a couple of days before. I remembered arguing with the bot, trying to make it see my side of the story and change its normal diplomatic response to something that more closely reflected my own indignation about what Zack – if it even was Zack – was planning on doing.

And now I knew he wasn't just planning – he was actually doing it. I'd seen him kissing Brooke. If I was absolutely sure that Anonymous was Zack, I'd feel obliged to have Adam tell him exactly what I thought. But I wasn't sure; it was only a suspicion, albeit a pretty cast-iron one.

That didn't matter, though. What mattered was that I had a duty and a deadline. It was time to put my feelings second and my career first, not time to burden my colleagues with additional stress because I wanted to tell some man who might or might not be my brother-in-law what I really thought of his actions.

So, frantic with haste, I opened my laptop and navigated to the tab where GenBot 2.0 was still open, the text I'd pasted into it still waiting there in the usual field.

I'd read the reply. I knew it was adequate. Not particularly hard-hitting and probably a bit overlong, but the subs would take care of that – it was their job to make the copy fit the allocated space, and they always needed to give everyone's work a fairly robust edit anyway.

I selected the text in the window, opened a new document and pasted it in. I added the usual identifying copy at the top – Ask Adam, my name and the date – scrolled down and typed [ENDS] at the bottom.

Then I saved the file, navigated to my email and attached the document to a new message, addressing it to the chief sub and copying Greg, with a quick note apologising for my lateness and explaining that I'd been confused by the time difference.

Then I pressed Send, closed my laptop and turned out the light. To my surprise, I fell asleep almost immediately.

When I woke the next morning, I felt strangely calm. I was still in New York – still in the same city as my sister. Perhaps she'd be able to see reason, once she'd had a chance to calm down. And if not, I'd keep messaging her, trying to FaceTime her, assuring her that whatever happened I'd always be there for her. I wouldn't let her feel like I'd abandoned her, or that I wouldn't forgive her for the things she'd said to me.

I just needed her to forgive me.

And I needed to tell her friends – who were worried about her too – that I'd seen her. Not about the baby – that wasn't my news to share. But I'd say I was here, that Amelie hadn't been well and was feeling better, and leave it to them to contact her too, make her feel supported and loved and not so far away.

I needed to try and forget about having made a fool of myself in front of Ross and accept that there was nothing more than friendship between him and me – never had been and never would.

I tapped through to WhatsApp and saw a couple of messages from Ross, which I only glanced at. Astro was okay.

He wondered whether I was okay, and why I hadn't been in touch.

Why do you think? Maybe because I'm not in a hurry to make a twat of myself over a man again, I thought.

I had a message from Nush, too, but I didn't read it – she was most likely wanting to check whether I'd spoken to Amelie, and I could update her along with all the others. So I opened the hen night group for the first time since I'd muted it months before.

Lately, it had been busy. Rosa had had a housewarming, Caitlin had got a new job, Eve had got a new tattoo. They'd all been out to celebrate these three things, and presumably it was then that they'd discussed their shared worries about Amelie, because the only mentions of her on the thread were bright and breezy @s, followed by *Wish you were here!*, *Miss you, babe!* and *Thinking of you always!*, all festooned with heart emojis in various stages of brokenness.

The latest social event appeared to have been Nush's birthday – cocktails followed by dinner at a Soho restaurant so on-trend even I had heard of it, followed by more cocktails somewhere else. Evidently, judging by the pictures of bacon sandwiches and glasses of squash that followed the next day, a good time had been had by all.

Especially one person. A post caught my eye and I stopped scrolling, then I scrolled slowly up again to try and make sense of it all. The birthday celebration had taken place last night, the evening I'd seen Zack and Brooke together. And the post-mortem had begun several hours previously, owing to the time difference.

NUSH:

OMG I am dying. Legit dead. Thank God clever sober me booked a day's holiday from work. I'm planning to leave my bed only to spew.

BRYONY:

I'm on the train to arsing Swindon for a shoot. Kill me now. Why did none of you bitches remind me of this when we ordered those mezcal margaritas at one in the fricking morning?

EVE:

We could have reminded you, but then you got kind of... busy.

NUSH:

Yes, you were otherwise occupied for the rest of the evening, weren't you, snogging girl?

ROSA:

Another night out, another hangover, another set of pics on my phone of Bryony's head practically disappearing down some random's throat, lol.

NUSH:

I don't know how you do it, babe. It's quite impressive actually. One minute we're having a perfectly normal night, the next – BAM, snog alert.

EVE:

At least this one was hot, not like the one last week. You seriously had your beer goggles on that time, chica.

BRYONY:

Was he hot? I actually can't remember. Oh well, go me, I guess.

But what about Ross? I thought, torn between fascination and outrage.

NUSH:

What about that Ross bloke you were seeing, anyway?

As if she'd read my thoughts, a whole seven hours before I'd thought them.

BRYONY:

Yeah, him, ahahaha. I suppose it's not ideal, is it? Three nights out in a row I've ended up kissing some other bloke. Do you think it's a signal from the universe?

EVE:

I mean, you do you. It's not as if you're married to the guy, right?

NUSH:

No, obviously. But if you're going round hooking up with randoms every time you leave the house, it's got to tell you something, right? I'm no relationship expert, but maybe you might just be trying to tell yourself something?

BRYONY:

Tell myself what? That Ross isn't that into me? I already know that. Hence the snogging, I suppose.

EVE:

Oh, babe. You never said! We thought it was going so well.

BRYONY:

Yeah, well. Denial's not just a river in Egypt, right? He's nice and everything, but whenever I've tried to have the exclusive talk he's got all weird on me and said he's not sure he's ready for a relationship. So I'm like, fine, you don't want to be exclusive, I won't be exclusive, and I'll snog whoever I like when I'm out.

NUSH:

Aw, mate. Maybe you're right – that's 'just not that into you' vibes right there. And maybe you're not that into him either…?

BRYONY:

I was, honest. Or I thought I was. But you know, you can't carry on flogging a dead horse. And besides, Charlie, the dude from last night, has already messaged me, so…

EVE:

Time to move on? One door closes…

BRYONY:

I guess. Is dumping someone by text still not cool?

NUSH:

It's been cool for ages. Do keep up. So long as you're not actually ghosting him after he asked you to marry him, you're all good AFAIAC.

ROSA:

Do it now. Quick and relatively painless.

BRYONY:

I would, but we're just pulling into fucking Swindon. Love you guys, feel better.

My relief was so overwhelming I forgot all about telling them that I'd seen my sister or even where I was. I barely knew where I was myself. Okay, I'd acted like an idiot over Ross. But at least he wasn't Bryony's boyfriend any more; at least the only person I'd betrayed and let down in that situation had been myself. My head felt as light as a balloon, as if it was going to float right off my body and out of the window into the bright morning.

TWENTY-NINE

For a few minutes, I just sat there on my bed, staring blankly at my phone. I felt as if the whole landscape of my life had shifted seismically since I'd woken up that morning – like I was standing on my head.

I'd thought I'd be able to go charging to Amelie's rescue and be greeted with gratitude and relief for my revelations about Zack. Instead, my sister was furious with me – and it mattered even more than I could have imagined, because now I was going to be an aunt. I'd thought I could finally abandon my crush – there, I said it – on Ross, because I'd forced myself to accept that it would only ever be a one-way street.

But now Ross wasn't taken any more. Bryony had seen to that; she'd simply, independently realised that not only was he not that into her, but she wasn't that into him, and she had taken decisive action to check out.

As for how I'd messed things up with him... well, unfortunately there was no squaring that circle, or not quite. I still felt totally cringy about what I'd done, but just enough time had passed for me to realise that he might not have seen it in quite the same way. For him, it might just have been a bit of fun – a joking way to play up the fact that I was in an iconic New York location, one that just about anyone would associate with that cheesy old movie scene. He wasn't to know that I'd been used and humiliated by a man I'd worked with before, and how violently and instantly I'd regretted what I'd done, once the initial impulsive urge to show off to him had passed.

Perhaps he—

But my thoughts were interrupted by the vibration of my phone in my hand. Even though I'd been staring fixedly at it, I was so startled I almost dropped the thing, like it had turned into a wasp and was about to sting the hell out of me. And when I saw Ross's name on the screen, I did drop it.

'Shit!' On hands and knees, I scrabbled on the ground, my hands suddenly slippery with sweat and clumsy with surprise. I'd been ignoring Ross's messages since the day before, but I was desperate not to miss his call now.

'Hello?' I gasped, my phone at last securely in my hand, although I was still on all fours.

'Lucy? Are you okay?' His voice sounded just the same as usual, relaxed and friendly.

'Yes. Yes, I'm fine.'

'Where are you?'

'I'm still in New York, obviously. I... Things with Amelie... I'll explain another time. Is Astro okay?'

'He's fine.' Ross's voice didn't sound quite so relaxed any more, but uncertain, almost nervous. 'Uh... where in New York, exactly?'

'Brooklyn. The Airbnb we found. I've only just woken up. Why?'

'Because... Lucy, please don't be mad at me. But I'm here, too. Can we meet up?'

'You what?' Ross was here? How? Why? What about work? And what about my cat?

'I'll explain everything,' he said. 'I know it's a bit of a

surprise. Please don't worry about Astro. But I'd like to see you, if you're free?'

Well, I was certainly nothing other than free. I had no Zack to stalk any longer; there was no hanging out with Amelie to do. Apart from filing another Ask Adam column, checking out of my Airbnb and catching a flight home, I was pretty much done with my visit here.

'I guess.' My own voice sounded just as uncertain as his had done.

'Can you meet me downtown? At the 9/11 Memorial Glade, in maybe an hour?'

I looked at my watch. It was just coming up to eleven; I'd been so lost in thought I'd barely realised that the sun was high overhead, beating down on the city like a grill element. I wouldn't have time to put on make-up or even wash my hair if I was to get to downtown Manhattan in an hour.

But why did that even matter? It was only Ross. Although apparently some new version of Ross who could bend the space-time continuum and be in two places at once: the place where he was meant to be and the place where he apparently was.

'Lucy? You still there?'

'Yes. Yes, I'm here. The Memorial Glade at noon? Sure. I can be there.'

'Great. I'll see you there. Don't worry, okay? Everything's cool.'

He ended the call and I showered and dressed at lightning speed, put my phone in my bag and hurried to the subway, my head feeling oddly disconnected from my body. I felt like I knew the route now, but I wasn't concentrating and realised too late that I'd got off at the wrong stop, and I had to use my phone to help me navigate. It was like one of those dreams where you need to be somewhere important but you get on the Tube going in the wrong direction and then you realise you've suddenly ended up in your sixth-form classroom and you've forgotten to put on any clothes.

But eventually, I found myself back on track, walking slowly towards the site I'd noticed during my day of sightseeing. Then, it had been quiet, only bustling commuters and a few tourists like myself passing through. Today, though, the space was busy – throngs of people moving slowly through the surrounding streets in little clusters, in pairs and alone.

But strangely, they weren't behaving like tourists. There was no laughter. There was conversation, but it was hushed. No one was slurping soda from take-out cups or scooping noodles from bowls with chopsticks. In spite of the crowd, there was a sense of reverence – like being in church.

I felt as if a cloud had passed over the sun, although the sky was clear and the day was hot. The sound of my own boots on the pavement seemed inappropriately loud, and I slowed my pace. Then the rhythm of my breath seemed too noisy, so I tried to still that.

I hadn't been to the Glade when I'd visited before – I'd barely been aware it existed. But my phone told me it was a separate memorial, a site dedicated not to the people who had died in the attacks on the World Trade Center, but to those who had been involved in the rescue operation, the firefighters and medics and municipal workers who had toiled over a period of years to remove debris of all sorts from the ruins of the buildings.

There was no debris now, no clouds of dust or heaps of ruined construction materials. There was only a spacious, serene square, lined with trees, half a dozen huge slabs of rock positioned around it.

I walked in slowly, matching my pace to that of the people surrounding me. It wasn't midday yet; I didn't need to rush, and hurrying would have felt inappropriate and disrespectful. I wished I'd brought flowers to lay alongside those that were already arranged around and on top of the stones, but I wondered if that would have been disrespectful too – I had no connection to this place and the tragedy associated with it.

And then I saw Ross. He was standing alone by one of the stones, his arms folded across his chest. He was wearing jeans and an open-necked, washed-out blue shirt. Sunglasses covered his eyes. Although I was some distance away, I spotted him immediately and I wondered how on earth I'd ever thought he was middling or ordinary to look at.

I mean, objectively, he was. Just another tallish, leanish young guy in a crowd of people. But to me he looked like a movie star. The clean line of his jaw, the sunlight glinting on his hair, the way his face was half-smiling even in repose, like he was remembering something that made him happy. Even standing still, there was a grace about him, an air of calm that seemed to dampen the murmur of the voices around me and the hum of the city beyond into silence.

He looked like the lead singer of some indie band posing for an album cover, alone in a strange city, thinking his thoughts and nursing his problems. Looking at him, I felt a moment of pure joy – *There you are!* – before struggling to recover my acceptance that nothing could ever happen between us.

He was out of my league. I could never again have a relationship with someone I worked with. I needed to stay single to protect my heart and my self-esteem.

And anyway, he'd abandoned my cat back in London.

Being Adam for all this time had made me let my guard down, I realised. I'd started to see men as human, as vulnerable, as people just like me. That had been my first mistake and I wasn't about to make it again.

I walked towards him, the solemn calm of the place seeming to slow my pace, like I was back in a dream again, trying to run from zombies but with my feet sticking to the pavement with every stride. When he saw me, he kind of unpeeled himself from the stone monolith he was leaning against and took a step forward, a hesitant smile on his face.

'Lucy,' he said. 'You came. I wasn't sure you would. This is all kind of weird.'

Weird? Yeah, I guess it is. Me acting out fake sex scenes from movies was properly weird. And as for promising you'd take care of an animal and then leaving it to fend for itself – well, just plain unacceptable.

Hearing his voice made a tide of emotions wash over me: happiness at seeing him, embarrassment at what I'd done, regret that so many obstacles stood between me and him – Bryony, even if things were over between them; Kieren, even though things between us had ended years before... But who was I kidding? Mostly, myself and my insecurities.

I tried to hide my confusion in light-hearted annoyance. 'Yeah, I mean, I guess it's not every day that a woman fakes an orgasm for you so convincingly that you ditch her cat and fly halfway across the world to meet up with her.'

'I'm sorry, Lucy. I know how this looks. I didn't mean to mess anyone around, especially not...' He hesitated, and I imagined the word 'you' forming in his mind before he abruptly changed it. 'Especially not Astro. Seriously, I wouldn't have come out here if I hadn't been able to get Nush to look after him. I felt terrible. But I did try to get hold of you, and I kind of needed to be here.'

So that must have been what Nush's message was about. And it was true – he had tried to get hold of me. But I wasn't going to let that get in the way of my righteous indignation.

'Look, if you'd told me you were going to up sticks and come out here on a whim, I'd have made another plan myself. I'd have found someone else to feed Astro. I'd have come home myself if needs be.'

'Really?' he said. 'In spite of your sister needing you? Because that felt kind of important to me. That's why I didn't keep trying when you weren't answering my messages and calls. I reckoned there was serious shit going down and you were too busy to sort it, so I made another plan myself. I wasn't going to just leave him on his own, Lucy. Come on.'

I wavered, and as if sensing my weakness, he produced his phone and held it out to me. 'Look. Nush sent me this earlier. Astro's fine.'

I leaned in, unable to resist. There on the screen was Astro, upside down on a pair of legs clad in ripped jeans I'd seen Nush wearing, his belly exposed for tickles and his paws in the air. My heart melted totally at the sight of my cat, although it remained only partially defrosted when it came to Ross.

'Fine,' I said. 'I accept he's not actually dead or been rescued by an animal shelter and trapped in a cage wondering why no one loves him. But still – come on. No one needs a holiday that badly.'

'Here's the thing.' He slipped his phone back into his pocket and folded his arms over his chest, almost defensively. 'It's not a holiday. I come here every year. I especially had to come this year.'

Something clicked into place in my mind, bringing with it a rush of embarrassment and guilt. Why hadn't I realised?

'You know what date it is today, right?' he asked.

THIRTY

I stared at Ross for a moment in shocked, baffled silence. You know what it's like when you're on holiday – you lose track of what day of the week it is, never mind what date in the year. But I should have known – of course I should. The banks of flowers propped up against the stone of the monument should have told me. The crowds of people, some smiling, some dabbing their eyes with tissues, all reverent, should have told me.

And if I'd been too thick to notice those clues, Ross's presence here should have filled in the final gap. But it hadn't.

'Oh,' I said. 'Oh. It's the eleventh of September.'

He nodded.

'And you had to come here... You had to be here today because...'

'Shall we go and get a coffee?' he asked. 'Somewhere not here?'

'Of course. Let's go.'

We threaded our way through the knots of people towards the exit and left the park. Beyond the shelter of the trees, the sun was fierce and I could feel the warmth of the sidewalk coming up through the soles of my shoes.

'You know what New Yorkers say?' Ross was smiling slightly. 'It's not the heat, it's the humidity.'

'It certainly is,' I agreed, relieved that he didn't appear to be actually furious with me.

For the first time since I'd arrived in the city, I didn't need to worry about finding my own way around – I just walked where Ross walked, our shoulders almost but not quite touching, turning corners and crossing streets together in silence amid the lunchtime bustle.

He led us down a side street – a quiet, unassuming road that seemed miles from the tourist trail even though it was still the centre of town. The pavements were lined with a mix of small stores selling vintage clothing, Asian food ingredients and second-hand furniture. Right at the end, we came to a diner, and Ross opened the door for me and led us to a Formica-topped table with two metal-backed chairs on either side, a steel napkin dispenser and bottles of ketchup and mustard on its top.

'This do?' he said. 'It's not much, but I like it.'

'Sure. It looks great.'

I was hungry, I realised, and thirsty and footsore from all the miles I'd walked. I was also tired – the confrontation with Amelie and now this encounter with Ross had left me feeling bewildered and wrung out, as if my brain had taken in all the surprises it could hold.

But I knew there was another surprise in store for me – or not really a surprise any more, given what his presence and his silence had already told me.

We sat down and a waitress brought us glasses of iced water. I took a grateful gulp and Ross did the same.

'You hungry?' he asked. 'The grilled cheese is great.'

I nodded and he ordered for us both.

'Do you always come here?' I guessed.

'Yeah. Sorry I didn't include it in my tour guide recommendations. It's not exactly the Top of the Rock.'

'Or Katz's Deli.'

He smiled. 'Right? But it's where I always used to come with my dad.'

'Do you want to talk about him?' I asked.

He nodded. 'I guess I should explain. It's not a long story, really. He was a firefighter.'

I felt a coldness settle in my stomach that had nothing to do with the iced water. 'And he was... there?'

'On 9/11. Yeah, he was. He was one of the lucky ones, in theory. He wasn't on shift when the planes hit the towers, so he wasn't involved in the initial response. But they were all called in, of course. He spent hours and hours there afterwards. But he survived.'

I thought of the scenes I'd seen on television – the planes hitting, the clouds of smoke, the chaos. I remembered Mum and Dad trying to explain to me and Amelie what was happening, but the memory was vague – it was a long time ago, we'd both been small girls, and they'd tried to make what they told us age-appropriate, not the stuff of nightmares it was.

Ross hadn't had the luxury of that emotional shelter.

'I was eight,' he went on. 'I mean, I knew Dad's job was dangerous. But it was also kind of cool, having a father in the fire service. I never thought anything bad would happen to him. And like I say, it didn't. Not right away. He was lucky and I was too. But afterwards... I mean, it wasn't just one day, you know.'

I nodded. 'It must have taken a long time. The rescue mission, I mean.'

He shook his head. 'Not that long. Once they knew they'd got out all the people they could, that part of it was over. But also, it never really ended.'

The waitress brought us our food and put the plates down on the table between us. The sandwiches smelled delicious, but I didn't feel like eating.

'He had post-traumatic stress disorder,' Ross said. 'He used to have nightmares, waking up screaming. Mum said it was natural, after something like that. She said he'd get help, talk it out and be okay in a few months. But he never was.'

'I can't imagine,' I said, 'how anyone could ever be the same after something like that.'

'Mum tried her best,' he went on, 'but she had to protect herself, and protect me. And he changed. His whole personality changed. He was depressed. He was violent, sometimes. To Mum and to me. So after two years she left and took me back to the UK with her.'

'Did he get better?'

'Mentally, yes. I think Mum leaving was kind of the catalyst for him to get more help. By the time I was in high school, I could come and visit him in the summer without Mum worrying too much what he'd be like with me. He even went back to work. But then he got sick.'

'From the... From what happened that day?'

Ross nodded again. 'He was diagnosed with mesothelioma a couple of years back.'

'Meso—?' I hadn't caught the middle of the word, but I understood the end. I knew that any medical condition ending in -oma was bad news.

'It's a type of cancer linked to asbestos inhalation,' Ross explained. 'It's really slow to develop. You can go for years without any symptoms, like Dad did. And once they knew, it was too late for them to treat it.'

'I'm sorry.' My voice came out in a whisper.

'The thing is,' Ross said, 'it's like I lost him three times. You know what I mean? The first, when he changed after the attacks. Then again when we moved to London, where Mum's from. And then, just when I thought I could rebuild a relationship with him, have a dad again, I found out he had this terminal illness, and I wasn't going to have him for long.'

'I'm so sorry. Ross, that's awful.'

'He died last year,' he said. 'Before Christmas. Last year was the last time I went to the memorial ceremony with him, but I promised I'd carry on coming here without him. Like it was the last thing I could do for him. So you see why I had to come.'

'Of course I see. I totally get it.'

'I tried to tell you.'

'I know you did. I should have picked up your calls. But I didn't. I was annoyed about... about the thing that happened yesterday.'

'What thing? I'm sorry, Lucy – I guess I did something to offend you, but I'm not sure what.'

'The *When Harry Met Sally* thing,' I muttered.

'Oh my God. Lucy, I... I mean, it was unexpected, that's for sure. It didn't seem like the kind of thing you'd do. But it was hilarious. You totally nailed it. Why's it a problem?'

To my surprise, I burst out laughing. 'I suppose you're right. I guess I'm not the first person to do that exact thing at that exact table, and I'm sure I won't be the last. But I felt really awkward afterwards, like I was hitting on you or something. Especially when I realised you were out with Bryony. I felt really stupid.'

'Um... Lucy. There's something I need to tell you, because it kind of changes things.'

I swallowed and looked at him, waiting for bad news.

'Bryony and me – well, we're not together any more. She dumped me. But if she hadn't, I'd have probably called it a day myself.'

'I know,' I said gently. 'I found out over WhatsApp. I'm sorry.'

I thought of the details – the guy Bryony had kissed on her

night out, and the others she'd mentioned. But there was no way I was going to tell him about that – it was for Bryony to reveal if she wanted to, and I'd have hated to say anything that might hurt him.

'Thanks.' He smiled. 'It's never nice when something ends. But if it means something else could begin...'

'Like what?' My voice sounded kind of hoarse.

'Lucy, I'm not going to lie, that thing you did in Katz's – it was... I know you were just play-acting and it was a joke and everything. But it was kind of hot.'

'Hold on.' I could see awkwardness radiating from him, and I tried to smooth it over with a joke. 'You think women faking orgasms is hot?'

'No!' he protested. 'I don't want you to fake any orgasms for me, ever.'

Then that familiar blush rushed up over his cheeks, and he pressed his hands over his face to hide it. 'Oh, Jesus. I'm just digging myself further into a hole here, aren't I? Forget I even said that.'

I giggled. 'No, I think you're all good. We can establish right now that I'll never fake another orgasm for you, and move on.'

He peered at me between his fingers and smiled. I smiled back. And I felt... something. Like a tingle that went from my lips right the way down through my body – a slow-motion electric shock. As I looked at him, I could imagine it flashing across the table, through his hands, meeting his own smile and then coursing deliciously downwards.

I fancy him. I really, really do. And I think he fancies me too.

'Ross?' I asked. 'Where are you staying?'

'You know what, I have no idea,' he said. 'I dumped my bag at Penn Station when I got the train in from JFK. I was planning to get a room in a Holiday Inn or somewhere.'

I took a deep breath. 'You can crash at my Airbnb in Brooklyn, if you like. There's plenty of room. It's booked for another two nights and I should probably get a flight back tomorrow – or even this evening – so you'd have the place to yourself.'

'Really? That sounds like an offer I can't refuse.'

Again, I felt that thrill run through me. I knew what it was now: desire. And with it, there came a sense of power – a power I'd never known I had. The ability to flirt with a man.

'Which offer?' I asked. 'The apartment with me, or the apartment to yourself?'

There it was again – that blush. It was intoxicating. I could do this to him any time I liked.

'I-I don't know,' he mumbled.

'Then it depends,' I said, 'on which option you'd prefer.'

'I think you probably know the answer to that,' he replied, and I felt my own face turn absolutely scarlet.

'Let's head back there now, then.' I felt overcome with shyness all of a sudden.

'But first we should eat,' he said. 'Hope you don't mind cold grilled cheese.'

'I can't think of anything nicer. Except maybe one thing.'

Our eyes met. We grinned and blushed in unison, and then we tore into our food like we hadn't eaten in weeks.

But before I'd finished the second half of my sandwich, I was interrupted by the thrumming of my phone in my bag. I realised that I'd momentarily forgotten about the situation with Amelie, and the incoming call brought my awareness springing back to her, like an invisible cord between us was being tugged.

I rummaged in my bag, located my phone and looked eagerly at the screen. But the number there wasn't my sister's.

'Greg,' I mouthed across the table to Ross, and his eyebrows raised in sympathetic anticipation. 'Hello, Lucy speaking.'

I kept watching Ross's face as I spoke to my boss. His expression went from curious to amused to concerned and alarmed, and by the time I ended the call he'd already asked for the bill and paid it, leaving a twenty-dollar tip for our patient waitress.

'Shit,' I said, dropping my phone back into my bag. 'We need to get back to Brooklyn, like, right now.'

THIRTY-ONE

The journey to Brooklyn seemed to take forever – actually, it did take forever, because instead of waiting for Ross, whose superior knowledge of the subway would have ensured we got an express train, I dragged him on to the first one that arrived and it stopped absolutely everywhere. In spite of the freezing air conditioning, I could feel sweat trickling down my back and soaking into my top, and the hand Ross was holding got so clammy I had to wriggle it free after a few minutes.

There was no point putting him off me before we'd even started, after all.

He asked, 'What's going on? What did Greg say?' several times before eventually giving up.

But all I could answer was, 'I don't know. I don't understand. I need to check my laptop.'

So, when at last we arrived at the apartment, that was the first thing I did. I perched on the bed – which to my shame I hadn't got around to making that morning, and my clothes were scattered everywhere, too – while he poured us glasses of water from the tap. I opened my laptop with trembling hands and tapped through to my email.

And there it was – the answer I'd sent through to the subs desk in the small hours of the morning, in response to the email I was sure had come from Zack.

Feeling like I was about to throw up, I opened my browser window. The *Max!* homepage was right there in the first tab, same as it always was. I hit Refresh and the new Ask Adam column appeared right at the top of the screen. I felt even sicker – normally it was about halfway down, below the news coverage and the sport, but above Neil's weekly financial advice segment.

I passed the laptop to Ross.

'Read that,' I said. 'I can't.'

He looked like he might be about to make some kind of a joke, but he changed his mind, balanced the computer on his knees and tapped the trackpad. The text appeared on the screen, but I couldn't look at it. I heard Ross take a sharp breath in, then hiss it out slowly through his teeth. Then he chuckled. Then I felt the warm weight of the laptop on my thighs as he returned it to me.

I still couldn't bring myself to read it – but I didn't need to, because I knew what it said.

Dear Anonymous,

Well, aren't you the catch with your fancy car and your big job and your luxe apartment and ego to match it all? I bet your new wife feels like all her dreams have come true, married to a guy like you. Not.

Seriously, Anonymous, when I encounter a man like you I feel frankly ashamed of my own sex. Not just because you're treating your wife appallingly – although you are – but because your lack of self-awareness shows in every word you write. You really do believe you're God's gift, don't you? And not only to your wife, but to your employer, your colleagues and the woman you're

*thinking of having – or, most likely, by the time this reply reaches
you, already having – an affair with.*

*Here's the thing, Anonymous – you're not. Without decency,
integrity, trustworthiness and kindness, you're nothing. Those
are the attributes that make a man, and I can see very little – to
be generous – evidence of any of them in your letter.*

*So what should you do? Come clean, mate. Tell your wife what
you've been up to and beg for her forgiveness. If you're lucky,
you'll get it – but most likely you won't, and I can't say I blame
your wife one bit for that.*

*Then, take a long, hard look at yourself. Why are you so blind to
what really matters in relationships and in life? Did you have a
distant father growing up? Quite possibly you'd benefit from
some counselling – if you go down that route, put the work in
with honesty and pragmatism.*

*As for the other woman, end it. She doesn't deserve you – and not
in the way you think.*

And moving forward, do try to stop being such a dick.

Yours,

Adam

'Wow,' he said. 'That's hot stuff.'

'Is it...?' I tapped the email window and opened the attachment I'd sent the previous day, unable to make myself read it. 'Is it this?'

Ross leaned forward to peer over my shoulder. I could feel his breath on my neck, tickling my hair, and smell his skin. He smelled a whole lot better than anyone who'd caught an overnight flight from London and had been walking the streets of New York ever since had any right to.

'Looks like the subs changed a few words here and there,' he said. 'Made it more Adam-like. The original's kind of stilted, like you wrote it in a hurry, so I guess they had more heavy lifting to do than usual. But it's – I mean, it's pretty punchy, right? Well done, you.'

'Here's the thing.' My lips felt so numb I could barely get the words out. 'I didn't write that.'

'What? Then who did?'

'GenBot 2.0, I think.'

'You think? Surely you must've told it what to write?'

In a rush, I explained what had happened. How overwhelmed I'd felt by the increased frequency of my deadlines. How I hadn't known how to respond to the letter, because I thought it was from Amelie's husband. How I'd been using GenBot to help me compose answers when I was stuck. How I'd remembered my overdue copy late at night and pasted the answer before sending it without checking it properly.

'But it wouldn't come up with this on its own.' Ross's brow was furrowed. 'I mean, it's done a decent job of copying Adam's style, which is pretty impressive given the column's only been running a few months. They must have updated the algorithm quite recently. But the content – it's dynamite. It's not like anything we've ever got from the AI when we've used it for research before.'

'I've been arguing with it,' I confessed. 'When I don't like what it writes, because it's kind of boring. I've been asking it follow-on questions and why it's not telling these men what dicks they are and stuff like that. And now it's gone rogue.'

'It's a piece of software, Lucy. It can't go rogue. You've trained it.'

'What?'

'You've trained the algorithm. When you didn't accept the responses it gave you, you made it change them, and it's learned. That's how these things work.'

Ross wasn't the only one who understood technology. I did too, and I knew he was right. I'd wanted the AI Adam to give answers that the real Adam – that I – couldn't. And now it had. And I hadn't checked my copy and it had gone live and it was all my fault.

'What did Greg say?' Ross asked. 'Is he spitting feathers?'

I forced myself to look at him. His face was full of concern. 'No, he's not, actually.'

'Jesus. He must really like you. But why not?'

'It's gone viral,' I explained. 'It's had the most hits of any Ask Adam column so far, like way more. It's had more hits than any *Max!* article ever, except the interview Marco did with Boris Johnson back in the day. The analytics are insane, Greg says. It's getting shared all round the web.'

Ross let out another long, slow breath. This time it came out as a whistle. 'So you got away with it?'

'Looks like it. But I feel terrible. I did a shit job. I was late and careless and it could all have gone horribly wrong.'

'I mean, yeah, I suppose so. But what's the worst that could have happened? The AI could've spat out some wishy-washy response about the guy talking to his wife and getting counselling and blah blah, and no one would've been any the wiser. Or if it really hadn't stacked up, the subs would've flagged it and Greg would have assumed you'd sent the wrong draft and made you do a rewrite.'

'I guess.'

'I mean, that's why we have processes in place, right? Checks and balances.'

'And I didn't follow them properly. I deserve to be sacked.'

'Well, you're not going to be,' he said. 'You're lucky, you'll learn from this – but also, you know what?'

'What?'

'I think this is good shit. I think it's better than the Ask Adam columns have been in the past, I'm not going to lie. You're a great writer, Lucy. You do your research and put a lot of thought into them. But they could be a bit more... you know? Punchy.'

'Like this?'

'Exactly. And this isn't GenBot, Lucy. This is you. GenBot wouldn't have come up with it if you hadn't fed it the ideas in the first place. I reckon, speaking as a man—'

'Don't say that! That's what men always say when they're about to start mansplaining.'

'Sorry. Speaking as me. I mean, when I wrote in to Ask Adam—'

'You what?' Suddenly I remembered the letter I'd responded to way back, from a guy who wasn't sure how to tell if the woman he was seeing was the one for him. At the time, something about it had struck a chord – and now I remembered why.

The conversation I'd overheard between Ross and Marco in the pub. The doubts he'd expressed then had been almost identical to what Adam's first anonymous correspondent had been worried about. And it was Ross – it had been Ross all along.

'So that was you?' I asked, astonished.

'That was me.'

'But why?'

'Two reasons. I genuinely wasn't sure what to do about Bryony. I needed advice. And also – oh God, I feel like a right pillock saying this.'

'Saying what?'

'I wanted you to know that I wasn't sure. I wanted you to know that I liked you.'

I looked up from my screen and met his eyes. He was blushing furiously.

I felt my own cheeks turn absolutely scarlet. 'I really liked you too. I still really like you.'

'Then maybe we should do something about that.'

'I...' I hesitated. Most of me wanted to throw myself into his arms, feel his body close to mine the way it had been at the foot of the ladder in the escape room. But a smaller, frightened part wanted to hold back, to walk away. 'I want to. But, Ross, I'm scared.'

He didn't throw his arms around me. Instead, he reached over and took my hand. 'Relationships are scary. At least, they are when there's something real going on. When you care about the other person a lot.'

'I haven't had a boyfriend in ages.' My voice came out in a whisper and I felt my eyes squeeze shut, like if I couldn't see him, he wouldn't be able to see me, know the truth I was about to tell him. 'Not for years. The last time I was with a guy, he treated me terribly. I don't know how to do this.'

'No one does,' he said. 'Not really. We can figure it out together, if that's what you want.'

'I do want to. I think. I think I'm ready. But, Ross...'

He squeezed my hand tighter. 'Lucy, I can promise you one thing.'

'What's that?'

'I'll try my very, very best not to be a dick,' he said.

And then he kissed me.

THIRTY-TWO

I hadn't set an alarm the previous night, what with one thing and another, but I woke at six in the morning anyway – because, what with one thing and another, I hadn't closed the blinds either, and the morning sun was streaming through the windows and piercing my eyelids. I turned to bury my face in the pillow but found there was no pillow there – instead, there was a shoulder. A warm, muscular shoulder, already smelling familiar.

Ross's shoulder.

He was asleep, one arm flung upwards over his head, his face still and peaceful, half-smiling as if he was having a particularly pleasant dream. The sunshine made his hair and the shadow of stubble on his jaw glisten like bronze.

I snuggled down, fitting my head into the hollow where his bicep and pectoral muscles met, and waited to see if I'd fall asleep again – but there was no chance whatsoever of that. I felt as excited as I'd felt on Christmas morning when I was little, conscious of the weight at the end of my bed that meant my stocking was there, filled, and Santa had been.

Then, I'd have leaped out of bed and gone next door to

wake my sister, so the two of us could prod and rattle and sniff the wrapped contents of our stockings until we couldn't wait any longer and had to burst into our parents' room like over-grown puppies, the stockings cradled in our arms.

Amelie. Thinking of my sister brought a stab of pain that was almost physical. Feeling it alongside the glow of happiness I'd woken up with was like stepping off a beach into a freezing ocean – part of me in the sunshine and gorgeously warm, part submerged by water and icy cold.

Sleep now out of the question, I took comfort in a daydream of the previous night. How our kiss had turned into more than a kiss – our hands exploring each other's bodies, our breath inter-mingling, our voices gasping and whispering.

I remembered how awkward I'd felt when I realised what was going to happen – almost frightened for a second, until Ross had paused, held me close and said, 'It's okay. Are you okay? Say if you want to stop.'

I'd taken a deep breath and said, 'I don't want to stop.'

But, as if he'd sensed the effort of will, the courage it had taken for me to commit to what we were about to do, he'd slowed right down. For the next half an hour, every touch of his fingertips or lips or tongue had silently asked that question. I half-remembered him even asking it aloud, one more time, just before I lowered myself on to him and took him inside me for the first time.

But he hadn't needed to ask, not then, and my body had given him all the answer he needed.

It had been perfect. Compared to those times with Kieren, it had been night and day. To do this with a man I liked, trusted and truly desired, rather than just wanting him to desire me – because I couldn't have been surer that he did – was amazing. It was a revelation.

I opened my eyes, as if to check that Ross was still there, he wasn't a dream, even though I could feel the gentle rise and fall of his chest under my forearm, the tickle of his hair under my skin.

To my surprise, he was awake, his eyes open too, gazing down at me.

'Morning,' he said.

'Morning.' When our eyes met, I expected to blush, or for him to, but it didn't happen. Whatever cringe factor there'd been between us was gone now, replaced with confidence and excitement.

'Sleep well?' he asked.

'Brilliantly. How about you?'

'So well. I could murder a coffee, though.'

'And some breakfast.'

'We don't need to get a flight until this evening.'

'So we have time...' I tilted my head and found his lips with mine. Last night, we'd kissed and kissed, all the way through, and then we'd kissed some more until we'd fallen asleep. I wanted to check that it was as good as I remembered.

And it was. Actually, it was better. There was less hesitancy now. There was no doubt in his mind that I wanted to be kissed, and none in mine that he wanted to kiss me. I felt no shyness in reaching down under the duvet, running my fingertips down the muscled ridges of his torso – all those CrossFit classes had done their job, I thought – until I found the warm, springy hardness of his cock, knowing before I touched it the sound of pleasure he'd make when my fingertips brushed his skin.

He knew, too. He knew where to touch me, and how firmly, and for how long. He knew when I couldn't bear to wait any more, and how quickly to move once he was inside me. He knew the instant when I was about to orgasm so that he could let go, too.

Afterwards, we showered together, splashing and giggling like loons, then dressed and ran downstairs, stepping hand in hand out into the morning.

It was eight o'clock, still cool and fresh. The air sparkled like it had been through a dishwasher. The stream of people on the sidewalk going about their Saturday business all seemed to be smiling. Even the little dogs on their early-morning walks seemed to have an extra spring in their steps.

We found a café, sat at a table in the window and ordered coffee. Ross had a stack of pancakes with bacon and maple syrup, and I had a smoked salmon and cream cheese bagel, and a portion of cheesy grits because he said it was my last day in New York, and if I hadn't tried them yet, I had to now. When I tasted them and made a face, he laughed and traded them for some of his pancakes.

'So, what's the plan?' he asked. 'We could take a walk in Prospect Park. Or we could go and explore Chinatown. Unless there's something you'd rather do?'

I licked a drop of maple syrup off my finger. The thought of spending the day with Ross was almost irresistible, but I knew what I had to do.

Ross read my thoughts as clearly as if I'd spoken.

'Sometimes when I'm out here I pay a visit to the fire station where Dad worked,' he said. 'I take them doughnuts. I'll do that. You—'

I nodded. 'I'll go and see my sister.'

THIRTY-THREE

As I approached the building on West Seventeenth Street, I felt my steps growing slower, as if someone had replaced the comfy AirWair soles of my boots with concrete. There was so much I wanted to say to Amelie, but I didn't know how I was going to say it – or whether she'd be willing to listen.

On the corner before my sister's apartment block, I paused outside a little arcade of shops, dithering. There was a florist selling enormous bunches of lilies and peonies, as well as hand-tied bouquets with ferns and all sorts of other things in them as well as the flowers. But I remembered Amelie telling me in the early days of their relationship that Zack had sent flowers to the office where she worked every day for a whole month until the girl who sat next to her got such bad hay fever she had to ask him to stop.

I didn't want to do anything that would remind her of the time when Zack made her so happy she used to sing all the time, out of tune and getting the words wrong, until all the people in her office had literally begged her to stop that too.

Next to the florist was a patisserie, its window filled with a wedding-themed display of pastel-frosted cupcakes and one towering three-tier extravaganza with ombré icing and sugar rosebuds cascading down its side. I definitely didn't want to remind my sister of her wedding day, either, but when I peered through the glass I saw a counter laden with things that looked more promising.

Ross was taking his father's old colleagues doughnuts for a treat, so I decided I might as well do the same. They were saving lives and needed calories, but my sister was growing one and would need them just as much.

After careful consideration, I selected four doughnuts – one matcha tea, one vanilla, one chocolate truffle and one raspberry jam – which I figured covered all bases. Clutching them in a paper bag, I pushed open the door to the street and almost collided with Amelie.

Her eyes were concealed behind huge black sunglasses, and the interior of the store was a lot dimmer than the bright day outside, so she didn't recognise me at first.

'Excuse m— Oh. It's you.'

'It's me.' Now that I was face to face with her, my determination to come and see her seemed more foolish than it had in Brooklyn an hour before. 'I wanted to... I bought doughnuts.'

The tight line of Amelie's mouth softened. 'Is one of them matcha?'

I nodded.

'Were you planning to eat them all yourself?'

I shook my head.

'Come on, then. Shall we walk?'

'Let's walk.'

I followed her down the street and up on to the disused railway line that had been turned into a park – or rather a kind of ribbon of open space, overlooked by buildings but lush with greenery – which my tourist research had told me was called the High Line.

'Are you feeling better?' I ventured. 'Since you're out of bed and everything?'

'A bit,' she said. 'I haven't puked since yesterday and I woke up this morning absolutely starving. So I came out for carbs. Imagine living here and not being able to eat – it's an absolute piss-take. When are you flying home?'

'This evening. Unless—' I stopped. If Amelie needed me, I'd stay longer, but she'd given no indication that she did, and I didn't want to break whatever tentative truce she had declared by pushing things.

'God, I can smell those doughnuts from here,' she said. 'Shall we sit down?'

We had to walk quite a bit further before we found an unoccupied bench on the shady side of the path, and then we sat. I opened the paper bag and held it out to Amelie.

She took out the top doughnut and turned it carefully in her fingers. 'This one's chocolate, I think.'

I removed the next one and inspected it. I could see a bit of pale green oozing out of one side.

'I reckon this is matcha.' I held it out to her.

She hesitated a moment, as if in the grip of some existential conflict. 'Are you sure you don't want it? They're the best by miles.'

'I got it for you. I'll like the chocolate better anyway.'

'I'll let you have a bite.'

'What if I think it's gross? It'd be a waste.'

'True.'

So we swapped doughnuts. I wasn't hungry, but I took a bite of mine anyway and its rich sweetness made me instantly forget how unhungry I was, and I took another bite and another. Amelie tore into hers as if she hadn't eaten in weeks, which I supposed she hadn't.

When she'd finished, I said, 'Vanilla or raspberry next?'

'Which do you want?'

'I don't think I want another. I had a massive breakfast earlier.'

Although her opaque dark glasses were still covering half her face, I could see that Amelie was rolling her eyes.

'Fine, I'll take the vanilla. Bet you eat the jam one anyway,' Amelie said.

'Bet you I don't.'

'Bet you d— actually, maybe not. Not with your rational mind and all.'

'What are you talking about?'

'You. You wouldn't stuff a doughnut down your neck if you didn't actually want it. You'd know that if you did, you'd feel sick and hate yourself, so you wouldn't do it.'

'Why would I hate myself? It's just a doughnut.'

'Because... Okay, maybe you wouldn't hate yourself. But you wouldn't eat it, because you'd know it wasn't worth it. Like with Kieren.'

'What on earth has Kieren got to do with doughnuts?' I asked, bewildered. Actually, I had no idea what he had to do with anything any more, but there was no stopping Amelie when she went off on one of her tangents.

'You had that thing with him, and you got hurt, so that was it. No more men. Because you didn't want to risk it happening again.'

Now didn't seem like the moment to reveal that risking it happening again was exactly what I'd just done – a leap of faith so breathtakingly thrilling and daunting I still couldn't quite believe I'd taken it.

'Whereas I,' Amelie went on, brushing the last doughnut crumbs off her mouth with her sleeve, 'make the same mistakes, over and over.'

'Do you mean with men or with doughnuts?' I felt it was important to bring some clarity to this conversation.

'Both. Luce, I know this sounds pathetic, but being the

pretty one hasn't been easy. Not that you're not pretty – you're stunning. But the label. It meant I always thought that was it – that was what I was worth. What I looked like to men.'

'And whether you could eat doughnuts?' I asked, floundering.

She burst out laughing. 'See? Logical. But yes. It's all part of the same thing. So I tried and tried to find someone who'd think I was good enough for them, and who everyone else would think was good enough for me. And then I found Zack.'

I nodded. This still wasn't really making sense to me, but at least now we were talking about the thing I'd come here to talk about.

'And Luce, the relief was just— I can't describe it. No more dates. No more swiping. I had my person. I had a ring on my finger. I could get on with what my life was supposed to be.'

'And eat doughnuts?'

'God, no. I mean, maybe now I can blame it on the baby. But you see, if I were to leave Zack, I'd be back where I started. I'd be alone again. I'd be back on the market. And I can't...' She sniffed. 'I just can't face it.'

'But you—' I began, but she carried on.

'I'm sorry about what I said to you the other night. I was horrible. I believe what you told me about him.'

Relief washed over me, followed immediately by a sense of weary resignation.

'But you're still...?' I asked.

'I'm still going to stay with him.' Her voice was calm. 'We're married. Once he knows about the baby, it'll stop. It'll be okay.'

'Amelie, this is... You don't have to do that.'

'I do. This is what I signed up for. I've got to make it work. Luce, promise me something?'

'Of course.'

'Don't hate me? Please?'

'Am' – I swivelled round on the bench so I could look at her directly – 'I know I'm meant to be the clever one of us, and we both know that's not actually true. But right now, I've got to tell you, you're being as thick as mince. Of course I hate what Zack's done. Right now, if he was standing here, I'd kick him in the balls so hard he'd have to swallow them back down. But you know what? If you forgive him, when you guys move back to London with your baby, I'll buy that man a Christmas present every single year until I die. Whenever I see him I'll smile so nicely everyone will think we're best buddies. I'll be your baby's godmother if you ask me, and I'll never say a bad word about its father. Why? Because you're my sister and I want you to be happy. Got it?'

'Got it. Maybe say about his balls again – I liked that bit.'

I said it again and Amelie nodded in satisfaction.

'Thank you, Luce. You're the best.'

'I love you, Am.'

'Love you more.' She managed a watery smile. 'I won't pull the radio silence on you again. I'm feeling better. FaceTime as soon as you're back in London and we'll chat, okay? I'll tell you what he says about... you know. Everything.'

'Okay. As soon as I'm home, I'll call you.'

'Speaking of home,' she said, 'I should get back. I'm bursting for a wee.'

'Okay,' I said again.

We stood up and walked slowly back the way we'd come. The shadows from the buildings that fell across the path were longer now, the benches on the other side in shade also.

As we got near to Amelie's apartment, her pace increased, but when we reached the entrance she stopped.

'Luce?'

'Am?'

'Are you going to eat that jam doughnut, or can I have it?'

'Of course you can have it. You're my sister.'

I passed over the paper bag, bunched and wrinkled at the top where I'd been clutching it in my hand. Amelie took it, then reached out her arms to me and we hugged as if we'd never stop.

THIRTY-FOUR

Dear Adam

I know your column is about answering questions about relationships, which this isn't exactly – although it kind of is. My mum and dad had a pretty traditional marriage – Dad was the provider and Mum looked after us kids and cooked for us and stuff. They were really happy, and I wanted my own kids to have a stable, loving home just the same as I did.

But my fiancée, who's absolutely brilliant and I love to pieces, doesn't see it that way. She's got a great job and she says she's not giving it up even if we have kids. She reckons we should share the job of parenting equally, and both take time off work when the kids are small or if they're ill and stuff like that.

I genuinely believe in equality so I can see where she is coming from. But aren't women naturally more nurturing than men and just better at stuff like that? I have a high-pressure, well-paid job and I know that taking time off work would set me back in my career, whereas it's expected that she as a woman would do that.

And come to that, I recently got passed over for promotion in favour of a female colleague.

It doesn't seem fair, Adam. I feel like whatever we do, men will end up being the bad guys.

So I wanted to ask you – has feminism gone too far?

Aaron, Cardiff

'Do you want the window seat or the middle?' I asked, hefting my bag into the overhead locker.

'Don't mind.' Ross slotted his bag in next to mine. They looked good together, I thought – two battered nylon backpacks with no pretensions to style. I imagined them being friends already, looking forward to more adventures together. 'You choose.'

'I don't mind either.'

'You take the window, then. Window's best.'

'If you like it best, you have it.'

'But I genuinely don't—'

'Excuse me, please,' snapped a woman behind us. 'Some of us would like to sit down, even if you don't.'

Apologising profusely, we slid into our seats, waiting until the woman had disappeared down the aisle before we allowed ourselves to giggle. Somehow, in the commotion, Ross had ended up in the window seat.

'Why don't you move to the aisle in a bit,' he said. 'Then you can move back if there's someone else in our row, and otherwise we'll have more room.'

'But then how will I hold your hand if I get scared?'

'You don't get scared on flights, do you?'

'Not really. Only climbing down ladders in the dark.'

We looked at each other and smiled, already taking pleasure

in the shared memory of the first time he'd touched me. I thought of building more memories together, and wondered whether there would eventually be so many that one would be forgotten. I hoped it wouldn't.

But the idea gave me a little lurch of fear, as if the plane was already airborne and going through a patch of turbulence. Where was this going? Where would it end? I liked Ross; as far as was possible, I trusted him. But what did I know? He was a man, and I didn't have a clue about men.

It could all unravel, and I could end up being hurt. And I knew already that the hurt I'd suffered over Kieren would be nothing compared to how I'd feel if things went wrong with Ross, because my hurt then had been largely down to my having been used, made a fool of; I'd let myself imagine something that hadn't ever really been there.

What was going on with Ross felt real. I felt far more vulnerable than I had with Kieren. I cared. I wanted it to work. And I was scared.

'What's wrong?' he asked. 'You look like someone just asked you to climb down a ladder in the dark.'

'I kind of feel that way, to be honest. Like I don't know what's at the bottom. You know – with us.'

Was it even okay to talk about 'us' already, after just one night together? Was I building up a fantasy relationship the way I had with Kieren, with someone who thought what we'd had together had just been a bit of fun, two people who vaguely liked each other finding themselves together in a foreign city and hooking up?

'Maybe lose the ladder analogy,' he suggested. 'It's not exactly encouraging, is it?'

'I mean, worst-case scenario at least you find yourself with your feet on the ground,' I joked.

'Still, though. I reckon it's more like climbing a mountain. You don't know what you'll see when you get to the top, but there'll probably be an amazing view, and more places to explore.'

'To explore together?'

He smiled. 'I hope so. I don't want to rush you, Lucy. But we like each other. I think this could be good. I'm... quietly confident.'

'Even though I don't understand men?'

'Hey, don't diss yourself. I've been reading Ask Adam every week for the past few months and I reckon you understand men a lot better than we understand ourselves.'

'Maybe that was just GenBot 2.0.'

'It wasn't. Not the good ones, anyway. Those were you.'

'Ross? Can I ask you something?'

'Sure.'

'What happened with you and Bryony?'

Now, for the first time since – well, since before what had happened between us happened – Ross blushed. I wasn't sure what to make of that – had I lost the power to make him do that, but Bryony still had it?

But he said, 'Oh God, Lucy. Not my finest hour, if I'm honest.'

I looked at him, waiting for him to carry on.

'I mean, it was just a casual thing. I didn't think anything would come of it after your sister's hen night. But then we started seeing each other.'

I nodded. What if I'd got it all wrong, Ross was devastated by Bryony ending their relationship, and I was just a quick rebound fling? In front of me, I could see the last few people straggling on to the plane and taking their seats – if what he was about to say wasn't what I wanted to hear, it was too late for me to run away.

He went on, 'It was just casual, really. On my side and on hers also. If I'm honest, I kind of expected it to peter out after a few dates. And then I wrote that thing to Adam, to see what you'd say if you knew how I felt about you.'

'And I didn't say anything,' I remembered. 'I got the AI to write back because I didn't know what the answer was.'

'But when you didn't... I mean, when I didn't get the answer I'd hoped I'd get from Adam, I let it carry on. I shouldn't have done that. I knew she and I weren't right for each other. But it just seemed easier, somehow. Easier than telling you properly how I felt, and easier than ending it with her.'

I didn't say anything for a moment. Ross was right – it hadn't been his finest hour. He wasn't coming out of this particularly well. A few months back, I'd have written his behaviour off as yet another failing of the male sex: too cowardly, too passive, too willing to take no-strings sex when it was offered to him.

But what had he actually done wrong? He hadn't cheated on her. He hadn't treated her badly. She'd kissed other men. She'd ended things when she'd realised it wasn't going anywhere. If there was one thing I'd learned in my months of being Adam, it was that men made mistakes. They weren't perfect; they were just people. And Ross at least acknowledged that.

'And now it's over,' I said.

'Totally, one hundred per cent over. It was all totally amicable. In fact, I may have...'

'You may have what?'

'When I asked Nush to deputise looking after Astro. I knew she'd be okay with it, but I had to give her an extra reason why, and I didn't want to tell her about Dad. It felt like too much information.'

'So you told her...?'

'I told her you were out here and I wanted to see you. I told her how I felt about you.'

'And what did she say?'

'She told me to go for it. She said it was...'

'She said it was what?'

'She said it was obvious you had a crush on me.'

'What? How did she know?'

'So you did have a crush on me?'

'Well, yeah. Course I did. A massive one.'

'I'm glad that was mutual, then,' he said. Then we laughed, and he reached across for my hand and squeezed it.

'Cabin crew, arm the doors and cross-check,' came the crackly announcement over the Tannoy.

While we were talking, the last of the passengers must have been taking their seats. But not all of them. From further up towards the front of the plane, I heard a familiar voice.

'I'm sorry, you can't possibly seat me in the exit row. You see, I'm pregnant.'

THIRTY-FIVE

Seconds later, a flustered-looking flight attendant hurried over, with my sister striding in her wake. Amelie was wearing a full-length silk dress that I remembered was by The Vampire's Wife – she'd agonised over its purchase before her first date with Zack. Hooked over her arm was a squashy, shell-pink leather bag; she had no other luggage. Her hair was straightened, her make-up flawless. Her oversized dark glasses were perched on her head and she exuded an air of, *Why the hell didn't you upgrade me to business class when I couldn't sit in the emergency exit row?*

'There's a space right here, ma'am,' said the flight attendant. 'Can I assist with your bag? If you wouldn't mind taking a seat, we're scheduled to take off in two minutes.'

Amelie thanked her graciously, gathered her skirt around her and prepared to sit down. Then she clocked me and her whole face changed. The air of superiority vanished and she squeaked, 'Lucy!' and bent down to hug me so quickly her sunglasses flew off and landed in my lap.

I couldn't say a word. I just pulled her close, squeezing her as hard as I could because I could barely believe she was real.

My sister, who I'd felt so guilty about abandoning to her fate with Zack but been unable to persuade to leave, was here. Right here, on an aircraft that would be landing in London in six hours. And she was sitting right next to me, and the cabin doors were locked, so there was no way she could escape and return to Zack.

'You're here,' I muttered once Amelie had sat down and fastened her seatbelt and I'd regained the power of speech. 'Are you... I mean, is this just a...?'

'I'm coming home,' she said.

'Home for, like, ever?' I asked hesitantly.

'Well, yes. Although given that home's going to have to be Mum and Dad's until I find a job and a place to live, I hope it won't be that forever.'

Then she noticed Ross, who was sitting silently next to me, half-watching our exchange while pretending to look out of the window as we taxied slowly down the tarmac.

'Hold on,' she said. 'I know you. You're Bryony's bloke.'

'Uh... I was,' Ross said. 'But not any more. Now I'm Lucy's bloke, if she'll have me, that is.'

'What?' Amelie squeaked. 'You came to New York to break up one relationship and ended up starting another, Luce? That's some going.'

'I... We... Ross and I...' I stammered. I wasn't sure whether my sister was still pissed off with me about having spied on Zack, and if she wasn't, whether she'd start being pissed off all over again for me having nicked her friend's boyfriend.

But part of me didn't care. She could be as pissed off as she liked – she'd come round eventually. For now, what mattered was that she was here and Zack wasn't.

Unless – a horrible thought struck me – he was here, basking in the luxury of business or first class at the front of the plane, with Amelie relegated to cattle class along with all the rest of us.

Surely that wasn't possible, though? Apart from anything else, my sister would never have stood for it.

'Ross and I will explain everything later,' I said firmly. 'But I need to know what's going on with you. And where's Zack?'

'Zack,' Amelie said, 'is at work. Or at the apartment. Or in bed with Brooke frigging MacIntyre. Or possibly having a swim in the lake in Central Park, and ideally being eaten by pumpkinseed sunfish. I don't know where he is and I don't care.'

'You mean you've—'

'Left him,' she confirmed. 'As of this afternoon. Right after you left, I gave my head a good wobble and I got changed and went to his office to talk to him. And that's when we had The Row. You know, the one where you call each other names you wouldn't even think of for your own worst enemy, and you know there's no coming back from it?'

I nodded. Although it was horrible to see Amelie's pain, part of me would have really loved to have been there to hear exactly what she'd said to Zack and see how small he must have looked in the face of my sister's rage.

'And that wasn't all. I remembered what you said, Luce, when we were on that bench on the High Line. I thought, if you could put what Zack did behind you to make me happy, I needed to do my bit and make myself happy, too. I realised I wanted to be with my family, and my family wasn't Zack. So I booked a flight and packed some things and got a cab to the airport. And here I am. Three doughnuts'll do that to you. I recommend it.'

Ross said, 'The seatbelt sign just switched off. If you two would like a bit of privacy, I can take a walk?'

I glanced at Amelie. I didn't want Ross to move – his presence there next to me felt stable and reassuring. But this was her personal crisis; if she didn't want a relative stranger knowing all the details of what had happened, that was up to her.

'No need for that,' she said. 'If you and Luce are an item,

you're part of the family, and you'd better get used to my dirty laundry. And there'll be plenty of that, especially once the baby's here.'

'Baby?' Ross said. 'You mean you're...?'

I realised that amid all the drama with Ross telling me about his father, and Greg's call, and then he and I spending the night together, it hadn't crossed my mind to tell him this vital piece of news about Amelie.

'I wasn't sure if you'd want everyone to know,' I said.

'Mum and Dad don't.' Amelie smiled. 'I reckoned when I turn up unannounced at their front door and say I need my old room back for the foreseeable, it might soften the blow a bit if I tell them I've got their first grandchild on board.'

'Don't be mad,' I said. 'They'll be thrilled to have you. And when they find out about the baby – oh my God.'

Amelie's face changed. Until that moment, she'd been all poise and bravado; now, her brow furrowed and her lower lip trembled a bit.

'I just feel so stupid,' she said. 'After the wedding and everything. I mean, Zack paid for most of it, but Mum and Dad paid loads. And it was all so perfect – all the time she spent on the phone to the bloody florist and having sleepless nights over the cake and shit. All for nothing.'

'Am, that's just the whatchamacallit. Sunk cost thing. Fallacy. All that time and money's spent regardless – no one would want you to stay with Zack and be unhappy just to get their money's worth out of the stupid flowers.'

'I know you're right,' she said. 'But there's so much else. All the wedding presents. We didn't even want most of them, but Mum and Dad's friends all wanted to buy something so we had that registry thing and now we've got three toasters we don't even need. I'm knocking the carbs on the head as soon as this baby's born. I could barely do up this dress earlier and it used to fit.'

'You're pregnant. Newsflash – pregnant people put on weight. And you can give the toasters to a food bank or sell them on Facebook or something. It's still not a reason to stay.'

'I know,' she said again. 'Seriously. I went through all that. After you left – and by the way, I was utterly shitty and I'm sorry—'

'I was an utter idiot and I'm sorry too—'

'Anyway, I was absolutely certain that I'd stay with him. I went through it all in my head. First I convinced myself that you were wrong – that you'd fucked up somehow. That Zack would never have sent that message to Adam, it was all a mistake, and even if it had been him, he wouldn't have actually done anything. And then I told myself that I've been a totally crap wife and I wouldn't blame him if he had – I could forgive him and we'd move past it, and our marriage would be stronger than ever.'

Given her wedding had only happened a few months before, I reckoned that was a fairly low baseline to set. But of course I wasn't going to say that.

'Why did you change your mind?' I asked.

'I didn't. Not at first. Like you saw, my mind was all made up. But then I thought – maybe I should be a bit more like you. A bit more logical. So I did a bit of digging. I'm not proud of it, but I went on the computer he uses when he works from home over weekends. I've never even looked at it before – he had no reason to set up a password or anything. And Teams was right there on the screen, with messages between him and this Brooke.' She spat the name out like it tasted horrible, which I supposed it did.

'Oh, Am. I'm so sorry you had to see that.'

'It was vile. I had to go and puke, and I hadn't puked for two whole days.'

I felt a surge of anger at Zack for doing this to my sister

when she was least able to cope with it. But then, there would never have been a good time, would there?

'And so I went to confront him. I told him I knew. I didn't tell him you'd seen him, or about the letter to Adam or anything. I just said I'd felt suspicious so I'd looked at his computer.'

'And what did he say?'

'He went off on one at me for snooping.'

'Of course he bloody did.'

'And then he tried to deny it, and he got his phone out and tried to delete the chat, but I'd taken photos and I showed him. And then he said it was all my fault because I'd been a disappointment to him as a wife and I didn't understand the pressure of his job and she did.'

'What a bastard!' Ross interjected from next to me. 'Sorry. It's none of my business.'

'You crack on,' Amelie said, with a watery smile. 'The more people call him a bastard the better. I need to hear it.'

'Then what happened?' I asked, reaching for Ross's hand and twining my fingers into his.

'Then I told him about the baby. And he started crying. Luce, it was awful. I ended up apologising to him. And he said he was sorry, and he would end things with her right away, and he just wanted us to be together and be a family.'

'Oh my God.' I could imagine Amelie, weakened by his tears and pleas for forgiveness and a misplaced sense of loyalty to a man who'd treated her appallingly, deciding to stay after all.

'I almost decided to stay after all,' she said, confirming my thoughts. 'And then he got up to get us some water and I looked at my phone – you know how you do: Russia invades Ukraine, you check your phone. House is burning down, you check your phone.'

'Queens Park Rangers get relegated, you check your phone,' said Ross.

'Exactly. So I checked my phone, just for something to do,

to kind of distract myself from what was going on. I had the Ask Adam column open in one of the tabs, and I refreshed it, and there was the question and your answer.'

It hadn't been my answer – it had been GenBot 2.0's. But I wasn't going to tell Amelie that now, and I wasn't sure I ever would.

'And that set me straight. Honestly, Luce, it did. He came back with the water and I threw my glass over his head – I know, I'm not proud – and I told him he was shit in bed and had a tiny cock, and I was leaving.'

'Good for you,' I said.

'Good for you,' said Amelie. 'Honestly, that column told me what I needed to hear. He's a dick, Luce, and he'll never change.'

THIRTY-SIX

Dear Adam,

I'm sure you don't remember, but I wrote to you a few months ago, about my daughter. I told you how I'd lost my wife to cancer, and I was worried about how I'd manage parenting my daughter alone as she goes through her teenage years.

Well, it was her thirteenth birthday yesterday and I found myself recalling your advice. Actually, that's not quite true, because what you wrote has been with me every single day since I read it. Your words gave me confidence, helped me to believe that I can do this, and that really meant the world.

I'm not going to say it's been easy, and we've still got a long road ahead of us. We still miss my wife like crazy. But I tell my daughter all the time how much I love her and how proud her mother would be of her. I talk to her about my feelings, too, and I know that if one day I meet someone else and I'm ready to embark on a new relationship, we'll be able to make that work together.

Adam, I wanted to thank you. I needed your advice and it helped me to find what was there inside me all along.

Jonno, London

At Heathrow Airport, Amelie said goodbye and got on the train in the opposite direction to us, back home to Mum and Dad, who'd been alerted to her arrival by text and were ready to welcome her with a freshly made bed, shoulders to cry on and Mum's legendary roast chicken.

Ross and I were headed east. He'd told me he was going to visit his own mother, as he always did when he got home from a trip to New York. She still felt a heavy burden of guilt, he said, over having left his father, and needed reassurance from Ross that it had been the only possible choice for her to make.

We said an early goodbye on the platform, standing there amid the crowds of suitcase-wheeling travellers, holding each other close then kissing on and on like two people at the end of a sad, French art-house movie.

'But I'll see you tomorrow at work,' I said, rubbing my face on his shoulder to wipe away a tear. 'Why am I being so daft?'

'Because when you've only had twenty-four hours together, twenty-four apart feels like a long time.'

'It really does,' I agreed.

We kissed again. Ross wasn't soft enough to actually cry, but his usual cheerful smile was absent.

'We could get a coffee together tomorrow before we go into the office?' I suggested.

'Deal.'

'Don't change your mind.'

'I won't. Scout's honour. Say hi to Astro for me.'

'I will. Promise.'

Then our train thundered into the station and we pushed

our way on, strap-hanging by the door because there weren't two free seats together.

When his stop came, he kissed me one more time, promised he'd text later and stepped off. I watched him until he disappeared around a corner, then the doors thudded closed and I was left alone.

My New York adventure was over. In a sense, I'd achieved what I'd set out to: Amelie was home, and we both knew the truth about Zack.

But it felt like a hollow victory. My sister was putting a brave face on things, as she always did, but I knew her heart and her pride were hurting badly. And her future looked uncertain, having to find somewhere to live and somehow get a job with a new baby on the way – a baby who would grow up with a mostly absent father, same as Ross had.

Inevitably, my thoughts turned to Ross. For him, the trip must have been a bittersweet one. Bitter because it was his first pilgrimage to the city of his birth since his father's death; I wondered whether he'd continue to visit every year, go to the shady park with the giant stones and remember what he'd lost. And I wondered whether every time, from now on, he'd remember meeting me there, and that would be the sweet part – the beginning of something wonderful.

But was it? He'd given me no reason to doubt him. In the months since I'd met him, I'd never heard him say an unkind word about anyone. I'd never known him to slag off a colleague or flake out on a deadline. He'd never treated me with anything but respect.

But what if us sleeping together had changed that? What if the memories I had of that night, which still made a wave of delicious pleasure wash over me, were something else entirely to him? What if...

For God's sake, Lucy, pull yourself together, I told myself sternly, gulping down the lump in my throat. *Keep the faith. If it's meant to be, it will be. If it's not, it'll hurt and you'll get over it, same as Amelie will, same as every woman does who's found a good man and lost him. And at least now you know men can be good.*

Because of Adam, I thought. Because of all the men – the young ones and the old ones, the arrogant and the diffident, the single and the attached, the dicks and the not-such-dicks, who'd confided their problems in Adam.

It must have been quite a leap of faith for all of them, I realised. Even if they genuinely believed in the existence of the smiley, bearded thirty-something chewing on his pencil, they'd put their future in the hands of a stranger writing an online column.

And what they'd got was me: Lucy Masters, twenty-nine and perennially single, who didn't have a clue about men.

I owed them all something, I realised. I owed them for their time and their trust and their honesty, even the dicks. They'd given me that and, in a roundabout way, they'd given me Ross.

In return, what had I given them? I'd never really thought about it before. I'd been so focused on getting the job done, meeting my deadlines, producing answers that I hoped made some kind of sense. Greg's focus on click rates and read-through had made me spend far more time considering the response of *Max!*'s readers to my replies than that of the men who'd actually written to Adam in the first place.

Jonno's email had changed that. I remembered how I'd felt writing my reply to him in the office all those months ago, shy and hesitant. I remembered showing the draft of it to Ross and how he'd reacted, and realised now that it must have reminded him painfully of the loss of his father.

But Jonno had read it and taken it on board. It probably hadn't changed anything – he'd clearly been a great dad before he'd read it, and he was still a great dad now. But it had given him confidence to keep on doing what he was doing – loving his daughter, talking and listening to her, parenting her.

I hadn't just done my job – I'd done a good job, and the knowledge filled me with satisfaction and pride. I wished I could meet Jonno, shake his hand and tell him how much his story and its sequel had moved me, although I knew that could never happen.

The train rumbled to a stop and I got out, surprised that the journey had passed so quickly. I was almost home, and suddenly, I was looking forward to that. My flat would feel different now – I'd be able to see the dent on the sofa cushion where Ross had sat and imagine him sitting there again, right next to me.

I'd probably need to invest in a second controller for my Xbox.

By the time I reached the stairs up to my flat, I was almost running, my bag thumping on my back. I was out of breath when I unlocked the door and flung it open, and when Astro came to meet me, I scooped him up and kissed him and told him how much I loved him.

By the next morning, my see-sawing emotions had settled down a bit. I'd unpacked all my stuff, done a load of washing and spent lots of time catching up with Astro and telling him all my adventures. I ate a ready meal and went to bed early, and woke up with a stomach full of butterflies at the prospect of seeing Ross again – not just that day, but maybe that night too, and every day in the office after that.

He was waiting for me when I got to the coffee shop, and we placed our orders together and walked to the office together. For the first time, I got into the lift with him and neither of us blushed. We walked across the office together and took our seats at our desks.

I was so buoyed up by happiness that it was only then that I realised something was wrong.

Well, not necessarily wrong, but definitely weird. There was an air of tension across the pod of desks. Although it wasn't yet nine thirty, everyone had their heads down and their eyes focused on their screens. Chiraag had already changed out of his cycling gear into his work clothes. Marco wasn't using the reflection on his screen to fuss with his hair. Neil got up and offered to make a round of drinks, but no one took him up on this once-in-a-lifetime offer.

Something was definitely going on, and I didn't know what it was.

Had the office grapevine somehow got wind of what had happened between me and Ross? But if that was the case, why weren't they relentlessly taking the piss out of us, like they had when Simon had snogged one of the girls from accounts?

Had they learned not only of what had happened, but somehow knew Ross had changed his mind about me? But there'd been nothing amiss between us that morning, and even now, when I looked up at him across the desk, I could see his face was just as puzzled as mine must have been.

And then it came to me. The reply to Zack that had gone viral and sent Adam's column shooting to the top of the *Max!* landing page hadn't been enough. Greg and the ad sales people had run the analytics and decided that Ask Adam wasn't washing its face; they'd run it up the flagpole and not enough people had cheered; the whole thing lacked long-term sustainability – or however they'd have phrased it in their meeting.

Ask Adam was for the chop. I was for the chop.

I knew how that felt. I'd experienced it before – not just a few months ago when Marion had told me my job was in jeopardy, but years before that.

After Kieren had ended things between us, I'd thought I'd never be able to show my face in the office again. But I knew I had to. Even though I'd spent the whole night crying, I forced myself to get up the next morning, shower, dress and go to work. My job mattered to me – it was my future. A future that would no longer have Kieren in it, but if I was honest with myself, I'd known that for a while.

So I needed to focus on what I could control. What I was good at. What I was doing that was for me, not for a man.

I gave myself this little pep talk, and it worked. Kind of. When I arrived at the office I was shaking, feeling sick and wanting to run away. But I was there. I squared my shoulders and forced myself to walk through the door, into the lift and to my desk. I didn't look in his direction.

You've got this, Lucy, I told myself.

But I hadn't.

It was mid-morning when the blow fell.

I'd been keeping my head down, getting on with my job as best I could, managing not to cry. There had even been moments when I was engrossed enough in my work to not think about Kieren for whole minutes at a time.

Then my desk phone buzzed with a call from my line manager. Deep down, I knew what was going to happen, but I made myself pretend I didn't. I stood up and walked as calmly as I could to his office, smiled, said good morning and sat down to wait for the words I knew were coming.

'As you know, Lucy, your probation period comes to an end next week,' he said, and I nodded.

'Your work here at the *Sentinel* has never been less than satisfactory,' he went on, and I listened mutely.

'But character matters to us as a business,' he pontificated, and I felt tears beginning to sting my eyes.

All I could do was sit there and wait while he fired me. I listened to the little lecture he gave me about conduct and professionalism and disrepute, and I knew every word of it was true. I knew I was getting what was coming to me.

And I knew something else, too. I knew that this wasn't going to happen to Kieren. He wasn't a junior working out a probation period; he was senior and valued. It would cost money to get rid of him. I knew he'd keep his job while I took the punishment for what we'd done.

When the lecture was over, I asked whether I was expected to work the remaining days of my probation.

'I don't think so,' he said. 'You'll be paid for them, but we think it's best if you pack your things and go. HR will be in touch.'

So I packed my things and went, and three days later Amelie came to my flat and found me there.

I'd picked up the pieces of my life and my career. I thought I'd learned my lesson – but here I was again, on the brink of being sacked from *Max!* in disgrace.

I'd managed before and I'd manage again, somehow. I was a different person now. I was more experienced, more self-assured, tougher. I'd find another job. But I didn't want another job – I wanted this one.

The prospect of leaving *Max!* made me realise how much my attitude to it and my colleagues had changed over the last months. I remembered walking into the office on my first day and seeing them all there – the man blob. Now they were just Greg, Neil, Marco, Chiraag, Simon and Barney. They were my colleagues and my friends.

Oh, and of course Ross. I knew that if things were going to work out between him and me, they'd do so whether or not I was sitting at the desk opposite his all day. Still, the stress of job-hunting and the challenges of adjusting to something new would place strain on our relationship – only days old – which I'd much rather avoid.

And then there was Adam. I was only just learning how to be Adam and I didn't want to stop learning. I didn't want to leave Adam's readers in the lurch; I cared about them all, even the dicks.

Damn it, I thought, *please don't let this be about to happen.*

More than anything, I wanted to talk to Ross – to confide my worries in him, hear him reassure me that whatever happened, it would be all right. I caught his eye across the desks and mouthed, 'Coffee?' even though we were still drinking the ones we'd bought together. He nodded, half-standing up out of his chair the way he had on that first day, when he'd ended up arse-planting on the floor.

But before we could get to our feet, Greg approached the pod of desks like the angel of death in a stripy button-down shirt.

'Morning,' he said. 'Good to see you two back. How was the Big Apple?'

His tone was genial, but I wasn't fooled.

'Good, thanks,' I muttered. 'Hot.'

'Yeah, great,' Ross said. 'Glad to be back.'

'Any chance you two could spare a few minutes?'

Here it was. I stood up and so did Ross. Everyone's eyes followed us as we walked behind Greg, back the way we'd come to the enclosed meeting room.

We pulled out chairs and sat. I could see a sweaty hand-print on the blank page of my notebook. Ross looked bemused but not afraid. He didn't know that something bad was about to happen.

'I suppose you're wondering why I've called you in today,' Greg said.

We both nodded mutely.

'As you know, here at Radiant Media, we're always looking for new ways to leverage opportunities and grow our business,' Greg went on.

And when those opportunities aren't working, they get the chop.

'The technology column has always been a high performer for *Max!*.'

In sharp contrast to Ask Adam.

'And therefore, the board has decided that now is the time to launch a dedicated technology portal, alongside the main *Max!* and *Fab!* sites. We're thinking of calling it *Future!*, but that's still under discussion.'

What?

'It will be a wide-ranging brief' – Greg was smiling, actually smiling – 'covering not only how we can keep our readers abreast of new and emerging technologies, but also lifestyle elements such as gaming and wearables.'

What was he saying? I looked at Ross and he looked at me, but he seemed no longer confused but only mildly surprised.

'Of course, the editorial lead on the project will need to have in-depth knowledge of all those facets of the world of tech. Ross, you've delivered outstanding work in your role as *Max!*'s technology editor. I know you'd be the perfect fit for the role.'

And the perfect fit for other things, I thought, stifling a nervous giggle.

'Wow,' Ross said. 'Thanks, Greg.'

'However, the scale of the brief means it's not a job for just one individual. The decision has therefore been taken to appoint a joint editorial team of two to spearhead the project.'

Oh. So that's where this is going.

'Lucy, since you came on board at *Max!*, the rest of the management team and I have been impressed by your talent and energy. You were given the opportunity to launch Ask Adam, and you did so to the best of your ability. Then, when expectations weren't quite being met, you were given the challenge of turning it around, and you did that, too. But I know your heart has always been in technology, so we'd like to offer you the opportunity to join Ross in heading up this new venture.'

'But what about—' I began.

'Of course, this would leave a vacancy to continue the Ask Adam column. I'm aware that it's been your baby, Lucy, and we'd hope and expect you to be an integral part of the recruitment process. We thought perhaps a man...'

I felt light-headed with shock. Five months ago, this would have been a dream come true. The axe that had been about to fall on me would have been lifted – there'd have been a thrilling new opportunity where before there had been only the prospect of joblessness and penury.

I'd have bitten Greg's arm off for it.

But that was five-months-ago Lucy, not the person I was now.

'Greg,' I said. 'I don't want the new job. I'd love to work with Ross on it – anyone would – but I want to carry on with the Ask Adam column more.'

'You do? But it's a very exciting opportunity, Lucy. Have you thought this through?'

I took a deep breath – maybe the deepest I'd ever taken in my life.

'Yes, I have,' I said. 'And there's something I need to tell you as well.'

I looked at Ross, who returned my glance with a smile so warm he might just as well have stretched out and squeezed my hand under the table.

'Over the past few months, I've been using artificial intelligence to help me out with the Ask Adam replies. I felt overwhelmed by the increased frequency of the columns, and I didn't think I could cope on my own. So I got GenBot 2.0 to point me in the right direction and compose a first draft of some of the replies. Then I edited them. Except...'

Greg was watching me, intrigued. 'Go on, Lucy.'

'Except I ended up changing the algorithm, so the answers the bot came up with were actually more like what I'd have written myself. That's what happened with the most recent column, the one that went viral.'

'Fascinating.' Greg leaned forward, his hands pressed together under his chin like a church steeple. 'So you'd say that the percentage of Adam – or rather Lucy – versus AI has increased over time?'

'Exactly. And I've learned something, Greg. I've learned that sometimes men – Adam's readers, that is, not necessarily all men – need gentle guidance, a hug and a handhold. And sometimes they need tough love and to be told when they're being dicks.'

'I think actually that is all men,' Ross said, and Greg chuckled.

I smiled indulgently at the two of them having their man moment together.

'And I believe I can do that,' I went on. 'I understand men so much better now. I don't need the artificial intelligence any more. I can do it on my own. But it's helped me – it's made me better at being Adam. And all the men who've written to Adam over the months have helped me, too. They've made me better at being me.'

The Lucy who Greg had first met – who Ross had first met – would never have dared to make such a soul-baring little speech. I half-expected them to hastily change the subject, or even laugh at me, but they didn't.

They both looked at me with something on their faces I didn't quite recognise, until I did.

It was respect.

'Sounds like your mind is made up then,' Greg said. 'And it certainly sounds like it's a great decision for you and for *Max!*.'

'I'm confident it is,' I said.

'Well, in that case, I'll let you get back to work, Lucy. Ross, we can have a chat about next steps if you can spare a little more time.'

'Sure,' Ross said. 'Catch you later, Lucy.'

'Later,' I said, and we smiled at each other in a way that must surely have told Greg what was going on between us, if he hadn't already guessed.

And so I returned to my desk, my fingers positively itching to compose a reply to Adam's still unanswered email from Aaron in Cardiff. I created a new document, pasted in his letter and started typing.

THIRTY-SEVEN

SIX MONTHS LATER

'Raaah, game over.' Ross dumped the Xbox controller on the sofa. Astro, who'd been snoozing on his lap, looked up, startled and affronted. 'Suppose I should get in the shower and head home.'

'There's no rush.' I sat down next to him. He slipped his arm round my shoulder and I leaned in for a kiss. I could hear Astro purring – and the feel of Ross's lips on mine made me want to purr myself. 'We've got another half an hour before anyone comes.'

'Half an hour, you say? Sounds like enough time to me.'

'We could shower together.'

'Maximise efficiencies, as Greg would say.'

'Exactly.'

Our eyes met and I smiled. Even after so many nights together, in spite of seeing him every day at work, although his body had become as familiar as my own, I still felt a tingling thrill of excitement when he looked at me like that. Sometimes it happened in the lift on our way up to the office, and we'd exchange a sneaky snog before arriving on the sixth floor. Sometimes it was as soon as he arrived at my flat, and we'd immediately take our clothes off and head to bed – or the sofa, or even, once, the kitchen worktop, although I wouldn't entirely recommend that. Sometimes it was on the Tube home after we'd been out together, and the journey would seem to last an eternity.

'Come on,' I said to Astro, 'I'm afraid you're going to have to move.'

Twenty-five minutes later, we were lying on my bed, slightly out of breath, still damp from the shower. Astro had joined us and was looking on disapprovingly from my pillow. Reluctantly, I peeled myself out of Ross's arms and opened my wardrobe, rifling through the hangers until I found the short, purple velvet dress I'd bought in a vintage shop a couple of weeks before.

It was the first garment I'd ever chosen because it was sexy, instead of just because it was cheap or practical or comfortable. In fact, it was none of those things, and it attracted cat hair so badly I had to spend ages lint-rolling it every time I wore it. But I didn't care – it made me feel fabulous.

'Look at you.' Ross slipped his arms round my waist from behind, moving my damp hair out of the way to kiss my neck, then eased the zip up. 'You look beautiful. I love the way that makes your eyes look the same colour as Astro's.'

'Sometimes I wonder if it's me you're here for or him,' I teased.

'I've got kind of fond of both of you.' He turned me around and kissed me again, on the lips this time.

'Just as well, since you'll be living here from next week. And just as well I quite like you, too, otherwise I might not be too happy about finding space for a bicycle and a load of vinyl records.'

'Love me, love my stuff. Although I'm going to sort through the LPs and take a load of them to the charity shop, like I promised.'

I leaned up to kiss him again, my hands behind his neck,

breathing in the clean man-smell of him. *I'll never tire of this*, I thought – but then I heard the doorbell and had to stop.

'You can stay if you like,' I said.

Ross followed me out of the bedroom and to the front door. I opened it and saw Nush and Eve, half-hidden behind a massive arch of pink and blue balloons.

'How exciting is this?' Nush squealed.

'You look amazing, Lucy,' Eve said. 'Hey, Ross. Are you going to play fairy godfather? Bet you beat us all in the blind-fold nappy-changing challenge.'

Ross looked alarmed. 'I was just leaving. I'm all for gender equality but I think baby showers are a female-only safe space, right?'

'It's never too soon to learn,' Nush said. 'After all, you might have your own baby's nappies to change soon, mightn't he, Lucy?'

'Steady on! Not for ages yet, if ever. One grandchild's more than enough for my mum and dad to handle.'

Together, we carried the arch inside and set it up over the kitchen door. Eve offloaded a couple of carrier bags of clanking champagne bottles.

'Where's the cake?' Nush asked. 'Can we see?'

'You can.' I lifted the lid off a large white box. 'But it won't give you any clues.'

It was true – the icing was as smooth, white and even as the box itself. Only Amelie, our parents and I knew the colour of the layers of cake underneath.

'It's a girl,' Eve said. 'I just know it, and I'm never wrong.'

'Well, you've got a fifty per cent chance of being right,' Ross said. 'I'm off. Hope you have a great time. Give Amelie my love.'

Soon, my flat was full of girls, just as it had been before my sister's hen night. Gifts were piling up on the coffee table. Outsize sugar dummies were hung round all our necks.

Miranda had brought a batch of her mum's famous pakora. The air was full of chatter and laughter.

There were no spangles or deely boppers this time, though – the most sparkly thing in the room was the diamond on Bryony's finger, given to her the previous week by Charlie, the guy she'd snogged just before she'd ended things with Ross.

It was funny how things worked out. Here I was, the one who'd been single for the longest, with a boyfriend who was about to move in with me and who I was sure as it was possible to be was my forever person. There was Bryony, who'd taken the wrong course but was now as happy as any newly engaged woman could possibly be.

And there was Amelie, more radiant and beautiful than she'd been even on her wedding day, her silk dress stretched over the bump that was Amelie's baby and my n— But that was still a surprise.

'So have you even heard from Zack?' Caitlin asked.

'Well, obviously my lawyer contacted his lawyer.' Amelie smiled, but I knew how much stress and heartache had gone into the back-and-forth over their divorce. At times, it had felt like only the excitement of her baby's arrival growing closer and closer, and the need to stay strong and healthy, had stopped her falling apart completely.

'Actually,' Nush said, 'he went round to Amelie's parents' place and begged her to forgive him and take him back, didn't he, babe?'

'He did,' Amelie confirmed. 'And once I'd finished laughing in his face, I told him no. But I was the bigger person – I said he can have contact with the baby once it's old enough, and we can co-parent in a civilised fashion. Which wasn't what he wanted, but it's all he's going to get.'

'You'll meet someone else,' Bryony said. 'Just wait and see.'

Amelie laughed. 'You know what? I don't care if I don't. I'm done with men – as far as I'm concerned they can all go off and watch Andrew Tate on YouTube and wank themselves into an early grave.'

Apart from Ross, I thought.

'Now,' Amelie suggested, 'maybe we should cut that cake.'

Everyone crowded round, their phones held up to capture the moment. Nush got a stack of plates and napkins ready. I found a breadknife in a drawer and handed it to Amelie, who raised it over the pristine white surface of the cake.

'Wait!' I said. 'Stop. I forgot something.'

I grabbed my sister's arm and hustled her through the crowd of her friends – who felt like my friends too, now – and into my bedroom.

'What's up, Luce? Has my lipstick gone wonky? If I look like shit in my Insta story, I'll be fuming.'

'No, you're all good. But we need these.'

I rummaged in my bedside table drawer. The envelope of letters from Kieren wasn't there any more. I hadn't burned them or anything dramatic like that, just chucked them in the recycling a couple of months before. They were irrelevant now – only a few pieces of paper that had once been important but now meant nothing.

I produced two small lengths of ribbon, one pink and one blue. 'Here, to tie on the handle of the knife. For the photos.'

Amelie took them from me, gazing at them like they were the most precious things she'd ever seen. 'Luce, I... Thank you. Thank you for making all of this perfect for me.'

'Don't be daft. It's nothing.'

'It is. It's a lot. You being here – knowing you'll always be here – it's everything.'

I could see her starting to tear up, so I pulled her close and hugged her.

'Just doing what sisters do. Now you are totally not going to cry, or you really will look like shit on Insta. Got it?'

'Got it.' She sniffed and pulled away, smiling. 'Thanks for the reminder.'

'You're welcome.'

Quickly, I tied the ribbons to the handle of the knife and we re-joined the group in the kitchen, waiting while everyone readied their cameras around the cake.

'Three, two, one...' Amelie slid the knife deep into its surface, once and then again at an angle, and lifted out a pale-blue slice.

'It's a boy!' everyone chorused.

I hugged my sister and she hugged me back, and everyone clustered round to congratulate her.

'I still think you should call him Adam,' I said.

'Well, I'm not going to,' Amelie said. 'Unless of course I change my mind. But one thing's for certain. We're going to make sure he doesn't grow up to be a dick, aren't we, Lucy?'

A LETTER FROM THE AUTHOR

Huge thanks for reading *The Love Hack* and joining Lucy and Ross on their journey. If you'd like to be kept up to date on future Sophie Ranald releases, please take a moment to sign up to my author newsletter.

www.stormpublishing.co/sophie-ranald

Ideas come to writers in different ways. Sometimes it's a chance snippet of overheard conversation. Sometimes it's events in our own lives that can only be worked through by making them happen – never in exactly the same way, of course – to fictional characters. Sometimes, more prosaically, it's through a conversation with an editor that might go something like, 'Sophie, you should write a Christmas book.' 'Okay, I'll try and think of one.'

In the case of *The Love Hack*, two seemingly unconnected pieces of news came together in a weird sort of alchemy. The first – which, to be fair, I'd have had to be living under a rock to miss – was the hullaballoo surrounding ChatGPT and other generative AI technology. For a writer, this was scary stuff: artificial intelligence was advancing at such a pace that it seemed to have the potential to do my job way better than I could. So I read every article I saw about it with a mounting sense of dread. Then I encountered another story, this one lamenting the dearth of sensible dating and relationship advice out there for straight men.

These two concepts pinged together in my mind like magnets – or, to be more romantic about it, like the eyes of soon-to-be lovers meeting across a crowded room. There was a book here, and I was going to write it.

And so, about eighteen months after the initial idea sprang into my head, here is the result.

I hope you enjoyed reading *The Love Hack*. If you have a second to leave a review, please do so – I read every single review of my books and hugely appreciate your thoughts.

If you'd like to stay in touch, you can follow me on Instagram, through my Amazon author page or via my website.

Thank you again for reading *The Love Hack*, and my very best wishes.

Sophie

www.sophieranald.com

 facebook.com/SophieRanald

instagram.com/sophieranald

ACKNOWLEDGEMENTS

Signing with a new publisher is a bit like starting at a new school: exciting of course, but also daunting. Will I understand the rules? Will I know anyone there? Will I be able to find my way around? Will they all hate me?

Fortunately, the welcome I have received from the wonderful team at Storm couldn't have been warmer. No one pulled my skirt up with their hockey stick. I didn't get put in detention when I asked for more time on my structural edit. Already, just one book in, I feel like I have made new friends.

Thanks for this, first and foremost, must go to my wonderful editor, Claire Bord. From the moment I first met Claire in April 2023, I knew I was in the best possible hands. Her expertise, commercial instinct and collaborative way of working have made the always somewhat tortuous process of writing a novel go as smoothly as it ever could. Thank you, Claire – you're a rock star!

Fortunately, I was to encounter many familiar faces as I navigated the corridors of Storm. Founder Oliver Rhodes is unfailingly kind and his reputation as a book whisperer is richly deserved. Editorial Operations Director Alexandra Holmes makes the complex juggling act of production look easy, never dropping a ball. Publicity Manager Anna McKerrow, brimming with ideas and enthusiasm, kept me up to speed on every step of the launch process. Thank you all.

And the new faces I've encountered are fast becoming familiar too. Thanks to Elke Desanghere for her support on the marketing side; DeAndra Lupu for making the copy edit go like a breeze; Becca Allen for smoothing over any remaining snags in the proofread; Harrie Dobby for bringing my characters to life in the audiobook narration; and of course Rose Cooper for the stunning cover design.

Behind the scenes, the indefatigable Naomi Knox takes care of myriad tasks from manuscript formatting to ordering author copies, while Chris Lucraft manages the all-important systems and databases that are ultimately responsible for this book to end up in my readers' hands – thanks to you both.

Throughout this transition period, I've been more fortunate than I can say to have the unstinting support of Alice Saunders, who's looked after me at The Soho Agency since 2017. With her wisdom and humour, encyclopaedic knowledge of the publishing universe and relentlessly positive energy, Alice is a joy to work with and a true friend. Thank you from the bottom of my heart.

Thanks must also go to my lovely friend Kelly, her husband John and daughter Evie for introducing me to their adorable cat Astro, who I have shamelessly borrowed as Lucy's feline companion in this novel. Another dear friend, the wise and wonderful Helen, allowed me to pick her brains for much-needed insight into the male psyche, which informed many of the Ask Adam problems Lucy encounters.

At home, I've been supported, comforted and often distracted by my darling Hopi and our two cats, Purrs and Hither. I love you all so much.

Made in United States
North Haven, CT
09 June 2024

53384539R10203